THE BRILLIANT HAILEY COTTON

THE BRILLIANT HAILEY COTTON

A Sunday School Detectives Mystery

No. 2

PEP STILES

INTRODUCTION

Racing from one idea to the next, the young man desperately searched for a solution to his problem. *There's that alley behind Washington Avenue... that would be quick, but does it go all the way to McPherson? Maybe I should just take Main. It would be fast, but there's so many cars and traffic lights!* The young man paused, glanced nervously at his watch and began to complain to himself. *Why did I pick such a stupid time? I'm gonna be so late! Her house is so far away – it's all the way at the end of Maple!*

The time was quickly approaching five o'clock on a Monday afternoon and Andrew Bayhill, an eighteen-year-old summer intern, was certain he would be late – quite late – for an upcoming appointment. Taking a deep breath, Andrew paused his worrisome thoughts to look through the tall rectangular window next to his desk, hoping that the view – eight floors above the downtown streets of Findlay, Ohio – would provide some needed inspiration. Peering through the glass, he tried again to envision the best route to his destination. *Maybe Beech to Hancock?* He could not make out the specific streets, due to the large covering of trees beyond the nearby YMCA, but he held his gaze for several seconds. *She doesn't like it when I'm late*, he thought, recalling his teacher's disapproving looks at the start of the previous week's lesson. *She'll probably remind me that she's got another student at 5:45!* Andrew shook his head in distress. *Five forty-five!*

Fiddling with his watch again, Andrew reviewed the steps he would need to follow to quickly reach his piano teacher's house. *At five o'clock I need to run... as fast as I can... to my car.* He pictured himself maneuvering around the many office workers in the tall building's hallways, then racing through the crowded lobby and speeding across the wide sidewalks to the large parking lot at rush hour. *That's gonna take me at least ten minutes to get to my car! Maybe even fifteen!* His lips pursed into a frown as he remembered that his car – an older model Oldsmobile – was parked in the very last row of the company's long parking lot across from St. Paul's, a downtown church. *Dad always said, 'Let the old people park close', but I wish I hadn't taken his advice today!* Andrew paused again, looking out the window at the crowded streets. He shook his head. *It's gonna take me forever to get to my car! Then, it's at least another ten minutes to drive over to her house! That's twenty minutes at least!* He woefully calculated. *She's not gonna like that. Why did I agree to a 5:15 lesson?*

In a flash, Andrew thought of a new idea. *What if I just ran? Mrs. Kulchar's house isn't that far away, right?* he reasoned. *I could just book it over there and not even have to worry about going to my car. Once I get beyond the YMCA, the sidewalks won't be crowded.* Andrew looked down at his brown lace-up dress shoes and pondered this new idea for a few hopeful moments. He smiled as he calculated the duration of this new route. *I could probably run there in twenty.* Soon, however, his optimism faded, and his face returned to its unhappy disposition. *Her house is at least a mile and a half away. That's too far,* he concluded, as he considered the difficulty of running in dress shoes. *I'll get there faster in my car.*

His previous thoughts of worry soon returned, and Andrew became more and more agitated – certain he could not keep his commitment. *Five fifteen! What a stupid time for a lesson! She should have known I couldn't get there in time!* He sighed. *Right when everyone is leaving work! I should call her. I should just call Mrs. Kulchar right now and let her know I'm not coming! I'll just call her and tell her I'm gonna be late – or, tell her I'm not coming over at all! Why should I even try! It's such a stupid time for a lesson!*

Andrew moved his hand toward the cream colored push-button telephone that sat on the left side of his neatly organized desk, but paused just before picking up the handset. He suddenly remembered his piano lesson from the previous week. *I wasn't too late last week, was I? That was also at 5:15. Maybe there's a chance I could make it. I would be cutting it close... really close. But, if I can run really fast to my car... and hit all of the green lights after leaving the parking lot... and if the traffic isn't too bad on my way to Maple... maybe... maybe I could get there. I'd be a few minutes late, of course, but I could get there close to my lesson's start time. Plus,* he considered, *I wouldn't have to call her.* Andrew took a deep breath and leaned back in his dark green office chair. *I think I can do this*, he thought – exhaling deeply and pleased with his plan. *I actually might be able to make it.*

Looking again at his watch, Andrew discovered that only a few minutes remained before his planned departure. Wanting to focus on something different, he turned his gaze to three carefully placed narrow white cardboard boxes on the right side of his desk. Small plastic wheels protruded from the tops of each box, displaying small stickers in a variety of bright colors. *I should do one more file*, Andrew thought. *That would take my mind off getting to my lesson on time.*

Pushing off with his feet on the hard-plastic liner under his desk, Andrew rolled his chair several feet across the grey Formica tiles of the office floor, eventually stopping at a nearby metal pushcart with tall wheels and two long rectangular metal trays. The cart had recently been delivered to Andrew's office by the Records Department and was filled with old file folders. Grabbing the nearest file folder with dog-eared white pages protruding from its worn forest green edges, Andrew rolled back to his desk and placed the old file near his telephone. In a quick movement, the intern grabbed an empty file folder from an open box under his desk and placed it near the white cardboard boxes with their brightly colored stickers.

Next, Andrew consulted a long printout that he kept on a nearby file cabinet. The printout – with alternating horizontal green and white lines – had been torn from a dot-matrix printer earlier in the day by Andrew's supervisor. On the printout, Andrew found the appropriate set of letters and numbers to use for the new file and underlined the information with a red pen.

Turning his attention to the narrow cardboard boxes with bright orange, red and blue stickers, Andrew moved the plastic wheels within each box to display the combination of letters and numbers that matched the underlined information on his computer printout. Next, he unpeeled the appropriate stickers from each box and carefully placed them on the front and back edges of the new file folder.

Focusing next on the worn folder that sat undisturbed on the left side of his desk, Andrew opened the old file and unclasped the metal binder that held the dusty contents. After carefully removing each piece of paper, he slowly placed them into their new home. Aligning the pages within the new dark green folder, Andrew then secured the papers tightly into place by pushing the folder's shiny metal clasp shut.

Exhaling, the young intern stood and briefly looked at his work, pleased with his accomplishment.

Next, Andrew grabbed the new folder from his desk and walked across the wide and large office, passing his co-worker's desks, and arrived at a second pushcart located near his supervisor's office. Andrew's manager, Roberta Duncan, would review the processed files the following day, and if she found them acceptable, would allow them to be returned to a new area of the Records Department. *Finished!* Andrew exhaled, as he dropped the file into the cart.

Returning to his desk, Andrew picked up the old and empty file folder and threw it into the trash can next to his desk. Then, moving to the file cabinet, he picked up the computer printout and placed a checkmark next to the set of letters and numbers that he had underlined earlier, indicating he had processed the file.

The work was tedious – there were thousands of company files to process – and Andrew had already lost track of the number of files he had completed in the four weeks he had been on the job. When he was bored – which happened frequently as he waited for someone from the Records Department to deliver another set of files – Andrew would read the contents of the files he had already processed, learning about the company's real estate transactions, antitrust litigation, trademark and other legal matters that had been documented by the company's attorneys. When he grew tired of reading the old files – and was still waiting on the Records Department – Andrew would turn his attention to the sights below his tall rectangular window, sometimes making rough pencil drawings of the First Lutheran Church or the top of the Elks' Club building located across the street from his office.

A small desk calendar sat next to the telephone on Andrew's desk, displaying the date in large black letters. Exactly four weeks had passed since the eighteen-year-old had started his summer internship. Four weeks of the same tedious tasks from Monday, June 9th to Monday July 7th, 1980. Four weeks of taking old papers out of old folders. Four weeks of unpeeling multi-colored stickers and aligning them on the covers of new shiny folders. Four weeks of taking files to his supervisor for review. Four weeks of staring out the window. Four weeks of waiting for new files to arrive from the Records Department. Four weeks of a boring summer job. And that day, Monday, July 7th, 1980, seemed to be just as boring as all the others. It soon, however, would be a day that Andrew Bayhill would not easily forget.

In later interviews, many of Andrew's co-workers noted that the day seemed to pass slowly. Many were tired, having just celebrated July 4th on the prior Friday. They recalled that the building seemed quieter than usual, with many workers out on summer vacations. Interestingly, most of the co-workers who saw Andrew on that hot July day provided the same word to describe him: *nervous*. "He was nervous the *entire day*," one of his co-workers explained, recalling how Andrew had tapped a pencil loudly on his desk and restlessly bounced his feet under his chair. Another recalled that Andrew spent much of the day fidgeting with a button on his suit jacket and looking at his watch. A third co-worker even stated that Andrew was perspiring more profusely than usual. They noticed too, that when the ticking clock in the office finally struck five o'clock, the young intern wasted no time in leaving – quickly grabbing his soft-sided briefcase that was located next to his desk near the trash can and racing out of the office. "See ya tomorrow!" he said loudly to his co-workers as he sped away.

Leaving his office, Andrew raced down a nearby hallway, flying by several other office workers and quickly pressed the large square *Descend* button when he reached the floor's bank of six elevators. Waiting for an elevator to arrive, Andrew heard the pitter patter of a new sound. Looking down at his feet, he saw that his brown dress shoes were uncontrollably tapping the shiny tile floor – a symphony of nervous energy anticipating a hasty exit. Looking over his shoulder, Andrew saw that his manager, Roberta Duncan, had joined him at the elevators with a group of several co-workers. "I guess we're leaving at the same time," Mrs. Duncan said with a smile. Andrew frowned, not replying to his manager. *I'm never gonna make it*, he thought, his mind focused on his upcoming appointment.

An elevator eventually arrived, and Andrew quickly entered the brightly lit car with the others. They descended, stopping momentarily – to Andrew's chagrin – at another floor to bring on more workers into the small space. A few moments later a loud ding announced their arrival on the ground floor and Andrew quickly exited, rushing past a number of workers who were moving through the building's wide lobby. *Maybe I'll make it*, Andrew thought to himself as he walked rapidly across the lobby's red marble floor, passing a large silver sculpture of an oil well derrick and pump. *I'm going pretty fast*, he reassured himself. He looked again at his watch and then toward a set of rapidly turning revolving doors at the lobby's exit. *I'm almost out of here*, he thought with a sigh.

A few feet from the revolving glass doors, Andrew felt a tug on the elbow of his dark suit, then saw a security guard move in front of him to block his exit. The guard had been standing near the elevators, and after being signaled by Andrew's supervisor, had quickly pushed his way through the crowd to catch the young intern in the busy lobby.

"Uhh," Andrew groaned, looking for a way around the wide-framed guard who glared at him. Andrew first hesitatingly moved to his right, then to his left, while the guard blocked his path.

"Excuse me sir," the security guard interrupted in a polite yet stern voice. "I need to check your bag."

"Who, *me?*" Andrew asked as his eyes fixated on the company logo etched on the shiny silver badge pinned to the front pocket of the guard's starched white uniform shirt.

"Yes *you*," the security guard replied curtly.

"Well, I... guess so," Andrew nervously coughed as he quickly looked down at his briefcase and then peered at his watch.

"Let's go over here," the guard said, pointing to the long marble desk occupied by several well-dressed receptionists.

"Ah... okay," Andrew responded meekly and followed the guard through the lobby.

The two arrived at the wide marble counter where Andrew set his briefcase down on the desk. "Here you go," he said, moving the bag toward the guard.

"Why don't you open it," the guard directed as he looked at the greenish tan soft-sided briefcase – a gift from Andrew's mother for his first day of work.

"Will this take very long?" Andrew asked impatiently. "I've got somewhere to go and I'm already late."

"I'm not sure how long this will take," the security guard replied in a serious tone. "Hopefully this will all be over soon." The guard paused for a moment, then looked at the three receptionists seated nearby. "Ma'am," he said in a deep John Wayne voice to the nearest worker at the long table. "Could you serve as a witness for me?"

"Well... sure," the young woman said cheerily, quickly standing and moving closer to Andrew and the security guard. Her perky smile had only moments before been saying 'Have a nice evening' to exiting workers, but now quickly turned to a serious and scornful expression after looking at the security guard and then Andrew. *She already thinks*

I'm guilty of something, Andrew thought, feeling bad for interrupting her cheerful goodbyes.

Andrew quickly unzipped the soft-sided briefcase and pulled out a wrinkled photocopied page of piano music and an old paperback copy of *Leaves of Grass* by Walt Whitman. "Just some poetry," Andrew explained nervously. "Nothing too exciting. I've had the book for a couple of years and still can't finish it," he laughed tensely. "Just some *lunchtime* reading," he added, overemphasizing the word *lunchtime*. He decided not to tell the two that earlier in the afternoon he had taken the paperback with him to Wilson's Hamburgers for a long afternoon break. *If they ask me why I was gone for so long, I'll tell them I was waiting for a new set of files from the Records Department*, Andrew reasoned, recalling his long break at the sandwich shop. His thoughts soon turned to wondering if someone had reported his extra time away from the office. *Maybe someone followed me over to Wilson's?* he speculated. *Maybe they saw I wasn't working! Maybe they saw me reading the book when I should have been processing files? Maybe I should tell them I left work for a doctor's appointment? Or tell them I'll make up the time tomorrow after work…that way there won't be any problems.*

"I think there's more in there," the guard said, interrupting Andrew's racing thoughts, as the examination of the briefcase continued.

"Re… really?" Andrew's voice was surprised. "Maybe just more piano music."

Not waiting for a response, Andrew quickly reached into his briefcase and pulled out several stapled documents and placed them on the wide marble countertop in front of the security guard and the receptionist. Andrew was momentarily confused as his mind struggled to understand the words stamped in red and blue upper case letters on each of the documents:

CONFIDENTIAL
FOR INTERNAL USE ONLY
EXECUTIVE USE

What are these? This doesn't make any sense? Andrew questioned as he viewed the papers on the marble countertop. "M… memos?" he said in a loud voice, as the significance of the crisp white papers slowly became clear. "There must be some kind of mistake," Andrew muttered. He momentarily thought about the first business memos he had learned to create in Mrs. Willigham's *Business Typing* class at Findlay High School, where he and his friends made up fictitious company names and filled many pages with the words *The Quick Brown Fox Jumps Over the Lazy Dog*. But there was no mistaking the origins of the memos placed on the marble countertop. The first page of each of the six documents displayed a large red "P" surrounded by a black hexagon border – the same logo that was prominently displayed on the nearby marble lobby wall – the logo used by the Peloponnesian Oil Company.

Andrew quickly flipped through the stapled documents, noticing their length – some were only two pages, others were three pages, while one was five pages long.

A sense of dread filled his mind, seeing the intended recipient for each of the memos.

> *To:* The *President* of the Peloponnesian Oil and Gas
> Company.

Next, Andrew's eyes raced through each memo and identified the author of each of the documents.

> *FROM:* The *Law Director* of the Peloponnesian Oil
> and Gas Company.

The Law Director! Andrew nearly shouted. *The boss with the big office down the hall from me! The person my boss – Roberta Duncan – reports to! What are his memos doing in my briefcase?* Andrew was astonished at the sight.

The severity of the situation overwhelmed the young intern as the words stamped in large red and blue letters at the top of each document stared back at him – *CONFIDENTIAL, EXECUTIVE USE* and *FOR INTERNAL USE ONLY.*

The three gathered around the documents were momentarily speechless. "These... these," the well-dressed receptionist began, but could not finish the sentence, her professional demeanor rattled by the shock of what she was seeing on her red marble countertop. Shaking her head, she adjusted a wide shoulder pad on her suit jacket and quickly regained a professional tone. "These are top secret company documents!" she said in a serious but hushed tone. "They should not be leaving the building!"

"I don't know how these got in here!" Andrew pleaded. "I didn't put them in my briefcase."

"Yeah, right!" the receptionist replied doubtfully, rolling her eyes.

"Really," Andrew continued in a pleading tone, glancing first at the receptionist and then at the security guard. "You've got to believe me! I have no clue how these papers got in here!"

"You've got a lot of explaining to do, young man," came the security guard's stern reply.

CHAPTER 1

The sounds outside my bedroom window startled me awake – chirping sparrows and robins enjoying the cool of the morning before the summer's day turned warm and muggy. It was Tuesday, July 8th, 1980, and I lay in my bed for a long time between blue and white *Star Wars* sheets, listening to the birds and wondering what adventures the day would bring.

Eventually, I heard my mother fixing breakfast in the kitchen and I quickly dressed and joined her. The aroma of my mother's breakfast – a one egg omelet and warm oatmeal with brown sugar – filled the kitchen. I smiled, seeing that on a nearby narrow wooden table, a bowl of *Cap'n Crunch* cereal and a glass of chocolate milk were waiting for me. As I ate my breakfast, I spoke excitedly about my hopes for the day, while my mother cheerfully listened to my frenetic words. "I'm sure you'll have a great day, honey," she told me with a smile.

After finishing my breakfast and sending my mother off to work with a warm, heartfelt hug, I went to the wide picture window in the living room, abandoning my usual habit of watching morning cartoons on the TV. At the window, I waited expectantly for an old friend to arrive, gazing hopefully at every car that passed. As I waited, I was struck with the thought that I had not seen my good friend in several weeks. *Not since sixth grade graduation,* I remembered. I was anxious to hear what he had been doing for the first month of our summer break and was concerned that I had done something that had contributed to his absence. *Maybe I said something really dumb at our graduation ceremony?* I wondered. *Prolly,* I admitted. *Maybe he's hanging out with some-*

one else now? I thought jealously, worried that he had picked a different friend to spend time with. Then, thinking of my friend's great skills and abilities, another thought crossed my mind: *Maybe he's been working undercover! That would be pretty cool,* I thought, imagining him dressed in different clothes or a disguise. *I hope he's okay.* Soon, my mind turned to an idea that was quite troubling. *Maybe he's asked someone else to write about his adventures!*

The friend I was waiting for was named Sneak Ryerson. We had known each other since we were infants in our church's nursery, but had become better friends when I switched to his elementary school in the second grade. Even at that young age, I discovered my friend was an amazing young detective, able to solve complicated and challenging mysteries with his photographic memory and analytical mind. To my surprise, he could solve crimes by simply reading about them in the newspaper or reviewing a dusty old police file. I had even seen my friend solve a mystery after only a few minutes of interviewing a witness. Several of our local newspapers described him as being "like a young Sherlock Holmes" and had called him *"The Amazing Sneak Ryerson"*. I had to admit, he was pretty amazing.

Sneak was not the eleven-year-old's given name – it was Steven, but only his mother and a few teachers still called him that. To his friends and everyone else who watched him solve mysteries in and around the city of Findlay, Ohio, the tall thin boy was *Sneak*, Sneak Ryerson.

I had a nickname too. My friends and even my parents called me *Pep*, even though I wasn't always very peppy. My dream at that time – and for many years afterwards – was to be a great newspaper reporter. I wanted to write about fancy restaurants and exotic destinations and politics, but above all, I wanted to write about complicated mysteries and the great detectives who solved them – like the fictional Doctor Watson had done in describing the mysteries solved by Sherlock Holmes.

I was deep in thought and worry that morning when I finally saw the Ryerson's long red Chevrolet Impala station wagon pull into the driveway. At first sight of *The Maroon Monster* I raced out of the house. Unfortunately, I left the house so quickly that I forgot to close the heavy wooden front door and I soon saw Mrs. Ryerson pointing back to the house when I approached her car. I returned to shut the door and was soon running down the driveway again, my faded green Whittier Elementary School gym bag flopping in my hand.

I was warmly greeted by the Ryerson family when I reached the car. I said hello to Mrs. Ryerson first and quickly noticed that Jennie Ryerson, Sneak's younger sister, was seated to the right of her mother. "Hi Jennie," I said, approaching the passenger side of the station wagon. "Hi Pep," Jennie said with a wave of her hand, as her pigtails bounced back and forth on her small head. "Mr. Knick Knack says 'hi' too," she added.

"Oh, hi, Mr. Knick Knack," I said to Jennie's imaginary friend as I waved my hand.

The car windows, I noticed, were already down due to the fast-approaching summer heat. I opened the car door behind Jennie and tossed my gym bag onto the floor, then quickly slid into the station wagon's back seat.

In my rush, I had not initially noticed the tall teenage girl seated next to me. "Oh, hey," I said awkwardly.

"This is Sara," Jennie quickly explained, seeing the confused look on my face as she turned around from the front seat. "She's our cousin from Seattle."

"Oh... hi," I said, as I waved at the tall teenager with long sandy blonde hair.

"Hey," the girl replied with a smile, revealing a set of silver braces.

"Wait a second," I said, as a memory came to mind while a smile came over my face. "Are you 'Little Baby Sara' that your grandparents talk about all the time?"

The car quickly filled with laughter.

"Well, I haven't been called that in a really long time," the teenager smiled.

"I just remember your grandparents calling you that," I added.

"Sara's staying with us for a few days before our *big trip*," Jennie explained, turning again towards me. "*She* just drove our grandparents all the way from Wyoming."

"Wow," I replied. "You can drive?"

"Yeah," Cousin Sara said, smiling brightly. "But I'm not sure why I volunteered to do that! It was such a long trip! And it was really hot, too! I didn't realize it would be so hot out here in the East."

"*The East!*" I said loudly as the others in the car laughed. "I thought we were in the Midwest!"

"Well, it's East to me," Sara explained.

"She's cool," Jennie added confidently, as she continued to face us. "She just turned sixteen."

"Cool," I replied in agreement. "So, what's this big trip you're going on?" I asked Jennie, unsure of the family's plans.

"Jennie, you'd better sit down now," her mother cautioned, as she carefully pulled the car out of the driveway and drove out of my neighborhood.

"We're going mostly to New England," my friend Sneak Ryerson explained from his seat on the other side of his cousin – the first words I had heard from him since I arrived in the car. "We're going up to Niagara Falls first, then across New York to Vermont, New Hampshire and Maine – and a few more places in Canada too. Then, we're going down to Massachusetts and then to Philadelphia and we'll stay a few days in Maryland, before coming home."

"Wow, that sounds cool," I replied, wishing I had been invited. "You got room for one more?" I asked hopefully.

"I don't think so," Mrs. Ryerson said with a laugh as she turned east at Fire Station Number Three on Tiffin Avenue. "I'm not even sure we'll have room for everyone who's going! We'll have such a packed car!" she added.

"Yeah, we're all going in *one* car," Sara explained with a frown, her freckled nose wrinkling with concern.

"So, it's you and the Ryersons?" I asked, pondering how challenging their trip would be with five people – Mr. and Mrs. Ryerson, Sneak, Jennie and their cousin Sara – in one station wagon.

"And our grandparents," Sara added.

"Your grandparents!" I nearly shouted. "So, like *seven* people? All in this car!"

"Well, eight if you count Mr. Knick Knack," Jennie interrupted. "But he doesn't take up very much space."

The car soon filled with laughter again at Jennie's words.

"Wow! That's a lot of people," I exclaimed.

"Yeah, two weeks on the road," Mrs. Ryerson said without much enthusiasm. "I guess it's good that we like each other – and that we're staying for a few days at some places along the way."

"That will be some trip," I declared, still hoping for an invitation.

As we passed the city limits and continued east on State Route 12, we were quickly surrounded by hundreds of tall green stalks of corn, many with small tassels on their tops, and bushy green, low to the ground soybean plants that filled the fields next to the two-lane road. Occasionally separating the fields were long ranch-style houses on big lots with lush green lawns or overgrown thickets of bushes or narrow old forests along property lines. Soon, Cousin Sara began asking Mrs. Ryerson questions as we drove – about the animals on her parent's farm and the crops they grew – while the rest of us listened quietly to their conversation, studying the countryside that sped by just beyond the lowered windows of the station wagon. As we drove, I noticed that an opened-topped wicker picnic basket filled with groceries and several orange plastic medicine bottles sat between Jennie and her mother on the front seat of the car. Without asking, I knew that Mrs. Ryerson had recently filled the picnic basket with things to take to her elderly parents so they would not have to "*go to town*", as they would say.

I liked Mrs. Ryerson's parents – Grandma and Grandpa Foster, as I called them, echoing the names used by their actual grandchildren. And I especially enjoyed where they lived – a large family farm located east of Findlay, between the town of Arcadia and the city of Fostoria, Ohio. The Farm – as the family called it – was where the elderly Fosters had lived and worked for nearly their entire lives. As we continued our drive along State Route 12, I wondered what adventures would be in store for me there. I knew the fun things that Sneak and I did at The Farm were very dependent on the weather. In warmer weather, we would run through his grandparents' large red barn, jumping among the bales of hay or climb through half-filled "corn cribs" and scramble over old wooden pigsties and piles of wood that reminded us of teepees. Sometimes we would even race through the narrow rows of sweet corn and field corn that surrounded the farmhouse. On especially exciting days, we might watch one of Sneak's uncles practice target shooting with a silver six-shooter or an old rifle. In colder weather, we might explore one of the upper floors or attics of the old farmhouse – small storage spaces within the angled eaves of the house that offered endless adventures. One indoor feature that was exciting for me, but not quite as exciting for my friend, was an old TV console that had been emptied of its contents, located in one of the Foster's cluttered upstairs storage rooms. If we were exploring that room, I would often climb behind the large empty television set and pretend I was a TV reporter, alternating between David Brinkley, Garrick Utley and John Chancellor of NBC. "Back to you John," I'd try to say in a deep voice. "Well, Pep, you sure have an active imagination!" Sneak's Grandma Foster once told me when she saw the ball of tape that I had attached to a long string and placed in my ear. "It's to help me hear my producers back in New York," I informed her.

On our drive to The Farm, after cousin Sara had finished asking her questions of Mrs. Ryerson, I decided to ask my friend a few questions. "So, Sneak," I began tentatively. "What have you been doing since our Whittier Graduation?"

He paused before answering and I shuddered, thinking he might have been spending time with another friend... or had asked someone else to write about his detective work.

"Mostly helping my grandparents," he replied with a sigh. "They've got another large garden behind the farmhouse again this summer."

"Ah," I felt both relieved and astonished. "So, *that's* the reason I haven't seen you all summer? I thought you might have been undercover or working with somebody else!"

"No, nothing exciting like that," my friend acknowledged with a frown. "Just spending time at The Farm."

"You've done a lot of good work for your grandparents," Mrs. Ryerson said encouragingly from the front seat. "They can't get around like they used to."

"It's just to keep me from working on cases," Sneak added remorsefully. "Until my punishment is over."

"Yeah," Jennie added, as I remembered – sadly – that my friend had been grounded from doing detective work since March after lying to his parents about a night-time stakeout at a cemetery and a dangerous ride on the back bumper of a suspect's car. Sneak's parents were understandably upset and had grounded him from doing any detective work until the end of the summer.

"Well, your punishment is almost over," I considered hopefully.

"Yeah, only *two* more months to go," my friend said, shaking his head.

Jennie turned to her brother, her smile revealing two missing teeth. "Mr. Knick Knack says it will all be over in a *jiffy*," she explained half-seriously, as the car filled again with our laughter.

Eventually, the Ryerson's long maroon station wagon turned off of State Route 12 and onto a narrow county road covered with loose gravel. The rocks crunched under the weight of the heavy car, rattling noisily around the car's wheel wells before shooting out as fast-moving projectiles behind the vehicle. After crossing a pair of uneven railroad tracks and driving for a few more minutes, our destination came into view – the white aluminum-sided farmhouse, large red barn and tall stone silo appearing first. As we grew closer, the smaller buildings that surrounded the barn and farmhouse became visible. We soon saw the small brown wooden garage next to the house where Sneak's grandparents parked their red Pontiac – a building where earlier generations had parked a black horse buggy. Other smaller buildings were also visible as we approached, including the small brown woodshed and red chicken coop located behind the farmhouse and three smaller red painted wooden buildings next to the barn. The Farm was like an island, I thought, after seeing how the buildings were surrounded in every direction by wide fields of corn and soybeans.

We soon parked in front of the house and raced inside to find Grandma Foster trimming snap peas in the bright, sun-drenched kitchen. Gathering around her kitchen table, Grandma Foster told us the latest news from The Farm as she continued her work above wide silver metal pans.

"Come on, let's go," my friend eventually said to me as we left the others talking in the kitchen.

"So, what are we going to do today?" I asked, as I followed Sneak through the dining room. "Do you want to climb up the side of the silo, like we did that one time?" I asked as I pushed open the metal screen door that was slamming shut in front of me and jumped off the long grey wooden porch that ran the length of the house. "That climb up to the top of the barn was pretty scary when it started to storm," I added as I continued following my friend who was now running across the wide lawn.

"I've got something different in mind," Sneak said with a smile, looking back at me, as we ran across a narrow stone path toward the red barn. Opening a gate, we entered an area enclosed by a white fence that separated the well-manicured lawn from a stone gravel driveway surrounding the barn and other red painted buildings. Turning to one of the small buildings next to a tall gasoline tank, my friend deftly opened a slanted wooden door. The door creaked as it opened, leading us into Grandfather Foster's dusty machine shop. The Shop was a small wooden structure located next to the narrow country road and dimly lit by two large dusty windows that overlooked the dark green lawn in front of the farmhouse. As we entered, we saw Sneak's seventy-year-old grandfather working on a metal gear with a long metal file at a sawdust-covered thick wooden workbench.

Grandpa Foster was a short man with salt and pepper hair, and glasses that fell low on his nose as he bent over the broken piece from the tractor. His typical work garb consisted of: a light blue denim work shirt, light blue denim work pants held up by faded green and yellow striped suspenders, and well-worn brown leather work boots on his feet.

"Hi Papa Foster!" my friend said enthusiastically when he saw his grandfather.

"Well, hey, Sneak," came the gravelly-voiced reply. "I've almost got this doggone thing fixed," he explained with a grimace as he focused on the metal gear he gripped in his powerful hands. "It's taken me longer than I thought. But I guess *Old Bessie* doesn't have anywhere else to go!" he said with a smile, referring to his old tractor, a forty-year-old rusted green International Harvester.

"So, what are we doing here?" I asked my friend as I followed him further into The Shop.

Sneak's grandfather looked up at me. "Oh, hello Pep. I didn't notice you come in."

"Hi Grandpa Foster," I said sheepishly. "It's okay," I added, following my friend through the dusty machine shop, between large metal tools and wooden barrels filled with rusted pieces of old farm machinery.

"We're doing this," Sneak said as he pulled out his bicycle, a bright red three speed Raleigh his parents had recently purchased at *Jim the Bicycle Man* on North Main Street in Findlay. "*Your* bike is over there," he said, pointing to an older black Schwinn – his grandmother's bicycle – that rested against the nearby back wall.

"We… we're going on a bike ride?" I asked hesitantly. "It's already pretty hot outside," I objected.

"It'll be fun," my friend said. "Come on," he added as he pushed his bike toward the door and grabbed a three-foot long T-shaped silver pipe. *I guess one of his tires is flat,* I assumed, thinking my friend had grabbed a tire pump.

"Do I at least get to pick which bike I'll ride?" I asked, as my friend left The Shop with his bike.

"I guess not!" Grandpa Foster replied with a laugh, seeing his grandson disappear out the door.

Not hearing a response from my friend, I put my faded green gym bag in a wide white wicker basket on the front of the bicycle – which, to my chagrin, was covered with pink plastic flowers. *I'd never put this basket on my bike*, I said to myself and soon began pushing the bicycle around the many barrels and crates towards the door. My friend's grandfather wished me well and I replied by saying, "See ya' Papa Foster," as I exited The Shop.

Sneak was already pedaling away, so I quickly jumped on his grandmother's bike and followed him along the country road, seeing that he was carefully balancing the silver metal object on the handlebars of his bike.

Although it was still morning, the temperatures were starting to rise. As I pedaled, I noticed the black tar that patched the country road was beginning to bubble from the sun's heat. Running beside us on our ride was Grandma and Grandpa Foster's collie, Lady, who had been waiting quietly next to the machine shop door while Grandpa Foster worked inside. The dog was tall, with a thick black coat, wide black paws and a white underside. She ran alongside us for several minutes, putting her nose close to our feet as we pedaled – so close that I was afraid we might accidentally collide. But she was careful not to get too close. After a few minutes, she grew tired of racing and turned back toward The Farm. "Will she be okay?" I asked, worried. I looked back to see her slowly trot back toward The Farm and the familiar white horse that was painted on the side of the red barn.

"She'll be fine," my friend reassured me. "She does that all the time when Jennie and I go on bike rides. There'll be some cold water waiting for her back at The Woodshed."

"Oh yeah, The Woodshed," I said, not wanting to admit that I couldn't remember exactly which small building The Woodshed was at The Farm.

We continued our ride after Lady departed, first going north, then heading west toward the small town of Bloomdale, Ohio. "Why are we going all the way over here?" I complained, as I quickly tired of the long bike ride, wanting to stop and mop the sweat from my forehead.

"I need to pick up some samples," the young detective told me.

"Samples?" I huffed, out of breath and annoyed that my Osh Kosh farmer's overalls were now drenched in sweat.

"Yeah, it's for my collection of soil samples. It won't take too long."

"But I thought you were grounded?" I asked, as we continued pedaling.

"I'm just grounded from investigating *cases*," my friend explained. "I'm not grounded from doing basic scientific research – like taking soil samples – or analyzing tobacco. I'm studying that this summer, too."

"Just like Sherlock Holmes!" I exclaimed.

"Yeah," Sneak replied with a knowing smile. "I'm also doing some research on plant and animal decomposition – but it's really stinking up the basement."

"Oh," I laughed, still struggling to keep up with my friend, not wanting to ask exactly what was decomposing in his basement and making such terrible smells.

"My Mom made me throw some of the samples away this week when Cousin Sara and my other grandparents came to stay with us," my friend said with a frown, turning his head so I could more easily hear him.

"Oh, that stinks!" I said with a laugh.

"It did!" my friend laughed.

I grew more and more tired as we continued riding along another country road. Eventually, I shouted to my friend in a frustrated voice, "I thought you already had a bunch of soil samples from Hancock County!"

"Well, we're in Wood County now," the young detective yelled back to me, his face displaying a wide smile. "I'm expanding my collection."

"What?" I asked, surprised.

"They've got *Hoytville clay loam* and some other interesting soil types that I want to study."

"Aww, man," I replied, as I tried to peddle faster to keep up with my friend.

Eventually, I caught up with the young detective when he stopped and dropped his bike on the side of the road and dashed into a nearby cornfield. Through the tall stalks, I could see that Sneak had darted between several rows of corn standing four or five feet high. He returned to the road a few minutes later carrying his long metal t-shaped object and a small brown paper bag filled with dirt.

"What is that thing?" I asked, pointing to the metal object.

"It's a soil probe," the young detective explained with a smile. "It's an early birthday present. And it's a lot better than using a shovel to get a sample. With shovels you get too much topsoil."

"Oh," I replied.

"And look how light it is," he pointed out proudly. "I mean, it would have been pretty hard to bike around with a Dutch auger."

"A Dutch what?" I asked.

"A Dutch auger," my friend told me. "It's a bigger version of this probe. *This* probe lets me go about ten to fifteen inches into the soil.

With a Dutch auger I could go down several feet, but I don't need to go that deep."

"Why don't you just grab some dirt from the top?" I asked.

"The topsoil?" he asked incredulously. "That would really mess up my results."

"Oh, right," I said knowingly, afraid to ask why exactly that would be the case.

After my friend returned to the road, he gave me a ballpoint pen and the small brown paper bag. "Can you label the bags?" he asked.

"Sure," I told him and followed his directions on how to properly label the paper bag before placing it into the basket at the front of my bicycle – the basket with pink plastic flowers.

We continued this process for what seemed like several hours, and I was glad that my friend stopped multiple times to collect his samples, giving me a chance to catch my breath and rest my tired legs. To my annoyance, however, immediately after giving me a new bag, the young detective would jump on his bicycle and peddle farther down the country road to the next location.

"Okay, we're finished!" my friend eventually said, after making his way out of a corn field and tossing me the final paper bag. "Let's go back to The Farm."

I quickly labelled the bag and started pedaling again – slowly, this time, in cadence with my friend.

"You wouldn't believe how much soil ends up at a crime scene," Sneak told me in a relaxed tone a few minutes later as we leisurely passed another long field filled with corn.

"R… really?" I asked, struggling for breath, my bike feeling heavy with the many bags that filled the basket in front of my handlebars. "I feel like most of it's on the front of my bike!"

"Being able to narrow down where soil at a crime scene comes from can sometimes mean the difference between solving a crime or not," my friend explained, ignoring my protests. "I'm really glad we were able to get all these today."

After a few minutes of riding, Sneak began talking about the *Sunday School Detectives* – a group he had helped form several months earlier. Realizing that he was going to be grounded by his parents and unable to investigate a case we called *The Case of the Mysterious Circles*, my friend recruited me and seven other friends from our church's Sunday School to help solve the mystery. I had assumed that our first case would be our last, but much to my surprise, the *Sunday School Detectives* continued investigating cases – even though our friend, the Great Detective, was unable to help. During the months of April and May, we helped several people find their missing pets and even gave Sneak's Uncle Charlie – a captain in the Findlay Police Department – a few ideas for solving some cases. And then, at the beginning of the summer – only a few weeks before my visit to The Farm – our group solved an exciting and dangerous case that I had called *The Adventure at Riverside Park*.

"That was a good newspaper article," Sneak told me as we rode back to his grandparents' farm.

"Th… thanks," I said, barely able to speak from the summer's heat and the exhaustion of the long bike ride. "I… I wondered wh… when you were going to talk about that."

"*The Adventure at Riverside Park* – that was a cool title. I liked how you named it like a Holmes mystery."

"Th… thanks," I said again, happy that my friend had read my first published newspaper story.

"And, I liked how you used some literary techniques – those are great in storytelling. Like the first person narration. I'll bet people could really relate to that. You know, seeing it from your point of view. And the MacGuffin – that was brilliant."

"Th… thanks," I said again, not wanting to ask what a MacGuffin was.

"Do you know who it reminded me of?"

"Wh… who?" I asked, feeling out of breath.

"Arthur Conan Doyle," my friend said appreciatively.

"*Sir* Arthur Conan Doyle?" I asked, surprised, able now to get all the words out.

"The one and only," the great young detective said encouragingly.

"Oh, come on," I replied, amazed by my friend's compliment. Sneak knew I loved reading Conan Doyle's stories about Dr. Watson and Sherlock Holmes. Only a few weeks earlier I had finished reading *The Adventures of Sherlock Holmes* and had recently started re-reading the famous novel called *The Sign of the Four*.

I was quite surprised by my friend's compliment, but that was not my only surprise of the day.

CHAPTER 2

It was after lunchtime when we finally returned to The Farm. Leaving our bikes outside the barnyard fence, we slowly plodded up the stone path where we were greeted with a welcoming smile by Sneak's grandmother. We were drenched in sweat from the high humidity and eighty-degree heat. As we approached, Grandma Foster asked us to "cool off" outside on the porch before coming inside and sitting on her nice furniture. "Sure," Sneak replied, as he sank into a white outdoor rocking chair while I relaxed on an old dark green wooden swinging glider. Leaving us on the porch, Grandma Foster went into the house and soon provided each of us with a tall glass of pink lemonade. "Can I make you boys a bologna sandwich?" she asked nicely, after giving us our cold glasses filled with large chunks of ice and the sugary liquid.

"Sure," said Sneak.

"That would be great, Grandma Foster," I replied.

"Mustard?" she asked.

"Sure," we both replied in unison.

"I'll be back in a jiffy," she said with a smile.

"Thanks Gram," Sneak replied.

"Ahh," I said, after the cold lemonade hit my throat. "That tastes so good."

"This is really good," Sneak added, after taking a big gulp from his glass.

We sat for a few moments in silence, my friend and I staring out at the lush green lawn between the farmhouse and the barnyard and the fields thick with corn and soybeans in the distance. As I drank my lemonade, I soon began studying the small, orange rectangular shapes on the tall cold glass in my hand – shapes that reminded me of the groovy patterns I had seen on furniture and artwork of the 1960's and 70's; shapes that seemed so out of place at The Farm, where most of the buildings had not changed their appearance in over one hundred years.

"So, Pep," my friend said with a smile, when we each had nearly finished our drinks. "I've been wanting to tell you something and I guess now is as good a time as any."

"What's that?" I asked lazily, leaning back on the wooden glider while letting my tired feet swing slowly below me as the aching muscles in my hips and thighs recovered from the long bike ride.

"Well," my friend said. "You are never going to guess where I'm going tomorrow."

"You want me to guess where you're going tomorrow?" I asked.

"Correct."

"Well," I paused, remembering that my friend was still grounded from doing detective work. "I can't believe your parents would let you go anywhere – except the garden behind your Grandma's house. So, I'm going to guess here… The Farm… that's where you're going tomorrow. Your parents won't let you go anywhere else, right?"

"Well, they are tomorrow," my friend said nonchalantly.

"So, you're not coming back here to The Farm, then?" I asked.

"Nope," he said with a smile. "Not tomorrow."

"Uh, wait, I know," I interrupted. "You're going on that trip with your family… where everyone is going to cram into the station wagon and drive to New Hampshire, right?"

"Nope," my friend replied. "We're not leaving on that trip until two days from now – on Thursday."

"Hmm, okay," I laughed. "Well, tomorrow is Wednesday," I said before pausing for a moment. "I don't know. I give. Where are you going tomorrow?" I asked.

"Prison," he said lazily.

"Did you say *prison?*" I coughed, as my eyes opened wide to stare at my friend.

"Yep," my friend explained calmly. "My uncle worked it out with my parents, and they said it was okay."

"Prison?" I asked, shocked.

"Yep," Sneak said again before taking another drink of cold lemonade.

"Wow," I replied. "I… I don't know what to say. Have you done something wrong?" I asked, thinking that my friend had to suffer some sort of additional punishment for holding onto the suspect's car while travelling over the frozen roads of a cemetery several months earlier.

"Did I do something wrong!" the young detective snorted loudly and let out a loud laugh – something quite uncommon for a boy who was typically sullen and morose. "Did I do something wrong!" he said again while pushing back the dark hair from his eyes. "Do you think I need to be *Scared Straight*?" he asked, referring to the 1978 documentary narrated by Peter Falk that followed juvenile delinquents who were temporarily placed in a prison with very scary and intimidating adult inmates, who scared them into avoiding future bad behavior.

"Well, I don't know, maybe…" I stammered. "This is the first time I've heard about it," I admitted. "And I thought you were still in trouble with your parents."

"It's okay, Pep," my friend said with a smile. "I'm still grounded until the end of the summer, but I was completely surprised when I got the invitation last week."

"An invitation?"

"Yeah, from the warden of the prison."

"A prison warden called you?" I asked, amazed.

"Well, he didn't contact me directly," Sneak clarified. "The warden called Uncle Charlie first. You know, to explain the situation and everything."

"Wow," I replied, as a confused look came over my face. "So, where is the prison that you're going to visit?"

"It's called The Lebanon Correctional Facility."

"So, you're going to another country tomorrow?" I asked. "How's that going to work with your trip to New Hampshire in two days?"

My friend let out another laugh. "No, no, it's not in a different country. The prison is in Lebanon, Ohio, not the country of Lebanon. It's near Dayton," the young detective explained.

"Ah," I replied knowingly. "Right… Lebanon, Ohio."

"It's where Russell Crenshaw is being held," my friend said matter-of-factly. "I'm going to go see him."

"*Mr. Crenshaw?*" I said with a jolt, surprised to hear the name of the mastermind behind *The Case of the Mysterious Circles*. A case that had turned out to be quite exciting, as the *Sunday School Detectives* tried to determine why an arsonist was setting fires to fields around Findlay, and why a letter-writer was claiming that the fires were being set by *aliens* to create UFO landing sites.

"Yeah, Mr. Crenshaw," my friend replied, as he rocked idly in his chair.

"But isn't he in the Hancock County Jail?" I asked. "Why isn't he there?"

"Because he already admitted to everything," Sneak explained. "Mr. Crenshaw took a plea deal, you know, to avoid a jury trial. So, he got a reduced sentence."

"Oh, yeah," I said knowingly, not admitting that I had never heard the phrases *plea deal* or *reduced sentence*. "So, he took a deal and will be out soon?"

"Oh no, he still has to serve a long prison term," the young detective explained. "Just not as long as a jury might have sent him away for."

"Oh."

"I mean, Pep," my friend continued, more animated now. "He did a lot of bad stuff. He set those fires and he framed – or tried to frame – Julian Davis for setting them. Not to mention, he encouraged Julian to run me over with his car! Plus, he tried to set that fire at that large seed barn off Warrington Avenue, where he had Julian Davis tied up inside!"

"Yeah," I said in agreement, before pausing for a moment. "He really did do some bad stuff." I shivered, thinking about the man's misdeeds while the ice-cold water condensing on the outside of my glass of lemonade numbed my fingers clinging tightly to the cold glass. "So, why exactly are you going to see Mr. Crenshaw?" I wondered.

"The warden says Mr. Crenshaw has some information – some *valuable* information, is what the warden called it."

"Ah," I replied. "Valuable information."

"But Mr. Crenshaw will only give it to me."

"Only give it to you?"

"Yep, that's what the warden says."

"Do you think it's a trap?" I asked, as I began rocking again on the dark green wooden glider. "You know, like how Julian Davis got you to go to Rawson Park and tried to run you over with his car?"

"I don't think so," the young detective replied. "I talked to Uncle Charlie about it, and he said Mr. Crenshaw would probably be in handcuffs the whole time – or maybe even behind a glass wall with a phone we'd talk into. Plus, my uncle said he'd drive me down there and go inside with me – he said I couldn't go by myself – so he'll be there the whole time. So, I'm not sure how Mr. Crenshaw could attack me or do something bad, especially if Uncle Charlie's there."

"Yeah, probably not," I said in a serious tone as I pictured Sneak's Uncle Charlie – a tall and fit man who could easily overpower the elderly Mr. Crenshaw. "It sounds like you'll be safe when you go visit him."

My comment, however, brought a wide smile over my friend's usually somber face – the kind of smile made popular by Lewis Carroll's *Cheshire Cat* from *Alice in Wonderland*.

"What?" I asked. "What? What's so funny? Is my barn door open?" I asked, looking at my overalls, then glancing at the tall red barn in the distance.

"No, no," my friend explained with a laugh. "Nothing like that. It's just that, well, there's a little bit more I need to talk to you about."

"What?" I asked nervously. "What about?"

"Well – it's just that, I'm not going to prison alone tomorrow."

"Right," I replied. "Your Uncle Charlie is going with you."

"With *us*," my friend clarified. "He's coming with us. You're coming with me," the young detective explained.

"What?" I asked again, more alarmed this time. "What do you mean?"

"You're coming with me and my Uncle Charlie to prison tomorrow," Sneak explained slowly.

"Me!" I nearly shouted. "I can't go to prison!"

"Sure you can," my friend reassured me. "When we get there, we'll do the same things we always do when we interview people for our cases. It won't really be any different. I'll be able to ask Mr. Crenshaw some questions and you'll write down his answers – just like you do when we interview witnesses or potential suspects. You'll probably even be able to bring your tape recorder with you – so, not really any different than interviewing people in Findlay."

"Not any different than interviewing people in Findlay!" I protested loudly. "It's totally different than interviewing people in Findlay, because instead of meeting a witness at *Oler's* or *The Rocking U* or *Wilson's* or somewhere like that, we'll be meeting a bad guy *in prison!* You know, the place where they lock people up and make it hard to get out!"

"Yeah, but we'll be with the guards."

"What if I get stuck in there?" I asked nervously. "What if someone, like, tries to get me with one of those homemade knives they have in there?"

"A *shiv*?" my friend asked.

"Yes a shiv! I think I saw that one time on *CHiPs*, when Ponch went undercover, or something like that. That's totally scary."

"I don't remember that episode. But you'll be with me and my Uncle Charlie the whole time," my friend reassured me. "You know Uncle Charlie – the police captain. He's a pretty tough guy and won't let anyone push him around – he still plays rugby up in Toledo on the weekends. I'm sure it will be okay."

"What if they put me in like an unmarked grave, or something like that? My Mom won't even know where to put the flowers."

"You mean like in that movie *Brubaker* that came out last month?"

"Yeah, one of my friends was telling me about it. His parents went to see it. It sounded so scary."

"It's going to be okay, Pep. It won't be like the movies."

"But there's, like, so many TV shows where the characters go – you know – undercover in prison, like *Charlie's Angels*..."

"Your Mom lets you watch that show?" my friend asked, surprised.

"Well, not all the time," I explained. "But I saw that episode where they went to prison to figure out why the sister of one of their clients disappeared."

"It's not like..."

"She *disappeared* in prison, Sneak!" I insisted. "The sister... dis... appeared," I said slowly. "In prison!"

"I like the smart one," Sneak interrupted, intentionally changing the subject.

"Yeah, Sabrina," I said dreamily as my thoughts were momentarily distracted from my protests. "I do too." But soon I returned to the previous subject. "I think I've even seen *two* episodes of *Police Woman* where Angie goes undercover in prison. Not *one* episode, Sneak, but *two episodes!* One episode was to get some information from an inmate to put a guy away. And in the other episode, she goes undercover to find out why *another* policewoman was killed when *that* policewoman went undercover in prison!"

"It's not going to be like TV," Sneak said reassuringly. "We're not going undercover, we're just going to visit. Wow, I didn't know you were watching that much TV," my friend added in a concerned voice.

"Well, re-runs," I explained.

"Oh," he said, before a realization came to his mind. "Pep, I bet you like *Police Woman* because Angie Dickinson's character is named *Pepper* Anderson, right?"

"Well, that is pretty cool," I smiled. "Pep... Pepper... it's cool." I said before pausing again. Soon, however, I became serious again. "I even think *Starsky & Hutch* went undercover for something like that."

"Okay Pep," my friend said strongly. "First, when *Starsky & Hutch* go undercover, it's for something funny – like to be longshoremen or hitmen or photographers, or something like that – I don't think they've ever gone undercover in prison. And second, it will be okay – it's not going to be like TV."

"Maybe you're right," I concluded, before pausing for a moment. "But, I've got to tell my parents, right? And they're never going to allow me to go," I added.

"Uncle Charlie's already talked to them and they both gave their permission."

"You guys already talked to my parents?" I wondered loudly. "Why didn't you tell me before today?"

"Because everyone thought you'd be too nervous to know about it in advance," Sneak said simply. "You know how you can get so anxious and excited about stuff."

I did not want to admit it to my friend, but I knew he was right – I did get anxious and nervous about a number of things. "So, that *guy*," I continued, trying to focus my thoughts to gain more information. "Mister Crenshaw..."

"Right, Mr. Crenshaw. He said he wanted to meet with me too?" I wondered. "How does he even know my name? I only saw him that night you caught him at the *seed place*."

"Well, technically *Hailey* caught him," Sneak corrected me, referring to our friend Hailey Cotton who, with his sister Jennie's help, had trapped Mr. Crenshaw in a net and later pulled off his plastic alien's mask while two newspaper photographers captured the moment.

"Right, right," I added. "I only saw him after *Hailey* caught him."

"Correct."

"But you and Jennie knew him from the Farmer's Market," I reminded him. "I haven't even been over there for a really long time."

"Yeah, Jennie's been reminding me of that," Sneak said remorsefully.

"...that I haven't been to the Farmer's Market?" I asked.

"No, no," my friend said with a chuckle. "Jennie keeps reminding me about that case and saying that she *called it* because when she first heard about *The Case of the Mysterious Circles*, she said our culprit would be someone from the Farmer's Market."

"Oh, yeah," I said with a laugh. "I sort of remember that. I guess she did sorta' *call* the case."

"Hardly," my friend said with a frown. "I keep telling her, 'Just because you guessed where the guy worked – for one day out of the week – doesn't mean you really knew who it was,'" the young detective explained while shaking his head. "She doesn't even use deduction. It drives me crazy."

"Yeah," I said again, not completely understanding what my friend meant.

We paused again, gazing at the beautiful countryside.

"So, if Mr. Crenshaw doesn't know about me," I asked, confused, "why am I going?"

"Well," Sneak explained. "When my uncle told me that Mr. Crenshaw asked me to visit him in prison, I said I wouldn't go unless you came with me."

"What!" I said, startled. "You mean I don't even *have* to go!"

"I won't go unless you do," my friend explained seriously.

"Why did you get me involved?" I asked loudly.

"Because, Pep," my friend said in a dramatic voice, again brushing his dark hair away from his eyes. "I know you'll write a great story about it one day – and I didn't want you to miss out."

"Yeah, but..." I began to protest, feeling frightened but also feeling grateful for my friend's appreciation of my writing.

"It will be okay," Sneak interrupted reassuringly. "Don't worry about it."

I sat in silence for a few moments thinking about the upcoming visit. I had never visited a jail or prison before, and the many pictures that flooded my mind were from what I had seen on TV. As I sat rocking back and forth on the green wooden glider, I imagined passing under tall prison guard towers and walking through an open door between two strong iron gates into a building that held dangerous prisoners – prisoners who had done some very bad things. "Dead man walking!" I imagined hearing someone yell when we arrived. As I rocked, I tried not to think about those TV shows of prison riots and detectives going undercover as inmates – but the more I tried, the more I struggled to forget them.

"So why does Mr. Crenshaw want to meet with you again?" I asked quickly, trying to turn my attention away from the scary pictures that were building in my head.

"I really don't know," Sneak replied. "I've been wondering about that since Uncle Charlie called me a few days ago to tell me the news. My uncle just said that the prison warden called him and said that Mr. Crenshaw wanted me to come visit him because he has some very valuable information. But he would only tell it to me – not the warden, or Uncle Charlie, or anyone else."

"Couldn't Mr. Crenshaw have just *called* you with the *valuable information*?" I wondered.

"Sure, I guess so," the young detective replied. "I'm pretty sure they can make collect calls from there."

"Oh, yeah," I said, unsure of what a "collect" call was.

"But," my friend added. "He probably thought it would be more fun to see me in person."

"In prison…" I added.

"Yeah, in *person* and in *prison*," my friend summarized with a laugh.

Just then, we heard the creak of the old metal screen door and saw Grandma Foster return to the porch. "Who's ready for some bologna sandwiches?" she asked with a smile, holding a tray filled with food.

CHAPTER 3

I'm going to prison tomorrow, I said to myself – still in disbelief – as my friend, Sneak Ryerson, quietly finished a second bologna sandwich and drank another glass of pink lemonade on the front porch of his grand-parents' farmhouse. "This idea is completely crazy," I said excitedly between bites of my sandwich. "And dangerous," I added quickly.

"It's not that crazy or dangerous," my friend reassured me. "Plus, you better get used to it."

"You don't think I'll be put away for something, do you?"

My friend laughed. "No. No. It's just that prison is where the bad guys go after we catch them," he explained in a serious tone. "So, both you and I will need to get used to visiting them there. If you think about it, there will probably be *lots* of times we'll need to interview prisoners over the next few years."

"Hopefully it won't happen too often. It still seems pretty danger-ous to me."

"Well, like I said, Uncle Charlie will be with us the whole time tomorrow. So, you don't have anything to worry about."

"I know, I know," I replied reluctantly. "I just don't like it."

As we finished our lunch on the front porch, I was grateful to talk about another subject. "So, when are we leavin' for the pool party?" I asked quickly.

"In a little while," my friend answered. "When we're done with lunch."

"Do we have to wait a half hour after we eat?" I asked, as my friend laughed.

"It will take us that long to get there," he replied.

After we finished our sandwiches, we sat quietly looking out at the wide green lawn and the fields in the distance. After a few minutes, I fell asleep on the porch swing, exhausted by the long bike ride and my friend's news about visiting the prison.

I awoke from my slumber later that afternoon. Eventually the five of us – Sneak, Mrs. Ryerson, Jennie, Cousin Sara and I – said our good-byes to Grandma and Grandpa Foster and made our way to the maroon station wagon that was parked alongside the narrow country road near the Foster's mailbox – a mailbox painted to look like the red barn with white trim. The maroon station wagon's back hatch and window were both open, and Sneak and I carefully placed the many soil samples – still in their brown paper bags – on the metal floor. When we had finished, Mrs. Ryerson turned her car key into a slot near the right brake light and simultaneously raised the back hatch while closing the glass "clamshell bubble" window.

We took our seats in the same places that we had initially occupied and after Mrs. Ryerson turned the car around next to the barn, we yelled "Goodbye" to Grandma Foster through the open windows while she waved to us from her porch. "Bye honeys," she called out. Mrs. Ryerson honked the horn in the pattern of the song, "Shave and a haircut... two bits".

Building up speed on the gravel-covered road, the station wagon crossed the bumpy railroad tracks and turned right onto State Route 12. We travelled west through the small town of Arcadia and eventually reached Findlay's city limits. Turning south at a Baptist church near the RCA building, we crossed Tiffin Avenue and soon arrived at our next destination – a long white brick home on Winterhaven Drive, around the corner from the house owned by Sneak's Uncle Charlie. Pulling into the driveway, we heard a loud and raucous party already underway in the backyard, prompting Sneak, Jennie, and I to quickly exit the car and run to a gate in the chain link fence at the back of the house. Mrs. Ryerson and Cousin Sara followed cautiously a few steps behind.

The ranch-style home belonged to the grandmother of Lisa Lavin. Lisa and her cousin Cressida Hudson were members of the *Sunday School Detectives*, who had invited our group to a pool party to celebrate the successful completion of our most recent case, *The Adventure at Riverside Park*.

I had been looking forward to the pool party from the time I received my invitation. And that morning, before the Ryersons had arrived at my house, I had checked and double-checked and then triple-checked my gym bag, making sure my light-blue swim trunks were inside. When I arrived at the party, I was relieved to see that the swim trunks were still in my gym bag, along with the voice-activated Panasonic cassette tape recorder that I always carried with me.

After quickly greeting Lisa and Cressida, I ran inside the house and quickly found a bathroom to change into my swim trunks. A few moments later, I eagerly joined the others who were in or around the pool.

Hailey Cotton was one of the first to greet me when I arrived pool-side. "Nice article," she said with a bright smile as she calmly pressed some hair in place with her right hand. Hailey had become the leader of the *Sunday School Detectives* when Sneak realized that he would be grounded by his parents and her bright personality and encouraging words were quite helpful to our group. This was especially true during those times when it seemed like our investigations had *gone cold* and we thought we had run out of clues – something that had happened on our last case as we struggled to find a solution to *The Adventure at Riverside Park*.

Like my friend Sneak Ryerson, Hailey Cotton was tall with high cheekbones and a high forehead below dark hair. Even though her hair was lighter than Sneak's, the two looked surprisingly alike and were frequently mistaken for brother and sister. Because of this, they would often greet each other with a laugh and say, "Hey Sis," or "Hi Brother." Despite their similar appearance, the two friends were quite different in a number of ways. Hailey's light green eyes were quite unlike Sneak's piercing blue ones. And their personalities could not have been more contradictory. Sneak could often be dark and moody – even solemn and morose – while Hailey was always cheery and upbeat, encouraging our group to keep looking for clues even when everyone wanted to stop.

Hailey's brother, Moscow Cotton, was also at the pool party. Like his older sister, Moscow was named after a town in Idaho that his parents had wanted to visit. But unlike his sister – who was unusually focused and disciplined for her age – Moscow was our group's daredevil, interrupting our discussions with reckless stunts that had entered his mind only moments before. During our investigations, Moscow would frequently tell us how bored he was and try to get our group to do something more exciting than discussing a case or looking for clues.

When I arrived poolside, Hailey was sitting with her feet in the water talking to Lisa's mother, Mrs. Lavin, while Moscow was doing crazy jumps and dives off the pool's small diving board. "This next move is illegal in at least twelve states," he claimed just before taking his next plunge.

I noticed that Lisa and Cressida, our party's hostesses, were now swimming in the shallow end of the pool opposite to where Moscow was diving, and they soon invited me to join them. Near the two cousins was Jennie's friend Michelle, who, like Jennie, was one of the younger members of our group. "Are we going to have a contest to show off our best dives?" I asked the girls when I approached them in the water.

"That sounds great," said Lisa as she swam near her cousin. "Do you want to dive too, Michelle?" she asked. Michelle quickly told us that she was not a good swimmer and stayed close to the edge of the pool, holding onto the side while the others splashed and swam.

I swam to the deep end, eventually joining Moscow Cotton at the diving board. We were quickly joined by another friend, Joel Hemlinger, who had just pulled himself out of the pool. Joel loved music and was humming a song when he came out of the water. "Have you guys heard the new song by Paul McCartney called 'Coming Up'?" he asked as he approached us.

"I don't think so," Moscow replied.

"It's really good," Joel told us, as he began singing the lyrics. He paused. "Okay, just imagine like a really funky bass line that goes like this." He hummed the bass part in a deeper voice. "And the trumpets sound like this," he added and then began making trumpet sounds.

"Trumpets?" Moscow asked incredulously. "In a rock and roll song? That can't be good."

"I've heard it," I said enthusiastically. "It's good," I reassured my friend.

"I like that song called 'The Streak'," Moscow said with a grin, referring to a Ray Stevens song that had been popular a few years earlier. "I like to show off my *physique*," Moscow added with a laugh as he began contorting his arms and legs in funny body-building poses, pretending to show off the muscles on his thin arms.

"Oh brother," I said, shaking my head.

"Alright Moscow!" yelled Lisa from the other side of the pool when she saw Moscow's funny stances.

"Moscow Cotton, what are you doing!" his sister Hailey scolded as she and the girls laughed.

"Have you heard of *The Plastic Macs?*" Joel asked me, ignoring our friend who continued with his body-building poses.

"I don't think so," I admitted.

"Nah," Moscow replied, as he stopped his funny moves to consider his next dive.

"How about *The Plastic Ono Band?*" Joel asked.

"I think you're making up those names," Moscow said with a laugh, and in an instant, he was running off the diving board, spinning and then hitting the water with a crash.

"There's Moscow coming up," Joel sang, when he saw our friend swim to the surface.

"Like a flower," I replied, as Joel smiled at my joke about the song.

After talking with Joel for a few more minutes, I dove off the diving board and into the heavily chlorinated warm water. Swimming underwater, I quickly arrived at the shallow end of the pool to splash Lisa, Cressida, and Michelle before swimming to Jennie and her cousin Sara who were nearby. I noticed Sneak had changed into his suit, but was in a deep conversation with Hailey Cotton at the edge of the pool and I thought it best not to interrupt them.

I loved swimming and did several circular laps around the pool. My Dad had taken me to the indoor YMCA pool once or twice a week for several years, so I felt confident diving deep below the pool's surface and swimming underwater. When I did return to the diving board at the deep end of the pool, Joel, Moscow and I took turns doing our tricks: cannonballs and belly flops, corkscrews, screwdrivers and jackknives.

I was happy being with my friends that afternoon. All of the *Sunday School Detectives* were there: Hailey Cotton, our encouraging leader, deep in conversation with Sneak Ryerson; the cousins, Lisa and Cressida, laughing and talking in quick high-pitched tones with Jennie and Michelle, the younger girls in our group. The guys, Joel and Moscow, were great fun. Jennie even assured us that her imaginary friend, Mr. Knick Knack, was swimming with us that afternoon!

We spent a lot of time splashing each other and laughing and joking about things that had happened during *The Adventure at Riverside Park*. Eventually, Lisa brought her grandmother's record player near the edge of the pool and began playing songs from her own record collection. As the music played, most of us gathered in the shallow end of the pool and struggled to do a synchronized dance called "The Hustle" while

Lisa played the 1975 disco song several times. At the end of the dance, I was preparing to dive underwater when I glimpsed a figure standing near the chain link fence that surrounded the backyard. "Who's that?" I asked, mid-dive, but was soon underwater. A few moments later, when I returned to the surface the figure was visible, standing poolside. To my dismay, I saw it was Roger, a boy who was not part of our group.

"Roger!" Sneak exclaimed. "Glad you could make it!" he added, greeting the tall, bushy-haired boy with a handshake. *He's not part of the group!* I thought, surprised by my friend's uncommon enthusiasm for his guest.

"Hey Roger!" Hailey said with a smile, as she joined Sneak in speaking to Roger at the edge of the pool.

"Hey Roger!" others joined in.

"What's he doing here?" I asked Sneak gloomily a few minutes later, when the young detective walked near me to get a chair for Roger.

"I invited him," Sneak explained.

"Yeah, but he's not part of the *Sunday School Detectives*," I protested. "He didn't do anything to help with *The Adventure at Riverside Park!* I thought that's why we're having this party!"

"Well, neither did my cousin – Little Baby Sara, as you like to call her," Sneak said with a laugh. "But she's here."

"Yeah, but she's from out of town," I replied.

Sneak's voice turned to a serious tone. "Roger saved my life, Pep. A car was coming right at me and he dragged me out of the way. I wanted to do something nice for him."

"Oh," was all I could say, but it still made me angry that Roger had been invited. A few minutes later I said in a loud whisper to Joel and Moscow: "He's not one of us. He's not a *Sunday School Detective*."

"Well, maybe he'll want to join us," Moscow said, unaware of my ill feelings.

"Did you hear how he said something about our last case being at River*bend* Park?" I said to Joel with a laugh. "It was River*side* Park."

"I get those parks messed up too sometimes," Joel replied. "But I won't get fooled again," he said with a smile, before singing a popular song and jumping in the water.

It bothered me that Sneak had invited Roger. I became even more irritated when Roger joined us in the pool and began swimming with Sneak. *Sneak didn't even get in the water until Roger got here!* I thought angrily. *I'm Sneak's friend – not this guy.* Sadly, while we swam, I made a few jokes to the others about our last case that I knew Roger would not understand. I was glad when Roger left a short time later, explaining that he had a baseball game at Swale Park.

CHAPTER 4

We were in the middle of a game of Marco Polo in the early evening when I heard the phone ring loudly from inside the house. When Lisa's grandmother answered the ringing telephone, she heard the request of a weak-voiced elderly man. "May I speak with Sneak Ryerson, the famous young detective? I was told he was at a party there at your house."

"Well, I guess so," Lisa's grandmother replied, and she set the plastic telephone handset down on her kitchen counter. Walking outside, she found Mrs. Ryerson, who then spoke with her son.

"Remember, no cases," Mrs. Ryerson said sternly as the young detective exited the pool.

"I know Mom, I know," her son replied as he quickly dried off with a towel and went inside. "Hello?" he said as he grabbed the phone.

"Hello... eh... is this Sneak Ryerson, the young detective?" the elderly man asked in his high-pitched voice.

"Yes, it is," Sneak replied curtly. "Who is this?"

"This is Doctor Bayhill," the elderly man replied.

"Who?" Sneak Ryerson asked, not immediately recognizing the name as his mind reviewed a list of area physicians that he had memorized from the telephone directory.

"Dr. Bayhill," the man said in a quivering voice. "...from the seminary."

"Ah..." Sneak replied. "Sorry, I was thinking of medical doctors."

"No, no, I'm not a medical doctor. I'm over at the seminary. We met when you came over here to meet with Professor Telson a few months ago. Do you remember that?"

"Yes, yes, I do," Sneak replied, surprised that the elderly man's voice on the phone sounded so different from the spry and energetic voice he remembered from his visit several months earlier. In March, the elderly man was bounding with energy, even interrupting Sneak's meeting with another professor to quiz him and learn more about "the great young detective." Now, the voice on the phone was quivering, sounding as if it was plagued by exhaustion and fatigue – the exact opposite of its earlier tone.

"You figured out I was a prisoner of war in World War Two," said the elderly man. "And you even knew the kind of soil I have at my farm… just by spending a minute or two with me. Do you remember that?" he asked.

"Yes, I remember," Sneak replied. "*Pewamo silty clay loam.*"

"That's right!" came the elderly voice.

"How did you find me here?"

"I got the number from your grandmother," the professor explained. "Turns out your grandparents have a farm not too far away from mine."

"Ah right," said the young detective as he remembered his grandmother's descriptions of the strange farming experiments conducted by the professor as he researched ancient agricultural methods. "So, how are you?" Sneak asked awkwardly.

"Well, not very good," the elderly man said in his exhausted voice. "I'm not very good at all."

"I'm sorry to hear that. What's going on?"

"Well, you see, my grandson, Andrew, he's in trouble. He's gotten himself in *quite* a lot of trouble actually, and he could really use your help."

"My help?" Sneak asked.

"Yes," the professor said in his fatigued voice. "My grandson has been accursed… Sorry, my grandson has been *accused*… accused of a crime he didn't commit."

"Ah, I see," replied the young detective. "What happened?"

"He was working as an intern," the professor explained, now speaking rapidly, "In the Law Department… and they've accused him of taking some important papers… some *very* important company papers. He had been doing a good job over there, but they fired him yesterday as he was leaving work. He's really upset about the whole thing – we all are, of course. He says the company might even press charges against him. It's pretty serious. He's afraid he might go to jail and lose his college scholarship."

"Wow," Sneak replied. "What company was he working for?"

"Peloponnesian," the elderly professor replied. "Peloponnesian Oil."

"They aren't known for making mistakes," the young detective said knowingly about the company his father and several of his friends' parents worked for.

"Yes, yes, I know," the professor replied in a worried voice. "But my grandson said he didn't do it – and I believe him. I guess I've got to."

"Yeah, I guess so," Sneak replied doubtfully, knowing that the large company would not have accused the young intern of theft without some convincing evidence. Sneak paused for a moment. "I'd really like to hear more about the case, Dr. Bayhill." The young detective paused to look out the large sliding glass door at the *Sunday School Detectives* playing in the pool and suddenly noticed his mother staring at him intently from a nearby chair. "Really, I would... but there's a slight problem."

"A problem? What's that?" the elderly professor asked quickly.

"It's just that – right now, I'm grounded," the young detective said remorsefully.

"Grounded? As in not flying planes?" the former airman asked in a confused voice.

"No, as in not being allowed to work on any active investigations... until the end of the summer."

"Ah," the elderly professor said in his shaken voice. "Sorry... I was thinking of something different. So, you're not allowed to be a detective until the end of the summer?"

"That's right. There are a few more weeks left before I can start again," Sneak confirmed.

"And you don't think your parents would change their minds, do you?" the professor asked desperately. "This is so important."

"*Other parents* might change their minds," the young detective explained with a laugh. "But not mine. My parents are pretty strict."

"Even if I spoke with them?"

"Probably not," Sneak replied. "Plus, we're leaving for a long vacation in a couple of days."

"I understand," the professor said, his voice turning to a sad tone. "You need to respect your parents and do what they tell you. That is the Fifth Commandment."

"Yeah," agreed Sneak. "But there is *someone* else who could help you," the young detective said with a smile as he looked toward the pool. "Let me go get her for you."

"Someone else?" the professor questioned. "Well, that would be… great, I guess."

Sneak left the kitchen and swiftly found Hailey Cotton poolside. "I've got a case for you," he said with a grin, and quickly provided Hailey with the information he had learned from the professor.

A few moments later, Hailey hurried into the house. "Hi Doctor Bayhill," Hailey said in her cheery sing-song voice when she picked up the telephone handset sitting on the kitchen counter. "My friend Sneak Ryerson told me a little bit about your grandson. I'm sorry to hear about what's going on."

"Thanks," the elderly professor replied wearily. "We've been so upset about it." He paused. "Now, who is this?" the professor asked hesitantly.

"Oh, sorry. I'm Hailey – Hailey Cotton. I'm sort of helping lead the group of investigators that Sneak Ryerson started a few months ago. We're called the *Sunday School Detectives*. Maybe you've heard about us?"

"Oh, yes… Yes, indeed I have," the professor said in his shaken voice. "I've read about your cases in the newspaper. That one at Riverside Park sounded like a real doozy," the professor added.

"It was!" said Hailey with a smile. "Definitely."

"So, my grandson Andrew – Andrew Bayhill – could really use your help. I was thinking your friend, the Young Sherlock Holmes, might be able to help, but it sounds like he's grounded for a few more weeks."

"Right," Hailey confirmed. "Till the end of the summer."

"Well, do you think your group would be willing to take the case?" the professor asked hopefully. "Andrew is in such a bad predicament. I'm just so worried about him. He's afraid he's going to go to jail. They've accused him of taking some rather sensitive documents from the Law Department."

"Well, I'll have to talk it over with the other *Sunday School Detectives*," Hailey explained. "You know, to make sure everyone is okay with taking the case."

"Oh, right… of course," came the professor's soft reply.

"But, I'd be glad to hear more about it," Hailey said.

"That would be swell," the professor said with more volume. "I'm out at my farm right now. Would you and your friends want to drive out here tonight?"

"Well… " Hailey paused. "We're all at a swim party right now," she explained, looking – as her friend did – out the large sliding glass door at the *Sunday School Detectives* who were splashing in the water. "Could we meet sometime tomorrow?"

"Definitely," exclaimed the professor. "I'll be working over at the seminary. I teach classes there in the afternoon, but I could meet you in the morning. Do you know where the seminary is located?"

"Oh, yes, definitely," said Hailey. "I was over there with my friends a few months ago to meet with Professor Telson."

"Oh, well, you'll know where to find me, then," the elderly professor said enthusiastically. "My office is right down the hall from where his office was located."

"Great, so it sounds like there won't be a *mystery* about that," Hailey added, as both she and the professor laughed.

"No, no mystery. You should be able to find my office pretty easily."

"Great!" said Hailey.

"So what time would you like to stop by?" the professor asked hopefully.

"Well, I'm actually going to meet a friend who works at the college at nine o'clock. So, after I meet with her, maybe I could stop by your office?"

"That would be great," Dr. Bayhill replied happily. "The college isn't too far away. I'll be in my office all morning. Just stop by whenever you can. When you get there, I'll call Andrew and he can join us too. He should be able to come over, since he isn't working."

"Right," agreed Hailey. "It will be important to talk to him."

"So, I'll see you in the morning?"

"Yep, I'll be over then," Hailey replied cheerily. "See you tomorrow."

"Thanks," said the professor. "I think you might just be an answer to prayer."

"I hope that's the case!" Hailey answered with a smile.

CHAPTER 5

When Hailey Cotton returned to the pool, we gathered around her as she quickly told us about the interesting conversation she had with Dr. Bayhill. Sneak Ryerson had already told us a few of the facts he had learned about the case, but we were interested in hearing Hailey's account too.

"It sounds like his grandson is a bunch of trouble," Lisa summarized, once Hailey had finished.

"Yeah, Dr. Bayhill is really upset about it," Hailey explained.

"Accused of a crime he didn't commit," Moscow said in a serious voice, repeating the phrase that Sneak had told us a few moments before, as a few of us laughed at Moscow's tone.

"A renegade," Joel said. "Now everyone's looking for him," he added, before singing a few lyrics from a song by the band Styx.

"I wonder what really happened?" Moscow asked, as Joel continued singing. "Did his granddad tell you anything else, Hailey?"

"No, not really," Hailey replied, deep in thought. "Just that his grandson was accused of taking some papers. He didn't say what they were, or anything like that." She paused for a moment. "It's weird. I haven't read anything about it in the newspaper. Has anyone else?"

"No," a few of us added.

"It must have been something pretty important," Sneak said knowingly.

"What do you think, *Joelsie*?" Michelle asked, looking at our friend, Joel.

"Michelle!" Joel protested loudly, abruptly stopping his singing. "I've told you a million times not to call me that!"

"Joelsie," Lisa paused. "That's a cute name, Joel. Why don't you like it?" Lisa's cousin, Cressida – who was reluctant to speak in front of the group – whispered into Lisa's ear. "Cressida thinks it's a cute name too," Lisa added.

"I don't want a cute name!" Joel said indignantly. "They won't let me in a rock n' roll band if I have a cute name."

"What kind of names do they have in rock bands?" Michelle inquired.

"Just regular names," Joel said. "Like Billy."

"Oh, right," Lisa said with a smile. "Like Billy *Joel*."

"Right on man!" Moscow laughed as he jumped back into the water.

"Or Rod, right?" I said. "Like Rod Stewart... I like him," I admitted. "Except Mr. Schroeder wouldn't let me play his album during fifth grade rainy-day recess last year."

"Oh yeah, I remember that," Sneak said with a laugh. "That was funny."

"He said it was too *risqué*," I explained, making air-quotes with my fingers.

"It probably was," Jennie replied seriously as she nodded to Michelle.

"Isn't the lady on the cover wearing, like, a tiger-print pantsuit, or something like that?" Lisa asked. "I saw it in the record store one time."

"I think it's snakeskin," I replied knowingly. "I wanted to get the poster, but my Mom said I couldn't," I added, as the others laughed.

"All I know is that guys in rock bands have regular names," Joel continued with his earlier subject. "Like the Beatles – they just have regular names like Paul and John and George. I'd get laughed out of a band – before I could even audition – if I had a *cute* name like *Joelsie*."

"Hmm, I hadn't thought of that," I replied.

"Take KISS, for example," Joel continued, in a thoughtful tone. "Regular names: Paul, Gene, Ace. There's no names like *Joelsie* in that band!"

"Well," I added. "I heard that the guys in KISS had their faces tattooed with their black and white makeup, so they can never take their masks off."

"What!" Lisa said loudly. "That's not even possible!"

"No, really, that's what I heard," I explained seriously.

"Where did you read that?" Lisa demanded.

"I didn't read it. I *heard* it from a person who knows about stuff like that," I said, not wanting to share the name of my Dad's coworker from the appliance store who had shared the information with me.

"Pep!" Joel protested.

"Come on, Pep!" Lisa replied bluntly. "That is not true. Plus, there was a picture of the band that just came out where they aren't wearing any makeup at all!"

"Yeah, I heard about that," I said. "But what I heard was that the guys in that picture are just *actors* the band paid. They were just *pretending* to be the real guys!" I paused dramatically, then continued my explanation. "Because the real guys in the band have their makeup tattooed to their faces!"

"Come on, Pep," Joel said, shaking his head.

"Oh brother," Lisa added, as she rolled her eyes.

"Hey, Lisa?" Jennie asked, changing the subject. "If you like music too, do you get *Tiger Beat*? My Mom won't let me get a subscription."

"I used to get it," Lisa explained. "But I haven't gotten it in a while. We used to read all about Leif," she added, glancing at her cousin who was in the pool next to her. Soon Cressida gave a wide smile and blushed slightly.

"Oh, Leif Garret," Michelle replied. "I like him."

"I always get him confused with Andy..." I began.

"Andy Gibb?" Michelle added. "I like him too."

"No... not him, that guy on the *Hardy Boys*," I replied, searching for the correct name.

"Shaun Cassidy?" Jennie, Lisa and Michelle all said in unison.

"He doesn't look anything like Andy Gibb!" Lisa scoffed.

"Pep! Come on," Michelle added, as she rolled her eyes.

"All I know," Joel said, returning to the earlier subject, "is that when I get in a rock band, I don't want you to call me *Joelsie*."

"All I know," Michelle replied with a smile as she looked at Joel, "is that when you're singing up on a stage with your rock band at a big concert somewhere, I'm gonna yell really loud, 'Joelsie! Sing us a song by *The Carpenters* – because you know all the words!" We all laughed, remembering how Joel sang a Carpenters' song to Michelle during an earlier case to keep her from feeling afraid.

"Oh brother," Joel replied. "I'm never gonna live that one down."

"Okay," Hailey said seriously from the side of the pool. "Let's talk about this new case for a few minutes. It looks like we don't have too much time before dinner," she added, seeing that Lisa's father was taking hotdogs from a nearby grill.

"Sure," several of us said.

"Dr. Bayhill said he's available to meet tomorrow morning at his office at the seminary," Hailey explained in a matter-of-fact tone. "And I've got a meeting near there in the morning at the college."

"Whatcha' doin' at the college, sis?" Moscow asked, trying to stay focused on the conversation, but also thinking of the next stunt he would perform off the nearby diving board.

"I'm meeting with Alice Williams…"

"Alice Williams!" I said, surprised.

"The girl from the picture?" Joel asked, referring to the young woman our group had identified in a photo when we were investigating *The Case of the Mysterious Circles.*

"Right!" Hailey said enthusiastically. "The same one from the picture."

"That's cool," said Joel. "She helped us with some clues. Why are you meeting with her now?"

"She invited me over to her biology lab tomorrow morning," Hailey explained with a smile.

"What for?" Michelle asked.

"I'm not really sure," Hailey admitted. "She said she wanted to talk with me for a few minutes."

"That's cool!" Sneak's sister Jennie added. "You'll like hanging out with the scientists!"

"Yeah," agreed Hailey. "I like learning about science." She paused for a moment. "Hey, do you girls want to go over there with me?" she asked, looking first at Cressida, then at Lisa. "We met Alice together the last time! And then, after we meet with Alice, we can go over to meet with Dr. Bayhill."

"Well, I'm definitely *not* going back down into that creepy basement ever again!" Lisa said, as she looked to her cousin.

"No way, me either," Cressida said quietly, remembering how scared they had been in the Science Building's dark and eerie basement on their previous visit.

"I'm sure we won't need to go down there tomorrow," Hailey said with a reassuring laugh.

"It couldn't have been *that* scary," Moscow said smugly. "I bet I wouldn't have been scared going down there."

"I bet you would have!" Lisa said. "It was really dark."

"I couldn't see anything," Cressida explained quietly. "It was so creepy."

"And there were some really strange noises too," Hailey added.

"Not to mention Mrs. Cotton's arm on my shoulder!" Cressida said with a laugh.

"Yeah," Moscow replied with a smile. "I heard about that."

"So, do you want to come with?" Hailey asked Lisa and Cressida.

"We could probably go," Lisa replied. "We're not doing anything, right?" she asked her cousin.

Cressida nodded in agreement. "I was going to go to *Children's Place* downtown to get some shoes. But we could do that after," she explained quietly.

"Cool beans," said Hailey with a smile. "We'll go see Alice first, and then go over to meet with Dr. Bayhill... and then go downtown to shop for some shoes!"

"It's good that you can meet with Dr. Bayhill tomorrow," Sneak added in a concerned voice. "He sounded really upset about his grandson. They could use some help."

"Michelle or Jennie," Hailey said, looking at the younger girls in our group. "Do you want to join us?"

"Tomorrow?" Michelle asked.

"The sun will come up," Joel sang with a laugh, reminding us of a song from a popular musical.

"We can't," Jennie explained. "We're going to Day Camp with our Bluebird group."

"It's gonna be really fun," Michelle said, smiling as she gave a thumbs-up sign. "Next year we get to do overnights at Camp Glenn."

"Oh, that should be a lot of fun," Hailey said. "I think we're going next week, right Lisa?"

"Yeah, I think so," Lisa confirmed, as her cousin nodded in agreement.

"We'll be there for a whole week," Cressida said softly as she smiled.

"You'll have a blast," Hailey reassured the younger girls.

"I'm really looking forward to day camp," Jennie acknowledged. "But I'm a little worried."

"It'll be okay, Jennie," Hailey told her. "Michelle will be there with you. And the camp counselors are super cool."

"Oh, I'm not worried about me," Jennie clarified.

"Is it Michelle?" Hailey asked.

"Oh, no, she'll be fine too," Jennie explained, while her friend gave her a thumbs-up sign from the edge of the pool. "It's just that… I'm not sure what Mr. Knick Knack is going to do while I'm gone. The camp is for *girls only*."

"Oh," Hailey replied seriously, as a few of us giggled. "That would make anyone worry," Hailey added sympathetically. "What are you going to ask him to do?"

"My brother's going to watch him," Jennie explained.

"Oh… right," Sneak said with a grimace. "I forgot about that."

"You better not leave him anywhere either," Jennie said sternly to her brother. "No funny business with Mr. Knick Knack."

"You got it, sis," Sneak replied with a smile. "No funny business."

"How about you, Joel?" Hailey asked, turning her attention to the member of our group who had been singing songs through most of her discussion. "Do you want to meet Dr. Bayhill in the morning? What are you up to tomorrow?"

"Well I'm definitely not going to be babysitting Mr. Knick Knack, if that's what you're wondering about!" Joel said with a laugh as many of us joined him. "Maybe I could go to Day Camp with Jennie and Michelle!"

"It's for *girls only*," Jennie said seriously.

"Yeah," Michelle added with a frown. "*Girls only*."

"I'm just kidding," Joel explained as the laughter ended. "I've got a really long piano practice in the morning."

"Can you skip it so you can come with us?" Lisa asked.

"Naw, I can't," Joel said in a serious voice. "I've got a concert coming up this weekend. And tomorrow will be my last time to practice with my piano teacher. Normally my practice is only thirty minutes long, but tomorrow it's like an hour and a half! Or maybe even two hours."

"Wow," someone said. "That's long."

"Yeah, it's only for me and a couple of other students," Joel explained. "And, it's in the morning. I wish I could meet with Alice and the professor; that would be cool."

"That's okay," Cressida said softly. "We can let you know how our meetings go."

"I'd really like to meet that girl from the picture sometime," Joel added.

"Maybe sometime," Hailey replied optimistically. "She was really nice when we met with her a few months ago."

"Yeah," Lisa added. "Just don't let her talk you into visiting the basement!"

We laughed.

"Oh, hey," Joel added with a smile. "If anyone wants to come, you're all invited to my concert. It's – you know – open to the public."

"When is it?" Michelle asked.

"Sunday afternoon," Joel explained.

"I definitely want to go, *Joelsie*," Michelle added with a smile.

"Oh brother," Joel frowned, shaking his head.

"It would be fun to hear you," Hailey added. "We'll see what we can do."

"Yeah," a few voices from around the pool replied.

"So about tomorrow," Hailey continued, turning to her brother. "I know what Moscow's answer will be… about going to *two* meetings in the morning – so I'm not even going to ask if he's interested in joining us."

"Boooring," her brother said as he rolled his eyes. "No way."

"How about you guys?" Hailey asked cheerfully as she looked at Sneak and me. "Sneak, I know you're grounded, but maybe your parents would let you come with? You know, if you told them I was doing the investigating? Or Pep, do you want to come?"

"We can't," Sneak said quickly. "We're busy."

In the flurry of the many activities – with our games of Marco Polo, attempts at synchronized swimming, and the crazy dives off the diving board – I had nearly forgotten the wild idea my friend had proposed to me earlier in the day, as my mind found respite under the hot summer sun from worrying about our upcoming visit to a prison. But suddenly, when asked by Hailey about my plans for the following day, it all returned. "Sneak and I can't go with you tomorrow," I replied quickly. "And you're never *ever* gonna believe where we're going."

With this comment, Sneak Ryerson gave me a long and piercing stare. I had forgotten that on our drive from The Farm back to Findlay, he had asked me not to tell the other *Sunday School Detectives* about our trip to the prison. He said he didn't want them to know about it just in case "things didn't pan out." In addition, his Uncle Charlie had insisted on limiting his prison visit to only one of his nephew's friends, specifically saying that he wouldn't take "that hyper kid named after a Soviet city" on a long car ride. "You know who I'm talking about," his uncle had told him. "The one who does all that crazy daredevil stuff."

"Are you going to The Farm tomorrow?" Joel asked, knowing the familiar name of Grandma and Grandpa Foster's farm.

"Nope," I said with a grin. "I was just there today."

"Riverside Pool?" Moscow wondered with a laugh. "So you can practice your dives off the high dive and finally be better than me?"

"Nope, not there," I replied.

"Okay, we give. Where are you going tomorrow?" Hailey asked.

"Yeah, where are you going?" Lisa questioned.

"Prison," I said with a smile, as I saw my friend shake his head.

"Prison!" Hailey replied in a shocked tone.

"Cool!" Moscow replied, suddenly becoming much more interested in the conversation. "Can I come?"

"We're the only ones permitted to go," Sneak explained seriously, answering Moscow's question. "We're going to visit Mr. Crenshaw."

"Old Man Crenshaw!" Moscow interrupted loudly.

"Moscow!" his sister scolded.

"Sorry, I mean, you're going to visit *Mister* Crenshaw?" Moscow said, correcting himself.

"Yep," I said with a grin.

"Why would you want to go visit him?" asked Lisa, with concern.

"He told the prison warden that he had some information for Sneak," I explained. "And that he'd only share it with him... in person... and in prison. So, the warden called Sneak's Uncle Charlie, who then told Sneak."

"No way!" Moscow said.

"Way," I replied.

"What do you think he wants to tell you?" Lisa asked, turning to the young detective.

"I have no idea," Sneak replied. "No idea at all," he shrugged.

"You don't think he'll be wearing that crazy alien mask, do you?" Hailey asked, laughing.

"I don't think so!" Sneak laughed. "Not in prison."

"That was *so* scary," Jennie added, wide-eyed.

"Yeah," Hailey agreed.

"So, I guess we've got two mysteries to figure out, huh?" Joel summarized. "We've got Dr. what's-his-name's grandson..."

"Bayhill," Hailey said.

"Right," Joel continued. "We've got the mystery with Dr. Bayhill's grandson that Hailey, Lisa and Cressida are gonna work on tomorrow morning. And we've got the mystery at the prison with Mr. Crenshaw that Sneak and Pep are going to learn more about."

"And maybe a mystery with Alice Williams at the science lab," Michelle added hopefully.

"That's right!" Joel replied. "There might be *three* mysteries to solve tomorrow!" The young musician paused for a moment. "I'm feeling a little left out having to go to a practice for my piano recital," Joel admitted.

"Maybe there will be a mystery there too!" Jennie said with a laugh.

"No, no mystery about the concert," Joel replied. "I'm playing Shostakovich!"

"Shosta-who?" Moscow asked.

"Shostakovich," Joel said again. "He's Russian."

"Oh," Moscow replied.

"You know, it's quite possible," Sneak interrupted in a thoughtful tone. "When Pep and I meet with Mr. Crenshaw tomorrow, we might discover that there isn't any mystery to solve at all. It might be a big prank or something like that."

"Yeah," Jennie said. "But it could be a big mystery, right?" she added, her smile showing her missing teeth.

"It could be," her brother replied. "But probably not. He probably just wants us to drive three hours to go see him and then turn around and drive three hours home. I mean, really, what mystery could he tell us about? He's been stuck in a jail or a prison since March! I think he just wants to make us drive six hours."

"Well, I'm hoping tomorrow's mysteries are *big* mysteries, like *The Adventure at Riverside Park*," said Lisa. "Looking for kids' missing pets was getting old – and boring."

"Yeah," her cousin whispered, as several of us agreed.

"So what do you think Dr. Bayhill's grandson – what's his name?" Joel asked.

"Andrew," Sneak and Hailey replied in unison.

"Right… Andrew," Joel continued. "What do you think really happened with him? Do you think he took the papers?"

"I'm not sure," said Sneak carefully.

"Anything is possible," said Hailey.

"Maybe he was the one stealing all of those missing pets we've been trying to find!" Lisa replied with a laugh, as the rest of us burst out in laughter.

"If he was taking all the cats," Michelle added, "he would be a cat burglar!"

"Nice one," Lisa said with a smile as we laughed again and several in our group began swimming and splashing in the pool.

"Maybe Andrew stole some sheep," I said in a goofy voice. "Because he had a hard time sleeping."

"Maybe it wasn't him, but Mr. Crenshaw!" Jennie said as she climbed out of the water and took a few steps away from the pool. "Maybe he stole a bunch of goats!" she added with a wide smile as she ran and jumped back into the pool. "Because he...." She hit the water with a loud splash, muffling the rest of her words.

"Hey Jennie, maybe he stole giraffes!" Sneak said to his sister when Jennie's head popped up to the top of the surface and she emerged coughing.

"Are you okay?" Hailey asked as she watched Jennie's small head bob up and down, pigtails held fast by several rubber bands, dripping with water.

"Yeah, I just sucked in some water," Jennie said as she paddled with her hands and feet to the side of the pool. "Hey Sneak! No giraffes!" she said of her favorite animal when she reached the edge of the pool.

"If that's what Dr. Bayhill's grandson stole, it'd be a pretty hard animal to hide!" Joel said with a laugh.

"Not if he hid it in Jennie's bedroom," Sneak joked. "There are so many toy giraffes in there, it would blend right in!" We laughed at our friend's words as we splashed and jumped around in the warm water, reminded of the many giraffe pictures, figurines and stuffed giraffe toy dolls that filled Jennie's room.

"Another giraffe would be easy to hide in there," Michelle agreed with a laugh, smiling at her friend.

"Maybe it's not giraffes he's after," Sneak continued. "Maybe he's a dog-napper! I know a dog named Ginger he could take off our hands!" he said with a laugh, referring to a dog owned by their neighbor, Mrs. Nelson, that Jennie spent time with and frequently took care of.

"Hey, don't you mess with Gingie-puppy!" Jennie replied with a pout from the side of the pool. "I love Ginger! And you know who else does too?"

"Who's that?" Sneak asked.

"Mr. Knick Knack!" Jennie continued. "And he wouldn't be very happy if his favorite animal was stolen." We laughed at Jennie's comments about her imaginary friend.

After swimming for a few more minutes, Lisa's mother called us to gather at a wooden picnic table for a meal of potato salad, coleslaw, hamburgers and hotdogs.

CHAPTER 6

While the *Sunday School Detectives* splashed in a backyard swimming pool and talked about potential cases, sixty miles to the northeast, in Sandusky, Ohio, a mysterious figure prowled along the shores of Lake Erie.

In later interviews, differing descriptions emerged of the shadowy figure who appeared at several marinas on that Tuesday afternoon. Some said the man was middle aged, while others described him as older. All agreed, however, that he was muscular with solid arms, a broad chest and dark weathered hands. Many agreed that he was dressed as a fisherman or boat hand and looked like someone who had spent long hours on the water. A scraggly blonde beard covered most of the features on his cheeks and chin, and a tattered, dirty, dark blue Greek fisherman's cap – worn low – covered his forehead and obscured his eyes.

In addition to the Sandusky Bay marinas, the fisherman was also spotted at two nearby "watering holes" located along the small waterway across from Cedar Point, the large amusement park overflowing with tall roller coasters and fast-moving rides.

Many of the locals who interacted with the stranger said the man talked with a deep, gravelly voice and asked about the weather, lake conditions and the boats that bobbed up and down in the choppy waters of the nearby docks. In particular, he inquired which vessels were for rent and which ones had owners who were "weekend warriors", who only came to the lake on Saturdays and Sundays or long holiday weekends.

No one was alarmed by the weathered fisherman's questions. He was knowledgeable about his profession and even boasted about the large fish he had caught off The Keys. He announced to several people that he was planning a big trip with some "fat cats" from out of town, who first wanted to fish near Kelly's Island and Put-in-Bay then travel across to Canada. Hearing about his plans, the locals offered a great deal of advice about the wind and weather conditions, while a few even walked with him through long docks filled with rocking boats to help him decide on the best vessel to use for the charter. Others provided the fisherman with their phone number, telling him to call them when he was ready to rent one of their fishing boats, or if he needed them to come aboard as a mate.

It was not until a few days later that the locals realized their friendship and hospitality would not be returned, discovering instead that the weather-worn sailor had not been looking for a boat to rent, but one to steal.

CHAPTER 7

Back in Findlay, Lisa's brother Brad Lavin joined our group at his grand-mother's house on Winterhaven Drive, after finishing his shift at Dietsch's Ice Cream. I had spoken to the older boy only a few times before, most recently when Sneak and I were considering joining the Boy Scout Troop that met in our Church's Annex. When I saw him approach, I expected him to chide me for not joining. But when he neared, he simply said coolly, "Nice article about that case at Riverside Park."

"Thanks," I said nervously.

"Just one thing Stiles," he said to me, seriously.

"Sure," I replied.

"Just don't make me into *Chuck Cunningham*."

"Oh, okay," I said uncertainly. "I… uh… just report… the facts."

"Yeah, sure," he said with a smile, before walking away.

Darkness had fallen on our party and I had already changed into dry clothes when Brad approached me again. "You seemed kind of con-fused when I talked to you earlier," he said to me with a smile.

"Uh, yeah," I uttered.

"I said don't make me into Chuck Cunningham."

"Right," I said hesitantly.

"Do you know who that is?"

"I don't think so," I admitted.

"He's the oldest son of Mr. and Mrs. *C* …. you know, from *Happy Days.*"

"Ah," I said, quickly remembering the minor character on the TV show. "He's the older brother of Richie and Joanie, who…."

"Went off to college, right?" I replied, remembering the television character.

"Right!" Brad said with a smile. "He was a basketball player who went off to college… and no one ever heard from him again!"

"That's right!" I replied with a laugh.

"Anyway, don't make me like him," Brad told me in a more serious tone. "I want to be in your newspaper stories too – just like Lisa and our cousin, Cressida."

"I'll see what I can do," I told him confidently.

"Thanks," came his reply. "Don't forget about me."

"I'll try not to," I nervously laughed.

Soon afterwards, my Mom arrived. She talked with some of the other parents who were at the pool party and then drove me home. I was exhausted from the day's activities and was ready for sleep, but my mother wanted to set out my clothes for my trip to the prison the following morning. Soon, we began to argue about what I should wear. I was insistent on wearing a common summer outfit – running clothes – for my visit. I was envisioning a red tank top shirt with three white stripes printed diagonally on the front, light blue running shorts, long white tube socks with three yellow stripes at the top and my black Chuck Taylor sneakers – a look that many of my friends shared at the time. My mother, however, maintained that the clothes I had picked were too casual for prison and insisted I wear something similar to what I wore to church every Sunday: a blazer with a dress shirt and dress pants. "Church clothes?" I whined. "There's no way I should wear that to prison. And there's no way Sneak Ryerson is going to be that dressed up," I told her adamantly, reluctant to admit that the real reason I wanted to wear my casual clothes was that I was dreadfully afraid of being mistaken for a prisoner if a riot or some mishap occurred. In my imagination, I envisioned something like an adult "food fight" happening in the prison cafeteria or in the prison yard, and the guards grabbing me and yelling, "Go back to your cell!" while I frantically tried to explain that I was only a visitor and not an inmate. "See, I'm wearing running clothes!" I imagined telling the guards.

"But you dressed up to go to the Foster's farm this morning!" my Mom had said in an exasperated tone.

"I wore overalls, Mom!" I replied loudly. "That's not dressing up!"

"Yes, but you didn't wear running clothes to go to their farm, you knew that wasn't the *appropriate* thing to wear. The same is true with visiting the jail."

"Prison," I corrected her.

"Right, prison," she replied, before taking a deep breath. "I don't know why your father and I agreed to such a thing. You'll be having bad dreams about this for a *month of Sundays.* Anyway, Pep, you need to dress up. According to Charles Foster, you'll be meeting with the warden first and probably other guards."

"Corrections officers," I corrected her.

"Pep!" she said loudly. "Don't you correct me to try to change the subject! I just want to make sure you don't look foolish – like you just came in from a jog!" The truth, she certainly knew, was that even though I wore running clothes, I didn't go jogging – I wore the clothes because that was how my friends dressed.

"So, you really think Sneak will be *this* dressed up?" I finally asked.

"Yes, I do," my mother affirmed. "And I'll tell you what," she added. "If Sneak Ryerson is wearing running clothes when he comes to pick you up tomorrow morning, you can change into yours. But for now, let's plan on wearing that new blazer I got for you."

"Okay," I said meekly as I watched her hang a red and white checkered blazer with a white shirt and red pants on the doorknob to my room. Secretly, however, I considered hiding my running clothes inside my green Whittier Elementary gym bag so I could change into them during our long drive.

I went to bed early that night, but my sleep was not sound, interrupted instead with images from crazy and uneven dreams. The setting of my first dream was a country road – a road that seemed to be near the town of Bloomdale, where Sneak and I had biked earlier in the day. In my dream, I was riding Grandma Foster's bicycle with the white basket covered in pink plastic flowers following my friend. Suddenly, on our bicycle ride we came upon a "chain gang" of prisoners working along the side of the road. Some of the prisoners – dressed in tan pants and tan short sleeve shirts – were cutting big boulders with long pick axes, while others moved dirt with shovels or pushed wheelbarrows. At first, I saw this chain gang from a distance. But then, as I approached to get a closer look, I found that I was no longer cycling. Instead, I was actually shackled among the prisoners of the road crew, breaking rocks along the country road with a long pickaxe!

"I shouldn't be here," I told the prisoner who was chained next to me. "I didn't do anything wrong."

"That's what everyone says," my partner in the tan prison uniform told me glumly. "Tell it to the warden."

Someone yelled for me to work faster, while I continued protesting, "I shouldn't be here! I shouldn't be here!"

I looked to my left and was surprised to see that some of the prisoners were people I recognized: Joel and Moscow from the *Sunday School Detectives*, Ponch and John from the television show *CHiPs*, Pepper Anderson from *Police Woman*, and three of the original "angels" from *Charlie's Angels*, as well as Chuck Cunningham from *Happy Days*.

"I don't belong here," I told them. "I'm just a visitor."

The pickaxe, heavy in my hands, seemed to grow heavier with every blow as I continued breaking rocks and watching my two friends cart the stones away in a wheelbarrow.

"This work stinks!" Chuck Cunningham told me.

"Yeah," I agreed.

Why does Chuck Cunningham look like Lisa's brother Brad? I wondered. *Isn't he supposed to be working at Dietsch's?*

Wait, I thought. *What's Joel doing here? He can't be on the chain gang! He's got a piano recital to go to!* I had a sense of panic and worry, uncertain of what was happening, but soon another idea dawned on me. *If Joel can't be on the chain gang, it must mean that I'm dreaming.* Then I quickly woke up.

I went in and out of sleep until sometime later in the night, when I had an even stranger dream. In my mind, I was walking along an open country road with Michelle, Lisa, her cousin Cressida from the *Sunday School Detectives*. Somehow I knew that the country road was located south of Findlay, just beyond the Greenbrier Apartments. As we walked along the barren road at sunset, we eventually saw a man and a woman in the distance standing near a stop sign at the next intersection. "Hey! Look!" Lisa told us loudly. "They're dropping something!" she exclaimed, as we watched the pair drop something into the low ditch next to the road.

"I think it's a package," Michelle said.

"Hey!" I yelled to the man and woman as they quickly disappeared down the road. "You forgot something!"

We quickly ran towards the package with hopes of returning it to the man and the woman, but when we eventually reached the stop sign, the man and the woman were no longer in sight. The four of us rushed down the road's steep embankment and found ourselves in a deep ditch filled with tall grass. We soon saw a large cardboard box. Opening it quickly, we saw that the box contained a baby, wrapped in a blanket. Shocked at the sight, we were relieved to see that the baby was sleeping peacefully inside its makeshift bassinet.

"What should we do?" I asked in a panicked voice.

"Let's take it to the hospital," Cressida advised quietly. "The baby's parents must have left it here for someone to find."

"Why would they do that?" asked Michelle.

"Maybe because they couldn't care for it themselves?" Lisa guessed.

We carefully gathered up the baby and its cardboard box and quickly carried it back to the city, rushing as fast as we could to Blanchard Valley Hospital.

"We... we... have a baby," I said out of breath to a worker at the admitting desk.

"A baby?" she asked loudly.

"Yes, we found it by the side of the road!" Lisa explained.

Soon, however, I was awake and wondering why I was having such a strange dream prior to my visit to the prison.

My sleep was interrupted frequently that night – partially because of the bad dreams, and partially because of a new plastic pad my mother had placed under my sheets due to an accident I had the week before.

Earlier that evening, in addition to arguing about the clothes I would wear, we had also argued about the plastic pad.

"I'm not going to pee my bed tonight," I had insisted. "I'm over that now."

"Let's go a few more weeks to make sure," my mother replied. "We don't want another accident, do we?"

Barely able to sleep, I had to admit that Sneak Ryerson – my friend and great detective – was probably right in waiting to tell me about our visit to the prison. I was overcome with such worry and anxiety about our trip that many strange thoughts and images continued to haunt me throughout my restless night.

CHAPTER 8

I raced out of the house when I saw the car coming down the street – a two-door 1977 Pontiac LeMans that was fast and loud and painted lime green. It was driven by Charles Foster, Sneak Ryerson's uncle, who soon pulled into our driveway. Uncle Charlie – a wide shouldered, former college football player – had wedged his tall frame into the car's black leather front seat and greeted me with a "Hiya Pep!" through the open car window, his wide smile visible under a thick, bushy moustache.

"Hiya Uncle Charlie," I replied.

Sneak Ryerson was in the passenger seat and quickly exited when he saw me, pulling his seat forward and initially greeting me with a mumble. Passing my friend, I moved to squeeze in behind him. "Oh, hey," Sneak warned as I tumbled into the back seat, avoiding two neatly folded sports coats behind the driver's seat. "Watch out for Mr. Knick Knack back there."

"Oh, okay," I replied instinctively. "Wait, what?" I asked, baffled at his cautionary phrase.

"Jennie's at camp today with Michelle, so she asked me to take Mr. Knick Knack with us."

"Okay!" I said with a laugh as I slunk down into the black leather seat. "I hope he moved over before I sat down!"

"I'm sure he did!" my friend laughed as he returned to his leather seat.

The morning of Wednesday July 9th, 1980 had started poorly for me. After a restless night of dreams and strange visions, I had spent nearly an hour wide awake in my bed. I was dreading the upcoming prison visit and my mind remained flooded with images of scary inmates surrounding me during a prison riot or working alongside me breaking rocks on a desolate county road.

"Pep! You better get going," I eventually heard my mother say loudly from the kitchen as she encouraged me to leave my bed. After rising, I quickly showered and ate a small bowl of *Cap'n Crunch* cereal and drank a glass of chocolate milk before putting on the clothes my mother had laid out for me: a red checkered blazer, white dress shirt and red dress pants.

After dressing, I found my Whittier Elementary School bag, which already contained my black Panasonic cassette recorder and extra blank cassettes, and jammed in my running clothes, in case I decided to change into them before entering the prison, to ensure the guards would know I wasn't an inmate.

Eventually, I moved to the living room and waited by the front window for what seemed to be a very long time but was likely only a few minutes.

After I situated myself in the back seat of Uncle Charlie's car, we left my neighborhood and were soon roaring past the muddy waters of the Blanchard River on East Main Cross Street. My mood quickly lightened as I heard my friend and his uncle laughing and talking in front of me. It was also a relief for me to see that I was not the only one who had dressed up for our visit to the prison. Sneak, I noticed, was wearing a white dress shirt and grey dress pants, while his Uncle Charlie wore a white dress shirt with a wide collar that was still in fashion from the late 1970's and black polyester pants. Sneak's uncle was usually dressed in his pressed blue police captain's uniform, and it was a surprise to see him dressed so differently. He seemed uncomfortable in the clothes, frequently referring to them as *civvies* or *mufti*, and explained that he had picked up those terms from some Australian troops he had served with in Vietnam.

We reached downtown Findlay in only a few minutes. The car was noisy, with sounds from the loud engine and the wind with the windows rolled down, but I could still hear Sneak and his uncle talking as we rode slowly past several banks, the post office and a grocery store. The two first talked about the news. Sneak's father received a number of newspapers and magazines, and Sneak had looked at most of them, hoping to find an interesting case to solve. Uncle Charlie also read the newspaper daily, so the two spent some time talking about the local news before turning their discussion to an important national news story: the hostage crisis in Iran. "I just read they've moved the hostages to about a dozen cities after that botched extraction in April," Uncle Charlie explained gloomily. "That makes a military rescue pretty difficult, if not downright impossible."

"Yeah," I added. "But maybe we could figure out a way to get them."

"I'm not so sure about that," the police captain replied morosely.

We were silent for a moment before Uncle Charlie changed the subject. "So, did you see that tennis match on Saturday?"

"What was it?" Sneak asked.

"Wimbledon," Uncle Charlie explained. "In England. Between Bjorn Borg and John McEnroe. It went to five sets and was just *incredible*. There was a long tie-breaker in the fourth – the match lasted over four hours."

"Cool," his nephew replied.

"Who won?" I asked.

"Borg. It was his fifth time winning it," explained Uncle Charlie. "But people are already talking about that being one of the best matches, ever. You know – one for the ages. Borg was relentless, nothing could stop him," he said, making a sweeping motion with his right hand like he was swinging a tennis racquet before grabbing the steering wheel again.

"Cool," I replied.

"I saw in the paper that the GOP convention is starting next week in Detroit," my friend said next. "Who do you think Governor Reagan's gonna pick for his Vice President?"

"It's hard to say. It could be Rumsfeld, or Senator Richard Lugar or Howard Baker – or even President Ford," Uncle Charlie reasoned.

"I like Phil Crane," I added.

"Yeah, he's got a chance too."

"Do you think George Bush has a chance?" I asked.

"Probably not," Uncle Charlie opined. "I don't think he and Reagan like each other too much. They really went after each other during the primaries – like they were having a knife fight in a phone booth! That's how I heard one person explain it."

Sneak and I laughed at the phrase.

"Oh, hey Pep," my young detective friend said, as he turned toward me from the front seat. "Did you hear that Monday was the 50th anniversary of the death of Sir Arthur…"

"Conan Doyle?" I inquired, completing the name of my favorite author.

"The one and only. Do you know what happens fifty years after a writer dies in England or America?" my friend asked.

"Does the Queen throw a party or something?" Uncle Charlie asked with a laugh. "Instead of a *birthday* party, is it a *death* day party?" We laughed at this comment. "I could see them doing something like that for a mystery writer," the police captain added.

"*No,*" his nephew replied in an incredulous tone. "Come on Uncle Charlie, they don't throw a *death day* party. Really, do you know what happens, Pep?" my friend asked me in a serious tone.

"No," I answered my friend. "I don't have a clue."

"Good one!" Uncle Charlie exclaimed. "Maybe Arthur Conan Doyle *didn't have a clue* either!" he added, laughing loudly at my unintended pun about the great mystery writer.

"Fifty years after the death of a writer," Sneak continued, ignoring his uncle, "the copyright expires."

"Oh, that *is* interesting," Uncle Charlie added.

"What does that mean?" I asked, perplexed by my friend's comment.

"That means that all of the characters that Sir Arthur invented, like –" my friend began.

"Sherlock Holmes!" Uncle Charlie said, interrupting his nephew.

"And Doctor Watson," I added.

"And all the others," Sneak continued. "Mrs. Hudson, Lestrade and everyone else, can be used by other writers without having to get permission from his estate..."

"Wow," I interrupted.

"...or pay royalties," Sneak added.

"Pep, that means that you could write a Sherlock Holmes story," Uncle Charlie said encouragingly.

"Right!" his nephew echoed. "That's why I thought of you when I read that article. You could write a Sherlock Holmes story and wouldn't have to pay any money to Lady Bromet or someone like that."

"Lady Bromet?" I asked. "Who's that?"

"That's Sir Arthur's daughter," the young detective explained.

"Sir Arthur Conan Doyle's got a daughter who's still alive!" I exclaimed, surprised at the discovery. "His stories seem so old. I mean they're set in, like, the 1880s, in what do they call it? *Victorian* England, right? I never figured any of his children would still be alive in the *1980s*. I mean, maybe like a great-great-grandchild or someone like that – I could imagine they would still be around, but not any of his actual kids!"

"It's weird, huh?" said my friend.

Sneak's Uncle Charlie found my comment entertaining and let out a laugh. "Well, I guess kids can live a long time!" he exclaimed.

"I was surprised to read that his daughter was still alive too," Sneak told me. "And, I'm with you, Pep. His stories seem so old. You know, with Holmes and Watson getting around London in a horse-drawn carriage and walking along foggy streets that that are lit with gaslights at night. But it was in Sunday's paper – not some old faded copy from a long time ago. Sir Arthur's daughter is still alive and her name is Lady Bromet!"

"Wow," I replied. "It would be cool if we could meet her sometime, wouldn't it?"

"Yeah, definitely," agreed my friend.

"The only thing I remember from last Sunday's paper," I told the two in the front seat, "was a notice that said *The Procrastinators Club* was holding their July 5th picnic on January 20th! And they said they have half a million members, but only 3,000 have gotten around to joining!"

"Now that's funny!" laughed Uncle Charlie.

The green Pontiac soon approached a Bill Knapp's restaurant and the Imperial House hotel near the western edge of Findlay and Uncle Charlie turned the car south onto the entrance ramp for Interstate 75. The car quickly picked up speed as we headed toward our destination – the Lebanon Correctional Facility – located several hours away. The rumbling of the car's engine and the blasts of wind from the open windows made it difficult for me to hear much of Uncle Charlie or Sneak's conversation, so I made a pillow with my checkered burgundy blazer and began gazing out of the small side window located behind the passenger seat. "Last night was the All-Star Baseball Game out in Los Angeles," were the last words I heard Sneak's Uncle say before I fell fast asleep.

Sometime later, I awoke briefly, my mind filled with a new mystery story that I thought my friends would enjoy. Leaning forward, I noticed that my detective friend had also nodded off to sleep. Uncle Charlie, meanwhile, had pulled out his collection of 8-Track tapes and was playing them on the car stereo. I awoke a few times again, hearing music from the 1960's and 70's: Mac Davis, The Doors and Glen Campbell.

CHAPTER 9

I had been asleep for at least an hour and awoke with a jolt as we were passing the tall buildings in downtown Dayton. The road was uneven, and traffic slowed as the highway curved around the city. Soon I saw signs for the Dayton Mall. Leaning forward, I was better able to hear the conversation in the front seat of the car. "We should eat lunch over there after our meeting with Mr. Crenshaw," I heard Charles Foster tell his nephew. "Meeting with prisoners always makes me hungry!" he added with a laugh.

"Wh… where exactly do you want to eat, Uncle Charlie?" Sneak asked sleepily, having also just woken up.

"The mall. Department stores have the best restaurants," his uncle explained confidently, pointing to the large shopping mall to our left.

"The food court?" my friend asked.

"Naw, not the food court. I want to eat inside one of the department stores. The restaurants in the stores are always better," Uncle Charlie explained. "I grab lunch at the restaurant inside J.C. Penney's at the Franklin Park Mall every weekend I'm up in Toledo. Let's plan on eating at one of the department stores here on our way back home."

"Okay," came his nephew's groggy reply.

We listened to Glen Campbell's popular song "*Rhinestone Cowboy*" on the car stereo a few times and soon saw signs for the cities of Franklin and Middletown. "It's not too much farther now," Uncle Charlie observed.

As we got closer to the exit for the prison, I found myself feeling more and more anxious about our upcoming visit with Russell Crenshaw

– a criminal we helped catch several months earlier – and I began fidgeting around the cramped backseat.

Eventually, Uncle Charlie rolled up his driver's side window and asked his nephew to roll up his, in order for me to hear him clearly. "You're moving around quite a lot back there," Uncle Charlie said as he looked back at me in his rearview mirror.

"Yeah," I admitted. "I'm getting pretty nervous."

"It will be okay. We won't be inside for long," he explained confidently.

"Okay," I replied meekly.

"But once we're inside," Uncle Charlie warned us in a stern voice. "Whatever you boys do, don't tell them I'm a police officer."

"Okay," I heard Sneak say. "Did you hear that too, Pep?" he asked, turning to me. "You're not always the best at keeping secrets."

"Yeah," I replied.

"Don't worry, if something goes wrong, we'll be able to get out. I'll make sure of it," Uncle Charlie explained, continuing his serious tone. "But it would be more complicated if they knew I was an officer of the law."

"Lew…" I said, using my favorite Inspector Clouseau voice.

"What?" the police captain asked, uncertain of my reply.

"Nothing," I told him with a smile.

"You understand what I'm saying," he said again, still sternly. "Obviously, Russell Crenshaw will know what I do because I arrested him. But if we meet any other prisoners, you don't have to tell them I'm a police officer. Got it?"

"Yeah," came the reply from his nephew.

"Right on man!" I said goofily, feeling anxious about the visit.

Eventually, we arrived at our exit and turned onto State Route 63 – an empty country road surrounded by farmland – and headed east toward the prison. We drove for several minutes along long rolling fields, and soon three sky-blue water towers appeared in the distance. Getting closer still, we passed several one-story white painted barns that were surrounded by white wooden fences. A sign near the side of the road zoomed by. It was dark brown, wooden and in the shape of the state of Ohio. I could only read a few words: "…operated by staff and inmates."

Seeing the word "inmate" caused my heart to race even faster. "I don't think I can do this," I told the others.

"It will be okay," Uncle Charlie said reassuringly as he glanced at me again in the rearview mirror.

"Pep, you don't have anything to worry about," Sneak said encouragingly from the front seat. "Just stick with me and it will be okay. You don't have to say anything to anyone; just write down what you hear."

"Yeah," I said in a sound that was just above a whisper.

As we drew closer to the entrance, I saw none of the chain gangs along the roads I had dreamed of the night before. Nor did I see any prisoners working outside in the summer heat and wearing the wide blue and white horizontal striped uniforms, like the Hamburglar on McDonald's TV commercials or the prisoners from the Keystone Cops from our downtown parades. Instead, the fields were empty, except for several large black and white Holstein cows that grazed peacefully nearby.

After turning into the prison's long driveway, several three-story red brick buildings came into focus. They all seemed interconnected. Built, I guessed, in the 1950s or earlier. Surrounding the buildings were tall chain link and brick fences, their tops wrapped with sharp silver concertina wire – the looping and twisted wire where thousands of sharp and tiny razors made escape nearly impossible.

Soon, we were in the prison's large parking lot and Uncle Charlie reversed the car into a spot – something he was trained to do with his vehicles in Vietnam, he explained.

After we parked, I tumbled out of the car with my green gym bag in hand. "Leave that bag in the car," Uncle Charlie told me sternly as he was working to get on a black tie and a dark blazer.

"But it's got my tape recorder," I told him. *And my gym clothes*, I wanted to tell him.

"You can bring that," he told me in sharp measured words, referring to my tape recorder. "Just don't bring that bag."

"Okay," I said meekly as I sensed Uncle Charlie's tension grow. And I quickly retrieved my black tape recorder from the bag and tossed the gym bag into the back seat of the car.

I waited for a moment as my friend also put on a tie and his blue blazer. And I suddenly felt under-dressed, noticing that I was the only one not wearing a tie.

I followed a few steps behind Sneak and his uncle, who were walking quickly through the long parking lot toward a large sign that read VISITOR'S ENTRANCE. We reached an open gate next to the parking lot, and were met by a serious looking guard – dressed in a starched white shirt and dark blue pants – who was stationed next to a small guard house. He asked for our names, checked them with a list he had on a piece of white paper attached to a dark wooden clipboard, and gave us permission to enter.

After walking through the open gate, we opened a thick metal door and entered an old red brick building where we found ourselves in another check-in area, behind three other visitors who had arrived before us. While waiting to proceed, I noticed that everything within the large open area – window frames, door frames, long wooden benches for visitors and even the guard's station – all seemed in need of a fresh coat of paint. "Wow," I said. "This place isn't too fancy."

"Right," Uncle Charlie replied. "They don't want the prisoners thinking they're on vacation here," he added with a measured laugh.

"I don't think they'll be confused," I told him, as I tried to see the car out in the wide parking lot through a narrow slit in a window behind thick metal bars – a grim reminder that I wasn't on vacation either.

We gave our names to another corrections officer at a check-in desk before going through a metal detector. The officer there spent several minutes looking at my tape recorder, taking out the cassette tape and then the batteries, to make sure I hadn't hidden anything inside it. Then, we waited for a few minutes more in the visitor's lobby before being met by yet another corrections officer who told us to follow him to the warden's office.

"I was hoping we'd meet the warden," I said with a smile to my friend.

We walked slowly, pausing for several heavy grey metal doors to open, then walked down several hallways and up a long staircase to the third floor of the building.

It was on our way to the warden's office that I saw the first "real" inmate: an old, disheveled man, whose wrists were bound by handcuffs and his ankles shackled with a thick metal chain. The prisoner, I noticed, was wearing "prison blues" – baggy dark blue pants with a dark blue short-sleeved shirt. He was escorted by two corrections officers. "Hi," I said instinctively to the prisoner as I hurried past him, trying to keep up with the corrections officer who was talking to Sneak's uncle as he guided us through the maze of locked doors to the top floor of the building.

Eventually, we found ourselves in a nicely decorated, wood paneled waiting area outside the warden's private office. A receptionist asked us if we wanted some coffee and Uncle Charlie accepted the offer of a warm beverage, while Sneak and I politely declined. We waited for a few minutes in leather chairs next to the receptionist's desk before being escorted into the warden's office – a spacious room in the corner of the facility's Administration Building.

The warden was a short man with receding salt and pepper hair. He wore black "browline" framed glasses that had been popular several decades earlier, with their thick dark plastic top and silver-wired chassis that held in the lenses. To my surprise, the warden was dressed like his visitors, wearing a checkered sports coat, white dress shirt and polyester tan "slacks" (as my mother would call them). The only difference in our appearance, it seemed, was the small bowtie he wore close to his neck. "Well, well, well," the older man said with a smile as we entered. "Isn't this something! I get to meet the young detective I've read so much about! And you must be Captain Foster, the boy's uncle?" he said, addressing Uncle Charlie.

"Yes, sir," Sneak's uncle said formally, making me think he had probably used those two words thousands of times during his military career.

"And which one of you is the young detective?" the warden asked, looking at the two of us.

"That'd be him," I said pointing to my friend.

"I'm Sneak… Sneak Ryerson," my friend said seriously as he shook the warden's hand.

"Nice to meet you," the warden replied, also formally. "And this must be your friend, the writer?"

"Well… I'm trying to be a writer," I explained awkwardly, not entirely comfortable with that description.

"You've had some stuff published already," Sneak interrupted.

"Yeah, I guess so," I added, shaking the warden's hand. "I'm Pep Stiles," I told him.

"Nice to meet you as well," the warden said, still smiling. "We usually get pretty good press here," he added with a laugh. "I hope that continues!"

"Oh, well… sure," I stammered.

"What I really mean is, I hope you don't write anything bad about me!" the warden laughed.

"Oh no," I insisted. "I definitely won't do that."

"My guards called me when you entered, concerned about that recording contraption of yours, but I told them it would be fine. Have a seat, have a seat."

"Thanks," I said, glad that I could record the conversation with the warden and our interview with Mr. Crenshaw.

The warden directed us to sit in large comfortable blue leather chairs in front of his long wooden desk, and once we were seated, to our surprise, began quizzing Sneak on the various cases the young detective had solved. The warden, it turned out, had been following Sneak's career closely for several years, and remembered a number of details about his cases. He was most interested in hearing about the work Sneak had done with the Police Department's "cold" cases – the older open cases that Sneak's uncle had asked him to look into.

"Wow, you sure seem to know a lot about my cases," Sneak concluded after the long review.

"Well, I've always liked reading mysteries. You know, Sherlock Holmes and that sort of thing."

"Us too!" I replied enthusiastically, and quickly began telling him the news I had learned earlier in the morning about the fiftieth anniversary of Sir Arthur Conan Doyle's death.

"I read that as well," affirmed the warden. But after a short pause, the warden continued with another set of questions to my friend about his old cases.

"So, is this the first time you boys have been to a correctional facility?" the warden finally asked, after concluding his long discussion of Sneak's cases.

"It is for me," I explained.

"Me too," said Sneak Ryerson. "I mean, I've visited some prisoners at the Hancock County *jail*, but this is the first real *prison* I've visited," he added in a noticeably energetic and eager tone – quite different than his typical somber demeanor. "I'm looking forward to talking to Mr. Crenshaw and hearing what he has to tell us."

"Well, we typically don't allow visitors your age in here – unless, of course, they're children of an inmate. It can be somewhat scary for a visitor coming in off the street."

"No kidding," I replied.

"It's punishment after all," the warden explained in a serious tone. "That's what some visitors forget. But you shouldn't. Don't ever forget that. The inmates in here," – I noticed that throughout our conversation, the warden referred to the prisoners as 'inmates', not 'guys' or any other casual term – "...they're in here for a reason. And that reason is *always* a bad one. Each of them has committed a serious crime – something heinous, something awful. Maybe they've killed someone," he motioned to Sneak, "Or tried to kill someone, like almost happened to you, right? When you were almost run over by that car. Or, they've forcibly taken someone's property with a weapon – in an armed robbery, a B&E or something like that. So, the word of caution I always tell our visitors is: *Don't let them fool you.* They've all done something really bad to be here," the older man said, staring intently at me first and then my friend. "Now, of course, some of them will tell you that they are innocent – that someone else did the crime and they shouldn't do the time – but no one's convinced me yet. They all deserve their punishment."

"Yeah," I replied, agreeing with the warden's assessment.

"You haven't had to set an innocent person free?" Sneak asked.

"Well, not too many," the warden said, as he paused for a moment before changing the topic and taking a warmer and friendlier tone. "I think you'll find our guards and staff are all top notch; they'll be with you the whole time and will treat you well. And," he added with a smile. "I've got a surprise for you. You boys are in for a real treat today."

"A treat?" Sneak asked. "I don't understand."

"Like ice cream or something at the cafeteria?" I asked, worried again about being caught up in a food fight that would turn into a riot.

"No, no," the warden laughed. "I'm not thinking of food from the cafeteria. We're not inviting you to lunch today!"

"Oh," I replied meekly.

"I didn't think you'd mind," the warden smiled. "But I've arranged for you to meet with *two* prisoners today, not just one!"

"Two prisoners?" Sneak questioned.

"What?" I asked loudly, already anxious about meeting *one* prisoner, and now shocked by the news that I would have to meet with *two*.

"That's right," the warden continued with his smile. "There are actually two inmates in here you'll be interested in meeting."

"Who?" Sneak Ryerson asked, now louder than normal, his brow wrinkling as his computer-like mind searched for an answer to his question.

"Well, it has to do with that case of yours up in Findlay – with the UFOs and the crop circles. Two of the individuals involved in that case are incarcerated here."

"Someone besides Mr. Crenshaw?" I asked, surprised.

"Yep," the warden said informally. "That young man he got to work for him."

"Julian Davis!" I nearly shouted.

"Yep!" the warden replied with a smile. "That's the one."

"What's he doing here?" I asked impatiently.

"Well, once he was found competent to stand trial," Uncle Charlie interjected from the seat beside me. "He immediately took a plea deal and got sentenced."

"Oh," I replied.

"I didn't realize he was sent down here already," Uncle Charlie continued.

"He hasn't been here too long," the warden explained. "Just a week or two."

"Julian Davis was found competent?" Sneak asked in a surprised tone, turning to his uncle. "I figured he'd be sent to some mental institution."

"He was found to be competent," Uncle Charlie said seriously.

"Well, between you, me and the fence post," the warden said with a wry smile, "I think he's crazier than a bed bug."

"Yeah," I agreed.

"I was hoping he'd gotten better," my friend said hopefully. "But, I haven't talked to him."

"Well, my C.O.s are telling me he still thinks the aliens are coming," the warden explained, shaking his head. "He says that any day now they're going to land in the prison yard and spring him from his cell."

"Oh no," Sneak replied with a grimace.

"Oh brother," I added.

"Well, that should be a pretty interesting conversation," Uncle Charlie concluded.

"Yes, yes it should," the warden added with a smile.

"So, I was wondering," I asked the warden. "Why aren't Mr. Crenshaw – and now Julian too, I guess – why aren't they closer to Findlay? There's a prison up in Marion, right? I've driven by it with my Mom before. And I think there's another one up near Toledo, too. It seems kind of far to be down here."

"Well," the warden explained seriously. "Once they're convicted, the prisoners go to a Reception Center – we've got two in Ohio, one in

Loraine and another in Orient – and from there, they could be placed at any of our prisons. But, you're right," the warden explained, "there is a prison in Marion and a few others in northwest Ohio. And, the Department of Corrections generally likes to keep inmates close to the areas where they're from. It helps if their families can visit them, but more importantly, if they need to go to court for an appeal or another case, it's not too long of a drive. But, I think there is some construction going on up in northwest Ohio and they had a shortage of cells, so the two got placed here. We've got a few from your area. And, Captain Foster can probably tell you, there's not much difference between the different correctional facilities in Ohio."

"Oh," I answered wearily, growing tired of the conversation that had lasted much longer than I had expected.

"But you probably noticed the one thing that sets us apart from a lot of other prisons – the farm," the warden said, nodding in the direction of his large window. "It provides a lot of the produce that the prisoners eat here at LCI."

"Oh," I replied. "That's cool."

"It's also an incentive for good behavior," the warden continued. "If they don't get into trouble, the inmates can get outside and into the sunshine and do something productive. They make license plates here too, but working on the farm is the thing they really want to do. Well, that, and get out of here for good!"

We laughed at the warden's comments.

"The farm is cool," I told him, feeling a little more reassured for my safety by the warden's comments that the prisoners would act better because they wanted to work on the farm. "Did you hear about that movie called *Brubaker*?" I asked, as Sneak and his Uncle quickly interrupted me and stood, thanking the warden for his time.

"Well, you're in for quite a treat with those two prisoners," the warden said with a smile.

"I guess so," said the young detective.

CHAPTER 10

A few minutes before nine o'clock that morning – while Sneak Ryerson and I were still on our way to the prison – a newer model Chevrolet Caprice station wagon navigated the narrow streets on our local college's campus. The copper-colored vehicle was driven by Hailey's mother, Mrs. Cotton, who was providing her passengers with the names of many of the college buildings located along the empty sun-drenched streets. "Here's the theater… and the local church on campus." She paused. "This campus sure is empty in the summertime," she added as her three passengers agreed. They drove further, and she was soon pointing to an imposing five-story red brick building. "Things have changed a lot since I was a student here. Most of our classes were there in the *Old Main*. Now, there's a building for almost every subject!"

A few minutes later, Mrs. Cotton passed a small planetarium, with its distinctive domed roof, and stopped her vehicle in front of the Science Building. "You girls have a good time," she said warmly. "Call me if you need anything. I just have to take Moscow to swim practice at the *Canterbury Club*."

The three passengers, all *Sunday School Detectives*, scurried out of the vehicle amid a chorus of "Thanks Mrs. Cotton!" and "See ya' later!" while Hailey Cotton added, "Love ya', Mom! Thanks for driving us over here!"

"Have a good time," they heard Mrs. Cotton say as they exited the car. Soon, the passengers heard Mrs. Cotton's favorite song called, "Sentimental Journey" – made famous by Doris Day in 1944, with the lyrics, "Seven, that's the time we leave at seven." The music trailed off as the car sped away.

The three young detectives – Hailey Cotton, Lisa Lavin and Cressida Hudson – quickly entered the building and ascended three flights of stairs to reach a biology lab on the building's top floor.

The girls had visited the lab several months earlier – while working on *The Case of the Mysterious Circles* – and found the large, well-equipped laboratory mostly unchanged with microscopes, glass cylinders, test tubes and other scientific equipment filling the large high-ceilinged space. After greeting the professor who oversaw the research, the three girls saw Alice Williams, a young researcher in her early twenties, leaning over a microscope on the far side of the room, carefully examining a specimen.

Like the other researchers, Alice wore a long white lab coat, and her hands were covered with blue latex gloves. As the girls approached, they noticed that she was slowly adjusting a dial on the microscope with her left hand while quickly scribbling information into a well-worn black composition notebook with her right hand. "Alice, you have some visitors," the biology professor announced, startling the young researcher.

"Oh, hey!" Alice said warmly after she turned to face the girls. "Y'all are here!" she smiled.

Hailey Cotton, who had led the others through the maze of lab equipment, thought that Alice seemed more relaxed than she had on their previous visit. And after hearing her say, "Y'all", Hailey smiled as she thought of how her friend, Sneak Ryerson, might have analyzed her accent: "Alice's voice conveys a southern accent with a soft border-state inflection."

"Is it okay that I brought my friends?" Hailey asked tentatively, gesturing toward Lisa and Cressida. "I know you just invited me."

"Oh, sure, that's fine," came the cheerful reply and soon the young scientist was complimenting the girls on their similar sundresses. "Do you want to look at some samples?" Alice asked a few moments later.

"Sure," said Hailey enthusiastically.

"I guess so," Lisa obliged.

Alice moved towards the microscope and began placing different slides under the lens while the girls took turns peering at the magnified shapes. The young researcher explained that the specimens were from moth larvae and had been taken at different points in their development, but after a few minutes of taking turns looking through the microscope, Lisa admitted, "I really can't tell any difference. They all seem the same to me."

"To the untrained eye, I can see how that might be the case," Alice said with a laugh. "It took me a while to see the differences."

"Is this what you do all day?" Lisa frowned. "Just look at the slides with your microscope?"

"Well, that's part of what I do," Alice admitted. "I count up what I see on one slide and then compare it with what I see on another one. That's what all these numbers are here," she said pointing to the quickly written numbers in the notebook on the countertop. "And that's what all these pictures and printouts are for too," she added, pointing to black and white experiment photographs and chromatography results, printed on narrow white pieces of paper, that overflowed unevenly from the notebook's edge. "And, when I'm not counting samples or taking pictures, I'm taking care of the moths!"

Hailey, being quite interested in science, asked several questions, but soon Alice noticed that the girls seemed bored with the scientific discussion. "Why don't we go out to the hallway," she said, and the four exited the lab. "Would you like some hot tea?" she asked when they arrived at a small table located in the hallway outside of the lab's large wooden door.

"None for me thanks," said Hailey.

"I'm okay too," Lisa said as her cousin whispered something in her ear. "But Cressida would like some."

"Great," Alice said with a smile, and she quickly grabbed an orange kettle. "Y'all are missing out," she said, smiling at Lisa and Hailey. "Why don't you go get some chairs and I'll go fill this with water."

The three young detectives found several plastic chairs that were spaced unevenly in the hallway and brought them around the small table. They waited quietly until Alice returned, her long blonde hair draped behind her white lab coat that swung like a pendulum, as she quickly walked with the orange tea kettle held tightly with both hands.

"So, how's it going?" Hailey asked in a friendly tone, as Alice prepared the tea for herself and Cressida.

"My summer's going great!" Alice informed the three *Sunday School Detectives*. "Last semester was pretty hard... you know... with my classes and my work here at the lab. But now that summer's here, I can relax a little."

"That's good," replied Hailey with a smile. "You look more relaxed than the last time we saw you."

"Last semester was *so* crazy," Alice continued warmly, but she quickly leaned closer to the three girls and lowered her voice. "You know, with all that stuff happening with *Julian Davis*. I'm surprised I didn't fail all my classes!"

The girls smiled as they remembered Alice's friendship with the young man who was involved in *The Case of the Mysterious Circles*.

"I was so distracted!" Alice admitted. "That whole thing was just so crazy."

"Yeah," Lisa agreed.

"Definitely," Hailey added.

"I was really worried I'd have to testify at his trial!" the young scientist confessed. "Even though I didn't really know anything."

"That would have been hard," assured Hailey.

"No kidding!" said Alice, raising her voice. Then, leaning toward Hailey, she added, "I'm so sorry I didn't call you back. I got your message when you called to check on me. And… I was going to call you back, but I didn't… I'm sorry about that."

"Oh, that's okay," reassured Hailey. "I just called to say *thanks* for helping us with the investigation. Plus, I wanted to make sure you were okay. I know Julian was a friend of yours."

"Yeah, well… he used to be. I haven't talked to him for a while."

The four paused for a moment.

"That whole thing was just so weird," the young researcher continued. "That's the word I keep using to describe it all… *weird*. And, I really should have called to check on your friend, Sneak Ryerson, too. I just couldn't believe it when I heard that Julian had run him over with his car!" Her eyes were now wide in wonder. "It was so unlike Julian to do something like that. He's not that kind of person – or at least I didn't think he was." She paused, then added with a shudder, "I've even ridden in that car with him."

"You heard that Sneak's okay, right?" Lisa informed the young scientist. "His arm was sore for a while and his parents got him a new bike – his old one was really mangled up. But he's okay."

"I'm so glad about that. I should have called to check on him… or sent him something," Alice said apologetically. "I was just so… you know… sad. It just really upset me. I've been going over everything in my mind, wondering if I could have *done* something different. You know… wondering what would have happened if I *hadn't* quit F.E.E.T.?

Maybe if I hadn't quit, Julian would have listened to *me* instead of listening to that old guy who told him to run over your friend! Then, *your* friend wouldn't have gotten hurt! And *my* friend wouldn't be in jail! I don't know, it just really bums me out."

"Those ideas are pretty deep," said Cressida – surprising her friends, as she rarely spoke in front of others. Feeling self-conscious, she quickly moved her hand to check one of the curls in her feathered hair, flipped back in a style made famous by Farrah Fawcett.

"Yeah," came Alice's faint reply. "I guess those questions are pretty deep."

"I don't know how you could answer those," Lisa interrupted abruptly. "Those are... what's the word... *guesses?*"

"Hypothetical questions," answered the young scientist. "And you're right, thought experiments aren't like the experiments we do here in the lab... there is nothing conclusive in asking what *might* have happened."

The four paused again.

After giving a cup of warm tea to Cressida and grasping her own hot cup tightly, Alice again leaned closer to the others at the table. "Did you know," Alice continued in a near-whisper. "Julian Davis hid out here."

"Hid out here?" Lisa asked in an alarmed voice.

"Really?" questioned Hailey, surprised by the news.

"Well, not *here* in the hallway," said Alice with a laugh. "Or in the lab," she added, looking over at the laboratory's open wooden door. "This area would actually be a pretty hard place to hide because there are so many people coming and going to check on their experiments at all hours of the day and night."

"Oh," Hailey said thoughtfully.

"It was actually on the night y'all came over here to interview me... and the very same night Julian tried to run your friend over with his car."

"Really?" asked Lisa, leaning forward.

"Yep," Alice continued seriously. "This was where he hid from the police, after he tried to run your friend over."

"Wow," Hailey replied, astonished. "I didn't know that. Where exactly did he hide?"

"In the basement," the young scientist began.

"Oh no!" Lisa interrupted loudly. "You're not gonna try to take us down there again, are you? 'Cause there's no way I'm going back down there!"

"Yeah, that place is really creepy," Cressida added softly.

Alice laughed when she heard the girl's descriptions of her work location. "You didn't think it was that bad, did you?" she asked. "I work down there every day!"

"Sorry, Alice," Hailey said with a smile. "I'm going to have to agree with Cressida, it was pretty creepy."

"...and dark," Cressida added.

"The moths need it to be dark!" Alice said with a laugh.

"It was pretty smelly too," Lisa admitted.

"Okay, okay," replied Alice, saying her words more quickly. "I'm *not* taking y'all back down there! I just thought you'd like to know that Julian hid down there on the same night y'all were here. Of course, I didn't know he had been here until he made his confession to the police."

"That was part of his confession, huh?" Hailey asked in an interested tone. "I don't think I heard much about that."

"Yeah," Alice confirmed. "And when the police found out where he had been hiding, they swarmed all over this place, you know, tryin' to find out as much as they could."

"Wow," said Lisa.

"But I think the investigators were pretty creeped out downstairs just like y'all were!" Alice explained with a laugh. "They ended up bringin' in a bunch of extra lights so they could see things more clearly. It really messed up my moths!"

"Oh no!" Hailey exclaimed.

"The moths are okay now," Alice said reassuringly. "Anyway, while they were down there, they found Julian's duffel bag."

"With clothes in it?" Lisa asked.

"I think there were a few clothes in it. They brought it up here to me in the lab. And you know what it had in it? All of the letters he... he had *translated* – I guess you could call it, or de-coded might be a better way of explaining it – from that so-called alien."

"*The Great Peggu*," Hailey sighed. "How could we ever forget about him?" she laughed as the others joined her.

"Yeah, *The Great Peggu*," laughed Alice. "What a crazy name for a space alien! Anyway, they let me look at some of the letters before they took them to the police station... I guess the detectives thought I was somehow involved and might give them more information. But I didn't know anything about what Julian was doing – I think they figured that out pretty quick."

"Right," said Lisa.

"I tell ya', I was flabbergasted to read some of those letters," Alice admitted. "I couldn't believe Julian fell for all that stuff... it just makes me so mad at that guy..."

"Mr. Crenshaw," Hailey clarified in a serious tone, looking knowingly to Lisa and then to Cressida, as she and the other *Sunday School Detectives* were reminded that Sneak Ryerson and I had an appointment to see Mr. Crenshaw later that morning.

"Right... Mr. Crenshaw," Alice agreed. "He said so many crazy things about alien spaceships coming here, and how Julian would be a great governor or emperor or something over lots of planets. It was just so unbelievable, but Julian bought it all." Alice paused briefly before slowly adding four more words in a deeply Southern accent. "Hook, line and sinker."

"Yeah," Lisa agreed.

"I just feel so bad for Julian," Alice continued. "Now that he's in jail, I can't imagine he's getting the help he needs. He's... you know... he's just messed up. Crazy – m*entally unstable* – I guess is the technical word for it. And that guy..."

"Mr. Crenshaw," Lisa answered.

"...he took advantage of him – making Julian believe he was getting letters from an alien!" Alice scoffed.

"It was pretty amazing," replied Hailey.

The three detectives waited for the young scientist to take a sip from her cup of hot tea, before Hailey asked, "So, did you want to talk more about *that* case?" Hailey paused to look at her watch, remembering that she had a second appointment to keep that morning, then added, "Is that why you invited me here?"

"I guess you're probably wondering why I called you out of the blue!" laughed Alice. "I've talked your ear off about Julian!"

"You didn't give me much to go on."

"I don't have a new mystery or anything like that to tell you about," Alice explained, sitting up in her chair. "I don't need y'all to solve anything *for me*."

"Oh, okay," said Hailey.

"Actually," Alice confessed, leaning forward again, closer to the three detectives. "I've been following your cases in the newspaper."

"Oh," Hailey replied.

"Yeah, it's been fun to read about your detective work. It sounds like you did a good job in handling some tough cases."

"Thanks," Hailey smiled.

"That case at the park seemed real excitin'," Alice continued.

"It was," Lisa answered. "But I think our friend Pep Stiles may have exaggerated a few things in his article." Lisa smiled and glanced at Hailey and then her cousin. "You know – to make it sound a little more exciting than it really was."

"Maybe just a tad," Hailey admitted.

"A little," Cressida said in an almost-whisper.

"Well, that article in the newspaper made the case sound super exciting," Alice said before pausing again. "So…" Alice continued, haltingly. "What I was wondering, is… it sounds sort of crazy as I say it out loud… but it's just that, well…"

"What?" Lisa interrupted impatiently.

"I'd like to help you out… you know, if I could," Alice explained.

"Oh, sure," Hailey said reassuringly. "If there's any crimes you come across …"

"Or evidence of a crime," Lisa added.

"Right," Hailey continued. "If you run across any evidence of a crime, you can always call us and we'll investigate it. Or if we can't do it, we can always give it to the proper authorities."

"Anytime," Lisa added.

"Definitely," Cressida whispered.

"Well," said the young scientist, even more sheepishly than her earlier tone. "I wasn't exactly thinking of *turning* evidence over to you."

"Oh?" Hailey asked with a puzzled look.

"I was actually thinking… this does sound crazy… but I was thinking that maybe I could join y'all?"

"Join us?" Lisa asked, perplexed.

"Yeah, like I was thinking maybe you'd want to take me on as, you know, an older detective – for your group."

Soon, the girl's faces changed from perplexed looks to ones of recognition as they began to understand Alice's request. "I wouldn't have to be a full-fledged member of your detective agency," Alice continued. "Maybe I could serve as a… consulting scientist? We have so much equipment here in the lab," she explained, gesturing to the open door. "And there's even more equipment in the other labs here in the Science

Building – some really powerful microscopes and a mass spectrometer and some other great things. I could use them to help you analyze evidence from crime scenes."

"Wow, that would be great," Lisa said.

"Yeah, but Sneak has a lot of scientific equipment too," Cressida said softly.

"That's just a few things in his *basement*," came Lisa's quick reply.

"Oh, well if you have that covered," Alice pulled back hesitantly.

"No, no," Lisa interrupted. "I'm sure Sneak doesn't have all of the stuff you have here. Plus, he's grounded."

"Oh," the young scientist replied. "I didn't know that."

"So," Hailey began slowly. "When you say you'd like to join us, does that mean you'd like us to bring evidence to *you* – for you to analyze – or would you like to go with us when we go out to investigate cases and interview witnesses and look at crime scenes?"

"I think I'd like to do *both* – be a scientist and a detective," Alice clarified with a smile. "I'm really interested in doing something other than spending all of my days and nights here with the *Ti. ni.*," she said, using the scientific name for the moths she raised in the lab. "The past few days I've thought, you know, maybe I could do something to make more of a difference," she continued. "Don't get me wrong; I like my work here in the lab. The research I do here is important and might even get into a scientific journal… *someday*. But I was thinking, what if I could do something right *now*, something that could really help people *today*, with problems that they are having. That would be pretty neat." The young scientist paused for a moment, and her voice changed to a more serious tone. "If I could stop a criminal – you know, someone like that guy who took advantage of my friend… Julian."

"Mr. Crenshaw," Cressida said softly.

"Right!" Alice said more forcefully, and her tone turned angrier. "If I could put someone like Mr. Crenshaw behind bars – so he could never, ever, take advantage of people again – it would be worth it for me. Before Mr. Crenshaw came along, Julian genuinely was a nice guy. He was a little *weird*, I admit!" At this comment the girls laughed, as did Alice. "Okay, maybe *a lot weird*! And you could say that Julian was misguided – you know, he dropped out of college because of his excitement to welcome aliens – but there isn't anything *criminal* about that. He wasn't mean or evil or anything like that – he was just *weird*. But when

Mr. Crenshaw got ahold of him and told him all those things about how the aliens were going to come and make him a ruler of a galaxy and stuff like that, it just made him…. crazy, you know?"

"Yeah," one of the girls responded.

"I just want to stop something like that from ever happening again," Alice said passionately.

The three *Sunday School Detectives* at the table soon looked at each other, trying to decide what to say next. "Wow," Hailey finally said. "That's a lot to take in."

"Sorry," Alice said meekly, with a smile.

"Thanks so much for wanting to help us," Hailey told the young scientist.

"Yeah, thanks," said Lisa.

"Thanks," Cressida added quietly.

"Well, sure," Alice replied.

"I had no idea *that* was what you wanted to talk about this morning," Hailey said with a laugh.

"Sorry to spring it on you," Alice said, smiling.

"Oh, that's okay," Hailey continued. "I'm just surprised, that's all."

"Surprised?" asked Alice.

"I thought you might have a case or something you needed our help with," Hailey laughed. "Not join us."

"Well… I mean, I don't want to take anything away from what *you* do," Alice said haltingly. "I mean, if Sneak Ryerson is already doing scientific investigations and forensic experiments, I don't want to get in his way."

"Oh, I'm sure we could work things out with him," Hailey continued. "Sneak could do experiments with the equipment he has in his basement *and* you could use the things here in the Science Building," Hailey paused thoughtfully, beginning to formulate a plan. "Or, maybe, you two could work together. He'd probably like the extra help and I'm sure he'd love to work with some of the equipment you have here."

"That'd be great!" Alice said with a smile.

"Yeah," Lisa agreed. "If you've got stuff that Sneak doesn't have, it could really help our investigations."

"That would be pretty cool," Cressida added.

"The only thing," Hailey said in a serious tone. "I don't know how exactly to say it…"

"Is it because I'm so much older?" Alice interrupted in a worried voice. "I am twenty-two... and y'all are just in junior high school, right?" She paused. "I should have thought of that! That might be kinda' *weird* working together, right? That's something I should have thought of before." Alice frowned dejectedly.

"Oh, I don't think that's a big deal," Lisa answered reassuringly.

"No, actually," Hailey continued. "It's not your age – that wasn't what I was going to say."

"Yeah, I wasn't going to say that either," Lisa said quickly. "Because I was thinkin' that we could really use your help driving us around when Brad can't," she said, smiling at the others.

"That's Lisa's brother... he works at Dietsch's," Cressida clarified. "And he isn't always around to drive us."

"Oh, I can definitely drive you... sometimes," Alice replied tentatively. "My car's not very big. It's just a Volkswagen Bug, so there's only room for a few *Sunday School Detectives* to fit. And, I'll still have work to do here in the lab, plus my classes will keep me busy when school starts again in the fall, so I couldn't drive you around *all* the time."

"Oh, that's okay," Lisa reassured. "We're always getting rides from our parents too."

"Oh, okay," replied Alice.

"Actually Alice," Hailey laughed. "I wasn't going to say any of those things! I hadn't even thought about you being too old or driving us around!"

"Oh, okay?" Alice wondered uncertainly.

"What I was going to say, is that we're called the *Sunday School Detectives*... 'cause we know each other from church."

"Oh," Alice said quickly, sitting back in her chair.

"When Sneak and I started our group, we were thinking it would be made up of kids from our church."

"Ah, I see," Alice said with a serious voice.

"So," Hailey continued. "Would you be interested in coming to church with us, too? Or do you go somewhere else?"

"Oh my gosh," Alice said, still leaning back in her chair. "I hadn't even thought about that," she continued. "I feel so silly, I should have known that a group called the *Sunday School Investigators*..."

"Detectives," Lisa corrected.

"Right, it's right there in your name, the *Sunday School Detectives*!" Alice continued. "I should have thought that with a name like that, your group would be made up of kids who went to Sunday School together! I feel so dumb not thinking about that."

"Oh, that's okay," Hailey said.

"Yeah, it's okay," Cressida added kindly.

"Well, it's not like you'd be in our *exact* Sunday School class at church anyway," explained Lisa. "It's by age group and we've just started going to the Junior High class. The Sunday School class you would go to is called –"

"*College and Career*," Cressida interrupted softly.

"Right, *College and Career*," Lisa agreed.

"The people there are pretty cool. We could introduce you. Would you be interested in going?" Cressida asked softly.

"Well, I guess I'll have to think about that," Alice replied haltingly.

"Have you ever gone to church before?" Lisa asked the young scientist.

"Well… yeah. When I was younger," Alice explained.

"Why'd you stop?" Lisa questioned.

"My Mom and Dad used to take me when I was really young, but then my Mom got really sick and after she passed my Dad stopped going."

"I'm sorry to hear about your Mom," Hailey said sympathetically.

"Thanks," said Alice. "It was a long time ago, and I was little. After that, I would go to Church sometimes with my Grandma, but she didn't live very close to my house, so I didn't go too often with her."

"Would you be interested in going with us?" Lisa asked hopefully.

"I don't know," Alice admitted. "I haven't really thought a lot about church for a long time. I'll have to think about it. I've got a lot of questions."

"What kind of questions?" Lisa wondered.

"Y'all really want to know?" Alice asked, with a doubtful voice.

"Yeah," the three said in near unison.

"Well, okay," Alice began. "I'll tell you, but I don't want it to, you know, make *you* change *your* mind about Church or stuff like that."

"Oh, that's okay," Hailey said with a smile. "I think we can talk about it, right girls?"

"Yeah, that's okay," smiled Lisa.

"Definitely," a smiling Cressida quietly agreed.

"Well, okay," Alice began in a serious tone. "I'm a scientist, or, at least I want to *be* a scientist…"

"Plus, a detective!" Lisa added.

"Right!" Alice continued with a laugh. "I'd like to be a scientist and maybe a detective too. I'll be finishing my Master's Degree this year and then after that I'll either try to get into a Ph.D. program or find a job working in a lab. I thought for a long time that my field would be Biology, but now, after thinking more about working with y'all to solve mysteries, I'm considering forensic science too."

"That would be cool," said Lisa.

"Yeah," agreed Hailey.

"But what does that have to do with going to Church, or not going to Church?" Lisa wondered.

"Ah… right," Alice said with a grimace. "Well, as a scientist, I've been trained to use what's called the *Scientific Method* to, you know, determine if things are true or not."

"The Scientific Method…" Lisa repeated.

"Right!" Alice said enthusiastically, in a tone that surprised the others.

"I've heard of it," said Hailey. "But I'm not sure if I could do a good job of explaining it."

"Well, what it is," Alice began. "Well… actually…. I'm pretty sure we have a poster around here that describes it. Do you mind if we go look for it?"

"No, I don't mind," said Hailey.

"As long as it's not in the basement!" Lisa added, as the others laughed.

"No, no," Alice laughed and stood with her cup of tea. "The poster's not in the basement! It's just at the other end of the building by the Science Library – at our other break room. It will only take a few minutes to get over there. Plus, I can show you some of the other labs."

Soon, the three young detectives were following Alice through a wide hallway as she began explaining some of the experiments being conducted by other scientists in the building, when suddenly they were engulfed by a putrid smell as the air around them filled with steam.

"Oh wow! What is that?" Lisa asked. "It smells like…"

"Like a wet dog," Cressida interrupted.

"Like rotten fruit is what I was going to say," Lisa added.

"It's coming from the Autoclave Room," Alice explained as they approached an open door. "Usually the door is closed, but someone probably just went in."

"Do we *have* to go in there?" Lisa asked, covering her nose. "That is disgusting."

"We can just look in from the hallway," Alice suggested.

"What's an Auto*cave*?" Hailey asked. "Sounds like a place with stalactites and stalagmites!"

"No, no, nothing like that," Alice laughed. "It's Auto*clave*, not cave. It disinfects our scientific equipment. We put our glass cylinders and beakers into it to get sterilized with steam."

"So, like a dishwasher?" Hailey asked.

"Right!" Alice said cheerily. "Only instead of just washing stuff off the surface, it actually kills all of the micro-organisms because it's so hot."

"So, how about your gloves?" Hailey continued. "Is that how you clean those?"

"No," Alice explained. "We actually have to throw those away. They'd get burned up if we put them in the autoclave – you know, because of the heat. Well, technically, we could put them in a biohazard bag and they wouldn't burn – but they'd shrink, so we don't do that. It's easiest for us just to throw the gloves away."

"Oh, that makes sense," said Hailey.

"In the lab, we use a lot of glassware and stainless-steel equipment. Those things are pretty expensive, and we couldn't just throw them away after only using them once. So, we put them in the autoclave."

"Cool," Lisa replied.

"Yeah, that's pretty neat," Hailey agreed. "But it sure is smelly."

"Definitely," Alice smiled.

The girls continued down the hallway and Alice paused at each door to explain the scientific research done on different plants and insects in each lab. At the end of the hallway, a large sign indicated the entrance to the Science Library where the girls could see a large room filled with books and journals on tall metal bookshelves. Next to the entrance, they found the breakroom, with a small table surrounded by plastic chairs similar to the table and chairs next to Alice's lab. A large coffee machine sat on a nearby counter. "So, there's coffee on this side of the building and tea on our side!" Alice explained. "Anyone want any coffee?"

"No thanks," came the reply.

"Hey, look at this funny cartoon," Lisa said, pointing to an old cartoon taped to a nearby wall. The drawing had been torn from a magazine and displayed a man with bulging eyes, sitting in a wide chair watching television. The caption read: "America's Drug of Choice."

"That's kind of funny," Hailey admitted.

"Yeah," Cressida agreed. "People do watch a lot of TV."

"Well, I guess they've left that old cartoon but have taken the posters down," Alice said with a frown as she looked around the hallway. "There was a really nice poster here that showed the steps of the Scientific Method, but it's not here any longer. I'll just get a paper and pen from the Science Library and draw it for you instead. I'm pretty sure I can remember everything that was on the poster."

The girls took seats at the small table as Alice walked quickly to the nearby Science Library. When she returned, she placed the blank piece of paper on the table and wrote the title **Scientific Method** at the top of the page as the girls moved their chairs closer to the table to read the words she was writing.

Alice drew a large circle and then drew several notches, similar to a face of a clock. "So, I've drawn seven dashes here," Alice explained. "These will show the seven steps scientists use to follow the Scientific Method."

"Sounds good," replied Lisa.

"So, the first thing we do is make observations." After saying this, Alice paused and wrote the words **Make Observations** on the first dash near the top of the circle. "During this step we notice things about nature."

"Like what?" Lisa asked.

"Well, anything, really. In our lab, like I probably mentioned to you when you were here the last time, we noticed that pupae change to moths. That's an observation."

"Oh, okay," said Hailey.

"Or, in history," Alice continued. "People observed a lot of things – like the sun rising in the East, or things falling to the ground when they're dropped. There are lots of things that people have noticed or observed."

"Makes sense," said Lisa.

"After making an observation, scientists ask a question." As she said these words, Alice wrote **Ask a Question** next to the second dash on the circle. "Another way of saying this is that we identify a problem."

"What do you mean by that?" Hailey asked. "How is it a problem? If you don't mind me *asking a question*."

"Nice one," said Lisa as she and the others laughed.

"Good one," Alice agreed. "Well, if our observation is that the sun rises in the East, we might ask the question, '*Why* does the sun rise in the East?' In our lab, for example, one question that we might ask is, '*Why* do pupae change to moths?' It's a question about our observation, but it is also identifying a problem – because when we start, we don't know the answer."

"So, you're asking *why*?" Hailey considered.

"Right!" Alice answered energetically. "We're asking *why* something happens, which then leads us to the third thing – and that is make a hypothesis."

"A what?" asked Lisa.

"A hypothesis," Alice repeated as she quickly wrote the words **Make a Hypothesis** next to the third dash along the circle.

"Oh yeah," Lisa added. "I think you said the questions you were asking earlier about Julian Davis were a hypothesis."

"Well," Alice clarified. "I actually said they were *hypothetical questions*, which is a little different. In the Scientific Method, to make a hypothesis is to make a guess about the answer. You're identifying why *you think* something happened."

"Oh," Lisa answered.

The young scientist pointed to the first dash on the circle. "So, we've seen some sort of phenomenon." Then she pointed to the second dash. "And then, we've asked a question about it." Then, pointing to the third dash she added, "And now, we're making a guess of why it's happening."

"Ah, got it," said Lisa.

"So, you're guessing the right answer," Cressida clarified softly.

"Right," said Alice with a smile. "And once we make our hypothesis – our guess – about why the event is happening, our next step is to gather information." As she said this, she wrote **Gather Information** next to the fourth dash along the circle. "What this means for me here in the Biology Department is I review the scientific literature and try to gather as much information as I can. I'll spend a lot of time over in the Science Library, looking through books and reading articles that are in scientific journals like *Science* or *Nature* or *Cell* or the *Proceedings of the National Academy of Sciences*."

"Wow," said Lisa. "That sounds like a lot of magazines."

"Yeah, it can be a lot to go through," Alice admitted. "But it helps me see if I'm doing something new and original – or working on something that someone else has already written about."

"Interesting," said Hailey.

"The next thing I'll do after I've gone through the literature, is design an experiment," Alice said, as she wrote the words, **Design an Experiment** on the paper next to another notch in the circle. "I'll want to make this a *repeatable* test – something that I can run over and over again. And then, after I *design* the experiment, I'll try to *run* the experiment." As Alice was saying these words, she wrote **Run the Experiment** on her piece of paper.

"This is what would separate scientists from everyday people, right?" Lisa asked the young scientist. "Doing the experiments?"

"I think you're right," Alice agreed. "I mean, lots of people do the first few things," she said, pointing to the first steps in her diagram. "Everybody makes observations and asks questions. Most people even take a stab at explaining why something happened and sometimes even try to gather more information. But I think you're right. It's really the experiments that set us scientists apart from everyone else – designing them and running them."

"That's probably the coolest part, right?" Hailey asked with a smile.

"Yeah, it's definitely pretty cool," Alice admitted. "Especially when it seems like you've discovered something that no one else has. But it can be pretty hard sometimes, too. Like, if the experiment you're running takes a lot of time. Some of our experiments might take eight or ten hours, or even longer, so you have to be around the lab for a really long time."

"Wow," said Cressida.

"Yeah, we even have cots so we can sleep here, if we have to be in the lab overnight."

"Wow," said the girls in unison.

"I hope the cots aren't in the basement!" Lisa exclaimed.

"No, no," said Alice, as the girls laughed. "They're up here on this floor."

The four paused, all looking at the paper.

"So, that just leaves one more thing," Alice said eventually, pointing to the last dash on the circle. "The last thing we do is draw conclusions." As she said these words, she wrote **Draw Conclusions** on the paper.

"That's when you explain what happened, right?" Hailey asked.

"Exactly!" Alice said enthusiastically. "That's when we put everything together! Maybe we just put it in our Lab Book – and those results help us with our next experiment. Or maybe we'll put it on a poster and present it at a conference or a seminar. Or, if we're really lucky, we'll write it up for an article in a scientific journal like *Nature*..."

"Or *Science*," said Hailey.

"Or, *Proceedings* of something," said Cressida.

"Right!" said Alice with growing enthusiasm. "We want to make sure our conclusions are consistent with our experiments. That's why we repeat them. We'll run them over and over to make sure they're right. And, if it's something that other scientists have already found, then there's not much of a chance our results would be published. But, if we find something new, well, that would be interesting to other people, and we might get our article published – and that would be a really big deal."

"That sounds pretty cool," Lisa admitted.

"Yeah, it's definitely really interesting to hear about that," Hailey agreed with a smile. "I'm really interested in science too," she admitted. "It's neat to see how you think about your experiments."

"Great!" Alice affirmed. "I'm glad you liked it."

"So," Cressida began, with a perplexed look. "I guess I'm having a hard time trying to understand it all. When we started talking about Church, you said you had some questions and then started talking about the Scientific..."

"The Scientific Method," the young scientist interrupted.

"Right, the Scientific Method," Cressida continued quietly. "I guess I don't understand how those two things are... connected?"

"Ah, right," Alice replied, now more seriously. "I guess I didn't really explain why I brought that up." She paused and took a deep breath, and then continued. "So, as a scientist, we're trained to look at *evidence* and use the Scientific Method to determine if things are valid and true."

"Right," declared one of the girls.

"But the thing is," Alice continued. "When I hear people talk about Church or you know, God or Christianity or things like that, I guess I want to look at the *evidence* to verify if it's true. I want to run it through the Scientific Method."

"Oh," Cressida replied. "So, you can't run those ideas through the Scientific Method?"

"Exactly!" affirmed Alice. "How can I determine if those things are true or not true if I can't run them through this," she said, pointing to her diagram of the Scientific Method.

"So, you'd say that everything that is real – or true – has a scientific reason or cause?" Hailey asked, glancing quickly at her two detective friends, as their faces betrayed faint smiles.

"Right!" Alice said loudly, growing more passionate in her explanations. "That's exactly right! We *can* get to the bottom of things. We can understand what is true or not true by doing analysis and measuring the results. And the *Scientific Method* helps us verify that," she added pointing again to the paper on the table. "It shows us the truth about *why* things happen – like, why the sun rose in the East and why my moths transform from one state or another and a million other things we might wonder about. As an undergrad I took a class on philosophy in college, and I think the name that best describes what I believe – or what I am – is what's called an *empiricist*."

"A what?" asked Lisa.

"An *Empiricist*," Alice repeated, thoughtfully.

"I've never, ever, heard of that," Lisa replied.

"Me neither," Hailey and Cressida nearly said in unison.

"It's just someone who wants to look at the evidence, and then, you know, make a conclusion based on that *evidence*," Alice explained. "It's someone, like me, who wants to use the Scientific Method to determine what is true. If you think about it, I would guess that most detectives are empiricists – like your friend Sneak Ryerson. He's someone who wants to look at the evidence and try to figure things out scientifically."

"Maybe," Hailey replied thoughtfully. "I'm not sure."

"Well, I'm pretty sure he is," said Alice confidently. "That's how your friend makes all of his discoveries for his cases! And for those of us in science, that's how we make so many discoveries," she explained, using her index finger to point to the door of the Science Library and a few pieces of scientific equipment sitting on carts in the hallway.

"So, in Christianity, we talk about faith…" Hailey began.

"And that's exactly where I have my problem," the young scientist interrupted. "The Christian faith that I learned from my Grandma, and I'm sure it's the same as what you've learned in Church – is something that can't be measured. It can't be analyzed like we do with everything else. Faith is just something people say they have or they don't have."

"Well," Hailey started.

"And since it can't be measured, I can't run an experiment on it," Alice continued, pointing to the words **Run the Experiment** on her drawing. "And because I can't run a *repeatable* experiment with it, I've got to come to the conclusion that it doesn't exist."

"Yeah, but," Lisa replied quickly. "What about hope?"

"What?" Alice asked with a puzzled look.

"Hope," Lisa said, as her two detective friends tried to conceal their smiles.

"Hope?" Alice asked.

"*Hope*," Lisa repeated. "You know, having a good feeling about something happening in the future. That's something that exists but can't be measured or analyzed with your Scientific Method," Lisa stated, looking down at the drawing. "You can't run an experiment on that," she added as she pointed to the words on the diagram.

"Hope?" Alice repeated.

"Yeah," Hailey agreed, and soon asked another question. "And what about your thoughts?"

"My thoughts?" Alice asked.

"Like, your consciousness," Hailey continued. "I think that's what it's called. And the thoughts inside your mind about what is real. You believe that our *world* is real, right? And that *you* are real… and that *other people* are real, right? And you can have thoughts that are like other people's thoughts, right?"

"Of course I do," Alice said seriously.

"Well, none of those things can be measured either," Hailey stated, looking down at the diagram.

"Well, just because I can't measure them *now*, doesn't mean scientists won't be able to measure them in the future," Alice protested.

"But you didn't say that about Christianity," Lisa objected.

"Yeah, and what about love?" Cressida asked, more firmly than in any of the words she had spoken earlier.

The effect, Alice explained later, was like receiving a 'a slap to the face' that left her momentarily dazed, and she sputtered some incoherent words, trying to process the challenging information from the young women.

"You told us a little bit about your Mom and Dad earlier," Cressida continued. "And your Grandma. I'm guessing they loved you and you loved them."

"Right," Alice said, unsure of how to respond. "A lot."

"But, love can't be measured either," Cressida said forcefully. "But that's something you probably believe in too."

"Well, yeah," Alice agreed. "Of course I do."

"And what about the basic ideas behind this?" Hailey asked firmly, pointing again to the drawing of the Scientific Method.

"What about it?" Alice asked.

"Well," Hailey continued, still looking down at the table. "If you start with the idea that the only things that are true are those things that have a scientific cause, then you've already ruled out any other options, right?"

"Well..." Alice began.

"But what if there are things that don't have a scientific cause? Like, faith?" Hailey asked.

"Or hope?" Lisa asked.

"Or love?" said Cressida.

"Well Einstein did say some things about the formulation of a problem..." Alice began, unable to continue her sentence. The young scientist, still seated at the small table outside of the Science Library, had found herself unsure how to proceed. She was taken completely by surprise with the sudden turn in the conversation. When she first mentioned the topic, Alice had worried that her explanations of The Scientific Method would persuade the young girls to abandon *their* faith in God and discard their beliefs about Christianity. She had even briefly worried that if the girls rejected their faith that their parents might somehow blame her as the cause! But now, as she reflected on how the girls had been so unpersuaded in her ideas and instead were giving persuasive arguments against her views, she was unsure of what to do or even say next.

"Triple-teamed" is how Alice would later describe the experience, borrowing a term from basketball. The young scientist unexpectedly found herself being triple-teamed by the three young detectives – and was now unsure how to proceed. "I'm not sure exactly what to say..." Alice finally replied. "I guess I'm actually more confused now than when I started. You've given me some really interesting things to think about. I mean, of course I believe in hope and love and ideas. And you're right, those things can't be measured or tested, or run through a repeatable experiment either. I can't believe you kids opened my eyes to that."

To Alice, the young girls' comments were profound, as they pointed to important shortcomings in her convictions. They also seemed spontaneous, as if the girls had just thought of them. But unbeknownst to Alice, our Sunday School class had been trained to do just what the girls had done in their conversation with the young scientist. In the months prior, our class had learned about different religions and philosophical views – discovering how each of them were different from Christianity and how each of them had, in some ways, shortcomings and inconsistencies. The words the young girls said to Alice cut through her beliefs and assumptions about the world, making her wonder if she really was on firm ground in holding them. Our coach and instructor in these matters was a lecturer at the local seminary and our part-time Sunday School teacher, Professor Nicholas Telson.

Still seated outside the Science Library, Alice Williams was flustered and continued to struggle in responding to the three young detectives. The young scientist had hoped to be persuasive in explaining why she could not accept Christianity, but instead, found herself confronted by the unsettling sense that her views had several major inconsistencies. "Y'all have brought up some really good points," Alice finally admitted, as she considered the objections the girls had raised. "I guess I have more questions about this than I thought. I've been rejecting Christian ideas for a while. Maybe I should try to get some answers."

"You know," said Hailey, as she was struck with a new idea. "Our next meeting this morning is over at the seminary."

"Really?" asked Alice. "Where they train *ministers?*"

"Yeah, I think that's what they do there," said Hailey.

"I'm pretty sure that's right," confirmed Lisa.

"Alice, maybe you could come with?" Hailey suggested. "You could see how we interview witnesses – if you decide you want to do detective work. Plus, you might be able to get some of your spiritual questions answered by the professor we're going to meet."

"Hmm," Alice replied as she considered the invitation. "That might be good… I could step away from the lab for a while to do that."

"Awesome!" said Lisa.

"Cool beans," Hailey added.

"Yeah, that's cool," replied Cressida.

"So," Lisa asked with a smile to her friends. "Does this mean I don't have to call my brother to give us a ride?"

"Yep, I can drive," Alice offered.

The four quickly returned to Alice's laboratory, where the young scientist checked on two experiments that were still processing before leaving her worn white lab coat on a coat rack by the lab's wide wooden door.

CHAPTER 11

One hundred and thirty miles south of Findlay, at the state prison near Lebanon, Ohio, Sneak Ryerson, his Uncle Charlie and I answered a few more of the warden's questions before finally being escorted out of his large office.

Following a Corrections Officer, we walked from the office down a set of stairs and then a long hallway. After waiting for a thick metal door to open, we found ourselves in another part of the building. Walking further, we eventually arrived at a large bland and dreary room with walls painted grey and small windows lined with thick black bars that brought in little sunlight from outside the prison's high guarded walls.

In the middle of the room was a long metal table with chairs on both sides. Heavy doors were at both ends of the room – used by the Corrections Officers to enter and exit from different parts of the building.

"You boys are going to ask the questions," Uncle Charlie said as my friend and I took seats on one side of the long metal table while Sneak's Uncle Charlie sat in a chair behind us.

"This room is usually used for lawyers to meet with their clients," the Corrections Officer who had guided us to the room explained. "It's a little quieter than the area where the inmates meet with their families."

"Th… thanks," I replied nervously.

As we waited, noises reached us through the labyrinth of hallways and distant corridors located deep within the prison – echoes and faint sounds of metal doors clanging shut, heavy chains dragging across floors and prisoners shouting between cells. Soon, we heard noises at the metal door opposite from where we sat and the rattling of a key in the lock. The heavy door slowly opened and two guards entered with a young man in his early twenties. The young prisoner was of medium height and slight build, and like the older inmate we had passed earlier in the hallway, wore the facility's "prison blues" – blue denim pants, a short-sleeved blue shirt and blue canvas shoes. He entered the room with his hands in front of him, bound by handcuffs, and walked slowly, due to the shackles around his ankles. I had met the young man once before – when I helped him get untied from a heavily knotted rope and safely away from a fast-approaching fire. But as he approached, I noticed that his face was more gaunt than I remembered, with deep bags under his eyes – which I guessed were from sleepless nights. As he came closer, I noticed that his eyes darted wildly about the room above a puzzled and confused expression. He mumbled a few words as he entered, "Big Dipper.... I saw the Big Dipper last night," he said quietly. "That's where they'll be coming from... not the Little."

"We'll see about that," one of the Corrections Office said, shaking his head in disbelief at the odd words the prisoner was saying.

"This should be interesting," I said, turning to my friend. "He seems crazier than a loon."

"We'll see," my friend replied quietly. "Maybe we can help him understand what *really* happened."

"Maybe," I answered doubtfully.

"Mr. Davis," Sneak Ryerson said in a formal tone as the young prisoner approached the table where we were seated.

"Julian," the young man clarified as he sat, staring down at his canvas shoes while the Corrections Officer locked the prisoner's ankle chains to a bolt on the floor.

"I don't know if you remember me or not," Sneak said in a serious tone after the chains were bolted.

"I do," Julian Davis said, finally turning his gaze to the young detective. "I tried to run you over with my car." His voice was calm and serious, and I shuddered at the strange tone of his words.

"Yeah," Sneak said with a blank look on his face. "You did try to run me over with your car."

"I am sorry about that," the young prisoner said, with an unchanged expression. "I said that in the apology letter I sent you. Did you get it?"

"Yes, yes I did."

"Good," Julian Davis said. "I went too far with that. I should have waited and let The Master take care of you."

"*The Master*?" I asked, perplexed by his statement.

"The Great Peggu," Julian explained. "He's coming," he continued, as surprised looks came over our faces. "...with the others. You'll see. They're coming for me."

"Oh brother," I heard Uncle Charlie say from behind us.

"Their timing is different... from what I originally thought," Julian explained quickly, now using short bursts of words. "But that doesn't mean they're not coming. They... they still want to use Hancock County for a landing area."

"Oh really?" my friend replied sarcastically. "I thought those plans had changed when we arrested you and Mr. Crenshaw."

"*You* didn't arrest me, the police did." Julian replied in a curt and serious tone. "And, no, the plans haven't changed. In fact, I've just recently heard from the Great Peggu," he said, pulling out a piece of paper from his front pants pocket. After looking furtively at one of the guards who had escorted him into the room, however, he changed his mind and returned the piece of paper back into his pocket. "They're definitely coming. Their timing is just a little different from what I was originally led to believe."

"You can't really believe that anymore," my friend replied. "After your arrest, didn't you hear that Mr. Crenshaw admitted to tricking you? He admitted that he was pretending to be your alien Master, The Great..."

"Peggu," Julian said, completing the alien's name.

"Yes... yes," the young detective said in an exasperated voice. "How could I ever forget that name? *The Great Peggu*! But Mr. Crenshaw confessed to everything," my friend intoned loudly. "Surely you heard that? Your lawyer would have explained all of that to you!"

"He did, he did," Julian replied quietly, before briefly pausing. "I had heard that Mr. Crenshaw *admitted* to being The Great Peggu, but that doesn't mean it actually *was* him."

"What?" I asked, perplexed.

"Why would he *admit* to it, if it wasn't him!" Sneak asked perceptively. "People don't usually confess to things they didn't do."

"How should I know?" Julian blurted out. "I can't read Mr. Crenshaw's mind. Nor do I want to."

"But he got sentenced to jail!" said Sneak.

"Prison," I said, correcting my friend.

"Right, prison!" Sneak added. "He got sentenced to serve – for a long time!"

"Yeah," I agreed.

"I guess if I had to come up with a reason," Julian began, now in a slow and thoughtful tone. "I'd say his reason was *fame*. He got pretty famous pretending he was an alien, didn't he? He was on the front page of a bunch of newspapers – all over the country. He could have just wanted the... the, you know, the *notoriety*."

"Notoriety, right!" Uncle Charlie chuckled softly behind us.

"But he took a plea deal and is in prison. He's in *this* prison!" Sneak Ryerson explained in an exasperated tone. "That's quite a big price to pay for just a couple minutes of fame!"

"He's not my problem," Julian Davis said nonchalantly with a shrug of his shoulders. "I'm not a mind reader. I don't know why he admitted to it... and I don't care. What I do know is that it couldn't have been Mr. Crenshaw. He's just an old guy. *The Great Peggu* is a brilliant lifeform. He's ushering in a great army of aliens. And with his help, I'll learn..." he paused momentarily to look back to the guard who stood near the wall behind him, as he searched for the right words. "I'll learn the secrets of the universe. I'll be in charge of a whole galaxy. I'm just waiting for my rescue," he added softly, looking back again at the Corrections Officer near the door.

"You might be waiting for a long time," Uncle Charlie said from behind us.

"But Mr. Crenshaw manipulated you," the young detective continued in an exasperated tone. "He got you to run me over with your car! And then he tied you up and set the building on fire! My Dad and Pep here had to rescue you! How do you explain that?"

"That wasn't Mr. Crenshaw, that was *The Great Peggu*," Julian told us.

"That was Mr. Crenshaw with a mask on!" Sneak replied angrily. "You were there when we pulled it off of him! My sister and our friend, Hailey, chased him as he left the seed barn and threw a net over him! And then they pulled his mask off!"

"I don't know. It could have all been a trick," Julian replied.

"But if it wasn't Mr. Crenshaw," Sneak questioned, "and it was really an alien named *The Great Peggu* that did those bad things, why did you get lured to the seed barn? And why did he tie you up? Why did you need *us* to rescue you? Why would you want to have anything to do with a *lifeform* that would do those things?"

"I don't know why *The Great Peggu* did that," Julian explained calmly. "He's a brilliant alien lifeform. I'm sure he has his reasons."

"Oh brother," I replied. "That doesn't make any sense."

"Maybe he was setting a trap for Mr. Crenshaw, or for you and your school friends?" Julian suggested.

"Our *Sunday* School friends," I corrected.

"I don't think we're getting anywhere with this," Uncle Charlie interrupted.

"I think you're right," his nephew added.

"Do you mind if I ask you a few questions?" I asked, gaining confidence as I repositioned my black tape recorder on the metal table with the microphone angled toward the inmate.

"Ask what you want," Julian replied, staring at the wall behind us.

For the next twenty minutes, I asked the disturbed young man one question after another about *The Case of the Mysterious Circles* – learning much about the case from his answers, including how *The Great Peggu* had communicated with him through coded letters, where he had been hiding after nearly running over my friend and how he had come to be tied up in that seed barn that caught on fire. (Years later, I included much of what I had learned from Julian Davis in my first volume about the Sunday School Detectives called *The Amazing Sneak Ryerson: A Sunday School Detectives Mystery*.)

Soon, one of the guards told us that we were nearing the end of our thirty-minute visit.

"So, what exactly has *The Great Peggu* been telling you now?" I wondered.

"The same stuff as before," Julian admitted in a tired voice, now more comfortable in answering my many questions.

"It looked like you had a note from him. Could you tell us what it says?" I asked.

Julian looked quickly at the guard behind him, who nodded his approval, then pulled the piece of paper from the front pocket of his denim pants.

"It's dated June 1st, and it's a little hard to understand," Julian explained.

"That's okay," I reassured him.

"It says, 'UFOs, UFOs, loitering on other kosmos – spelled with a k," he added.

"Hmm," came the words of my detective friend – his first comments after silently listening to my interview with the prisoner. "Is that it?"

"Well, no," Julian Davis said in an incredulous tone. "*The Great Peggu* is smarter than that. He wouldn't just give me that short of a letter."

"Oh," I replied.

"He says," Julian continued. "'Ask Them: Mary York?'"

"Ask them Mary York?" I repeated.

"Correct," Julian Davis replied.

"Who's that?" I wondered.

"How should I know," said Julian Davis, still in an incredulous voice. "I think that's who I'm supposed to ask for when the aliens come to get me."

"Oh, right," I replied knowingly. "So, is that all there is?"

"Well no. My letter ends with the words, 'Please leave a correct eulogy'."

"A correct eulogy?" I asked. "What's that?"

"Those are the words said at someone's funeral," Sneak's Uncle Charlie explained from behind me.

"Who's having a funeral?" I wondered.

"Well, I think there will be a lot of funerals when the aliens arrive," Julian Davis said confidently.

"I'm not so sure about that," Sneak Ryerson said sternly. He paused for a moment, then added, "The letter doesn't make any sense to me. How about you Pep?"

"I don't understand it," I admitted.

"Don't you see?" Julian Davis asked as a crazed smile came across his face and he quickly put the paper back into his pocket. "It shows they're still out there. The Great Peggu – and the other aliens. They're coming."

"Hmm," I replied. "I don't know about that."

"They are," Julian Davis reassured us. "You just wait and see. And I'll ask them about Mary York and give a eulogy and they'll know it's me. They'll know it's *The Great Julian Davis*... ruler of a cosmos. And they'll ask me what galaxy I want to be governor of, and I'll have a hard time choosing, because there are a bunch of different galaxies that I could choose from. And then I'll make my choice, and everyone will be amazed that I'm the governor and nobody but me saw this coming."

"Alright, time's up," one of the Correction Officers told us in a serious voice as he tapped on his watch.

"Is there anything you need?" I asked Julian Davis, concerned about the young man who was clearly mentally unstable. "We might be able to help you, right?" I added, turning quickly to Uncle Charlie.

"Naw," the young prisoner replied. "My *friends* will be coming soon," he said assuredly.

"Do any of your friends from F.E.E.T. ever come to visit?" I asked, referring to a group called *Findlayites Entertaining Extra-Terrestrials.* "You had some friends in that group, right?"

"They aren't making a trip down here too, are they?" Julian asked in a concerned voice.

"Not that I know of," I told him. "I just thought of them, that's all."

"Well, they aren't friends of mine anymore!" Julian said with a laugh. "They haven't believed me for a long time, so I don't need any of them to come visit! I need my other friends, from up there," he said, pointing upwards.

"Ah," I said. "Okay."

"Until then, I'm spending as much time as I can in the prison library. The library is actually pretty good here," Julian told us. "They have a lot of Isaac Asimov books, and I like reading those."

"Alright, let's go," the guard said as he unlocked the ankle chain that had been secured to the floor and started escorting Julian Davis out of the room.

"Usually I'd say, 'See ya' later'," Julian said as he was leaving the interview room. "But I'm not sure if I will."

We smiled at this comment.

"You're laughing now," he continued. "But you'll believe me in a few months – just wait and see. They'll be coming for me."

"Okay," I replied skeptically. "See ya' later, or maybe we won't."

The prisoner and his two guards exited the room quickly and the echo of the heavy metal door slamming shut reverberated throughout the room. Then the room was quiet. "Wow, that guy's really messed up," Uncle Charlie concluded. "We need to be praying for him."

CHAPTER 12

Sneak Ryerson, his Uncle Charlie, a Corrections Officer and I waited quietly in the prison's large interview room for several minutes until we heard a key turn in the thick metal door.

Some have asked – and I've wondered myself – if I knew I would be coming so close to the face of evil when that thick metal prison door opened. Did I know how dark the person's heart was that I would soon meet? Did I know the danger Russell Crenshaw would bring to the *Sunday School Detectives*? Did I ever imagine that my friend, Sneak Ryerson, the great young detective, would be brought to the brink of death because of that man? Did I have any sort of premonition or sense of the evil that we would be facing? During our interview, did I understand the challenges that would come?

The short and uninteresting answer is no, I did not. I was as surprised as most people were to discover the malicious depths of Russell Crenshaw's heart and the large path of destruction that it created.

Before meeting him, I certainly knew the crimes Mr. Crenshaw had committed. I knew that he was charged with arson and attempted murder and was serving time in prison now as his punishment. But the thought that he could be involved in additional sinister crimes never crossed my mind. The one time I had seen him – outside of that seed barn, when he was caught – left me with the impression that he was simply a weak older man. He seemed thin and frail and looked harmless – and at the time, I was naïve enough to think that appearances were more important than the heart and mind and soul. I had seen scary looking criminals in the

Scared Straight movie narrated by Peter Faulk. And Mr. Crenshaw didn't seem like any of them. At the time, I wasn't afraid of him at all.

After my visit to the prison, however, that would change.

After turning the lock, the heavy metal prison door opened and Mr. Crenshaw was led into the room by two Corrections Officers. Like the other prisoners, he wore his "prison blues" – blue denim jeans, blue shirt, and blue canvas shoes. However, unlike Julian Davis whose clothes were disheveled and in disarray, Mr. Crenshaw's clothes were starched and neatly pressed – maybe even dry cleaned.

Like Julian, Mr. Crenshaw's wrists were handcuffed and attached to a thick chain that reached his shackled ankles. He entered the room slowly, taking methodical steps to reach the table and carefully sat down across from us with the help of one of the guards. "Thank you," he said meekly to the guard as he was seated.

Then, a thin evil smile came over the old man's face – a grin I will never forget – that instantly communicated his ill will towards us. For a moment he seemed to be silently "sizing us up" – looking first at Sneak Ryerson, then myself, and then Uncle Charlie.

"Wow! What a place, huh?" he asked loudly, as his eyes brightened.

Not knowing how to respond, I sat quietly – as did the others.

"Well, I'm glad you came," he said cheerily as we continued staring at the older man who was clearly pleased that we had come to visit him. "Captain Foster, I expected you would be here. And the amazingly great and exceedingly brilliant young detective, Master Sneak Ryerson, it is good to see you too! And this young man, I don't believe we've met, have we?"

"Not officially," I began. "The only time I saw you was outside the seed barn a few months ago."

"Ah, at my *coming out* party!" Mr. Crenshaw said with a creepy maniacal laugh. "You must be Pep Stiles! I read your story about *The Case at Riverside Park*."

"The *Adventure* at Riverside Park," I quickly correcting him, feeling both surprised and filled with dread at the news that the prisoner knew about our recent case – as well as my name.

"That article was pretty good," Mr. Crenshaw said in a complimentary tone. "I liked the MacGuffin."

"Uh...?" I replied hesitantly.

"You had something to tell us," Sneak Ryerson interrupted impatiently before I had a chance to thank the older man for his praise of my writing.

"Yes, yes, yes! I'll get to that," Mr. Crenshaw said offhandedly, as he smiled widely. "I'm sure you're *dying* to ask me some questions about that request of mine. But before I answer your questions, I wanted to ask some questions of my own."

"Here we go," Uncle Charlie interrupted. "I knew this wasn't going to be easy."

"It's okay, Uncle Charlie," Sneak Ryerson replied firmly, quickly looking over his shoulder at the muscular police captain. Then, turning back towards the prisoner he continued. "I expected there was something you wanted from *us* before you would turn over *your important information*. So, I've decided to answer your questions – but only about my cases."

"Why of course, I wouldn't think of asking you about anything else," Russell Crenshaw replied with another maniacal laugh.

"Good," Sneak replied. "Go ahead."

"In fact, I don't have questions about *all* of your cases," the prisoner explained. "Just about one."

"Okay, go ahead," the young detective said again.

"Well, I was wondering," the older man began. "With that case I was involved in with you..."

"*The Case of the Mysterious Circles*," I explained.

"Ah," Russell Crenshaw replied. "What a quaint name."

"Well, it made sense to me," I told him.

"I'm sure it did," Mr. Crenshaw replied, turning again to Sneak. "When we last met, at the seed barn – as Pep here so lovingly called it. You tracked me down before I had a chance to get out of the parking lot. I hadn't expected your arrival so quickly. So, I was wondering, how exactly you were able to catch me? I mean, I hid my identity from Julian Davis – that young nitwit who believes all that UFO business..."

"You manipulated him," Sneak interjected.

"He's totally nuts," I added as I twirled my finger in the air next to my head.

"Unstable," Uncle Charlie added from behind me.

"You can't blame me for everything," Mr. Crenshaw objected. "He already believed all that stuff before I ever got to know him. You wouldn't believe how gullible he was with all that *Great Peggu* stuff," Mr. Crenshaw said with a laugh. "What a chump! And when I gave him those coded notes, he took that story about the alien invasion... hook... line... and sinker."

"How did you even meet him?" Sneak asked.

"I was just taking a break from one of my walks at the Mall," Mr. Crenshaw explained with a laugh. "Just sitting on one of those benches they have there – near *The Toggery* – and he came up and started talking *to me* – trying to get me to join his F.E.E.T. group. I didn't even start it. He's the one who got me on this track."

"Ah," I said.

"I thought it was a joke at first," Mr. Crenshaw continued. "I mean, come on, a group of people who created a club to invite aliens to visit Findlay! I really thought that any minute Allan Funt was going to jump out with his Candid Camera!"

The three of us sitting across the table from Mr. Crenshaw were silent, staring at the older man, refusing to join him in his laughter.

"Anyway, I'd been thinking of a way to make some money – some *real* money. You know, for retirement. And the fires seemed like a great idea... and, like I said, Julian took the bait and started writing those letters to the newspaper editor."

"Manipulating him wasn't a very nice thing to do," Sneak replied.

"You have to understand," Mr. Crenshaw explained, holding out his hands towards us, palms up. "I didn't have to do too much. Julian was enthralled with the coded messages I was sending him – he was so gullible. But I have to tell you, he wasn't very smart. In the beginning, when I helped him *discover* the notes from *The Great Peggu* behind that bench near *The Toggery*, I had to help him out and decode them for him. We'd just sit there at the mall and I'd give him clues on how he could translate the alien letters. I couldn't believe he didn't catch on that it was actually me who had written all of them! I mean come on – a leader of an alien army who leaves coded messages outside of a men's store at the mall! It was just ridiculous if you think about it."

We listened without comment as the older man boasted about the many times he had manipulated the feeble-minded younger man. "So you just led him on," Uncle Charlie eventually summarized.

"Pretty much," Russell Crenshaw said with a smile. "...down the garden path as they say. Or, the cemetery path."

"I was wondering about that," I said. "Why did you leave notes in the cemetery, if you could give him notes at the mall?"

"Well, I thought we'd get noticed if we were at the mall too often. Plus, those notes at the cemetery had my specific plans for each of the fires, so I didn't want them to get into anyone else's hands. It was all pretty easy. But, I have to tell you," he paused to laugh and shake his head. "I was quite surprised to see you at the cemetery that evening, young Master Ryerson. You almost got that note... holding onto the back bumper of Julian's car! But, after you left, I stopped and talked to the woman who was bringing in her groceries. Actually – you'll find this interesting – she didn't really see you. But, I talked to her for a long time and gave her enough information, so after a while she was convinced she *had* seen you. And, based on my advice, she called the police to complain."

"Thanks," my young detective friend said somberly.

"Well, after all, I needed to make sure you were out of the way. That's why I encouraged Julian to take care of you – but unfortunately, that did not work out as planned."

"No, unfortunately for you it did not," my friend replied.

"But I didn't know that," the older man continued. "I thought he had taken care of you – at least put you in the hospital. I thought I had gotten away with everything, until you meddling kids caught me at the seed barn and stopped that fire."

"You were close to getting away with it," Sneak admitted.

"I was! I was!" Russell Crenshaw declared, before pausing. "So how did you figure it all out? That's what I want to know! You weren't suspicious of me when you came out to my place to interview me about the first fire at my farm."

"No, I wasn't suspicious," Sneak answered. "At least not during the first interview. I thought at first you were a victim. There wasn't anything suspicious when I first interviewed you."

"So what was it, then?" Russell Crenshaw asked, leaning forward. "What gave me away?"

"Well, it was elementary," Sneak explained.

"Of course it was!" Mr. Crenshaw said with a laugh as he slapped his leg, rattling the heavy chain around his wrists. "Elementary!" he said again before asking in a more serious tone. "But specifically? What gave me away?"

"Well, it wasn't just one thing," the young detective clarified. "It was several things... and they all added up to your guilt."

"Like what?" the older man asked.

"Well, one thing was that I learned you were from Salisbury, England."

"Salisbury, England... okay?" Crenshaw replied. "I was born there, but came to the States as a child after a jury awarded my family a lot of money in a personal injury trial. I don't talk with an English accent, but I do remember telling the Fire Inspector I was from Salisbury. Why did that matter?"

"Well, when we were researching crop circles, we learned that some of the biggest circles are from that area – near Old Sarum," Sneak explained.

"Old Sarum! I haven't been there in years!" Russell Crenshaw roared.

"Well, I knew that Old Sarum is only one or two miles away from Salisbury – where you're from. So, I reasoned that you must have known about crop circles – for a long time, no doubt."

"So that was it?" Mr. Crenshaw said with a frown. "I got caught simply by a matter of geography!"

"Well no, there were other clues too," Sneak Ryerson continued. "Another clue was that you were the first victim."

"The first victim?"

"Right – and that gave me the idea that you might have been testing things out. You know, figuring out your process for starting the fires on your own land first, before moving on to other fields."

"That's good," the older man replied as he raised his eyebrows and nodded his head. "And correct."

"And then..." Sneak Ryerson began.

"Wait? There's more?" Russell Crenshaw asked.

"Of course, there's more," the young detective replied. "A lot more."

"Well, then, please continue."

"There was the alien's name – *The Great Peggu*," Sneak Ryerson said seriously.

"I kind of liked it," Mr. Crenshaw replied with a laugh. "What was wrong with that name?"

"It was such a ludicrous name," Sneak said seriously. "It didn't take me too long to realize that it was the creation of someone who was frequently writing the name Peg – a nickname for Margaret. Which was also the name of your late wife."

"Peg, God rest her soul," said Mr. Crenshaw as he briefly shut his eyes.

"Once I realized it was you, all of the other pieces fell into place. When we learned that Julian Davis was going to meet *The Great Peggu* at the seed barn on Warrington Avenue – in a note that was really easy to decipher, by the way – I made a quick call to the newspaper and found out you owned the only other seed barn in town."

"Nicely done," said the older man approvingly.

"And that helped to answer the only other part of the mystery that remained unsolved: your *motive*. That was one of the hardest things with that mystery – trying to figure out *why* someone was doing those things. But it all became clear when I learned the seed barn you owned was the only other seed company in Hancock County."

"Bravo, young man," the prisoner said approvingly.

"Plus, I also learned from the newspaper that your wife had died only a few months before the fires started," Sneak Ryerson continued. "Which told me that you probably weren't thinking straight."

"That had nothin' to do with it," Mr. Crenshaw said sharply.

"Okay," the young detective said, continuing his monologue. "But, hearing that you owned the other seed company helped me deduce your ultimate plan – to be the only place in town that had seeds to sell to farmers in the Spring. Once you were the only one selling seeds, you could raise your prices and make a bunch of money, right? When I figured that out, it became clear that the crop circles really didn't have anything to do with your ultimate purposes – they were all just a diversion to pin the fires on Julian Davis. And once we knew you were going to set fire to the seed barn on Warrington Avenue, we called the Findlay Fire Department and rescued Julian Davis from the fire. You were really close to getting away with it too, weren't you? And really close to having everyone blame Julian Davis for the fires! I guess you're going to have a lot of time to think about that, huh?"

"I could have gotten away with it," the older man said, his voice turning to an angry tone. "If it wasn't for you kids. My summer would have looked a lot different than it does now." He paused for a moment, then continued angrily. "If it wasn't for you, I'd be flush with cash, sittin' on a beach somewhere and enjoyin' all of my profits. I was lookin' for one big payday for my retirement."

"But Sneak almost got run over by a car!" I exclaimed.

"And Julian Davis almost got burned up in that fire at the seed barn," Sneak Ryerson added calmly.

"Well…" Mr. Crenshaw said haltingly. "Julian could have easily gotten out of those ropes, they weren't tied very tight at all. If he hadn't panicked, it would have taken him only a few minutes to untie himself. I just needed some time to get away. He could have been free before the fire ever got close to him."

"That's incredible!" Uncle Charlie said from behind us. "I don't believe you for one minute. I don't think Julian Davis could have gotten free from those ropes. My brother-in-law said they were on pretty tight."

"It's true! He could have easily gotten free," Russell Crenshaw asserted. "I was planning to raise a ruckus around the neighborhood, so a lot of people would see him leave the building as it went up in flames."

"I'm not so sure about that," Sneak Ryerson replied. "My Dad and I had to really work at getting those knots loose."

"And me too," I replied.

"Yeah, and Pep too," Sneak added.

"He probably just wrapped himself up in them tighter when he was sitting there," Mr. Crenshaw proposed. "He's really not that bright."

"I don't think we're getting anywhere with this," Uncle Charlie interrupted, using the same words with Mr. Crenshaw as he had used in the earlier interview with Julian Davis. "Crenshaw, you pled guilty to the arson and conspiracy charges, so let's talk about why you asked the boy to come here."

There was a pause in our conversation and I looked down at my black Panasonic tape recorder, seeing the cassette tape turn slow circles around its black box. Turning, I saw my friend Sneak Ryerson continue an unflinching stare, carefully observing Mister Crenshaw's every move.

"So why did you want us to come here?" my friend asked abruptly, interrupting the awkward silence. "You told the warden you had some valuable information, or something like that, right?"

"That's right," the older man said in a quieter tone, as another sinister smile appeared on his face. "I do have some information. Some *very* valuable information."

"Well," the young detective asked. "Who gave you this *valuable* information?"

"I can't reveal my sources!" the older man exclaimed in a higher pitched voice. "But I can tell you *where* I got it."

"And where..." Sneak asked impatiently.

"..the County Jail," Mr. Crenshaw interrupted. "– back in Findlay. I got it at the Hancock County Jail."

"Why didn't you tell anybody then?" I asked.

"Well, I tried to. I hoped to use it for some leverage, but I had already taken the plea deal. My lawyer actually thought we might be able to use it to get a reduced sentence or better accommodations, but the Prosecutor wasn't interested in making any further deals. So, I've been waiting... trying to make something out of it."

"Not much luck, huh?" Uncle Charlie interrupted.

"Well, I was able to get this meeting," Mr. Crenshaw said smartly.

"True," Sneak's uncle replied.

"So, what's the news that we've come so far to hear?" Sneak asked.

"Well, it's this," the older man said seriously, leaning closer to the table that separated him from our group. "Something *big* is going to happen this week – on Thursday, in fact."

"This Thursday?" I asked, surprised. "Like tomorrow?"

"Correct," Mr. Crenshaw said seriously. "*Tomorrow.*"

"But that's the day you're going on vacation!" I said without thinking, as I turned to my friend – who gave me a stern look.

"So how exactly did you acquire this information?" the young detective asked the prisoner, ignoring my comment.

"Well," Mr. Crenshaw explained. "When I was locked up in the County Jail, the word among the inmates was that whoever was released by this week should have a really good alibi for this Thursday – because something *big* was going to happen. Something *really big.*"

"An alibi?" I asked. "Like having a witness say where you are?"

"Correct," the prisoner responded.

"Alright. So, what exactly is supposed to happen tomorrow?" Uncle Charlie asked in a professional tone.

"I have no idea, Captain Foster," Mr. Crenshaw replied calmly. His voice suddenly changed to a more pitiful tone. "I'm just a simple country farmer. All I know is what I told you: the word among the prisoners was that if you are getting out, make sure you have an alibi for this Thursday, because something big is going to happen. All the prisoners were talking about it and the word was even being spread to all the local criminals around Findlay, too. *Everyone* should have an alibi tomorrow."

"So, like *when* tomorrow? Will it happen in the morning or afternoon?" I wondered.

"The sense I got," Russell Crenshaw replied while leaning closer, "was that the criminals were to have an alibi for the *whole day* – and the *whole night* too."

"Wow," I exclaimed. "All day and night!"

"That's it?" my friend – the great young detective – said with a shrug.

"Well, yeah," replied the prisoner, surprised by his comment.

"That's not really all that *valuable*," Sneak frowned.

"What do you mean it's not all that valuable?" Mr. Crenshaw objected. "Of course it's valuable! I'm telling you that something's going to happen tomorrow! Something *big*! That's what all the criminals in Findlay are being told, so it must mean that it's going to happen somewhere in or around *Findlay*. I'm telling you that a crime will take place! A big crime! For a detective like yourself, it doesn't get much more valuable than that!"

"Yeah, but," my friend retorted. "We don't know exactly *when* it will occur. I mean it could happen anytime during the day *or* night."

"Well, at least you've got a *date* to go with," Mr. Crenshaw replied.

"And you don't even know *what* is going to happen! It could be anything really, or it could be nothing at all. Someone could have just been pulling your leg. We don't even know *where* this information came from to be able to confirm it. I mean, the rumor could have been started by a guard at the jail to keep the crime statistics down on Thursdays, or something like that," Sneak speculated – wildly, it seemed to me.

"Started by a guard!" Mr. Crenshaw exclaimed.

"I don't think..." Uncle Charlie began to reply.

"I'm thinking bank robbery," I interjected. "That would be something *really* big. Don't you think? Maybe at Diamond Savings and Loan? I've got my money in the *Squirrel Club* there. It's not a lot but a lot of kids I know keep their money there too. If someone blew up the bank vault or a safe at the bank with dynamite or something like that, and they took all the kids' money, that would definitely be big."

"Or, it could be absolutely *nothing*," Sneak said again blankly. "I think you've led us here on false pretenses, Mister Crenshaw. Leading us down the garden path like you did with Julian Davis."

"False pretenses!" the elderly prisoner replied loudly – loud enough to get the attention of one of the guards who had brought him into the room and was standing next to the heavy metal door.

"Who told you this news?" Sneak continued. "*The Great Peggu?*"

"Don't be ridiculous!" Mr. Crenshaw said loudly.

"Or maybe it was *Mary York?*" the young detective asked, trying to trap the older prisoner.

"Who?" came the reply. "I have no idea who that is!"

"Everything okay over there?" the guard asked, concerned with the loud conversation.

"Yes!" Mr. Crenshaw said with a scoff.

"I don't think everything's okay," Sneak said angrily to Mr. Crenshaw. "I mean, you made us drive all the way down here. How long was the drive Uncle Charlie?"

"About three hours…one way," his uncle calculated.

"….then you ask us all sorts of questions about the case where we caught *you*," Sneak continued in protest. "And then when you finally got around to the part where you're *supposed* to tell us some *valuable* information, it turns out not to be valuable at all! I mean, my sister could have told me more valuable information than that – and she's *six*! And she doesn't even use deductive reasoning!"

"This is outlandish!" the older man replied. "I asked you to come down here because I thought *you* could make some use of this valuable information and maybe put in a good word for me to the warden. I thought with this valuable information, maybe *you* would want to have the police stake out a high-crime spot – like a bank or someplace important! Or, I don't know, maybe *you* could use your spectacular world-class detective skills to solve the crime before it happens! How would that float your boat? Maybe the reporters are wrong about you being such a great hot-shot detective! I don't know! And frankly, I don't care anymore!" And with these words Mr. Crenshaw indicated he was concluding the interview. "Good day gentlemen," he added, leaning back in his chair. "Guard! I'm ready to go back to my cell now," he said, turning to the nearby Corrections Officer. "I've probably got to go to the Infirmary again to see Nurse Ratched, er, whatever her name is."

"Okay," the guard said as he approached the table and unlocked the chain at Mr. Crenshaw's ankles from the floor. Slowly, the guard helped Russell Crenshaw from his chair and began escorting his prisoner toward the thick metal door.

"Oh, by the way *Crenshaw*," Uncle Charlie said loudly as the prisoner turned his head. "I'm going to tell the warden that you're still writing letters to Julian Davis and pretending to be *The Great Peggu*. He'll put a stop to that."

"Hmmph," the old prisoner mumbled as he walked a few feet forward before turning sharply. "Sneak Ryerson," he said in a voice that dripped with evil and contempt. "You think you're so smart. You probably think you're smarter than me, but you're not! I'm one step ahead of you! I'll always be one step ahead! You better watch out for those UFOs! They'll get you sometime!"

I was taken aback by the prisoner's strong words and sensed that Sneak's Uncle Charlie was moments away from defending his nephew. But then, suddenly, the prisoner's face changed from a smirk to a smile as he sang part of a song that I had heard many times at my grandmother's house. "Au revoir, Adios, Auf Weidersein. Good night!" He said with a flourish before turning his head toward the open hallway. A moment later, Russell Crenshaw was out of the interview room.

Again, I was soon startled by the heavy metal door slamming shut and the loud echo that followed. For a few moments, we could hear the prisoner continue his singing as his chains rattled along the floor of the long hallway.

CHAPTER 13

"Wow, you were sure worked up," I said to my friend Sneak Ryerson, as we sat behind a metal table, deep inside a prison in southwestern Ohio. I paused for a few seconds to listen to the final sounds of Russell Crenshaw's chain drag loudly over the concrete floor and I wondered how far away he was from the interview room, as he slowly walked down a hallway singing a song from a popular television program. "I don't think I've ever seen you that angry," I confided in my friend.

"Oh, I wasn't angry," Sneak Ryerson replied calmly. "I wasn't angry at all."

"But..." I paused. "I thought you told him you were mad because we had to drive all the way down here to get such measly information. You said his clue was basically worthless."

"Oh no," my friend replied cheerily. "I actually thought it was pretty cool to get to visit someone in prison – two prisoners, actually."

"But I thought you said that..."

"It's something we planned," Sneak's Uncle Charlie interrupted with a laugh as he stood and nodded to the Corrections Officer who had been with us on our side of the room, near the heavy door we had used to enter.

"What?" I asked.

"We've been talking about this meeting with Russell Crenshaw for a couple of days," explained my friend's uncle.

"Yeah," my friend added. "And Uncle Charlie said that if it seemed like Mr. Crenshaw was holding back on us, I should try to act – what did you call it?"

"Slighted."

"Right, slighted. We thought Mr. Crenshaw would be willing to tell us more if I complained a lot and pretended to be angry. That's why I was grumbling about how far we had to drive and stuff like that."

"Ah, got it," I replied.

"Sneak, you done good," Uncle Charlie added, echoing a catch-phrase used by the actor Joe Don Baker in a recently cancelled TV detective show called *Eischied*. "Unfortunately, old Mr. Crenshaw didn't have much to offer us, did he?"

"No, he didn't," Sneak sighed.

"What do you think he meant by *something big* happening tomorrow?" I wondered. "Do you think it's a bank robbery?" I asked excitedly.

"I don't know," my friend said with a shrug of his shoulders. "I really don't know. Maybe the warden will have some information we could go on."

Soon, we were escorted by the Corrections Officer out of the interview room and back through the labyrinth of hallways to the warden's office. "Well, did you learn anything interesting?" the warden asked us warmly when we sat down again in the leather chairs across from his desk in his large and spacious office.

"Hmm? Did we learn anything?" Sneak asked. "I don't know, maybe."

"Yeah, maybe." I added.

"You came down here to get some *valuable information*. What did Russell Crenshaw tell you?" the warden inquired.

"Not much," I summarized. "Just that he heard that something *big* is going to happen tomorrow – in Findlay."

"So, some jailhouse scuttlebutt?" asked the warden.

"Yeah, sounds like it," replied Sneak's Uncle Charlie. "He said he got the information while he was incarcerated up in Findlay – at our county jail."

"So, nothing happening here, apparently," the warden added, with a look of relief on his face.

"Right," Uncle Charlie confirmed. "Nothing going on here." The police captain paused for a moment, then asked, "Would you mind if I used your phone?"

"Sure, you can use the one here or outside the door, at my administrator's desk. You can talk freely on it. Your call won't be recorded like most of our phone calls are in here!"

"I'll be right back," Uncle Charlie replied with a concerned look. "I'm going to have my guys start looking into this."

"Perfect," the warden replied with a smile. "That will give me a chance to ask this young detective a few more questions!" Soon, the warden was asking Sneak Ryerson more questions about his older cases – questions he had forgotten to ask when we were in his office earlier that morning.

Eventually, Uncle Charlie returned.

"Did your detectives know anything about what is supposed to happen tomorrow?" the warden asked the police captain.

"No," Sneak's uncle replied with a grimace. "They hadn't heard anything about it. But they're going to check in at the County Jail and get in touch with some of our *CI's* – our confidential informants," he explained, seeing the puzzled look on my face. "Maybe they can enlighten us further."

"Oh, that's a good idea," I said encouragingly.

"I hope so," added Uncle Charlie. "Maybe by the time we get home, they'll have something for us to go on. And, we can prepare for whatever is supposed to happen."

"Yeah," I replied hopefully.

"Well, thanks for your help, sir." Uncle Charlie said formally to the warden as he shook his hand. "We've got a long drive ahead of us."

"Safe travels," the older man replied. "Let me know if you need anything," he added as we walked out of his office and into the large reception area.

"Oh, there is one more thing," Uncle Charlie said, as he turned toward the warden. "It looks like Julian Davis is still getting letters from Russell Crenshaw. Crenshaw's using the name *The Great Peggu* – that alien he pretended to be up in Findlay. You can put a stop to that, right?"

"Of course, of course," the warden replied with a serious look. "We can put an end to that right away. Those two are already housed in different units, but I'll make sure my Officers know about the letters."

"Thanks," Uncle Charlie replied.

"Absolutely," said the warden warmly.

"Oh, and actually there was one thing I wanted to ask you about," Uncle Charlie continued.

"What's that?"

"The letter that Julian Davis had in his possession referred to a woman."

"A woman?" the warden asked.

"Do you remember the name, Sneak?" Uncle Charlie asked his nephew.

"Mary York," came the quick reply from the young detective with the photographic mind. "I tried to get Mr. Crenshaw to tell us who she is, but he said he didn't know her."

"That's right," Uncle Charlie continued. "Mary York. Does that name ring any bells with you?"

"Mary York?" the warden asked with a puzzled look. "Hmm, I don't think so."

"Is there *anyone* here at the prison with that name – maybe someone in prison administration?" Uncle Charlie asked. "Or maybe she's a teacher who's taught a class here, or someone who visits regularly from a church or something like that?"

"I always review the names of all of the volunteers who come through here... and I know all of our workers... I don't know anyone by that name," the warden confessed. Turning to his administrator, he asked, "Leslie, does that name sound familiar to you? Mary York?"

"No sir," the prison administrator replied. "I can have Human Resources check on it."

"Thanks," the warden replied, before pausing. "Oh, wait, you know, we did have a prisoner here a number of years ago by the last name of York. What was his first name?"

"Frank," came the response from the Corrections Officer standing nearby. "Frank York."

"That's right!" the warden replied. "Wow, that was a long time ago."

"Was his wife's name Mary? Or, maybe his daughter?" Uncle Charlie asked.

"I can check on that for you," said the warden. "If we find out, we'll let you know."

"Thanks," Uncle Charlie concluded. "We appreciate the help."

"Yeah, thanks!" I added. "This has been a cool visit."

A few moments later we exited the warden's office and retraced our steps, walking down a set of stairs and then several long corridors to return to the Visitor's area. We stopped to drop off the Visitor's Badges we had acquired at the check-in desk and walked in silence out of the red brick building where we were greeted by the warmth and sunshine of the late summer morning. A few moments later, we came to the small guard house with the same serious looking guard dressed in a starched white shirt and dark blue pants. He asked us for our names again and after we had provided them, he made a notation to a piece of paper on his wooden clipboard and instructed us to "Have a nice day" in a deep baritone voice.

Passing the large VISITOR'S ENTRANCE sign and entering the parking lot, I let out a long and sustained laugh. "Yes!" I yelled, looking up in the air. "Yes!" I said again, raising both of my hands in the air, while still clenching my black Panasonic tape recorder in my right hand.

"What's wrong with you?" my young detective friend asked, momentarily embarrassed by my display of emotion. "Put your hands down."

"I'm so relieved to be out of there!" I said in a loud ecstatic voice, thrilled that I was now outside the prison walls. "I was *so* worried about going in there. And I did it!" I added as I lowered my hands. "We did it!"

"You done good," commented Uncle Charlie.

"Yeah," Sneak agreed.

"I was expecting to see Mr. Crenshaw," I said to the others excitedly. "But seeing Julian Davis. Man, that was weird."

"No kidding," my friend replied. "You asked some really good questions, Pep. I hope you got it all recorded."

"I think so," I said, looking at my black Panasonic tape recorder. "I put new batteries in last night and I checked it a couple of times to make sure the tape was moving."

"Good," said my friend as we arrived at his uncle's car. Soon, he and his uncle placed their blazers in the backseat.

"So, what do you think's gonna happen tomorrow?" I wondered as we returned to our seats in Uncle Charlie's two-door Pontiac.

"I have no idea," my friend admitted from the front seat. He exhaled deeply, tired from our meetings with the two prisoners and the prison warden. "But we've got a couple of hours to think about it, huh?"

"Yeah," I agreed.

"Hey, don't forget about Mr. Knick Knack back there!" Sneak said with a smile as he looked toward the backseat.

"I hope he had a good nap while we were locked up!" I replied.

"We weren't exactly locked up!" Uncle Charlie said with a laugh.

"Well, it felt like it," I laughed as the car pulled out of the prison parking lot. "Hey, wouldn't it be funny if we told Jennie that we accidently left Mr. Knick Knack inside the prison?" I added, leaning forward as the others chuckled.

"Jennie would probably insist we drive back here tonight and get him!" laughed Uncle Charlie.

"Prolly," I smiled.

"She never lets me forget that time we left him tied to a tree," Sneak added.

"What!" Uncle Charlie asked.

"That was so funny," I began.

"It wasn't intentional," Sneak added seriously.

"Yeah, we didn't mean to do it," I agreed.

"Tell me what happened," Uncle Charlie prompted. "My mind could use a break from thinking about those two bozos back there."

"We were playing *Cowboys and Indians*," I began. "And…"

"And we were having a really fun time," Sneak interrupted.

"But the problem was everyone wanted to do the same thing," I explained.

"And it doesn't really work if everyone wants to do the same thing," Sneak expounded. "There have to be two *different* groups."

"Right," Uncle Charlie added with a laugh. "You need one group of kids to be the Cowboys and another group of kids to be the Indians."

"Right," I continued. "But when all of our friends got to the Ryerson's house, everyone wanted to be a cowboy."

"When was this?" Uncle Charlie asked.

"It was a long time ago," I explained.

"Like two years ago," Sneak answered.

"Right," I persisted.

"Do I happen to know any of these friends of yours?" Uncle Charlie asked with a smile.

"Moscow and Joel were there," I added. "And a couple of kids from school."

"Right," said Sneak.

"And we had talked about playing *Cowboys and Indians* a few days before, so a bunch of us showed up at the house with our cowboy hats and toy guns," I continued.

"Ah," said Uncle Charlie. "I think I see where this is going."

"Mom even had some different colored bandanas for us to wear," Sneak added. "So we could be different Cowboys."

"I could see her doing that," Uncle Charlie said of his older sister, as he continued driving down the narrow state highway that led away from the prison.

"Yeah, but before we could even start," I continued, "there was a big argument because everyone wanted red bandanas. But there weren't enough, so a few of us had to settle for blue ones."

"Right," Sneak replied.

"So anyway, we were having fun running around the yard shooting at each other with our toy guns and then someone..."

"Moscow, I think," Sneak added.

"...said we should stop and play *Cowboys and Indians*," I explained.

"Makes sense," Uncle Charlie added.

"But no one wanted to take off their bandana and be an Indian."

"Oh," said Uncle Charlie. "So, Indians can't wear bandanas?"

"Not on that day," I explained.

"Oh," replied my friend's uncle.

"So anyway," I continued. "Mrs. Ryerson brought out all these cool Indian things she made for us too."

"Like what?" asked Uncle Charlie.

"Like feathers stapled onto a headband," I explained.

"Oh," said Uncle Charlie.

"And some tomahawks," Sneak added.

"Yeah, those were pretty cool," I said.

"Sounds like it," Uncle Charlie agreed.

"But, once everyone saw that stuff," I continued, "everyone wanted to be an Indian. So, we took off our cowboy stuff and everyone grabbed the feathers and the tomahawks and started whooping and hollering and chasing each other around the yard. We even scared the neighbor's dog."

"Yeah, Ginger," Sneak explained. "She didn't know what was going on, so she stayed on Mrs. Nelson's porch just looking at us the whole time. So, then someone..."

"I think it was Moscow," I added.

"....had the bright idea to tie someone up to the big maple tree in the back yard, so that some cowboys could ride up on their imaginary horses and rescue them."

"Sounds about right," Uncle Charlie said.

"It wasn't such a bad idea," I added. "But nobody wanted to be tied up. We even asked Mrs. Ryerson, and she was like, '*Absolutely not!*'"

"Yeah," Sneak agreed. "Grandma Foster was visiting that day and we almost talked her into it, but she said she wanted to keep talking with Mom."

"I would have paid money to see that!" Uncle Charlie said, laughing at the thought of his elderly mother being tied up to a tree as the boys ran around her.

"We couldn't get any adults to do it," I explained. "So, I volunteered to be tied up first."

"Big mistake," Sneak commented.

"Those bozos," I began, using Uncle Charlie's word from earlier.

"Yeah, it didn't work out exactly as we planned," explained Sneak.

"What happened?" Uncle Charlie asked.

"Well," I continued. "They tied me up with an old rope they found in the garage."

"It was an old clothesline," Sneak explained.

"And they said they'd come back and get me," I said in a disappointed tone. "But then, everyone ran to the front yard – and I was there in the back yard – and I guess there was a big argument about who was going to be Chief of the Indians and if it was going to be *freeze tag* when you got shot and how to get unfrozen…"

"Yeah, we should have worked out the rules ahead of time," Sneak added as Uncle Charlie laughed. "We had some differences of opinion – no tag backs and that sort of thing."

"Ah," Sneak's uncle said in a knowing voice.

"So, I was just tied up waiting for everyone to come to the back yard and after like five minutes, I got free and went to the front yard and had to break up this big fight," I explained.

"It wasn't that bad," Sneak replied.

"I think it was," I continued. "I almost got decked."

"We eventually worked everything out," Sneak explained.

"Yeah," I continued. "And then they wanted to tie me up again!"

Uncle Charlie let out a loud laugh at this comment. "I'm sure they did!"

"But, I was like, '*No way!* Tie someone else up!'" I continued. "But they were like, 'We want to rescue someone!' Because, by then, everyone was tired of being an Indian and had changed back to being a Cowboy again."

"Wow," Uncle Charlie replied.

"So," I continued, "We went back to the back yard and Jennie was swinging on the swing set."

"Just minding her own business," Sneak added.

"Yeah, so we tried to convince her to be a *damsel in distress* that we could rescue, but she wouldn't agree to it."

"She didn't want to play," Sneak added.

"Then someone," I began.

"I think it was Moscow," Sneak said.

"He thought of her imaginary friend and asked Jennie if we could play with Mr. Knick Knack."

"I love it," Uncle Charlie laughed.

"Jennie said that Mr. Knick Knack mostly just played games with her," I continued. "But he hadn't played with boys for a while and might like it – so she agreed. But then when we said we were going to tie him up to a tree to be rescued she said '*No way*'."

"I would think so," Uncle Charlie said with a chuckle.

"But we said it would only be for a few minutes – just enough time for us to run around to the front of the house and then come back to rescue him," I explained.

"Right," Uncle Charlie added.

"So, we tied up Mr. Knick Knack to the big maple tree in the back yard and went to the front yard again," Sneak said.

"And, then we began arguing… again," I explained. "Someone…"

"I think it was Moscow," Sneak added.

"…said that maybe we could pretend that Mr. Knick Knack was a famous Chief – like Sitting Bull or Geronimo – and that we should be Indians who go and rescue him."

"Yeah," my friend replied.

"So then," I continued, "We couldn't agree if the cowboys would do the rescue or the Indians."

"Yeah, there was a lot of arguing again," Sneak said.

"I definitely thought we were all going to get in a big fight," I explained. "But by then we had moved on from freeze tag to shooting our plastic cap guns in the front yard. But then we discovered that we were all out of ammunition – our red plastic circles had all run out. I mean, there's only eight pops in a circle, and everyone had shot them all by then."

"I was getting tired of all the arguing," Sneak explained. "So, I just said, 'Let's go to the basement and play with my model train set'. So, we all went into the house from the *front* door and then went down to the basement and played with my trains."

"Yeah, that was pretty fun," I continued. "Then, a little while later, our parents came over and picked us up, and we all went home."

"Also, from the front door," Sneak explained. "So, nobody had gone to the back yard – and Jennie had gone inside before we started playing with Mr. Knick Knack."

I interrupted my friend with a smile. "Wasn't it at dinner when Jennie asked you about Mr. Knick Knack?"

"Yeah," Sneak replied as he shook his head. "We were all eating dinner and Mom asked if I had fun with my friends," Sneak explained.

"And then…" I said with a laugh.

"And then," my friend continued. "Jennie asked if we had fun playing with Mr. Knick Knack."

"Classic," I added.

"And then I said, 'Oh yeah, we had a lot of fun playing with him'," Sneak continued, muffling his laughter. "And then Jennie asked me, 'So, was Mr. Knick Knack tied up to the tree for very long? Or, was it only for a few minutes?' And…" Sneak grimaced. "I couldn't lie to her. She would have known if I was lying," he explained. "I just looked at her with a surprised look on my face and said 'I think we forgot to untie him'."

At this comment, both Uncle Charlie and I were laughing heartily.

"So, what did Jennie do?" Uncle Charlie asked.

"When she heard the news, she let out a giant scream. '*Mr. Knick Knack!*' she yelled. And Mom said, 'Jennie, no singing or screaming at the dinner table', but by then, Jennie had booked it out of the house with Mom and Dad following her – with me following a few steps behind. Sure enough, when Jennie got outside she saw that the clothesline was wrapped tightly around the tree. And Jennie started yelling, 'Mr. Knick Knack! Mr. Knick Knack! What have they done to you?'"

With these words, the car filled with the loud laughter from all three passengers.

"Eventually, she got the clothesline off the tree," my friend continued. "And then she started yelling at me – and that lasted for a really long time. 'You left Mr. Knick Knack out here all afternoon!' she was screaming. 'I'm never going to let him play with you guys ever again!'"

My friend paused for a moment, then concluded. "I was really sorry about that, but it was only a few days later she asked to play with us again."

"Yeah," I said.

"Wow," Sneak's Uncle Charlie exclaimed. "That was quite some story! It definitely helped get my mind off those guys back there at the prison."

"Definitely," I agreed.

"Let's go get some lunch! I'm starving!" Uncle Charlie declared as the car increased speed and entered the northbound lane of Interstate 75.

CHAPTER 14

While Sneak, his Uncle Charlie and I were interviewing prisoners, three *Sunday School Detectives* – Hailey, Lisa and Cressida, along with Alice Williams, a young scientist and researcher at our local college – arrived on the campus of our local seminary in Alice's orange Volkswagen Beetle.

The four exited Alice's car, talking rapidly as they entered the three-story seminary building. Moving quickly, they quickly passed the first floor that held a large auditorium and a second floor where smaller classes were held. "This is also the way to Professor Telson's old office," Hailey Cotton said with a smile as they climbed the stairs to the offices on the third floor of the building.

"He was pretty cool," Lisa Lavin said to the others.

"Yeah," her cousin Cressida Hudson said quietly.

"So, who was this?" Alice Williams asked, following a few steps behind the younger girls.

"He was sort of like an advisor to the *Sunday School Detectives*," Hailey explained.

"Yeah, and he was also our Sunday School teacher sometimes too," Lisa interrupted.

"Right," Hailey confirmed, continuing up the stairs.

"He taught us some pretty cool things," Cressida said in her soft voice.

"But he doesn't teach here anymore?" Alice questioned.

"Right," explained Hailey. "He was just a visiting professor here."

"He's gone back to the East Coast – to finish his Ph.D," Lisa added. "His school will start in the fall."

"But this summer he's on an archeological dig in Israel," Hailey explained.

"Wow, that sounds cool," said Alice.

"It sounded pretty boring when he explained it to us," Lisa said with a frown.

"Really?" the young scientist asked.

"Yeah, he said the last time he was there all he did was just sit around in the desert for a few weeks waiting for the right permits to arrive. And then, once they got all the permits, they spent three days and nights digging in the desert..."

"...and didn't find anything," Hailey added.

"...and then he had to come home," Lisa concluded.

"Wow, those first few weeks must have been really boring," Alice observed.

"Yeah, really boring," Cressida agreed.

The four quickly rounded the corner of the stairway where they saw a long row of offices on the third floor. "There's Professor Telson's old office," Hailey said, pointing to a door that opened to an empty room. The four stopped in the open doorway and looked at the bare office, furnished only with an empty metal desk and two blue chairs.

"When Professor Telson was here, this room was packed with books," Lisa exclaimed, as she stared at the open space while bright sunlight streamed in through a long dormer window on the far side of the office.

"Yeah," her cousin agreed. "It was really crowded."

"Are you looking for Professor Telson?" a female voice asked from behind them.

Turning, the four saw a middle-aged woman wearing a double-stranded white pearl necklace, a long yellow dress and blue high-heeled shoes. Her pretty face, the girls noticed, had strong features and she wore wide eyeglasses low on the bridge of her nose.

"No, no, we're not looking for the professor," Hailey said with a laugh. "We were just looking at his old office. It sure looks a lot different without all of his books!"

"Yes, quite a lot different!" the woman said cheerfully.

"Our Sunday School Class had a goodbye party for Professor Telson a few weeks ago," Lisa added.

"Oh," the woman said with another laugh. "I was going to tell you that he's gone, but it sounds like you know that already!"

"Yeah," Cressida replied softly.

"He's out on some archeology dig," Lisa commented.

"Sounds like it might be kind of boring," Alice added. "At least I heard his last one was."

"I guess you know that story too!" the woman said with a smile as the girls laughed. "It's funny, Nicholas didn't even remember signing up for this latest dig. But the paperwork arrived and so did his airline ticket, so he packed up his office and sent his books out East and then, off to the desert he went!"

"He didn't remember signing up for the archeology dig?" Lisa asked incredulously.

"Nope," the woman said with a smile.

"Well, he used to say he could be an absent-minded professor!" Hailey said, smiling.

"I've heard him say that too," said the woman as she laughed. "I'm Dr. Driver," she added abruptly, stretching out her hand in greeting. "I don't think we've met."

Hailey introduced herself first and then the others shook Dr. Driver's hand as they told her their names.

"So, do you work here?" Alice asked.

"I do!" said Dr. Driver. "I teach Counseling and Psychology."

"That's interesting," Alice said with a smile. "I might need some of your help!" she admitted. "I just realized earlier today that I've got some questions that I need to find some answers to."

"Well, we do have some good resources *downstairs* in our Counseling Center," the professor added in a serious tone, making the girls feel a bit out of place among the offices of the learned professors.

"We're on our way to see Dr. Bayhill," Hailey explained quickly. "Is his office down this hall?"

"Yes, it is. I can take you to him," offered Dr. Driver cheerfully. "With the summer term, it's kind of slow around here and I'm not too busy right now. I was actually just on my way to make a copy of a recipe, Maryland chicken," she explained, holding up a clipping from a magazine.

"Oh, that sounds good!" Lisa exclaimed.

"Yeah," one of the others agreed, as the four followed the professor down the long hallway.

"It's nice to be here in the air conditioning, isn't it?" Dr. Driver said. "Probably a big difference from what Professor Telson is experiencing in the desert, huh?"

"Yeah," the girls agreed in unison.

"Definitely," one of them added.

"He's probably so bored," Lisa concluded.

"Definitely," said another.

CHAPTER 15

"I think you'll really enjoy meeting Dr. Bayhill," Dr. Driver said with a smile as the three Sunday School Detectives, along with a young scientist, followed her down a long hallway. "He is quite a character."

"Does he have as many books as Professor Telson had in his office?" Cressida Hudson asked curiously, in her quiet voice.

"No, no. Not even close!" Dr. Driver laughed. "It would be pretty hard to match Professor Telson's books! Actually, Professor Bayhill is semi-retired. He just works here part-time now. His office is also used as a conference room for our faculty and staff, so he doesn't have many of his personal things in there anymore."

A few moments later, they arrived at an open door and peered into a large office where an elderly professor was seated at a large wooden conference table, carefully studying a book. The rectangular table was surrounded by chairs and uncluttered, containing only the book the professor was studying and a solitary black rotary telephone in one corner.

"Dr. Bayhill?" Dr. Driver asked in a calm voice. The older professor, however, did not reply but continued reading from the orange and black covered paperback textbook. "Dr. Bayhill, you have some guests," said Dr. Driver, this time in a louder voice.

"Yes?" the older professor asked weakly, as he glanced up and a surprised look overtook his tired and weary face. "Oh, the detectives!" he added with a smile. "I'm glad you've arrived!" His voice was now more animated and high-pitched. The professor stood slowly, holding tightly to the chair as he rose. "Thank you, Nichole," he said to his colleague at the doorway.

"Sure, thing Sam," Dr. Driver replied with a smile. "I'll let you know how this recipe turns out," she said as she waved the magazine clipping with the recipe.

"Oh, please do," the elderly professor replied. "I'm definitely interested in that Maryland chicken! It should taste a lot better than my last cooking adventure – a mummified Cornish Hen!"

"Well, I hope my chicken turns out better than that!" Dr. Driver laughed. Then, turning to Hailey Cotton she added, "And I hope your meeting goes well too."

"Thanks. I'm sure it will," Hailey added optimistically.

"See you later," Dr. Driver said with a smile and wave, before turning and walking quickly down the hall.

"So, you're the young detectives who are going to help my grandson," Dr. Bayhill said in his high-pitched voice.

"Well, we can't make any promises," said Lisa Lavin. "But I hope we can help."

Turning to Alice Williams – the oldest member of the group – the professor asked, "Were you the one I talked to yesterday?"

"No, sorry," said Alice.

"That would be me," Hailey interrupted, as she stretched out her arm to shake hands with the professor.

"Oh, very good," the professor replied, shaking her hand. "Very good, indeed. I'm Dr. Bayhill."

Each of the girls introduced themselves to the professor and were soon seated around the table. "Do any of you know my grandson, Andrew?" the professor asked as he sat in a high-backed wooden chair. "He just graduated from high school."

"No," several replied. "I don't think we do," replied Lisa.

"Well, that's neither here nor there," the elderly professor concluded, as his face turned grim. "He's in so much trouble," the professor explained, slowly shaking his head while nervously moving the palm of his right hand across his forehead and then over the top of his bald head. "I'm so very glad you're here to help," he added with a sigh.

"Could you tell us more about the trouble your grandson is in?" Lisa asked quickly.

"It's bad – really bad," the professor said in a serious tone. "He's been accused of taking some important company papers."

"That's what you told me on the phone," said Hailey.

"When did this happen?" Lisa questioned, taking a small black notebook from her purse.

"It was Monday," the professor said in a sorrowful voice. "Just a couple of days ago, when he was leaving work. I honestly can't believe it."

"So, what exactly happened?" Lisa continued with her questions.

"Well, he was walking out of the building and a security guard stopped him."

"Really?" one of the girls replied.

"You know, it would be best if Andrew told you himself," the professor explained. "I've been so upset about it, I'll probably leave out some of the details. We just can't believe it – his parents and my wife and I. It's just so shocking. My mind has been in such a fog. I feel almost like I've fallen into a deep abyss. It's been so strange – not being able to think straight. Last weekend, he was out working on my farm – helping me try to replicate an ancient Mesopotamian farming technique – and then, the next day he finds his whole world is turned upside down. I've been so confounded by this whole matter. And, if *I'm* feeling so upset about this, I can't even imagine how my grandson is feeling. He's so young to have something like this happen. I mean, they might even press charges against him! We had such high hopes for that boy. When you meet him, you'll see that Andrew is a little different – I'll give you that – but he's always been such a good boy. But now – now, he's in so much trouble." The professor paused for a moment, then looked at the black rotary phone on his desk. "Let me phone Andrew and get him over here. He lives just a few minutes away. He can be here in a jiffy."

"I think you're right. It would be good if we could talk to Andrew," Lisa said in a serious tone. Soon, Dr. Bayhill picked up the phone receiver and dialed his grandson.

While the professor spoke with his grandson, the girls studied their surroundings. The elderly professor, they noticed, was dressed casually, wearing a short-sleeved white dress shirt with pencils and pens filling black plastic pocket-protectors in both front pockets of his shirt. His tan pants were flat-fronted polyester above simple brown lace-up Hush Puppy shoes, occasionally revealing white socks around his ankles. Appearing quite frail, with a hunched back, weak voice, and eyes betraying great worry and lack of sleep, the professor seemed to also be suffering from a neurological condition that made his right hand sporadically shake with a tremor. When the tremor occurred, he would cross his arms over his stomach, holding his right arm steady with his left.

Dr. Bayhill's office, the girls noticed, was quite different than Professor Telson's. While the younger professor's office was small and cluttered with books and academic journals, Dr. Bayhill's large office was neat and orderly, containing only two tall bookshelves along one wall that were partially filled with books. The books on the shelves were neatly organized by subject, with labels on their spines betraying their origins as being on long-term loan from the seminary's library. Unlike the younger professor's desk that overflowed with materials, Dr. Bayhill's long wooden desk had only one lonely book titled THE ANCIENT NEAR EAST with an orange and black cover that contained a black and white photograph of an Egyptian statue. The subtitle read, *Volume 1: An Anthology of Texts and Pictures by James B. Pritchard.*

Although sparsely decorated, the large office reflected the professor's interest in ancient history. Several old vases and terracotta pots were prominently displayed on the bookshelves, while ancient oil lamps and a wide clay bowl with black-figure images stood on a wooden table next to the office's sole window. The walls, although mostly bare, contained two large framed maps – one of ancient Assyria and the other ancient Babylonia – while two thin stone tablets that listed the Ten Commandments were mounted on a wall near the table.

"Okay, detectives," Dr. Bayhill said in a more upbeat tone after hanging up the telephone. "Andrew will be here in just a few minutes."

"Great," one of the girls replied.

"Would any of you like something to drink?" the professor asked. "We have some instant coffee out in the hallway."

"No, I'm okay," Hailey replied.

"Us too," Lisa said, looking at her cousin.

"I'm okay," replied Alice, who was seated in a chair furthest away from the others – positioned to observe rather than participate in the discussion.

"So, what exactly do you teach here, Dr. Bayhill?" Lisa asked, after studying the large office.

"Well I teach…" the professor began and then paused. "Actually, maybe you should tell me! Can you figure that out by using your detective skills, like your friend Sneak Ryerson?"

"Hmm," one of the girls replied.

"Did you know that young detective was able to figure out I had been a Prisoner of War, right after he met me?"

"That sounds like Sneak," Hailey said with a laugh.

"He even knew the type of soil I have on my farm, just by looking at some dirt on my shoes!"

"That doesn't surprise me either," said Lisa as the girls laughed.

"So, you want us to figure out what subjects you teach?" Hailey asked.

"Well, you could give it a try," the professor encouraged.

"What clues should we look for?" Lisa asked, while scanning the room.

"Well, by looking at the Two Tables of the Law over there," the professor said, nodding his head toward the stone Ten Commandments displayed on the wall. "You might deduce that I teach..."

"Something from the Bible?" Lisa queried.

"Yes!" said the professor with a smile. "Yes, indeed," he added with a chuckle. "And specifically, classes about the..."

"Old Testament?" Cressida guessed quietly.

"Correct!" said the professor. "I teach some theology classes too. But I mostly teach classes about the Old Testament and the Ancient Near East," he added, looking down at his orange and black textbook.

"Did you call the Ten Commandments, *tables*?" Lisa inquired. "Did I hear you right?"

"Yes, yes, I did call them that," said the professor, in an animated voice – a voice that surprised the girls in its dramatic change from the haggard and weak sounds they had heard earlier when they had first entered the room. "The Ten Commandments are actually called different things by different scholars – maybe just to make us sound smarter than we really are!" At this comment the professor and his audience laughed. "Sometimes the Ten Commandments are called *The Decalogue*," the professor continued.

"Decalogue," several girls repeated.

"Right! It comes from two words in Greek... *deka* meaning ten and *logoi* meaning..."

"Commandments?" Lisa asked.

"Well, close," the professor said enthusiastically. "It's actually *words*. Logos means words." The professor paused for a moment. "So, *Decalogue* means *Ten Words*."

"Ten words," one of the girls repeated.

"Your guess was close," the professor said encouragingly to Lisa. "We sometimes call the Ten Commandments the *Decalogue* and sometimes we call them..."

"But there's more than just ten words there, right?" Lisa asked, as she studied the tablets on the wall.

"Oh yes, of course," said the professor. "Saying that those are *Ten Words* doesn't mean that there are *just* ten words. It just means we're talking about Ten Commandments."

"So *Decalogue* is a way to say *Ten Commandments*, without actually saying *Ten Commandments*," Lisa summarized with a smile.

"Yes... yes it is," laughed Dr. Bayhill.

"Did they look like that?" Alice, the young researcher, interrupted, pointing to the stone tablets on the wall and leaning forward in her chair – surprising the others with her question. "You know, were they written on stone like that, when the people read them in the Old Testament?"

"Another very good question!" the professor replied enthusiastically. "Well, I'd say The Ten Commandments probably looked something like that," he admitted. "But I don't really know for sure."

"Oh," replied Alice.

"I mean I'm old, but I'm not that old!" the professor said with a loud laugh. "I wasn't there when Moses presented them to the people!" With this comment, everyone in the room laughed as Dr. Bayhill's high-pitched laughter filled the room. "The Ten Commandments that Moses presented to the people were on two tablets, so they certainly could have looked like the ones I have on the wall. But... well... there are, of course, some differences," the professor admitted.

"Like what?" Alice asked.

"Well, for one thing, they weren't written in English like mine..."

"Oh, right." Alice agreed.

"It was Greek, right?" Cressida asked.

"Well, no, actually the originals would have been written in Hebrew," said the professor.

"Ah, Hebrew," Cressida replied.

"And another difference, of course," the professor continued, "was that the very first tablets were written by God's own hand."

"Written by God?" Alice asked in a surprised voice.

"Correct. It was when Moses spent forty days and forty nights with God on the mountain. But then it was Moses who chiseled out the second set."

"So, there were two versions?" Alice questioned.

"Right!" said Dr. Bayhill with growing enthusiasm.

"So, which one was the right list of commandments?" Alice continued. "I guess the first one, right, because God wrote it out?"

"Well, the first version and the second version matched," the professor clarified. "They each contained the same words."

"They were the same?" confirmed Alice.

"Right," the professor continued. "What happened was that Moses got the original tablets from God on the mountain…"

"When he was there for forty days and forty nights?" Lisa offered.

"Correct! But, sadly, when Moses came down off the mountain, he saw that the people had made an idol – a golden calf to worship – while he was gone. He was so angry that God's people were worshipping an idol instead of worshipping the one true God, he threw the tablets down in disgust."

"So, the one that God made broke into a bunch of pieces?" Lisa asked.

"Right," the professor confirmed. "But after that first version was destroyed, God – in His great mercy – allowed Moses to chisel out another set, with the same words on them."

"Wow," Hailey replied. "I guess I don't remember that from Sunday School."

"Me either," Cressida admitted.

"It can be found in Exodus – chapters twenty through thirty, I think – but don't quote me on that," the professor added with a laugh.

"So, they were in a different language," Alice, the young scientist, summarized, keenly interested in learning more. "And the first set was written by God and a second set was written by Moses. Are those the only differences between what's in the Old Testament and what's here on your wall?"

"Well, there are a couple of other differences I can think of," the professor added, after pausing for a moment to look at the tablets. "Another difference is that the original version didn't have numbers like they have over there."

"Oh," one of the girls replied.

"If there were numbers," the professor began with a laugh, "it would clear up a little disagreement us Protestants have with our Catholic friends."

"They don't believe there's Eleven or Twelve Commandments or anything like that do they?" Lisa asked rapidly as the group laughed.

"Oh no, no," the professor replied quickly. "All Christians would say there are Ten Commandments. The differences between

Catholics and Protestants on the Ten Commandments are about how they are grouped."

"Grouped? What do you mean?" Cressida asked in her soft voice.

"Well, all of us – Protestants and Catholics – use Exodus chapter twenty as the basis for describing the Ten Commandments. At the beginning of that *pericope*, God explained two important things – *Who* He is and *what* He has done."

"And *who* did God say He is?" asked Alice, still deeply interested and leaning forward in her chair.

"Well, first He began by saying that He is *Lord*," the professor explained.

"Ah," one of the girls replied.

"And not just *any* Lord, but He said that He was *their* Lord – the One who rules over His people."

"So that's *who* He said He is," Alice summarized.

"Right! And then, after he explained who He is, God went on to explain *what* He had *done*."

"And what was that?" Alice wondered, as the professor quickly continued.

"...that He had brought His people out of Egypt. The *Land of Slavery* is what He called it."

"So, the Ten Commandments don't start with commands but with God explaining who He is and the things He has done?" Hailey summarized.

"Correct," said the professor. "And because God is the Lord and the Deliverer of His people, He had the right to tell them how to live," the professor said forcefully. "You see, God makes it clear that He's the one with the authority. He's the one who can set the standards for how people should relate to their God and one another."

"Interesting," one of the girls said.

"And that's just the introduction!" the professor said enthusiastically. "After His introduction, God gave His commandments. The First Commandment – and all Christians agree that this is the First Commandment – God said, 'You will have no other gods before me.' So that means..."

"We shouldn't worship other things, right?" Lisa asked.

"Like a golden calf," Cressida added softly.

"Right!" the professor agreed. "Nothing should be put above God. Nothing created – like a golden calf – or any other thing. God was saying that He is the *only one* that deserves worship and devotion."

"Because He is the Lord, right?" said Lisa.

"Precisely," said the professor.

"So, if both Catholics and Protestants believe the same things about the First Commandment, do the differences occur later in the list?" Alice asked.

"Yes, actually. It's at this point that Protestants go on to the *Second Commandment*..."

"Hey," Lisa said to her friends with a smile. "Do you remember in Sunday School when Pep Stiles confused the Second *Commandment* with the Second *Amendment* and told our Sunday School Teacher that it was something about Americans having guns?"

"That's funny," said Dr. Bayhill, as the others laughed.

"It's an easy mistake to make," said Hailey sympathetically.

"You're right about that," agreed Dr. Bayhill. "It's not the Second *Amendment* that we're talking about here, but the Second *Commandment*. And it actually says, 'You shall not make a graven image.'"

"So, sort of sayin' the same thing again, right?" asked Lisa. "Don't make a golden calf or something like that, right?"

"Correct," replied Dr. Bayhill. "Where the first commandment spoke about not worshipping anything but God, the Second Commandment says not to *make* anything and worship that thing you've created. The Bible says that God is an uncreated being – unmade by humans. He is far above anything that we could ever *make*."

"So, what's the difference between Protestants and Catholics on that?" Alice wondered.

"Well, what's interesting," said the professor. "Is that Protestants place the words I just described in the Second Commandment, but Catholics actually add those words to the First Commandment that we talked about earlier."

"So, they combine the words about the *graven image* with the First Commandment and make it into a longer sentence?" Lisa asked, looking at the tablet on the wall.

"Right!" the professor agreed. "Well, technically, it's several sentences, but you get the gist."

"So, if they combine our first two commandments into one big commandment, how come they don't end up with Nine Commandments?" Alice asked.

"Another good question!" replied the professor. "They get to Ten Commandments, by…"

"Let me guess," Hailey interrupted. "By separating out another commandment that we group together?"

"Precisely," replied the professor. "For Protestants, when we get to the Tenth Commandment, we group all of the *coveting* prohibitions together…"

"The *what*?" Alice asked.

"The Commandments about *coveting*," the professor replied in a serious tone.

"That's not a word you hear too often," said Alice with a laugh.

"No, I guess not," the professor admitted.

"What does *coveting* mean?" Alice asked.

"Well, it's sort of…" the professor began, searching for the best word. "Desiring… things."

"Does it mean like wanting stuff that you shouldn't have?" Lisa asked. "I think I remember that from Sunday School."

"Yes!" the professor agreed. "That's a very good definition. 'Wanting things you shouldn't have.'"

"Ah," said Alice.

"So, in the list of commandments on the wall over there, you'll see three types of commandments against coveting. There is coveting your neighbor's *house*, your neighbor's *wife*, and other things owned by your neighbor. Those three are all grouped together in my version over there," the professor explained. "But in the Catholic list, coveting your neighbor's wife is separated out, becoming the Ninth Commandment. And then, the rest of the coveting prohibitions are in the Tenth Commandment."

"That's interesting," Alice admitted.

"Well, I like to think so," the professor said with a smile.

"So, really not much of a difference between Catholics and Protestants?" Lisa asked.

"Well, not in this case," the professor chuckled.

"…just how the Ten Commandments are organized," Alice summarized.

"Right," said the professor.

"Hmm," said Lisa.

"But you also said something about the Ten Commandments being *Two Tables*, or something like that, right?" Alice continued. "Or did I misunderstand?"

"Ah, yes," Dr. Bayhill said with a smile. "You didn't misunderstand me; that's still another way of discussing the Ten Commandments. Sometimes scholars will talk about the *First Table* of the Law and the *Second Table* of the Law."

"First and Second Tables?" Lisa asked quizzically.

"Exactly!" the professor said in his animated tone. "The First Table of the Law refers to the first three commandments on the left side of the tablet over there."

"Hmm," Lisa said as she stood up to get a closer look at the stone tablets. "First, second and third commandments, huh?"

"Precisely," said the professor. "You'll notice that those commandments have to do with a relationship with *God*."

"Oh, yeah, I can see that," said Lisa as she began reading. "Don't put any gods before me… don't make images – we talked about those already – and don't take the Lord's name in vain."

"Right," the professor replied.

"So, if the First Table of the Law has to do with our relationship with God, then what does the Second Table deal with?" Alice asked curiously.

"Mostly other people," the professor explained.

"Ah, I can see that too," said Lisa, looking closely at the tablets. "Commandments four through ten have things about other people: honoring your parents, not murdering, not stealing, not giving false testimony – which I guess that's not lying, right?"

"Right," said the professor.

"And all that coveting stuff we talked about," Lisa continued, "is at the end."

"You got it," said the professor.

"Interesting," said Alice. "So, the First Table is about relating to God and the Second Table is about relating to others."

"Yep," the professor said with a smile. "And what's really interesting in talking about the commandments this way, is that is precisely how Jesus summarized the Law to his followers."

"He did?" one of the girls asked.

"He did," the professor smiled. "He did indeed. I'm thinking of Luke chapter ten where Jesus summarized the Law by saying, '*Love the Lord with all your heart, all your strength and with all your mind.*' Can you see how that might be a summary of the First Table?"

"Yeah, I think I could see that," said Lisa, still standing in front of the stone tablets. "About how people should treat God."

"I think so," said the professor.

"And how did Jesus summarize the rest of the commandments?" asked Hailey.

"He said, 'Love your neighbor as you...'"

"Love yourself, right?" said Cressida with a smile. "I remember that from Sunday School."

"Correct!" said the professor.

"That really does summarize Commandments four through ten," Lisa said, gazing at the stone tablets on the wall. "Love your neighbor as you love yourself."

"Yep," said the professor.

"Wow, that's pretty cool," said Lisa, turning to look at the professor. "So, Two Tables, instead of Ten Commandments."

"Well, it's still the Ten Commandments," the professor said with a laugh. "Saying *Two Tables* is just another way of talking about them." The professor paused for a moment, then reflected. "I tell ya', I'm really blessed to be able to talk to you about these important things."

"It seems like so much to learn," Alice said in an exasperated tone. "*Decalogue*... Ten Words... Ten Commandments... Two Tables... if my math's right, that's like twenty-two or twenty-three things right there!"

"Well, it can seem like a lot," said the professor. "But I tell my students: when it comes to theology, it can be helpful to start with just two things. Once you have a good understanding of these two things, the entire Bible makes sense."

"What are those?" asked Lisa as she turned to the professor.

"Law and..."

"Order?" Lisa asked.

"Close!" the professor said encouragingly. "I could see how you detectives would choose that word! I was actually thinking of Law and Gospel."

"What do you mean by that?" asked Lisa, quizzically.

"Well, we could spend hours talking about it – and I take whole classes through those topics – but generally when we talk about *Law* we are talking about God's *standards* – His commands."

"So, just like what we've been talking about this morning," Lisa said emphatically. "When we were talking about the Ten Commandments."

"Exactly!" Dr. Bayhill agreed. "When we talk about Law, we're talking about what God tells us we *ought* to do."

"Makes sense," said Alice, still seeking to understand the older professor. "So, what about the other one?" she asked next. "Not Law and Order, right?"

"Right," the professor continued. "Law and *Gospel*, is what I said. When we talk about the Gospel, we're referring to God's *promises* – about what God has done *for us*."

"So, is it sort of like the Old Testament versus the New Testament?" Lisa asked.

"Well, some people might talk that way, but I think it's a little bit more complicated than that. The Old Testament, as you would guess, has a lot of references to the…"

"Law?" asked Lisa. "Like we talked about," she added, as she returned to a chair near the long conference table.

"Right!" the professor exclaimed. "The Ten Commandments can be found in the Old Testament. But interestingly," the professor said, before pausing dramatically, "it also has some important things to say about the Gospel too. In fact, we learn that God's promises were actually preached to *Abraham*!"

"In Genesis?" Cressida asked.

"Yep, all the way back in Genesis – the first book of the Old Testament," the professor said in an animated tone. "In fact, we can find God's promises all throughout the Old Testament."

"So, the Old Testament has both Law and Gospel?" Hailey summarized.

"Correct," said Dr. Bayhill. "And, when we turn our attention to the New Testament, we can see that it has quite a lot to say about God's promises, but it also has some pretty good explanations of God's Law too."

"So, Law and Gospel are two big topics to learn about in Christianity?" Alice, the young scientist, summarized.

"Precisely," the professor said. "They are kind of like a *one-two punch* in boxing," he said, humorously striking the air with his clenched fists, as the girls laughed at the elderly man's new-found energy and meager boxing techniques. "Law," he said, punching the air with his left fist. "Shows us how far we've fallen from God's standards – letting us know we need a Savior. And the Gospel," he said, now punching the air with his right fist, "shows us the great love of God – the things He's done for us. Those topics will knock you out!"

The professor and his audience laughed.

"It still sounds kind of complicated," Lisa admitted.

"Well, maybe a little," Dr. Bayhill exhaled, ending his shadow boxing. "But I could explain it in more detail, before Andrew gets here…"

"Actually, if it's going to take a while to explain, professor," Hailey interrupted, talking quickly. "Maybe we could talk about that later?"

"Oh?" the professor replied with a quizzical look. "Okay."

"I think we have some *other* questions for you that you could help us with first."

"Oh, well, sure," said the professor, haltingly. "I'm sorry, I didn't know you had more questions for me. I'll try my best to answer them." He paused for a moment. "What kind of questions do you have?" he asked, rubbing his forehead again. "Is it about Andrew's situation?"

"Oh, no," Hailey began, glancing at Alice. "You see, our friend Alice here is a scientist."

"Or, at least I want to be," Alice admitted.

"Maybe even a *forensic* scientist, to examine crime scenes," Lisa added, from her chair near the table.

"Well, that's great!" the professor said enthusiastically. "The world needs more Christian Scientists – er, I don't mean the denomination, but you know what I mean – more scientists who are Christians."

"Well, that's just the thing," said Alice. "I don't know if I'd call myself a Christian. I've got some questions."

"Oh… okay," the professor said with a surprised voice. "I didn't realize… I thought… oh, never mind what I thought!" He paused again for a moment. "I'd be glad to help you – if I can. What exactly are you wondering about?"

"Well, as a scientist, I try to use the Scientific Method to, you know, determine facts in order to know what is true," Alice began, continuing quickly. "Using the Scientific Method, we start by observing phenomena, then we come up with a hypothesis; then we create experiments that can be conducted over and over again. It's those repeatable experiments that help us verify if the hypothesis is correct or not. Does that make sense?"

"Oh, definitely," said the professor. "I had a lot of science classes in college."

"Great," said Alice.

"...way back in the Stone Age," the professor added, as the girls laughed.

"So, I guess as I think about Christianity," Alice continued, "I guess I don't really see how it could fit within the Scientific Method. You know, I mean there's no way for me to do a repeatable experiment with something like *faith*."

"Ah," the professor said. "I see."

"And, I thought I had it all figured out too," Alice continued, as she looked briefly at the three Sunday School Detectives who were seated nearby. "But when I explained it to the girls this morning, they asked me some really good questions. And they pointed out that it's not just *faith* that can't be measured by the Scientific Method, but there are a lot of other things too like *love* and *hope*."

"...and our *thoughts*," Hailey added.

"Ah, very good!" said the professor. "That actually sounds like something Professor Telson would say!"

"Well, maybe a little," Hailey answered with a smile.

"Yeah," Cressida admitted. "A little."

"So now, what exactly are you wondering about?" Dr. Bayhill asked Alice.

"Well, I guess I'm kind of stuck," Alice began. "I can't put Christianity and faith through any of my experiments and run them through the Scientific Method. Plus, I learned a few years ago – when I was an undergrad in a Philosophy class – that the Bible is full of inconsistencies and isn't really historically accurate. So, I guess I'm wondering: Where do I go from here? I mean, I'm sort of interested in the Christian faith... I guess I have to be if I want to be a *Sunday School Detective...*"

"We didn't say that!" Hailey interrupted.

"I know, I know," Alice admitted. "But, Professor, when I look at the evidence, Christianity just doesn't really seem to be – you know..."

"Reliable?" Dr. Bayhill asked.

"Right!" said Alice.

"Well, you've brought up some very interesting questions," the professor began, as he rubbed his forehead again. "Some *very* important theological questions."

"And, real quick," Lisa broke in. "What does *theological* mean?"

"Ah, another good question," the professor replied. "I guess I've used that word quite a lot, haven't I?"

"Yeah," one of the girls replied. "A little."

"Well," the professor said, before pausing for a moment. "The word *theology* is actually like another word we talked about earlier."

"Gospel?" one of the girls asked.

"Commandments?" asked another.

"Well, no," said the professor with a laugh. "Sorry, I guess we've used a couple of words this morning! I was actually thinking of the word *Decalogue*."

"Oh, yeah," one of the girls replied.

"We said that word was a combination of two Greek words: *deka* meaning ten and *logoi* meaning…"

"Words!" said Lisa.

"Correct!" Dr. Bayill exclaimed. "We said that Decalogue means *Ten Words* in Greek. And the word *theology* is like that too. It's also a combination of two Greek words. The first part – the first four letters – is *theo*, which means *God*. And the second part of the word is from the Greek word *logia* meaning…"

"Words?" asked Lisa.

"Well, you're definitely on the right track; that's the root of the word we're looking for," the professor explained.

"So, it's not exactly the same word we used earlier?" Lisa asked.

"Not exactly," said the professor. "The root of *logia* is *logos*, which means *words*, but over time, the word *logia* developed into something a little different. *Logia* can be translated to mean *the study of*."

"The study of," one of the girls repeated.

"Precisely," replied the professor. "And, it's not just theology that uses the Greek word *logia*. There are a lot of other words that end that way too, like *zoology* – the study of animals. And then there's *sociology* – the study of society."

"And biology!" Alice said. "I'm a biologist."

"Excellent! Biology means the study of life. Bio means *life* in Greek and *logia* means *the study of*. And so, theology is the study of…"

"God!" several girls said in unison.

"Exactly!" said the professor. "Theology is the study of God."

"Thanks for helping me with that," said Lisa. "Sorry, if we got off track for a few minutes."

"Oh, that's okay," the professor replied, before turning to Alice. "So now, I think I was saying that your questions were theological questions, right?"

"I guess so," Alice agreed.

"Well, what I find helpful when I first encounter a theological question, is to take a step back and put down any preconceived notions I'm holding and take a neutral position. And then, after I've examined all of the evidence, make my decision."

"So, take a neutral position?" Alice asked.

"Correct," said the professor. "Just step back and put aside what you think you know is true, and really look at the evidence."

"Hmm," Alice wondered out loud.

"But, professor," Lisa interrupted. "Nobody can really be totally neutral."

"Well, sure they can," the professor began.

"I'm not so sure about that."

"Now, why in the world would you say that?" the professor asked.

"Because of what God has done in our lives," said Lisa.

"Right," Hailey continued. "As Christians, we've been changed. We are new creations. We can't just stop being transformed, can we?"

Lisa then added, "And for non-Christians, they can't really be neutral if they don't want to follow God, right?"

"And," Cressida began, before pausing briefly.

"Wait a minute!" Dr. Bayhill said in his loud and shrill voice. "Wait just one minute! These are the same arguments I used to have with Professor Telson! This isn't his doing, is it?"

"Well, maybe a little," Lisa admitted with a laugh.

"Yeah, a little," said Cressida.

"Oh, brother," the professor said, lifting his hands in disbelief. "We used to go around and around about this very point."

"That's funny," said Hailey.

"Well, we're not going to solve this before my grandson gets here," the professor said, shaking his head. "Let's just agree to disagree, okay?"

"Okay," declared Lisa as the other girls smiled.

"Okay, well," the professor said, turning his attention again to Alice. "So, even if you're not able to take a *perfectly* impartial or neutral position, I still think it can be helpful to take a look at the evidence."

"As a scientist that makes a lot of sense to me," Alice agreed.

"So, you mentioned that you had heard from your philosophy professors that the Scriptures weren't accurate, right?"

"Right," said Alice.

"That wasn't at our college here in town was it?"

"No, I went to a big school south of here," Alice explained.

"Oh, okay," said the professor. "So… essentially, you're wondering about something being historically accurate, right?"

"Right."

"Well, before we start talking about the Scriptures, maybe we can take another example from history. Would it be okay to think about that first?"

"Sure," Alice agreed.

"Okay," said the professor in his animated, high-pitched voice. "Now, what if I were to tell you that during World War Two, I was a POW – a Prisoner of War?"

"You mentioned that earlier," Alice replied.

"Yes, well, Sneak Ryerson figured that out just by talking to me for only a few minutes! But, what if I told you that I became a POW when my B-26 was shot down over Italy. And after hiding for a few days, I was captured by the Germans. And after they caught me, they took me to a Prisoner of War camp in Poland."

"Okay," said Alice, as her face displayed a confused look. "I guess I would respond by saying, 'Thank you. Thank you for serving our country'."

"You're very welcome," said the professor with a smile. "Okay, so let's think for a moment about what I just told you. I just told you about several events that I'm claiming are true. But, the important question is, how would you *know* if what I've been saying is true or if I am just making it all up?"

"Well…" Alice began.

"Would you go talk with some college philosophy professors?" Dr. Bayhill interrupted with a smile. "They certainly would be able to tell you some interesting things – maybe about the nature of war, or the nature of justice, or something like that. But could they help you figure out if I am telling you the truth about *historical* events from the Second World War?"

"Well no, probably not," Alice admitted with a laugh. "I don't think I'd want to talk with philosophy professors about that! They wouldn't know anything about you or your service during the War."

"So, where would you check?" the professor questioned. "What would you do to confirm I was telling the truth?"

"I don't know," Alice pondered. "I guess maybe I would check first with the Air Force, to see if they had any record of you being a pilot or had any records of your plane being shot down."

"Good thought," said the professor. "That is good. Technically, I flew with the U.S. Army Air Corps, but I think you're on the right track. You could check with them to see if they had my service records."

"And there might even be some records in Germany or Poland from when you were a prisoner."

"Right!" the professor encouraged. "You could look there too."

"And other witnesses," interjected Hailey. "Alice could see if there are any other prisoners of war or guards who were at the camp at the same time you were there, and she could ask them if they remembered you."

"Yes, that's also a possibility!" the professor agreed.

"You could also review the professor's statements," Lisa added.

"What do you mean by that?" the young scientist wondered.

"I'm interested in hearing what you mean by that too," said the professor, as he turned to listen more closely.

"It's something we do in our cases with the *Sunday School Detectives*," Lisa explained. "Most of our cases are pretty boring because they're just about someone's lost pet or missing jewelry, but sometimes we have to do interviews with witnesses and sometimes we end up interviewing them more than once. When that happens, we're able to check their statements for any differences. When the professor told us what happened to him, he said he was sent to a camp in Poland, but if we interviewed him again, and he told us he was sent to a camp in England – or somewhere different – it would tell us that he's probably not telling the truth."

"Amazing!" the professor exclaimed, sitting back in his chair. "Absolutely amazing! You've all just given some prime examples of what we call *internal* and *external* evidence. It would have taken me a month of Sundays to explain that to you!" The girls laughed at his funny midwestern expression as the professor gestured with his hands and continued. "When scholars talk about internal evidence, we're referring to those things *within* a document that point to it being accurate. So, if my statement had been all jumbled or was different each time I told it, you might have suspected I wasn't telling the truth, right? That's the internal evidence we look at. And when scholars talk about external evidence, we mean those things outside of a document that point to its accuracy. You had all of those great ideas: talking to other witnesses, checking my service record or looking for documents from Germany... all of that external evidence could also verify if I was telling the truth."

"That makes sense to me," said Alice. "We should look at internal and external evidence."

"Exactly! And you can probably see where I was going with this," the professor added with another smile. "If that approach can work for something that happened forty years ago, it can work for something that happened two thousand years ago as well."

"Hmm," Alice considered.

"If you look into it, you'll find very strong evidence for the truth of Christianity. And you'll also find some very strong evidence for the Bible being accurate and reliable too."

"Like what kinds of evidence?" Lisa asked, leaning forward.

"Well," the professor paused, as he thought of his response. "Let's start with the first four books of the New Testament."

"Matthew, Mark, Luke and John, right?" said Cressida.

"Correct," said the professor. "We call those four books *The Gospels* and they were written by four different writers from their own eyewitness accounts or from the testimony of different witnesses. What is interesting, is that even though they were written by different people, they all describe the same thing! They're all about the life, death, and resurrection of Jesus."

"And there's good evidence to substantiate what they've written?" the young scientist asked.

"Definitely," said the professor. "Lots of good evidence."

"Like what?" Alice asked, still leaning forward in her chair.

"Well, there is both internal and external evidence!" the professor smiled, as he waved his hand dramatically.

"I've heard that somewhere before," said Hailey.

"I'm just a broken record!" the professor laughed. "For *external* evidence, we could point to a Roman historian named Tacitus and a Jewish historian named Josephus who both wrote about Jesus. They both wrote that Jesus was killed by a Roman punishment called *crucifixion* and that Jesus' followers were called *Christians*."

"So, non-Christians wrote about Jesus?" Lisa asked, surprised.

"Oh, yes, definitely," the professor explained. "Those non-Christian historians verified some of the basic truths taught in the Gospels. Another example of external evidence that comes to mind are the many letters and sermons from members of the Early Church. They wrote all about Jesus too. In fact, if we just had those early documents, we could probably piece together everything found in the accounts of Matthew, Mark, Luke and John."

"So, the external evidence comes from both Christian and non-Christian writing?" Hailey summarized.

"Indeed, it does," the professor agreed.

"And what about the *internal* evidence?" Alice asked.

"Well, there's a lot there too," the professor explained. "One of the things you'll see if you read the four Gospels is that they are incredibly *consistent* in their description of Jesus. There is some variation, which is what you would expect from four different people writing about the same things, but much of it is very, very similar."

"What are some of the differences I might notice?" Alice asked.

"Well, the differences are really minor – so you might not even notice them the first time you read through them! But really, it comes down to a matter of emphasis. The different Gospel writers emphasized different things, probably because of who they were writing to. So, for example, many scholars think that Mark's Gospel was written to a Roman audience while Matthew's was written to the Jewish Church and so on. But, overall, if you read one account after another, you'll notice that their description of Jesus – of what He said, how He interacted with people, what He did – are all very consistent. In fact, the first three Gospels are so similar, they're actually called *The Synoptic Gospels.*"

"Synoptic," one of the girls said.

"Yep," said the professor. "That's just a big word for saying that they are *similar* in their content and their order. It's like our word *synonym*... meaning a similar word. With the Synoptic Gospels, you get a similar story."

"But there are four Gospels, right professor?" Lisa asked.

"Correct," the professor affirmed.

"So, if the first three are similar, is the fourth one really different?" Lisa asked.

"Well, that is a very good question! The fourth Gospel, if you remember, is the Gospel According to John."

"Oh, yeah," Lisa recalled.

"And John," the professor said wistfully, "was a very interesting fellow."

At this comment, the girls laughed.

"Maybe you've learned about this in Sunday School, but John was one of Jesus' disciples. He was said to be the 'beloved disciple' and the 'one whom Jesus loved'. In addition to writing the Gospel, he also wrote three letters that we call First, Second and Third John, as well as the Book of Revelation – which is at the end of the New Testament."

"So, he wrote *five* books in the Bible?" Lisa asked.

"Correct," said the professor. "And the one thing I love about John – and I could read his letters over and over again – is that he doesn't forget it's all about a person."

"A person?" asked Alice. "What do you mean by that?"

"Well, for me… being here at seminary and reading so many scholarly works, I can get pretty wrapped up in a lot of the technical details – you know, the little things: the Greek and Hebrew words, the different opinions and controversies about things; the little details about Assyrian and Canaanite rituals. But what I love about John, is that every time I read him, I'm reminded that our faith is not based on some lofty scholarship or theological principles. It's based on a person. It's based on Jesus."

"But, Jesus was more than just a person, right?" Lisa asked.

"Well sure," Dr. Bayhill said with a smile. "We believe that Jesus is God's Son, who came from Heaven to die for our sins. But we also believe that He is a person – a human, with real human emotions and feelings."

"That's kind of hard to understand," Alice admitted.

"Well, I'd be the first to admit that I don't understand it fully," the professor said with another smile. "But that's what we believe."

The five paused for a moment.

"So," the professor continued, still facing Alice. "I'd encourage you to look at the evidence. Read the Bible – maybe start with the first four books in the New Testament. It won't take you too long, maybe a few hours at the most."

"Maybe I will," Alice replied, thoughtfully.

"I really think you'll like it," Dr. Bayhill encouraged. "From the beginning to the end, those books are packed with powerful truths. Oh, hey, you'll like this," he said, turning to Lisa. "Because I know you found our earlier word study so interesting! You'll be interested to know that John starts his Gospel account by saying, 'In the beginning was the *Logos*...the...'."

"Word!" Lisa said loudly.

"Exactly!" the professor nearly shouted as the girls laughed.

"It's the only Greek word I know," Lisa admitted with a smile.

"Well, it's a pretty good one," the professor laughed. "John uses *Logos* to say that Jesus was *The Word*."

"What does that mean?" asked Cressida.

"Well, if we think about our words, they come out from us, right?" the professor motioned with his hands, indicating words coming from his mouth. "John was saying the same thing about Jesus. Jesus not only was God, but He *came* from God – He was God's very Word. It's quite a beautiful picture."

"Wow, I guess so," said Hailey.

Suddenly, they heard footsteps approach the office and a knock on the metal doorframe.

"That will be Andrew," said the professor.

CHAPTER 16

Andrew Bayhill took the occupants by surprise as he stood in the doorway of his grandfather's office. The eighteen-year-old's wild appearance was a stark contrast to his grandfather's. While the older man's orderliness was clear from the ancient pottery expertly placed on bookcases in an uncluttered office, his grandson, by contrast, stood before the group with hair that was entirely unruly, wrinkled and worn grey dress pants and an equally wrinkled white dress shirt. The former intern tried to force a smile as he looked first at his grandfather and then to the young women seated around the large table, but was unable to hide the weariness and strain on his face.

"Andrew, you look terrible," his grandfather began, still seated in a high-backed wooden chair.

The three *Sunday School Detectives* – Hailey Cotton, Lisa Lavin and Cressida Hudson along with Alice Williams – stared in surprise at the young intern, who remained leaning against the doorway, propped up by the door's metal frame, as he paused for a moment to reply to his grandfather. "Sorry Grandpa, I guess I've had a lot on my mind." The young man talked slowly, first looking at his clothing, then back to his grandfather – his eyes betraying a lack of sleep and a mind filled with grief and worry. "I tried to get here as soon as I could," he added.

"Well, come in, come in," said Dr. Bayhill. "Let me introduce you to these people."

"Okay," replied the weary former intern.

"These are the detectives who will be helping you," the professor explained as the young women introduced themselves and shook hands with Andrew.

"Grandpa, can I talk to you for a minute?" Andrew asked, refusing to sit in one of the empty chairs near the table.

"Well, sure," Dr. Bayhill replied with a surprised voice, then stood and slowly moved towards the back of the office near the window.

"Grandpa," Andrew said a few moments later in a loud whisper as he rested his hands on a small wooden stand that held an ancient bowl. "I can't believe these are the detectives you've hired. They're just kids."

"They're the *Sunday School Detectives*," his grandfather explained. "I've read all about them in the newspaper. They're pretty good."

"I can't imagine they'd be able to help," Andrew whined, leaning closer to his grandfather. "Did you see how young they are?"

"I think you'll be surprised at how good they are," Dr. Bayhill replied. "Don't you remember me telling you about their friend Sneak Ryerson who was able to figure out all kinds of things about me after meeting me for only a few minutes – like the type of soil on the farm. Do you remember when I told you about that?"

"Yeah, I remember," said Andrew glumly. "But I'm in so much trouble – the company might press charges, which means I could get picked up by the police at any minute! It just seems like we should work with some detectives who are more, you know, experienced."

"Let's give them a try," Dr. Bayhill said optimistically. "Let's see what they can turn up."

"But, we don't have much time!"

"Just trust me on this, please! I think they'll do a good job. Let's give them a couple days, and if nothing turns up, we'll hire a… a professional. Okay?"

"Okay, okay," Andrew said nervously, as he wiped his hands down the sides of his wrinkled grey dress pants. "But I don't think I have much time."

"Let's go talk to the detectives," Dr. Bayhill said, nodding in the direction of the young women, as the professor and his grandson returned to the table.

Meanwhile, the young women had been watching and listening to the conversation between grandfather and grandson. The office, although bigger than many on the third floor, was not very large, and as the professor's hearing was weak, his grandson had talked loudly.

"So, why don't you tell *your* detectives about the case," Dr. Bayhill said, after he and his grandson had taken seats next to each other.

"We haven't agreed to take the case yet," Hailey explained in a serious tone.

"Right, we haven't taken the case," Lisa said as she turned toward Andrew. "And it sounds like you don't really want our help," she added indignantly.

"I… uh… I didn't say that, exactly," stammered Andrew. "I was just thinking…you know, someone more professional… would… uh."

"Maybe we should go?" Lisa asked.

"No, wait," Dr. Bayhill interjected, pleading with the young women. "Andrew really needs your help. He's in so much trouble. I think you could really help him."

Then, turning to his grandson, the professor implored, "Why don't you go on and tell them about the case? About how you've been accused of something you didn't do – tell them about the papers!" Then, turning again to the young women, the professor added, "That would be okay, right? Just listen for a few minutes? Just hear what happened. And then, if you don't want to take the case, I'll understand."

"Okay," said Hailey. "That would be okay, don't you think so girls?"

"Yeah, it's okay with me," said Lisa.

"Yeah, me too," Cressida said softly.

Dr. Bayhill and Andrew turned to Alice who was seated several feet away from the others and waited for her reply. "I'm just here to listen," Alice said with a laugh.

"Okay, then. Andrew, why don't you start," Dr. Bayhill said, turning to his grandson.

"It happened when I was leaving work," Andrew began nervously. "A security guard made me open my briefcase, as I was walking out."

"Actually," Hailey began, as she grabbed a small black notepad from her purse while Cressida did the same. "I'd like to start by asking you some of our standard questions. Is that okay?"

"Oh, okay," Andrew replied. "Yes, that's fine."

"So, we've got your name…"

"Andrew Bayhill," the young intern said gloomily as Hailey wrote his name on her notepad.

"Could you give us your age and your address?" Hailey asked.

"And your phone number, too," Lisa added.

"Uh... sure," said Andrew, first looking at his grandfather before giving the girls the information. Soon the girls were writing Andrew's age – eighteen – and his parent's address – located a few streets away on the north side of Findlay – and his home telephone number.

"We always like to begin with some standard questions," Hailey explained as she quickly looked at a small sheet of paper she had taped to the inside cover of her black notepad that listed the following questions:

What is the mystery?

When did it happen?

Who did it happen to?

What evidence has been gathered?

Who are the witnesses?

What really happened?

Why did it happen?

Who did it?

After reviewing the questions, Hailey returned to the page with Andrew's information. "So, let's start with the mystery you've asked us to solve. What is it that you've been accused of?"

"Okay," Andrew said, letting out a deep breath. "I've been accused of taking... I honestly can't believe they think I'd do this... but I've been accused of taking some important papers from Peloponnesian Oil Company."

"Hmm," Cressida said as she wrote some words on her notepad.

"And you're claiming you didn't do it," Lisa asked seriously, while Alice let out a faint laugh a few feet away.

"Of course I didn't do it!" Andrew exclaimed. "That's why my grandpa hired you to find out who did!"

"Okay, okay," said Lisa with a smile. "I just wanted to make sure we're not wasting our time."

"Grandpa!" Andrew cried as he turned to Dr. Bayhill. "Really?"

"It's okay," his grandfather affirmed. "Keep going. Keep going."

"So," Hailey continued. "You were working there, right?"

"Right, as an intern," Andrew replied.

"Okay," Hailey resumed. "Why don't you tell us about your job at Peloponnesian and how the folks there thought you'd taken some of their important papers. Maybe start from the beginning."

"Yeah, tell us as many details as you can remember," said Lisa.

Soon, Andrew was describing the feeling of joy he had experienced a few months earlier – near the end of his senior year of high school – when he was offered the summer job at Peloponnesian.

"So, when did you start working there?" Hailey asked.

"Well, I guess the Monday right after I graduated," Andrew explained. "I graduated from Findlay High and we always have our graduation on the first Sunday of June, so whatever the day was after that."

"I think it was June ninth," Dr. Bayhill added. "I was trying a new Mesopotamian farming technique at the time."

"That sounds about right," Andrew added.

"So, what sort of work did you do at Peloponnesian?" Lisa asked.

"I worked in the Law Department – with their old records," Andrew explained. "They are converting their old company filing system to a new one with new file folders. So, I was helping them do that."

"And what exactly did you do?" Lisa asked.

Next, Andrew explained the details of his job – how he would take the old company files from the cart delivered from the Records Department, remove the papers from the old folder and use multi-colored stickers to create the new file folder. And when he was finished, he'd place the new file in a cart by his supervisor's office for her to review.

"So, the new files would go into a different cart, next to your boss' office?" Lisa asked.

"Correct," Andrew said.

"Did you work with the files after that?" Cressida asked.

"Nope," Andrew explained. "Once I finished with a file and gave it to my supervisor, I'd never see it again."

"And what is your boss' name?" Hailey asked, pen poised above her notepad.

"Mrs. Duncan – Mrs. Roberta Duncan," Andrew clarified, as the detectives wrote down her name.

"So, you did that every day," Lisa began. "You didn't go to different places to do different things?"

"Nope," Andrew continued. "I did the exact same thing every day. And, you know, I was pretty good at it – or at least I thought I was," he added with a small laugh. "I was getting pretty fast at converting those old files to new ones, but once I got faster, I had to wait around for the next batch of files to come from the Records Department."

"So, things were going good," Lisa continued as she wrote a few words in her notebook. "But then what happened? Why did they think you took the papers?"

"Well," Andrew began, now speaking more nervously. "Like I said, things were going good. There were times when I had to wait for the Records Department, so I'd read a book, or I'd look out the window, or something like that."

"Sounds kind of boring," Lisa said.

"Yeah, sometimes," Andrew admitted.

"So, what happened?" Cressida asked, in her soft voice.

"Well, all of a sudden everything just sort of blew up."

"Dr. Bayhill said it was on Monday. Is that right?" Hailey asked.

"Yeah, Monday," Andrew replied.

"This Monday?" Hailey clarified.

"Yes," Andrew and his grandfather answered in unison.

"Okay, let's see," Hailey continued. "That would have been July..."

"July 7th," the professor said quickly. "Monday, July 7th."

"Thanks professor," Hailey smiled as she wrote down the date in her notepad. "So what happened? Try to give us as many details as you can."

"Well, things were going along just like *always*," Andrew explained. "Really, nothing out of the ordinary. I guess I'd been working there for about a month, and really had my routine down. I processed a ton of files that day...."

"Okay," said Hailey. "So what happened?"

"Well, I was on my way out of the office – I was sort of in a hurry to get out of there – and I was almost out the door, when all of a sudden a security guard stopped me."

"A company security guard?" Lisa asked, as she and the other detectives wrote quickly in their notepads.

"Right!" Andrew said anxiously. "He was like this big mean guy – and he asked me to open up my briefcase."

"Had you ever seen that security guard before?" Hailey asked.

"Not that I remember," Andrew admitted. "But, I'm not sure."

"Did you get his name?" asked Lisa.

"No," Andrew replied. "I didn't."

"So, the security guard asked you to open up your briefcase?" Hailey began.

"Right!" Andrew continued. "And the papers were right there! I couldn't believe it! They all said things like CONFIDENTIAL and TOP SECRET and stuff like that."

"So the papers were just there in your briefcase?" Lisa asked.

"Right," Andrew agreed.

"And you didn't put them there?" Lisa asked in a serious tone, while the other detectives tried to hide their smiles.

"No, I didn't put them there!" Andrew protested. "Grandpa!" he said again, turning to his grandfather.

"Just continue, continue," Dr. Bayhill told his grandson.

"So, how many papers were in there, like fifty or one hundred pages? Something like that?" Lisa asked.

"Oh, no. Not that many," said Andrew. "There were maybe five or ten different sets that were stapled together. And each set was only a couple of pages long."

"So, what can you tell us about these papers?" Hailey asked.

"Well, they were memos and they were all written from the head of the Law Department to the President."

"Of the United States?" Hailey asked. "Wow," she added, sitting back in her chair.

"Oh, no, sorry," Andrew said. "Not the President of the United States. They were written to the *company* president." Hearing this comment, Dr. Bayhill and Alice both laughed.

"The President of Peloponnesian Oil Company?" Lisa clarified.

"Right," Andrew confirmed.

"That's still a big deal," Alice admitted.

"Well, it's not quite the Pentagon Papers," Dr. Bayhill said with a laugh. "But, you're right, it is a pretty big deal."

"And had you ever seen any of the papers before?" asked Hailey. "You know, were these in the files you worked with earlier that day, or the week before, or anything like that?"

"No," the young intern said nervously, again wiping his hands across his grey dress pants. "I'd never seen them. Or at least I don't think I had seen them. I mean, I've processed thousands of files over the last few weeks, with lots of papers inside them. I guess it's possible they were in one of the folders I worked with. But I don't remember seeing them in any of the files I processed."

"Is it possible they were on another person's desk, like your boss' desk?" Lisa asked.

"Well, I guess it's possible!" Andrew replied in a frustrated tone. "Anything's possible! But I don't remember seeing them! I'm pretty sure I would have remembered seeing a set of documents labelled TOP SECRET, or something like that!"

"Alright, alright," Dr. Bayhill said to his grandson as he moved his shaking right hand and placed it on his grandson's shoulder. "No need to get worked up right now. The detectives are here to help."

"We'll see about that," Andrew said bitingly.

"Hmm," Hailey began, as she looked over her notes, ignoring Andrew's outburst. "So, they discovered the papers in your briefcase when you were walking out of the building, right?"

"Right!"

"When you were coming out of the office building on Main Street?" asked Lisa.

"Correct," said Andrew. "Well, technically the lobby isn't on Main Street."

"And you don't have any idea how the papers got into your briefcase?" Hailey asked, as she wrote more words into her notepad.

"I don't," Andrew admitted while shaking his head. "I have no clue."

"So, where did you keep your briefcase before you left?" Hailey asked.

"On the floor – next to my desk," Andrew explained quickly.

"Could the papers have fallen into your briefcase when you were working on the files?" Cressida asked in her quiet voice.

"Right," Lisa continued with the idea. "Like, did you keep your briefcase open on the floor and maybe the papers fell off your desk and accidentally went inside the briefcase?"

"No, that's not possible," Andrew admitted in a dejected tone. "My briefcase isn't one of those hard cover ones, like you're probably thinking of. Mine is soft-sided and zips at the top – and I always kept it zipped."

"Oh," said Lisa.

"Plus, when I pulled out the papers in the lobby, they weren't all jumbled up like a bunch of papers that just fell off my desk – they were all neatly stacked inside."

"Oh, okay," said Lisa as she wrote more words in her notepad.

"Could we look at your briefcase?" Hailey asked. "You know, to see if there's anything we might notice?"

"Sure, I've got it out in the car. I can go get it."

"That would be great," Lisa replied, as the others agreed.

"But before you go get it, I've got a few more questions," Hailey said, continuing the interview.

"Okay," replied Andrew.

"Did you notice anything unusual when you were getting ready to leave your office? Like, did anyone borrow your briefcase, or did it feel heavier than usual?"

"No, there wasn't anything unusual."

"Could someone have switched briefcases with you?" Alice wondered, from her chair nearby. "Maybe you grabbed someone else's brief-case, by mistake?"

"Oh, that is a good question," Dr. Bayhill said in his high-pitched voice. "That's a very good question, indeed."

"No, sorry," Andrew admitted. "It was my briefcase. It even had the book that I was reading earlier in the day. That was the first thing I saw when I opened the briefcase for the security guard."

"Oh," said Alice.

"Was the briefcase ever out of your sight?" Hailey wondered. "You know, when someone could have put the papers in it?"

"Well, yeah, I guess," Andrew confirmed. "There were a couple of times that day when I didn't have it with me. I left my briefcase in the office when I went to lunch and when I went to the bathroom."

"Hmm," said Hailey.

"So, it sounds like we've got to figure out who put those papers in there on Monday," said Lisa. "When you were away from your desk."

They paused for a moment.

"Wait a second," said Alice. "Are you sure the papers were put in there on Monday?" the young scientist asked.

"Another good question," Dr. Bayhill said.

"What do you mean?" asked Andrew.

"Well, we're all thinking someone put the papers in your briefcase on Monday because that was the day you got caught. But, is it possible that someone put them in your briefcase last Friday, or maybe some other time last week?" Alice asked.

"Ah, I see what you mean," said Andrew. "I guess it is possible. I didn't work on Friday because of the July 4th holiday – so, maybe some-one could have put them there on Thursday. But, I keep a book in my briefcase too and I don't remember seeing any papers in there. You've got to believe me, I didn't see the papers until the security guard stopped me at the end of the day – on Monday."

"So, before you got caught with the papers, when was the last time *you* opened up your briefcase?" Alice asked.

"Well, that would have been a little earlier on Monday afternoon. I went over to Wilson's to read for a little while – I was pretty bored – and I took my book with me to get a malt."

"Can you tell us exactly what you remember when you opened your briefcase to get your book?" Alice asked.

"Sure," Andrew said slowly. "I remember looking at the clock and seeing that there was still a lot of time left in the afternoon, and the cart with new files from the Records Department hadn't arrived yet, so I reached down – quickly – and unzipped my briefcase, pulled out my book and zipped the briefcase back up again."

"And you didn't see the papers in your briefcase then?" Alice asked.

"No," Andrew replied. "But, I wasn't really looking for them either."

"You said you got your book quickly," Alice observed. "Why were you in a hurry?"

"I wasn't in a hurry, I just didn't, you know, want anyone to see what I was doing," Andrew admitted. "I didn't want them to know I was taking an afternoon break away from the office."

"Oh," said Lisa. "And how long were you gone?"

"To *Wilson's*?" Andrew asked. "Ten minutes, maybe a little more."

"To walk all the way over there and then read a book?" his grandfather challenged.

"Okay, well, it was probably longer than that. Maybe twenty minutes," Andrew admitted.

"And what time was that?" Lisa asked.

"Probably between three and three-thirty, I'd guess."

"So, maybe even thirty minutes?" Dr. Bayhill asked with a smile.

"Well, that's probably more like it," Andrew agreed.

The detectives glanced at each other before Hailey concluded, "That's probably when the papers were put inside there, right? That's when someone had the best *opportunity* – but we can't be sure."

"That makes sense," said Andrew.

"Someone would have had a lot of time to put the papers in there without you noticing," Lisa added.

"Unless…" Alice began.

"What?" Andrew wondered.

"Oh, never mind, it's just a silly thought," Alice said apologetically.

"Go ahead," Andrew prompted.

"Well," Alice began. "I was just thinking, what if the security guard put the papers in your briefcase, to – what's the word – to *frame* you?"

"The security guard?" Andrew exclaimed.

"It would explain why you didn't notice the papers until you got to the lobby," said Alice.

"I don't think so," asserted the former intern.

"Why not?" asked his grandfather. "You've got to look at all the possibilities."

"Was there…" Alice began, before pausing. "Like, a big distraction, maybe a loud noise or something like that? You know, a time when you weren't paying attention when the security guard could have slipped the papers into your briefcase without you noticing?"

"No. I mean, I was pretty surprised when he stopped me and dragged me over to the receptionist's desk, but there wasn't a loud noise or anything like that."

"He dragged you?" Dr. Bayhill asked in a shocked voice.

"Well, no," Andrew admitted. "He didn't exactly drag me, he just told me to go over to the front desk."

"Ah, okay," said Andrew's grandfather.

"But," Andrew paused as he thought for a moment. "I don't think there was any time he could have put the papers in there. I had to unzip the briefcase and when I did, the papers were already there. He asked a receptionist to be a witness too and she saw them at the same time I did."

"A receptionist?" asked Hailey as she wrote another note in her notepad.

"Right," said Andrew.

"Do you know the receptionist's name?" Lisa asked.

"No, sorry," said Andrew.

"Did they give the briefcase back to you then, or did they keep it for a while?" Hailey asked.

"Oh, they gave it back," said Andrew. "They just kept the papers!" he added with a laugh. "That was after I had a big meeting with the Company's chief of security – he wasn't very nice. And after that, they escorted me out of the office building and told me not to come back again."

"Oh no," said Alice.

"That stinks," said Hailey with a frown.

"It was terrible," Andrew explained. "I was so embarrassed. There were still a lot of people leaving – some people I knew too – and they saw me."

"And those papers?" Hailey began.

"I said I'd never seen them," Andrew insisted in a whiny voice.

"Right, right," Hailey replied. "I know you hadn't seen them, but what were they about? Maybe that could give us some clues about this mystery?"

"I have no idea," Andrew said in an exasperated tone as he slumped in the chair.

"Did you have time to read any of them?" asked Lisa.

"No, I just saw that they were from the Law Director and written to the company President."

"Can you describe them?" Hailey asked. "Were they written on three-ring notebook paper or something like that?"

Andrew stared at her with an incredulous look on his face, before saying, "The Law Director at a big company doesn't write to the Company President on three-ring notebook paper!" He paused for a moment. "The letters were on nice white paper."

"Okay," said Hailey. "So, were they typed?"

"Of course they were!" replied Andrew. "And they had the company logo on the top."

"The Big Red *P*?" asked Cressida.

"Yes," Andrew replied incredulously.

"But, you didn't read any of them – to know what they were about?" Hailey asked.

"No, I didn't have time. I just looked at who they were *from* – and who they were *to*. And I knew right then, I was in big trouble."

"I guess we'll have to do more research on those papers – to figure out what they were about," Hailey said as she wrote down more words in her notepad. "Is there anything else you can tell us about them?"

"No, I don't think so," said Andrew.

"Well, I think I've run out of questions," said Hailey. "How about you girls?"

"What time was it?" Lisa asked abruptly. "When the security guard stopped you?"

"Around five," Andrew explained. "When everybody was leaving work."

"And was he stopping lots of people?" Lisa wondered. "You know, going through everybody's briefcases and things, or just yours?"

"Just mine, I think," said Andrew. "I didn't see him go through anyone else's."

They paused for another moment.

"So," Cressida began quietly. "Has this ever happened before?"

"To me?" asked Andrew. "This is a nightmare! I hope nothing like this ever happens to me! Never... ever... again! I mean, I really needed that money this summer... and now... well, I've got to start looking for something else. And I've got to figure out how not to tell my next employer that Peloponnesian thinks I stole something from them! It stinks, it really stinks!"

"Yeah," Hailey agreed.

"I guess I was wondering," Cressida continued in her quiet voice. "Did you ever hear of anything like this happening before in the Law Department? Or, in any other department at the company? Maybe sometime earlier this year? Or with last year's summer intern?"

"That is another good question!" Dr. Bayhill affirmed.

"Not that I know of," Andrew replied dejectedly. "If it did happen before, no one ever told me about it."

"And did you have any problems..." Lisa began.

"I've got so many problems," Andrew replied, as his haggard look remained on his face. "I lost out on a bunch of money! The company I used to work for might press charges against me! My face could be plastered all over the newspaper and TV! It's unbelievable!"

"That really does stink," Hailey said again.

"I guess I was wondering," Lisa clarified. "Did you have any problems at work before Monday?"

"Why do you want to know that?" asked Andrew quickly.

"I'll tell you in a minute," Lisa replied. "But first, tell us if you had any problems with anyone at the office. You know, like, was anyone mad at you or anything like that?"

"I don't think so," said Andrew. "I mean, I wasn't best friends with the people I worked with, but I think I got along fine with everyone."

"Hmm," one of the girls replied.

"Why were you wondering that?" Alice asked.

"Well," Lisa explained. "I was thinking that maybe someone put the papers in Andrew's briefcase and then told the security guard *in order* for Andrew to get caught."

"Oh," Andrew replied.

"That would be a dirty trick," Hailey said as the others agreed.

"I can't think of anyone who would want to do that to me," Andrew said meekly.

The young detectives paused for a moment, thinking of additional questions.

"Well, let's move on to witnesses," said Hailey, looking to the others.

"Sounds good," said Lisa.

"So, you talked about the security guard and the receptionist – they witnessed you opening your bag," Hailey summarized, looking at her notes.

"Right," Andrew said in an exhausted voice.

"And we don't have their names yet," Hailey recalled.

"Right," Andrew replied with a laugh. "I don't know their names!"

"Okay, well, maybe we can get those," Hailey said hopefully.

"Good luck with that," the former intern scoffed.

"So, let's move on to the people in your office," Hailey continued, ignoring Andrew's comment. "You said your boss is Mrs. Roberta Duncan, right?"

"Right."

"And was she in the office on Monday?" Lisa asked.

"Yeah, she was there all day," Andrew recalled. "I think she even rode down on the elevator with me on my way out of the office."

"She rode in the elevator with you?" Lisa asked. "On the day you got caught?"

"Yeah," Andrew said meekly. "I was on there with her before they found the papers in my briefcase."

"That's interesting," said Hailey, writing more words in her notepad.

"Could she have slipped the papers inside your briefcase – on the elevator – when you weren't looking?" Lisa asked.

"I don't think so," Andrew replied. "I'm pretty sure my briefcase was zipped shut."

"Okay," wondered Lisa. "Could she have opened it, when you weren't looking?"

"No, I don't think so," Andrew laughed. "I was in a hurry, but I don't think she could have done that. She wasn't even standing very close to me."

"Okay," Lisa shrugged.

"So, who else worked with you in the office?" Hailey asked, her pen readying to write additional names in her notepad.

"Well, just a couple of other people," Andrew began, as he searched for his coworkers' names. "There was Paula Bigelow – she works on Tuesdays, Wednesdays and Thursdays."

"Paula Bigelow," Hailey said slowly, as she and the other detectives wrote the name of Andrew's coworker in their notebooks. "And was she working in the office the day you got caught?" Hailey asked.

"Yes," Andrew affirmed.

"Wait a minute," Alice interrupted from her seat away from the table. "You got caught on Monday, right?"

"Right."

"But you said Paula only works on Tuesdays, Wednesdays and Thursdays!" Alice said proudly.

"That is a good observation!" Dr. Bayhill affirmed.

"Why was she there?" asked Alice.

"I'm not sure," Andrew replied. "She never works on Mondays. But she was definitely in the office."

"That's interesting," said Lisa. "Really interesting."

"Yeah," Cressida agreed.

"Well, I guess we have our first *real* suspect," Hailey said, writing more words in her notepad, as the other detectives agreed.

"Naw," Andrew insisted. "She wouldn't have put the papers in my briefcase. I'm sure of it."

"Why's that?" asked Hailey.

"Because she's – well, she's not that kind of a person. She's a Christian... " said Andrew.

"As are most of the people here," his grandfather said, looking around the table. "Christians aren't always perfect – we make mistakes too, you know."

"Well, yeah, Grandpa, I know that – and she has some really weird ideas, but I don't think she'd do anything sneaky like stealing papers and putting them in my briefcase. She's always been really friendly to me. I don't think she'd want to get me in trouble."

"You never know," said Hailey, before pausing briefly. "We'll need to talk to her. If she didn't commit the crime, maybe she witnessed something earlier in the day, right?"

"Maybe," said Andrew doubtfully, as his face became more dejected. "I mean it's already been a couple of days and if she saw someone put some papers in my briefcase, I'm sure she would have said something by now, right? She wouldn't let me struggle all week, would she?"

"Well, you're probably right," said Hailey. "But, if she was guilty, she wouldn't say anything. And, there's still a chance she saw something and didn't realize it was related to the case. We won't know until we ask her."

"Okay, okay," agreed Andrew.

"So, besides your supervisor – Mrs. Duncan – and Paula Bigelow, was there anybody else who worked in the office?"

"Yeah, there was Jason – Jason Compton."

"Oh," Alice said in a faint voice nearby.

"What can you tell us about him?" Lisa questioned.

"Just that he's kind of weird," Andrew replied.

"Why's that?" Hailey asked.

"He's into some really weird stuff – antiques and old clocks – and he's part of that F.E.E.T. group."

"The F.E.E.T. group?" Dr. Bayhill asked loudly.

"Oh brother," said Hailey and Cressida simultaneously.

"Do you know him?" Lisa asked quickly, turning to Alice.

"Yeah, I know Jason," Alice admitted with a smile. "I didn't realize he worked at Peloponnesian... but I'm not surprised, he's really smart."

"He's more of a know-it-all, if you ask me," Andrew replied, looking glum. "How do you know him?"

"I was part of F.E.E.T. too," Alice explained.

"Oh," Andrew frowned.

"Findlayites Entertaining Extra-Terrestrials," Dr. Bayhill said, remembering the name of the group. "I read about them in the paper."

"I'm not part of the group anymore," Alice clarified. "But I was at a lot of meetings with Jason Compton."

After glancing at her notes, Hailey turned to Andrew and asked, "So, what else can you tell us about Jason? Was he in the office on Monday?"

"Yeah, he was there. I can't remember what he was telling me about on Monday, but sometimes he'd talk to me about flying saucers and UFOs and stuff like that, and other days he'd tell me about old grandfather clocks and antiques. He was always talking about weird stuff."

"So, you two didn't get along too well?" Alice asked.

"Well... I guess not too well," Andrew replied. "We weren't best friends or anything like that." The young intern suddenly paused before continuing. "Actually, if you were to ask me to pick *one* person from the office who might have put those papers in my briefcase, I'd pick him."

"Really?" Hailey asked, looking up from her notepad. "So, I guess we have our *second* suspect."

"Well, I don't know if you should call him that," Andrew said quickly. "Calling him a suspect seems kind of... strange... like he's already guilty. But he's sort of a strange guy. And now that I think about it, we didn't really get along."

"Alice, is there anything you can tell us about Jason Compton?" Lisa asked, turning to the young scientist.

"I'd be really surprised if he was involved in something like this," she said firmly. "He's not that sort of person. I mean, he can be *quirky* – but that doesn't mean he did something illegal, right?"

"You didn't think your friend Julian Davis could have done anything illegal either, right?" Lisa questioned.

"You're right, you're right," said Alice holding up the palms of her hands towards Lisa. "I'm not the best judge of character."

"Okay, well, we'll need to check out Jason Compton," Hailey said as she finished writing more words in her notepad. "So, besides Mrs. Duncan, Paula Bigelow and Jason, who else was in the office on Monday?"

"Well, there were a ton of paralegals who were in and out of the office."

"Paralegals?" Hailey asked, as she wrote down the word in her notepad.

"What's a paralegal?" Lisa asked.

"It's someone who works with the company attorneys," Andrew explained. "When the attorneys need help writing a *brief* or need someone to do some research, the paralegals help them."

"So why were they in your office?" Lisa asked.

"Well, they all report to Mrs. Duncan too," Andrew explained. "And to get to *her* office, the paralegals have to walk through the office where Paula, Jason and I work."

"So, how many paralegals walked through your office on Monday?" Lisa asked.

"Oh, lots," said Andrew. "There's so many of them."

"So, they *all* went through your office to see your boss?" Lisa asked.

"Well, I don't know if every single one of them came in to see Mrs. Duncan, but a lot of them did," Andrew clarified.

"Did they walk by your desk?" asked Cressida. "Or, was your desk, like, in another place?"

"No," Andrew explained. "They all had to walk by my desk to get to Mrs. Duncan's office."

"Wow," said Lisa as she looked at Hailey and then her cousin.

"This case just got a lot more difficult," said Hailey.

"Yeah," Lisa agreed. "I thought we'd have maybe two or three suspects, but now it turns out we've got a lot more than that."

"Do you know how many paralegals are at Peloponnesian?" Cressida asked. "Is it just a few?"

"Oh, no," Andrew clarified. "There's at least thirty... maybe even forty... I don't really know. It could be more than that."

"Oh my," said Cressida.

"Is that how many people walked by your desk on Monday?" Lisa asked.

"It could have been that many," said Andrew. "I don't always pay attention and they don't always stop and talk to us, especially if they are really busy. On some days, there might be only a few paralegals to stop in to see Mrs. Duncan, but other times there can be a lot."

"Wow," said Lisa, again shaking her head.

"So, the paralegals..." Hailey continued her questioning.

"Oh, yeah," Andrew interrupted. "And Jimmy Mannix has a desk in our office too, but I hardly ever see him. He's never around, he's got another desk down on the seventh floor."

"Why does he have two desks?" Lisa asked.

"He's an intern like me, but he's doing some different kind of work – helping with a new computer project called *Project 81*. He's always going from one place to another. Sometimes he comes up to our office, but he's usually on *Seven*, and I think he does stuff on *Four* too."

"Jimmy Mannix. It seems like I've heard his name somewhere before," Lisa said, writing his name in her notepad.

"He's part of Findlay *royalty*," Andrew explained in a serious voice as the girls laughed.

"What does that mean?" Dr. Bayhill asked in his laughing high-pitched voice.

"Well, you know," Dr. Bayhill's grandson replied. "He's really rich – or at least his dad is. His dad's a bigshot at *Peloponnesian*. Jimmy's always talking about fancy trips and cool cars and stuff like that."

"Oh," one of the girls replied.

"So, did you see him on Monday?" Hailey asked.

"No," Andrew replied. "Like I said, he's never around our office, he just has a desk there."

"Okay, thanks," said Hailey as she wrote the information in her notepad. "So, is there anything else you can tell us?"

"I don't think so," Andrew admitted in an exhausted tone.

"I guess I wasn't out of questions like I thought I was a while ago," Hailey laughed. "Maybe you could go out and get your briefcase? That will give us a chance to talk about the case."

"I'll be back in a minute," Andrew said as he quickly rose and walked to the door.

CHAPTER 17

Are they chasing the lion, or is the lion chasing them? Alice Williams wondered as she gazed at the ancient pottery in Dr. Bayhill's office. Noticing that several figures on the vase were holding spears and lunging at a large animal – a lion or a bear – the young scientist pondered the spear holders in the scene and wondered what they were doing. *Are they a group of hunters going after a large animal? Or are they villagers protecting their homes from an attack?* She paused for a moment. *Is there a right answer to my question?* she wondered. *Maybe I should look closer for some evidence to determine the truth?* She smiled, remembering how similar her thoughts were to the advice that Dr. Bayhill had given her earlier regarding the search for answers for spiritual questions.

Alice had always been interested in learning new things, and her thoughts turned next to the work she was doing in the biology lab. At the lab, Alice could conduct one experiment after another in hopes of learning more about *Ti. ni.* – the small creatures that had consumed most of her days and nights for the past year. But now, she thought about the possibility of new adventures in helping the *Sunday School Detectives* solve mysteries. It seemed so exciting: interviewing witnesses… chasing bad guys… searching for evidence… uncovering the truth. In some ways, she realized, her work at the biology lab and the work she would do to help the young detectives were really not that different – both required her to be an investigator. In the biology lab, she had been a scientific detective, uncovering the truth about larvae and moths. With Hailey Cotton and her friends, she could continue to be a scientific detective too, searching for the truth in the cases they would be working on together. *This should be pretty interesting*, Alice thought hopefully.

Soon, however, Alice's thoughts turned to the discussions she had earlier with the girls and Dr. Bayhill about theology. In some ways, she felt like a scientific detective in that area too – trying to uncover what was true about spiritual things. For her, those things had seemed so hidden and cloaked in mystery for such a long time but seemed so clear to the girls and Dr. Bayhill. As she pondered the idea further, she realized the things they had been saying were not that mysterious at all, and the reality of God and His presence in the universe somehow made perfect sense to her. It was as if she had known this truth for a long time, yet suddenly was just informed about it. Her feelings of interest grew as she continued thinking about other spiritual questions. *What does it mean that there is a God of the universe?* she wondered. *And what is my place in it?*

While Alice studied the pottery, three *Sunday School Detectives* – Hailey Cotton, Lisa Lavin and Cressida Hudson – talked about Andrew Bayhill's case in his grandfather's office.

"We should take the case, right?" Hailey asked her friends in an energetic tone. "It would be pretty interesting, don't ya think?"

"I don't know," said Lisa as she looked at her notes. "There are so many suspects. I mean, there are definitely some interesting ones, like Paula. She wasn't supposed to be at work on Monday."

"Yeah," Cressida agreed. "She's definitely high on my list of suspects."

"And Jason too," said Lisa, continuing to look at her notes. "It sounds like there wasn't any love lost between him and Andrew."

"I don't know about that," Alice said confidently, interrupting the girls' conversation and her thoughts on spiritual questions. "I've known Jason a long time. I really can't imagine he would be involved."

"Okay, okay," said Hailey reassuringly. "But we still should check him out."

"And, then there's Andrew's boss," Lisa said.

"Roberta Duncan?" Cressida asked, looking at her notepad. "You think she's a suspect?"

"Well," said Lisa. "I thought it was really weird that she rode the elevator down with Andrew – *just before* he got caught. She could have put the papers in his briefcase, right?"

"Like right in front of the security guard?" Cressida asked with a laugh.

"Okay, maybe not," Lisa admitted. "It would have been hard to do that with all of those people around."

"Yeah," said her cousin.

"But, you do have to admit there are a couple of really interesting suspects," Hailey added optimistically. "This could turn out to be a really interesting case."

"Yeah, but what about all those paralegals," Lisa frowned.

"Yeah," Cressida added quietly. "Andrew said thirty – or even forty – of them went by his desk on that Monday. That's a lot."

"Right, that's what has me worried," said Lisa in a serious tone. "If one of those paralegals is guilty, it would be so hard for us to figure out which one it is. That's why I'm leaning toward *not* taking the case."

"Yeah, me too," her cousin agreed.

"What?" Dr. Bayhill interrupted. "Oh, please, please don't do that!" the professor pleaded. Prior to his outburst, the professor had been sitting nearby, intrigued by the girls' conversation. But, hearing them suggest that they might *not* take the case, he felt compelled to implore them to do the opposite. "Andrew is in such trouble! It's bad, it's really bad! They might press charges against him – and if that happens, he'll be arrested! Please don't let that happen!"

"I'm just not sure how we can investigate a case with forty suspects," Lisa said matter-of-factly.

"Right," her cousin agreed.

"But, maybe you could give it a try, couldn't you?" Dr. Bayhill asked. "Right?" He paused for a moment. "You never know what you might turn up?"

"I think you're right, Professor," agreed Hailey. "You never know what we might turn up." Then, turning to the other detectives, she added optimistically, "Lisa, what if we give it a try for just a few days? Then, if nothing turns up, we could stop our investigation. What do you think? Could we give it a day or two?"

"Well, maybe," said Lisa.

"I think we could do that," said Cressida quietly.

"How about you, Alice?" Hailey asked the young scientist.

"Oh, I'm just here to observe," she smiled. "Y'all are the real detectives."

"Yeah, but what do you think?" Lisa asked.

"What do you mean?" asked Alice.

"About the case. Do you think we should take it or not?"

"Well," Alice paused for a moment. "There are definitely going to be some challenges with the investigation – like tracking down forty paralegals!"

"Exactly," said Lisa.

"But," Alice continued. "I can definitely tell ya' that y'all can eliminate one suspect. I guarantee you won't find anything on Jason Compton. He'll be totally innocent after you check him out."

"So, instead of forty-three suspects, there are only forty-two?" Lisa laughed.

"Yeah, I guess something like that," Alice replied.

"So, should we take the case?" Lisa asked the young scientist.

"I think it would be pretty fun," Alice finally said with a smile. "And I'd like to help too."

"Okay, so Alice and Cressida are in," Hailey summarized. "Lisa, I'm not sure if you agreed – you said *maybe*."

"I guess we could give it a try," Lisa reluctantly agreed.

"Okay, that's everyone who's here," Hailey concluded. "Dr. Bayhill," she added, turning to the professor. "It looks like we're taking the case."

"Thanks be to God!" the professor replied.

A few moments later, Andrew Bayhill, the professor's grandson, returned to the office with his briefcase. "I've got some good news for you, my boy!" Dr. Bayhill declared upon seeing his grandson. "The girls are taking your case!"

"Well, it's right here!" the young intern said, as the group laughed at seeing him hold up a greenish tan soft-sided bag.

"Well, I think they'll take that case too!" Dr. Bayhill laughed as he explained that the young detectives had agreed to work on the investigation.

"Thanks, I appreciate it," said Andrew in a serious tone as his briefcase was passed among the girls who each examined the bag.

"Well, there's no secret compartment or a tricky way to put things into it," Lisa explained after handling the briefcase.

"Yeah," Cressida admitted. "I don't think anything could get into it without unzipping the top. You'd definitely notice it."

They paused for a moment at the long wooden table.

"So, what do you think our next step should be?" Lisa asked Hailey. "We've got a lot of possible suspects we could start talking to."

"I've got an idea that might help us get a lot of answers pretty quick," Hailey replied with a smile, before turning to the professor. "Dr. Bayhill, can I borrow your phone?"

The professor eagerly agreed, and Hailey quickly dialed a familiar number on the black rotary phone. After a brief conversation she hung up the receiver and shared her plans with the others. "That just might work," Lisa said.

"Yeah, I like it," said Cressida.

"Me too," said Alice.

A few minutes later, the young women stood and prepared to leave the office.

"Thanks again," Dr. Bayhill said to Alice and the young detectives. "You have no idea how relieved I am that you are taking the case."

"Hopefully it will only take us a couple days," Hailey smiled.

"I hope you're right!" Andrew said, smiling as he stood. "You have no idea how nervous I've been about this whole thing. I mean, I'm out of a job... I'm worried I might go to jail... it's been so crazy." Then his voice turned to a serious tone. "I am glad you're taking the case too."

Soon, the three *Sunday School Detectives* and the young scientist left the office and retraced their steps down the seminary building's long third floor hallway. "It's so weird seeing Professor Telson's office so empty," Lisa said as they approached the open doorway.

"Yeah, it is," Hailey agreed.

"I hope he's not too bored in the desert," Cressida said softly.

CHAPTER 18

Around that same time in the Negev Desert – the large wilderness that encompasses much of southern Israel – the afternoon was slowly marching towards evening. There, a young linguist was sluggishly returning to his tent, exhausted from the day's activities. His body ached from the day's strenuous effort and he craved sleep, hoping to get a few moments of rest on his lumpy cot before being awakened for dinner. He walked carefully, avoiding cracks between the large rocks that led to his tent, but his mind was focused on getting rest, undaunted by the dirt and sand that caked his khaki shirt and pants. *I sleep, you sleep, we sleep*, he conjugated in several languages.

The twenty-eight-year-old was exhausted, and as he glanced at his watch, seeing that the time neared six o'clock – seven hours ahead of his hometown in the eastern United States – he knew that there would still be several more hours of work to do that day.

The man's day had started over twelve hours earlier with a pre-dawn growl from a stern Scottish voice yelling into his tent, "Alright ye Gits! Time to get goin'! Now!"

"Urgh," the young linguist groaned – as did several others – as bleary eyes adjusted to the lantern held by the Scotsman.

"I said it's time to get goin'!" the Scotsman yelled before raining down a hail of expletives on the men. "Five minutes! Time to get up!"

Good old Mr. McGregor, the twenty-eight-year-old thought as he checked his boots for yellow scorpions and quickly donned a clean khaki shirt and pants. *Good thing old Mr. McGregor is moving on to the next tent*, he thought as he heard the same announcement being yelled nearby – and then again to another tent, as the Scotsman continued his morning reveille.

The group followed their lantern-bearing leader out of their tents and across the rocky terrain to a nearby mess hall. Their breakfast together was quick and quiet, kept separate from the Israeli Army at the base in a room so discreet that even the kitchen staff could not see them.

Soon, the group was on the hiking trail – rucksacks full of water – feet slowly following the person in front of them, one foot forward, then the next. There were twelve of them: four who spoke Russian, four German speakers, three from England and the young linguist, the lone American. The group hiked quietly, in single-file formation, led by an Israeli guide who could hike so quickly over the rugged terrain that the group frequently had difficulty keeping up. As always, the team was trailed on their hikes by the Scotsman, *good old Mr. McGregor*. The Scotsman never revealed his name to the group, but the young linguist liked thinking of him as the gardener who chased poor Peter Rabbit around his garden in the Beatrix Potter stories. In those stories, Peter escaped Mr. McGregor's grasp by leaving his jacket and shoes behind. *I'd gladly give my dirt-covered jacket and shoes to get Mr. McGregor off my back*, the young linguist thought wistfully as they hiked that morning.

"*No names!*" That was one of the first rules he had been told before entering the back of a truck in Jerusalem, which would take him to the secret Army base deep in the Israeli desert. "No first names, no last names, no nicknames, no names," he had been sternly warned. "And speak in English only," he had been directed. "We realize that you know German and all of those other languages, but in front of the others, it's English only. Okay?"

"Okay," the young man had reluctantly agreed, barely comprehending the directions, as his mind flooded with the new and confusing information. He had not realized until much later that the precautions regarding the secrecy of their names and the languages to be spoken were designed for one purpose – to prevent members of the group from being identified.

The hike that morning had been strenuous – navigating around boulders, up steep hills, down dry gullies, and across barren landscapes for many kilometers. Earlier in the summer, during his first few days of training, the young man's body had revolted as he experienced cramping in his feet and legs, an upset stomach, and lungs that gasped for breath. But as the days progressed, the hiking became easier for the twenty-eight-year-old and eventually he came to enjoy it – even as his feet blistered and his muscles ached from the strenuous activity.

After several hours of determined hiking, the guide stopped high atop a hill and the group collapsed on the dry and dusty ground. The group swiftly pulled canteens and jugs from their packs and drank their water quickly. The linguist's throat was parched, and he eagerly gulped the liquid into his dry and sandy mouth. Pausing to look out across a wide valley, the young man saw in the far distance the tiny figures of Bedouin herdsmen tending their animals. *Are they sheep or goats*, the young linguist wondered, unable to see the animals clearly in the distance.

He thought of the Psalm: *He led forth his people like sheep and guided them in the wilderness like a flock.* "The Negev is beautiful in the early morning, isn't it?" the young linguist asked the others who were seated near him, as they watched the sun rise over a large mountain range to the East.

"Early in the morning our song shall rise to thee..." an Englishman in the group replied to him with a smile.

"Casting down their golden crowns around the glassy sea," the linguist replied, smiling.

"No sea around here," *Mr. McGregor*, their Scottish minder, growled. "Maybe after the training is over ye'll all go down to Eilat for a swim, hey?"

"It feels like we marching all the way down there this morning," one of the Russian speakers joked in broken English.

"The Red Sea would do ye good!" the Scotsman said with a gruff laugh. "Wash off that dust on ye!"

"Technically it's the Gulf of Aqaba," the Englishman said with a smile as the others laughed, knowing that *Mr. McGregor* did not like being corrected.

"Alright!" *Mr. McGregor* replied in a flash of anger. "Let's git goin'! Double-time back to the base," he commanded, as the team began returning their canteens and water jugs to their backpacks.

The group eventually returned to the Army base by following a more difficult trail on the return route. After a thirty-minute break, they gathered in an open area, still segregated from the Army troops, for hand-to-hand combat training. There, they studied the techniques of *Krav Maga* – the attacking and self-defense methods developed for the Israel Defense Force – where the young linguist frequently found himself on his back, failing to land punches or kicks against his Israeli trainer during the drill.

After a long lunch, the group was in the field again, practicing with an arsenal of weapons – rotating between small arms and larger weapons – learning to fire quickly as well as disassemble and re-assemble the equipment in only a few seconds. At the end of the afternoon, the group was physically challenged again on an obstacle course, running around barriers, scaling walls, crawling under barbed wire, and swinging on ropes, with occasional live rounds of ammunition fired in their direction.

It was after this training that the young linguist found himself heading for the lumpy cot in his tent, exhausted and hoping to get a few minutes of sleep before the next activity.

Later that evening, after a short break, a quick shower, and a meal, the young linguist walked with his team to a different building on the Army base where they separated individually into their own classrooms. In the classroom, the young linguist had more training focused primarily on East German nuances and geography. The training varied each evening – one evening his instructors might emphasize the many streets of East Berlin. Another evening his teachers might have him learn about Rostock, the large port city in East Germany. Another evening his instructors might focus on different escape routes from behind the Iron Curtain. Later in his training, he would be required to memorize pages from *Jane's Fighting Ships* on the ships within the Soviet fleet. The subjects covered seemed endless: Red Army tank formations, Swiss accents, German accents, Austrian accents, disguises, codes and cyphers. And then the learning was repeated – but that was the point. The more that things were repeated in the classroom, the less likely they would go wrong in the field – at least that was the plan.

The young linguist had mixed feelings about the training. On one hand, he liked learning new things. Hearing about the potential missions he might undertake behind the Iron Curtain and the methods for executing them seemed quite exciting. However, the secrecy within the group of trainees – the avoidance of personal matters, of not disclosing one's name or talking about one's family or one's past – was difficult. Knowing the German language well, the young linguist was able to understand the conversations between the four German speakers, but was forbidden to speak to them in German. Similarly, after being with the Russians for several weeks, he was able to understand their conversations – but did not let them know he understood. After spending six weeks with the group, the young man was frustrated that he did not know more about the others. He had shared meals, tents, and a training course with them, but he did not really know them: their interests, their backgrounds or their motivations.

Several years later, one of the Russian speakers found himself on the cold concrete floor of a secret military prison in Czechoslovakia – after having been drugged, beaten, and starved for several days. Opening his eyes upon hearing the heavy door to his cell open, the man was relieved to see a new face enter.

Entering the cell with a slow and deliberate stride, a short muscular man appeared before him. He reminded the prisoner of a devout priest, with a calm stoic face below short cropped silver hair. His clothes were all in black – including a long greatcoat that added to his pastoral demeanor.

"I just arrived," the man said calmly to the prisoner in Russian as he removed his black leather gloves while his reverent eyes looked down at the prisoner on the floor. "You will confirm a few things for me," the man said directly, indicating that no other options were available. "When I am done, you will be exchanged for a Soviet prisoner held by the Western dogs," the man continued, as his muscular chin relaxed after each sentence. "You are ready to cooperate now, of course?" he added.

"*Da*," the prisoner said in agreement, as a mixture of sweat and blood dripped from his forehead and into his eyes and his mind calculated the remote possibility of actually being traded for a Soviet spy.

"Chair," the man commanded to those who were waiting outside the cell. A wooden chair was swiftly brought into the dank room. "Lights," the man commanded tersely, as additional lights were turned on.

Next, two guards entered and lifted the prisoner onto the newly provided wooden chair. Soon, one of the guards began binding the prisoner's wrist to the chair's arm.

"Not necessary," the man in black said firmly. "Correct?"

"*Da*," the prisoner said again, and the guard released the prisoner's wrist from his grasp.

A metal cart was wheeled into the room, and the prisoner saw that it overflowed with packs of cigarettes, bottles of water, canned fish and other food. "There is nothing to worry about now," the man in black said calmly. "You will be well taken care of." When he had finished speaking these words, the man in black turned to leave the cell.

"Where are you going?" the prisoner asked in a worried voice, concerned that he would be forced to confess his transgressions to others. The man in black, however, left without reply.

Reluctantly, the prisoner began eating the food on the cart, hoping for his priest's return.

After nearly two hours, the man in black returned with two new assistants who brought files and stacks of papers into the room. Then, he had the food cart removed and took a seat in a wooden chair that had been placed in front of the prisoner. The two now stared at each other – one man commanding, strong and muscular; the other broken by days of starvation, punches and kicks.

"Are you the one they call *Shpionski Stalker*?" the prisoner asked weakly in a mix of Russian and English.

The Spy Stalker.

"Da," the interrogator replied. *Yes.*

The prisoner's eyes blinked several times, trying to comprehend the severity of his situation.

The Spy Stalker continued staring, unblinking, at his prisoner.

"Tell us what we need to know…" one of the other interrogators started from nearby.

"Where do you want me to start?" the prisoner interrupted, broken by the days of torture and the newfound knowledge of his interrogator's identity. The prisoner knew *The Spy Stalker* would get the information he wanted – whether he cooperated or not.

"Start at the beginning," the Spy Stalker directed in a firm and unwavering voice. And soon the prisoner was telling his interrogators about his youth in a Soviet mill town, his recruitment into a spy ring and then his espionage work behind the Iron Curtain.

"And your network?" one of the interrogators interrupted, after the prisoner had described his many activities. "Give us their names." The prisoner began sharing the many names of agents and contacts in his spy network while the two assistant interrogators busily wrote down the information. Meanwhile, the man called *The Spy Stalker* continued staring – observing, watching, and analyzing – unmoved in his position in his wooden chair. Eventually, the interrogators brought books of photographs to the prisoner, demanding he identify the photos of the men and women in his spy network.

"That is it, comrades," the prisoner finally said in an exhausted low voice. "That is all I know."

"The training camp in the Negev?" the Spy Stalker asked. "You have not told us about that."

The prisoner blinked, surprised that the man in black knew that detail about his life. "Ah, yes, that was quite an experience," said the prisoner. "My first time in the Middle East." Soon the prisoner was telling his captors about the darkened windows in the transport bus taking him to a training camp (exact location unknown) somewhere in southern Israel... led by a Scottish commando, probably from the Royal Marines... lots of marching, hiking, shooting... studying codes and street maps of Prague in his evening classes, memorizing safe-houses and exits. "Some good that did, huh?" the prisoner asked rhetorically as he remembered how clumsy his attempted escape had been.

"And the others in the camp?" the Spy Stalker asked.

"We did not talk much," the prisoner explained. "It was forbidden."

"Let's see if you can confirm them for us," the Spy Stalker said, as one of the interrogators pulled a folder from his briefcase titled *Covenant Training – Group 8* and took out a stack of photographs.

"The first one, yes," the prisoner began – already confirming what The Spy Stalker knew. "The second one, no. The third one, yes." Again, confirming what the Spy Stalker knew. "The fourth one, no. The fifth one, yes."

The prisoner continued through the stack, identifying two additional members of the training group – people *The Spy Stalker* had suspected – who could now be found and arrested.

"So, with you that brings the number we have identified to seven," the Spy Stalker said.

"Understood," said the prisoner said dejectedly.

"And what about the American in your group?"

"He was not in any of the photos you showed me," the prisoner replied weakly.

"But what can you tell me about him?"

"He was religious, you know," the prisoner said. "Like you."

"Like me?" the Spy Stalker asked, in a surprised voice.

"Reverent... thoughtful... devout," said the prisoner.

"I see," said the Spy Stalker. "Is there anything else you remember about him?"

"No," the prisoner said after a moment of reflection. "Religious... that is the best name for him. He would quote from the Bible in English."

"Did he study the streets of Prague, like you?"

"I don't know," the prisoner replied. "We went to different classrooms. For me it was Prague and Red Army formations; for others I think they learned about missiles while others learned about the Soviet Navy. I only know what they taught me – and what I could hear from other instructors through the classroom walls."

"Do you know which country the American focused on?" asked the Spy Stalker. "The U.S.S.R. maybe? Or East Germany?"

"I don't know," the prisoner replied.

"You have done well," the Spy Stalker reassured the prisoner. "We have some more photos for you." Soon, one of the assistants presented more photographs. Some were in color while others were in black and white. Each was taken from a different distance – some close, others far away – and varied in quality. Some were blurry while others were very clear.

In one of the black and white photographs a distinguished-looking man – fit and proud, the very essence of a Swiss banker – stood on a Zurich sidewalk waiting to cross a street. The man wore a traditional hand-tailored suit with a luxurious silk tie and an expensive unbuttoned camel hair overcoat. Thick dark-rimmed glasses surrounded the banker's eyes while his hands, protected by fine Italian leather gloves, held an expensive leather briefcase.

"How about him?" The Spy Stalker asked. "Does he look familiar?"

"No, definitely not."

"Are you sure?" one of the interrogators asked.

"I've never seen that man in my life," the prisoner said, not recognizing the man.

"You are sure?" the second interrogator asked, repeating the words of his colleague.

"No, never," the prisoner said. "I have never seen him."

"Then let's look at some others," The Spy Stalker said in his reassuring voice, as more photographs were distributed.

So complete was the transformation that even after spending weeks together in the desert, eating in the same mess hall, training in the same camp and hiking over the same narrow dusty trails, the prisoner could not recognize the man in the photo – dressed as a successful banker in fine clothes and poised to cross a fashionable Zurich street – as the young linguist and adjunct seminary instructor, Professor Nicholas Telson.

CHAPTER 19

Back in Ohio, I was grateful that Sneak Ryerson's uncle, Charles Foster, drove his lime green Pontiac LeMans at a high rate of speed, creating more and more distance between myself and the prisoners we had visited at the Lebanon Correctional Facility. We drove north on Interstate 75 for our return to Findlay, and soon passed the cities of Middletown and Franklin before exiting at the Dayton Mall, where Uncle Charlie wanted to eat a late lunch. After parking the car in the suburban mall's large parking lot and asking for lunch recommendations, we arrived at a department store called *Rike's*. "Come back at Christmas and visit the downtown store," one of the helpful mall workers told us when we asked for directions. "They have a great Christmas display down there."

We arrived at the restaurant located on the second floor of the department store and ordered sandwiches, which soon arrived. "That was just so weird," I said hungrily as I ate my grilled cheese sandwich and fries.

"What's that?" Uncle Charlie asked.

"I mean, I can't believe we were actually in *prison* and got to see Julian Davis! I mean, who would have thought we'd be able to talk with him? Not me! And hearing him talk about all that UFO stuff – that was really weird too!"

"He seemed so," Uncle Charlie began. "I don't know the best word for it – *confused* – I guess."

"Yeah… confused," I continued. "I felt sorry for him."

"Me too," my friend, Sneak Ryerson, added softly.

"And what about Mister Crenshaw?" I continued. "He was so mean and creepy – asking us about how we caught him and telling us something 'big' is going to happen tomorrow. Sneak, you were looking at him pretty closely. Did you figure anything out?"

"I did, Pep, I did," my friend began.

"You did! What was it?" I asked.

"He wasn't telling the truth."

"Really?" Uncle Charlie and I both responded.

"What gave it away?" I wondered.

"Did he have a *tell*, or something like that?" Uncle Charlie asked expectantly. "If he did, I didn't notice it."

"That's the funny thing," explained the young detective. "I don't have anything to prove it. I just got the sense that he was lying to us."

"Oh no!" Uncle Charlie replied pretending to be shocked. "The great *Sunday School Detective* from Findlay, Ohio has stopped using deduction! He's basing his ideas on his feelings!"

"You're starting to sound like your sister," I smiled.

"I know," the young detective agreed seriously. "It's driving me crazy." Uncle Charlie and I laughed when we heard Sneak's comment. "I guess we'll see if my deduction is correct tomorrow, huh?"

"Right," I replied.

"You mean your *hunch*?" Uncle Charlie teased his nephew, as the young detective continued his explanation with a weary look.

"Yeah, I guess that's all it is. I don't have any factual evidence to prove Mr. Crenshaw wasn't telling us the truth. He just seemed... you know, happy to be stringing us along... making us drive all the way down here... making me explain things about the *Case of the Mysterious Circles*... and then was really vague about the *big thing* that will happen tomorrow. I don't know... it just seemed like there was a lot he wasn't telling us."

"Yeah," I agreed.

"Well, I hope he was lying," Uncle Charlie said quickly. "Because that would mean 'something big' *isn't* happening tomorrow and I don't have to keep my department on alert!"

"Maybe," said his nephew.

Uncle Charlie soon wiped his face with his napkin and told us, "I'm going to pay the bill and check in with my detectives again – maybe they've turned up something by now. I hope they have! I'm pretty sure I saw a pay phone on our way in here. Why don't you boys finish up with your lunch and meet me at the front door."

"Sure," we both replied as he quickly walked to the counter.

As I finished my lunch, my attention was drawn to two girls who were seated at a nearby table sipping strawberry milkshakes and talking in quick, short phrases about an upcoming vacation to Arizona. The pair were apparently sisters, who looked to be a few years older than me.

"It's going to be so cool to see the desert," the older one remarked, as her ponytail moved quickly back and forth as she spoke and took sips from a long straw while her restless leg tapped nervously on the side of her chair.

"Yeah, but those javelins make me nervous," the younger sister said with a smile.

"Javelins?" the older sister asked.

"Yeah, those wild pigs – or whatever they are – those things they are always telling us about," the younger sister explained nervously.

"I don't think that's what they're called," said the older sister.

"I'm not so sure I want to go out there," the younger sister admitted in a fearful tone.

"Well, we're going," the older sister said confidently. "Whether you like it or not! I just hope you don't do anything to embarrass me."

I paused for a moment after looking at the girls, then turned to my friend who was deep in thought. "Wouldn't it be weird if we met those girls, you know, like when we were older?" Hearing no response, I repeated my question. "Wouldn't it be weird if we met those girls when we were older?"

"What?" my friend finally replied.

"Those girls," I said, glancing in the direction of the nearby table where the girls were seated. "It would be weird to meet them when we are older."

"You mean, like, if we came back to this restaurant again?" my friend asked.

"No." I said. "You know, like in twenty years if we were in a different city," I explained. "And ran into those girls there."

"Pep," my friend said in an exasperated tone. "The odds of that happening are infinitesimal."

"Yeah. I guess you're right," I replied, not wanting to ask the meaning of the word *infinitesimal* – as my friend looked gloomily at his half-eaten sandwich, and wondered what crime would occur in our hometown the following day.

CHAPTER 20

After lunch, Sneak Ryerson and I joined his Uncle Charlie at the department store exit and soon walked outside into the warm summer sun. We crossed the mall's wide parking lot and returned to the car where I again slid into the backseat. Returning to the interstate, we resumed our drive north, each deep in thought. Uncle Charlie murmured something about "maybe getting someone to help Julian Davis", but other than that short phrase, the three of us were quiet for a long time as we reflected on our earlier visit to the prison.

Driving north, I stared out the small car window located behind the passenger seat watching the sights as we passed a large papermill, then the office buildings of downtown Dayton, and eventually the signs for Little York Road and the city of Vandalia. After we had passed that exit, my friend turned to me from the front seat and with a smile began, "Hey Pep."

"Yeah?" I asked.

"Do you have a story for us? I really need to get my mind off that weirdo Mr. Crenshaw. I just can't stop thinking about what he meant by *something big* happening tomorrow – something *so big* that all the local criminals need to have alibis."

"Yeah, I've been thinking about that too," I told him.

"But do you have a story?" my friend asked hopefully. "Maybe something to get our minds off those guys for a while."

"I actually have been thinking of a story," I admitted with a smile – and should not have been surprised that my friend, the great young detective, had uncovered it. The idea had been floating around in my mind from earlier in the day, and I had even written a few sentences in the small notebook I carried in my green gym bag.

"Cool," my friend replied.

"For real?" said my friend's uncle. "Like a detective story?"

"Well it's not a *love* story if you were hoping for that!" I laughed, as Sneak and his uncle joined in my laughter. Pausing dramatically for a few moments, I continued. "I've actually been thinking about it since this morning. I think the idea came to me because of something Uncle Charlie said... or maybe it was you, Sneak."

"Well at least someone listens to me!" Uncle Charlie laughed, as his nephew added, "Hey, *I* listen to you!" as if he were offended. "So, what did I say that was so insightful?" Uncle Charlie asked.

"It was about Sherlock Holmes," I continued. "You know – that it's been exactly one hundred years since his death... or," I paused to correct myself. "Actually, it's been one hundred years since the death of Sir Arthur Conan Doyle."

"Right," replied Uncle Charlie. "I remember talking about that."

"Technically, I think it's been fifty years," my friend said.

"Okay, fifty, one hundred. Anyway, now anyone can make up a story and not have to pay his family," I resolved.

"Right!" both Uncle Charlie and his nephew affirmed.

"So, I was thinking about that," I explained.

"About how Sir Arthur Conan Doyle died?" Uncle Charlie asked.

"Well, no," I replied hesitantly. "About those kinds of mystery stories and our group."

"Your group?" Uncle Charlie asked with a puzzled look.

"Do you mean the *Sunday School Detectives?*" Sneak questioned.

"Yep."

"What do you mean?" questioned Uncle Charlie.

"Well, I sort of came up with a story with the *Sunday School Detectives* as... the characters," I explained.

"No way," Sneak replied, smiling at me.

"Way," I told him.

"I'll bet this will be good," my friend said encouragingly.

"This should be interesting," Uncle Charlie added as he pressed a button to pop out the 8-track tape from his car stereo – ensuring that the music would not play while I told my story. "Do you have a name for this story?" he asked.

"It's called," I paused dramatically, then said in a serious voice. "*The Case of the Blue Cressida.*"

"*The Blue Cressida?*" asked Sneak.

"This does sound interesting," Uncle Charlie declared from his driver's seat.

"Are you ready for it?" I questioned.

"Of course," said the driver.

"Sure," added his nephew encouragingly, as they rolled up the car windows to better hear me.

"Okay," I said, clearing my throat with a cough as I moved closer toward the gap between the two leather front seats – speaking near the ears of the driver and my friend. "The year was 1880," I began dramatically. "Exactly one hundred years ago."

"Nice," said Sneak.

"I was tired and had just finished working at my doctor's office when…"

"Wait!" Uncle Charlie said with surprise. "Pep, you're in the story?"

"Come on, let him continue," his nephew urged.

"I just wasn't expecting Pep to be in it," Uncle Charlie confessed.

"He said it was about the *Sunday School Detectives*!" Sneak scolded his uncle. "Who do you think the characters will be?"

"Okay, okay," said Uncle Charlie. "Keep going."

"So, the year was 1880 – exactly one hundred years ago. The place was London, England and I was tired, having worked a long day at my doctor's office. I was wondering what mystery I'd learn about that evening, as I was riding through the foggy streets of London in the back of a horse-drawn carriage."

"A handsome cab," my young detective friend said to himself with a smile.

"Eventually the carriage stopped, and I stepped out onto the uneven cobblestone road, carrying my heavy doctor's bag. And after walking a few steps and passing a tall gas light, I got to the sidewalk and then, after taking a few more steps, I came to the front door of my apartment at…"

"221B Baker Street!" Sneak said instinctively.

"Yes, 221B," I continued. "I opened the door and limped up the stairs. I was limping because of a wound I received while I was in the Army, when I was a soldier in the War in…"

"Afghanistan, right?" Uncle Charlie asked.

"Excellent!" Sneak replied. "Uncle Charlie, it sounds like you've done some reading about the great detective too."

"Well, a little bit. When I was a kid."

"Afghanistan is correct," I added. "The doctor got wounded in Afghanistan."

"But now," Uncle Charlie said, shaking his head. "Instead of the British being in Afghanistan, it's the Soviets who are fighting over there. The more things change…"

"When I arrived at the top of the stairs," I continued, "just before turning the doorknob to my apartment, I heard a loud voice greet me from behind the closed door. 'Come in, Doctor!' said the voice. 'Come in! I'm just about to get some tea from Mrs.…'"

"Hudson!" Uncle Charlie exclaimed.

"Excellent," Sneak said approvingly.

"I was amazed that my friend knew I had arrived even before I entered the room, but then I remembered he was a great detective – the first-ever consulting detective to Scotland Yard. Eventually, I made my way into the rooms I shared with him and saw that he was sitting in a big leather chair, holding a violin in one hand, while our landlady, Mrs. Hudson, stood next to him."

"I like it," Uncle Charlie replied with a smile.

"Having just come back from the War in Afghanistan," I continued, "I had only a few things in my bedroom. But, the rest of the apartment, I noticed, hadn't changed much since I left for work that morning. It was cluttered with all kinds of things for the consulting detective's scientific experiments. Things like… tobacco and soil samples… and gunpowder."

"Sounds like Sneak's basement!" Uncle Charlie said with a laugh as he glanced at his nephew.

"Yeah, just a little," my friend agreed. "But Mom said I couldn't have a firing range down there," he admitted with a frown.

"She's such a downer," said Uncle Charlie while smiling at his nephew. "So, Pep," the older man asked, still smiling as he looked at me in the rear-view mirror. "What did this famous detective – the first consulting detective to Scotland Yard – look like?"

"Well," I explained. "He looked a lot like your nephew."

"Really?" Uncle Charlie exclaimed, in mock surprise. "I would never have guessed that!"

"Yeah," I continued. "He had long black hair that fell into his eyes that he kept trying to push back, even though he was wearing one of those hats with a cap on the front and the back."

"A deerstalker!" both Uncle Charlie and Sneak said nearly at the same time.

"Is that what it's called?" I asked.

"Yeah," my friend confirmed.

"Okay," I continued. "Anyway, besides wearing the hat, he wore a robe... not the kind that we have that go over our pajamas, but different.... valor, right?"

"Velour," Uncle Charlie corrected.

"Right, velour," I replied. "Anyway, when I walked in, I saw that the consulting detective wore his velour robe over his black pants and a nice white shirt – ready to rush outside and into the London fog to work on a case at a moment's notice!" I explained.

"I think they call that a dressing gown," Uncle Charlie explained.

"Sounds right," I replied.

"Or a smoking jacket," Sneak added. "I think he wears that sometimes, too."

"You might be right on that," Uncle Charlie added. "Or maybe a London Fog," he said whimsically.

"So anyway," I continued. "I saw my friend, the great consulting detective, sitting in his chair wearing his jacket and smoking his long pipe."

"Sometimes he smokes one of those long curved pipes that is really big at the end," explained Sneak.

"I think it's called a Calabash pipe," Uncle Charlie clarified.

"I remember reading that he kept his tobacco in like a slipper or something like that," Sneak added.

"I can't remember," I said. "But he was coughing, and saying, 'How do people smoke these things'?"

The two laughed at my words as Uncle Charlie added, "That sounds about right! Smoking isn't good for you!"

"Then, Mrs. Hudson came in," I said, continuing the story.

"I thought she was already in the room?" Uncle Charlie asked.

"Oh, sorry," I explained. "She was just coming into the room when I got there."

"Ah, got it," said Uncle Charlie with a smile.

"And who did *she* look like?" Sneak asked curiously.

"Uh, well, earlier, when I was thinking about the story, I was thinking she looked a little like Hailey Cotton."

"Oh oh," Uncle Charlie replied grimacing. "You might be on thin ice with that."

"Well, that was earlier," I explained. "But then I remembered that Mrs. Hudson doesn't really do much in the stories, so Hailey wouldn't be a good choice, because I'd like Hailey to do a lot of cool stuff in my story."

"That makes sense," Sneak replied.

"So then I thought, 'Well, if it's not Hailey Cotton, how about *Moscow* Cotton?' And I imagined Moscow coming into the room and doing a bunch of back flips while still holding a pot of tea, and then doing crazy stuff when he's pouring the tea for the doctor and the consulting detective and their clients – maybe from the top of a ladder or someplace high up, into a teacup on the floor."

"That would be funny," Sneak said with a laugh.

"That kid," Uncle Charlie said with a smile.

"But then I thought – like I did with Hailey – it would be cool if Moscow did some other cool stuff in the story too."

"Yeah, I don't think Moscow would be happy just pouring tea," Sneak told me.

"Makes sense," said Uncle Charlie.

"Then I thought of your mom, Sneak," I explained.

"Really?" my friend replied. "To be Mrs. Hudson?"

"Well, yeah," I explained. "I thought she'd be better than Hailey or Moscow. She's always so friendly and always makes sure the kids have snacks or Hawaiian Punch, or something like that when we come over."

"I think she gets those nice traits from her brother!" Uncle Charlie said of his sister.

"Exactly!" Sneak replied with a laugh to his uncle. "Her *older* brother!"

"Naw!" his uncle argued. "It's your mom's *younger* brother! That's where she learned all of those good qualities!"

"Maybe," Sneak replied with a chuckle. "But you're right, Pep," my friend said as he turned to me. "My mom is nice and she'd make a good Mrs. Hudson in your story. But I don't think she'd like to be in it," he said matter-of-factly.

"Why's that?" I wondered.

"She doesn't like drawing attention to herself," Sneak suggested.

"That's true," Uncle Charlie said of his sister.

"Okay, well," I continued. "I was thinking that she would just come into the room and serve tea and then say something about how messy the apartment is because of all your experiments."

"Now, that's definitely something your mother would say!" Uncle Charlie said with a laugh.

"Definitely," my detective friend added. "Just like she does now."

"Okay," I said, trying to continue the story. "So Mrs. Ryerson it is."

"Now, Pep, sorry to interrupt you," Uncle Charlie added with a chuckle. "Just so we're clear... and I understand things correctly... in your story, you imagine Sneak – your best friend here – as the great consulting detective living at 221B Baker Street with his mother playing the role of Mrs. Hudson?"

"Well, yeah," I explained.

"And she's serving him tea and cleaning up after him?" Uncle Charlie asked with a smile.

"Yeah," I replied.

"So, basically he's still living with his mother when he's all grown up!" Uncle Charlie roared.

"There could be some advantages to that," Sneak replied, as his uncle continued his laughter. "She bakes some pretty good cookies."

"Well, that's true," Uncle Charlie agreed as he continued laughing.

"Well, actually," I interrupted. "I didn't really imagine Sneak or me... or any of the other kids who are in this story, all grown up," I explained. "I have a hard time doing that. I don't have any idea what we'll look like in twenty years. I just imagine we're the same age as we are now."

"That makes sense," my friend replied.

"So, in the story, you're just like you are now," Uncle Charlie summarized. "But living in London in the 1880's!"

"It's just a story," I explained.

"Yeah, a fictionalized version of ourselves," Sneak explained smartly.

"Right," I agreed, assuming my friend was correct with his description.

"Okay, okay," said Uncle Charlie. "Sorry to interrupt. I just wanted to understand – and tease my nephew about living with his mother when he's older," he added with a laugh. "Keep going, Pep. Proceed."

"So, anyway," I persisted. "Just when your Mom was scolding you for making a mess...."

"You mean Mrs. Hudson," Sneak corrected.

."What?" I asked.

"It was Mrs. Hudson, who was scolding *the great consulting detective* from the 1880's about the mess in his room," Sneak corrected.

"Right, right," I said in agreement. "So right when she was scolding the great consulting detective, the detective turns to me – the doctor – and says, 'Doctor, it appears that we're going to have a visitor.' And then he turns to the owner of the house and says loudly, 'Mrs. Hudson! You better make tea for one more person – a princess from Bohemia, if I'm not mistaken. She'll likely be alone.'"

"Nice," Sneak smiled.

"And just then," I continued. "To my amazement, there came a faint knock on the door."

"Nice," Sneak repeated.

"I had not even heard anyone walk up the stairs at 221B Baker Street," I continued. "So, I turned to the great consulting detective and asked, 'How in the world did you know someone would be at the door?' And he turned to me, smiling as he walked over to answer the door and said, 'It's elementary...'"

"Yeah, Whittier Elementary," Sneak interrupted with a smile, including the name of our elementary school in the famous phrase.

I paused my story, shaking my head at my friend.

"You're doing great so far, Pep!" Uncle Charlie said encouragingly. "Don't pay any attention to the distraction on my right."

"So, what did she look like?" Sneak asked me quickly. "The princess from Bohemia."

"Well she looked like..." I began before pausing. "Hey, wait a minute, how did you know it was a *'she'* at the door?"

"Deduction," Sneak replied with a smile. "It was elementary... as you would say."

"That's pretty good," I told my friend. "You knew that the person at the door was a *she*."

"Oh, come on," Uncle Charlie admonished his nephew. "You had a fifty-fifty chance! Plus, Pep already told us it was a *princess* from Bohemia that was going to join them for tea!"

"Oh... right," I stammered. "Anyway, you are correct," I said, continuing with the story. "It was a young woman at the door."

"Did the person at the door look like Hailey?" Sneak asked.

"No," I replied.

"Lisa?"

"Wrong!" I said loudly.

"Cressida?"

I refused to answer because I had not intended to tell that part of the story at that time. "The young woman had hair like Farrah Fawcett," I explained.

"Okay, so the person at the door was basically Cressida," Sneak replied.

"Yeah, but she wasn't dressed like we normally see her," I explained hastily. "She was wearing one of those really big poufy dresses with lots of ruffles made of *crackoline*."

"Crinoline," Uncle Charlie corrected with a chuckle. "I can't believe I know that! I guess it's because I've been married a long time."

"....and have a daughter," Sneak added.

"Right," Uncle Charlie replied. "That probably has something to do with it too."

"So," I continued. "When he saw her, the great consulting detective said, 'Miss, I see that you are royalty...from a small kingdom in Europe... Bohemia... if I'm not mistaken. You are left-handed. You don't like to speak very much. You've just arrived in London. And you are very distressed.'"

"Nice," Sneak replied with a smile, enjoying the consulting detective's many deductions.

"The young woman," I explained, "was totally amazed at the great detective's skills."

"I guess that's one way to get the girls to like you!" Uncle Charlie added with a laugh from his driver's seat. "Girls like it if you notice things about them!"

"Come on Uncle Charlie!" Sneak protested with a smile.

"Yeah, come on!" I added, joining my friend's protests. "So anyway, the young woman – of course – was amazed at the many deductions made by the great consulting detective."

"Of course she was," added Uncle Charlie.

As I continued the story, and said the words of each character, I tried to sound like the people the characters in the story were based on. For the princess, I tried to sound like our friend Cressida, who spoke in a very soft Jacqueline Kennedy-like tone. "'Every one of those things you mentioned is correct.' the princess said. 'I am left-handed, I don't like to speak in public and I am a princess. My name is Princess Cressida of Bohemia and just like you said, I am very distressed. You're my only hope.'"

"So, she's basically our friend Cressida who talks like Princess Leia," Sneak commented with a frown.

"It gets better. I promise."

"Let him continue, Sneak," Uncle Charlie advised. "He's doin' good."

I paused for a moment, uncertain if I should continue.

"Keep goin' Pep," Uncle Charlie said encouragingly. "You're doin' good."

"It was then," I said seriously, after deciding to continue with the story, "that Princess Cressida began her tale of woe."

"That's good," Sneak said approvingly. "*Tale of woe*. I like that."

"Princess Cressida sat down in an empty chair in the apartment and said to the great consulting detective and the doctor: 'You see, my father, the King of Bohemia, gave me the best, most expensive and most famous jewel in our kingdom – a beautiful blue sapphire ring surrounded by diamonds – with instructions to deliver it this week to the Queen of England.'"

"That'd be Queen Victoria, during that time in English history," Uncle Charlie added.

"Right," I agreed, hoping my friend's uncle was correct. "So, Princess Cressida continued, 'I was supposed to give the jewel to Queen Victoria to finalize the peace treaty between our two countries. But....'"

"It was stolen," Sneak added.

"It was stolen," I said, continuing in the voice of the princess and ignoring my friend. "'And now without that ring – my country's promise of peace – our two countries will probably go back to war again. I'm so upset.'"

"I like where you're going with the story, Pep," Sneak said approvingly. "You've set it up to be a pretty good mystery – and I should know, I've read a lot of them."

"Thanks," I said with a smile. "I've read almost all of the same detective stories too."

"Yeah," Uncle Charlie added. "As long as you don't have the great consulting detective pull out the jewel from his desk drawer and say that he's already solved the case, I think you've got a pretty good mystery going."

"You're not going to do that, Pep, are you?" my friend questioned.

"Oh, no," I reassured him. "I've got a lot more to go."

"That's good," Uncle Charlie affirmed.

"So, why is it called *The Adventure of the Blue Cressida*?" Sneak asked. "Is it because she's sad?"

"Oh, I forgot that part," I replied. "So, anyway, the doctor and the consulting detective were in the apartment listening to Princess Cressida's *tale of woe*, when Mrs. Hudson comes in with more tea from the side door."

"'Oh, your majesty,' Mrs. Hudson said, when she saw Princess Cressida."

"So, she recognized the princess?" Uncle Charlie asked.

"Did she do a backflip when she entered the room, like Moscow Cotton would do?" Sneak asked with a smile.

"No, no. I changed that part, remember? Mrs. Hudson didn't look like Moscow; she looked like your mom."

"Oh, yeah, right," the young detective replied with a smile.

"So, anyway," I continued. "Mrs. Hudson entered the room with more tea, and when she saw the princess she said, 'Oh, hello, Your Majesty. I read about you in the newspaper and the wonderful jewel that you're bringing to our country, *The Blue Cressida*.'"

"I think I just got passed by a *blue Cressida* on the highway," Uncle Charlie said quietly, referring to the small car made by Toyota.

"Ah," the young detective said from the passenger seat in front of me. "It's the name of the jewel."

"So then," I said, continuing my story. "The doctor asked, 'So, Princess, why is the jewel called *The Blue Cressida*?' but he was immediately cut off by Mrs. Hudson who said, 'I know the answer to that, Doctor. I read all about it in the London newspapers. It's because when the jeweler made the ring, he said the blue in the sapphire matched the blue in Princess Cressida's eyes."

"Nice," Sneak replied in front of me. "The jewel matched Princess Cressida's eyes, so he called it *The Blue Cressida*. And now that the princess has lost the ring and is really sad about it, you could call her *The Blue Cressida* too."

"Well isn't that a *coinkydink*," Uncle Charlie said in a funny voice, as we laughed at the funny Midwestern term for the word *coincidence*.

"Pretty good, huh?" I said.

"Pretty sneaky Sis," Sneak said, reminding us of the TV commercial for a game called *Connect Four*. We all laughed at the joke, but Uncle

Charlie soon asked, more anxiously than his usual measured words, "So what happened next, Pep? Keep going, you're tellin' a pretty good story."

"Okay," I said, then paused dramatically. "Well, after the princess explained what the ring looked like, the great detective asked her where she had lost the ring,"

"Or, when she last *saw* the ring," Sneak added authoritatively, knowing what a consulting detective would ask a witness.

"Right," I said. "He asked her where she last saw her ring, and Princess Cressida explained that she had the jewel with her all the time she was on the long boat ride from Bohemia to England – sometimes keeping it in on her finger and other times keeping it in her purse, because it was so heavy."

"Makes sense," my friend said.

"And then when she arrived in London, she went to stay at the giant mansion of her cousin…"

"Her cousin huh?" Uncle Charlie asked with a smile.

"Yeah, her cousin," I explained. "Lady Lisa."

"Lady Lisa," Sneak smiled, pleased with how I had woven the name of Cressida's real cousin into the story. "Nice one."

"So," I continued. "Princess Cressida continued her *tale of woe* to the three that were gathered in the crowded apartment, which included Mrs. Hudson – because Mrs. Hudson wanted to stay and listen. 'It was just after I arrived at the house of my cousin Lady Lisa, that I first noticed that the ring was missing. I was finishing tea with my cousin in her sitting room. At first, when I noticed it wasn't on my finger, I immediately checked my purse. Because, like I said, I sometimes keep it there. But when I couldn't find it in my purse, I thought it might have fallen on the floor, or fell into the couch where I was sitting and taking my tea. So, we looked for it there in the sitting room, but we couldn't find it. Then we started looking through all of my bags and my belongings. They were still at Lady Lisa's front door because there had been a mix-up of some sort with the luggage. But we still couldn't find the ring! And then we looked all through my carriage and even the place where I had stepped to get out of my carriage. But it wasn't there. And it was then – when we were sure it wasn't in the sitting room or in any of my bags or the carriage or the area where I walked from the carriage to Lady Lisa's mansion – that we sent a message to Scotland Yard to come and help us, and soon the police and a bunch of detectives swarmed all over the house, searching all of the servants and their rooms and every part of Lady Lisa's big mansion. There were already a lot of English police officers and soldiers guarding me when I got to the mansion, and as soon as we called for Scotland Yard's help, the whole area filled with police. We all looked and looked for the jewel, but none of us – not the soldiers, or the policemen or the detectives or the people who came with me from Bohemia, or the people who worked for my cousin Lady Lisa, could find it.'"

"Yikes," said Sneak as he listened attentively.

"Soon," I continued in a serious tone, narrating the story, "the three listening to the *tale of woe* at 221B Baker Street were ready to ask the princess some questions. 'Are you sure you had the jewel when you arrived at your cousin's house?' the great consulting detective asked. 'You didn't leave it on the boat from Bohemia?' 'I'm positive I had it with me,' Princess Cressida told him. 'I remember having it with me when I was in my carriage on my way to Lady Lisa's house.' Then Mrs. Hudson asked her, 'Did you make any stops before you arrived at your cousin's mansion?'"

"Good question," my friend said.

"'No, no stops,' the princess explained."

"That would have been interesting," Sneak told me.

"Then Mrs. Hudson asked another set of questions," I continued. "'So, you went straight from your carriage to the sitting room at your cousin's house? There were no interruptions or visits with other people?'"

"More good questions," Uncle Charlie added.

"'Well, not exactly,' Princess Cressida said. 'There actually were several interruptions. First, when I got out of the carriage, the horses got really scared and started bucking up on their back legs. The grooms told me there was a rumor that a big hound from the Baskervilles had gotten loose and was panicking the horses.'"

"Nice one," Sneak added again.

"A hound from the Baskervilles, huh?" Uncle Charlie said with a smile.

"'And then,'" I continued in the voice of the princess, "'There was a big mix-up when I arrived at my cousin's big mansion. My rooms weren't ready, so they had to leave all of my bags by the front door and said they would take them in later.'"

I paused dramatically.

"'And was that all that happened?' Mrs. Hudson asked. 'Were there any other issues that you remember?' 'Not *before* I got to the sitting room,' the princess continued. 'But *after* I got to the sitting room, there was something that was strange. Instead of being alone with my cousin to take our tea, I saw that she already had a visitor. He was a red-headed man who said he was from *The Red Headed League* and was hoping my cousin could give his club a big donation.'"

"Excellent!" my friend said loudly, as his uncle laughed and I continued with the story.

"'It took my cousin a long time to get the red-haired man to leave – he kept asking for money for his club, but eventually he left her mansion.' Then the princess asked the great detective and the others, 'Do you think he could have taken *The Blue Cressida*? Could it have been that man from *The Red Headed League*?' 'Maybe,' said the doctor, as he thought about the possibility. 'It is a possibility,' the great detective agreed. 'I'm aware of that group's activities already.' Then the doctor asked the princess, 'What time was it when you noticed the jewel was missing?' 'It was just this morning,' the princess replied, '...just as I was finishing my tea with my cousin. That's when I looked down and saw the ring wasn't on my finger. And I've spent the entire day looking for that jewel! And now,' Princess Cressida added, 'since it's so late in the day, and I still haven't found the precious jewel, I've come here to Baker Street – to the most famous detective – who is even known by my people in faraway Bohemia! I really need your help. You're my only hope.'"

"You don't have to keep saying that line," Sneak interrupted. "It reminds me too much of *Star Wars*."

"I don't mind it," Uncle Charlie added with a laugh. "This is turning into one heck of a story."

"Uncle Charlie's right," my friend agreed. "This is shaping up to be really good."

"So what did they do next?" Uncle Charlie asked, captivated by the mystery.

"Well, after they heard the princess' *tale of woe* – as I like to call it – the consulting detective said in a loud voice, 'We must go, the game is a foot!'"

"I think that's afoot," said Uncle Charlie.

"Anyway, the doctor got on his heavy coat and the consulting detective took off his smoking jacket and put on his fancy black cape and they decided to take a carriage with Princess Cressida to visit her cousin's mansion – to investigate the..."

"...scene of the crime," Sneak added.

"Going to the scene of the crime is important," Uncle Charlie agreed.

"But just as they were about to leave the apartment," I said dramatically, "they got a telegram from the detective's older brother."

"Mycroft!" Sneak and Uncle Charlie said in unison.

"The telegram employed them..."

"Implored," Uncle Charlie corrected, "I think is the word you want."

"Right. The telegram *implored* them to meet Mycroft at his club to talk over some important matters of national security."

"Nice," Sneak added.

"So, the two sent Princess Cressida back to her cousin's mansion with her soldiers and guards, and they said goodbye to Mrs. Hudson and after the consulting detective adjusted his hat with the two caps..."

"The deerstalker," Sneak said.

"...and the doctor got his medical bag, they went downstairs and out the door of 221B Baker Street and into the London fog, and soon they hailed a carriage to go to..."

"The Diogenes Club," Uncle Charlie and Sneak said together.

"Right! The Diogenes Club," I added. "And after a few minutes of riding through the London fog in their carriage, they arrived at the club where talking was a no-no, and they eventually found Mycroft – the detective's brother – who was having dinner in the Visitor's Room. They were glad that he was having dinner in the Visitor's Room because that's the only room in the club where they could talk!"

"Please don't tell me you were thinking of me playing the role of Mycroft!" Uncle Charlie protested. "Isn't he pretty boring?"

"No, no," I assured Uncle Charlie. "Well yes – he is boring, but I wasn't thinking of you."

"Oh good," replied Uncle Charlie.

"I was actually thinking of Professor Telson in that role."

"The Professor isn't like that, is he?" Sneak's uncle asked.

"Well, maybe a little," Sneak explained.

"I thought he was a lot like me!" Uncle Charlie replied, remembering the seminary professor who was in his bowling league.

I ignored the comments and continued with my story. "So they found Professor Telson, I mean Mycroft, at the Diogenes Club reading a big thick book. And you know Mycroft knows all about the British government."

"I think in one place," Uncle Charlie began, "they said that Mycroft..."

"...*is* the British Government," uncle and nephew said together.

"Wow, that was weird," I said, surprised at how well they both knew the stories. "So anyway," I continued, "the great detective met his older brother at the Diogenes Club along with the doctor..."

"Seven years older," Sneak added. "He's seven years older."

"Okay," I said, before pausing. "So they met with the detective's brother *who was seven years older* and asked him why he wanted to meet. And then Mycroft said in a serious voice, 'I've called you two here because of a matter of grave importance involving national security. As you've probably heard, the gem called *The Blue Cressida* has been stolen and if it's not recovered, our nation will go back to war with Bohemia.'"

"Oh, oh," replied Uncle Charlie.

"That would be bad," said Sneak Ryerson.

"That's exactly what the consulting detective in our story said!" I replied. "Then Mycroft continued, 'It will be a disaster for our country to go back to war with Bohemia right now. We've lost a lot of soldiers in the war already and we've been counting on being at peace. And we've got a big secret, but I'll tell it to the two of you,' he said, whispering to the doctor and the consulting detective. 'Our soldiers aren't ready to go back to war right now. We need time to get more guns and do our drills. We just aren't ready! So, it would be a disaster if we sent our soldiers back into battle right now. We'd surely lose! But getting the Blue Cressida sapphire was part of the Peace Treaty with Bohemia, and if the Queen doesn't get that ring, Parliament will insist that we go back to war *right away*. And if that happens, thousands of our soldiers will die. You need to find that jewel right away! You two are our only hope!'"

"Wow, you really like using that phrase," Sneak replied.

"It's a good one," I explained.

"Okay, stop interrupting," Uncle Charlie said, scolding his nephew with a smile as he summarized my words. "So, Mycroft told them that they really, really, really, needed to find that ring because if they didn't, their country would go back to war with Bohemia – and a lot more soldiers would die because they aren't ready to return to the field of battle."

"Yep," I agreed. "That was pretty much what Mycroft told them."

"Well, I guess wars have been fought over less," Uncle Charlie said somberly from the front seat.

"Okay, so what happened next?" Sneak asked.

"Well, after they met with Mycroft they went to the scene of the crime," I explained.

"Princess Lisa's mansion, right?" Uncle Charlie added.

"Actually, *Lady* Lisa's mansion," Sneak corrected.

"Ah, right, it's *Princess* Cressida and *Lady* Lisa," said Uncle Charlie.

"So anyway," I continued, "the doctor and the consulting detective left the Diogenes Club and went to Lady Lisa's mansion. And when they got there, they saw that it was still swarming with soldiers and police officers – just like the princess had told them. And one of the police officers was Officer Athelney Jones."

"Yes!" Sneak said enthusiastically, slapping his leg. "Yes!" he said again looking at his uncle.

"Who's *Athelney Jones*?" Uncle Charlie asked.

"He's a police officer," I explained. "Who happened to look a lot like you, Uncle Charlie."

"Uh oh," my friend's uncle replied. "I'm not sure if I like the sound of this," he added. "Couldn't James Bond make an appearance in your story, instead? I'd rather be on *Her Majesty's Secret Service* than on the London Police force right now."

"Nope," I replied seriously. "No James Bond in this story. Just Officer Athelney Jones."

"Yes!" Sneak said again, laughing.

"Why's that so funny?" Uncle Charlie asked his nephew. "I've read a lot of the stories and I don't even remember a police officer with that name. What is it again?"

"Athelney," I repeated. "Athelney Jones."

"Didn't Athelney arrest everyone in *The Sign of Four* book?" Sneak laughed expectantly.

"Yep," I replied.

"Well, that's not so bad," Uncle Charlie said reassuringly. "I like to be thorough, too."

"When I say he arrested *everyone*, I mean *everyone*!" Sneak explained with a laugh. "He literally arrested everyone in the house – and then had to let them all go, after Sherlock Holmes proved that none of them were guilty."

"Well, I don't think I've ever..." Uncle Charlie began.

"So back to my story," I continued. "And because he couldn't find the jewel, Athelney Jones was about to do the same thing at Lady Lisa's mansion, right when the doctor and the consulting detective arrived."

"I love it," Sneak said approvingly. "He's not very smart," my friend added.

"Hey, watch it now," Uncle Charlie said sternly.

"Sorry," came Sneak's meek reply.

"And what kind of name is Athelney, anyway?" Uncle Charlie wondered.

Ignoring the comments, I continued with my story. "So there was this great commotion when they arrived at Lady Lisa's mansion – not just because Officer Jones was going to arrest everyone, but because some of the police officers didn't like the consulting detective showing up there."

"Kind of like *you* at the Findlay Police Department," Uncle Charlie said with a smile as he glanced at his nephew.

"Hey!" his nephew replied. "Most of the force appreciates what I do."

"Yeah, but not everyone, unfortunately," his uncle chuckled.

"So then," I continued, "the great consulting detective said in a really loud voice, 'Before you arrest everyone again Athelney – I mean Officer Jones – I'd like a chance to interview the suspects.' So Officer Jones let him interview all the people who were there when the ring went missing. They interviewed the soldiers and then the police officers who had been guarding Princess Cressida, and then they interviewed Lady Lisa's workers: her cooks and cleaners and butlers and the people who worked in the gardens. Lady Lisa said she could vouch for each of her workers, telling the doctor and the consulting detective that 'They've been with me forever'. Next, they moved on to talk to Princess Cressida's people – you know, those people who came with her from Bohemia – her maids and guards and servants."

"Makes sense," Sneak replied.

"Then, they even interviewed the group of soldiers that had been assigned to guard her while she was in England," I continued.

"I think you said them already," my friend said.

"It was a pretty exhaustive interview," Uncle Charlie added.

"Okay," I continued. "I guess you're right. So, eventually after they had interviewed each person, they got everyone in a line and started asking questions to the whole group. And it wasn't going anywhere. No one saw anything. And they were just about to stop the interview when the doctor – all of a sudden – noticed an older guy, who was hunched over, in the group of people who worked for Princess Cressida. The doctor stopped and said to the consulting detective, 'Wow, he looks familiar. It seems like I've seen him before.' 'Maybe we have,' the consulting detective said to his friend. 'But that gentleman wasn't with the other people we interviewed earlier.'

"Hmm, now it's getting interesting," Sneak said from the front seat of the car.

"They asked the princess who that older gentleman was – and, I forgot to tell you, the person looked really old. He had white hair and a white beard and was sort of stooped over."

"Kind of like you are in the back of my car," Uncle Charlie said apologetically.

"Yeah, kind of," I concurred, as I leaned forward to continue telling my story from the small backseat. "Anyway, the Princess said that his name was... just a second." I paused to find the name I had written earlier in a notebook. "His name was Sadvi Demopopulous."

"Sadvi Demopopulous?" Sneak asked, his face wrinkling in unrecognition. "I don't remember him in any of the stories."

"That was his name," I said with a smile.

"Hmm," Uncle Charlie added.

"Anyway, the princess said that Sadvi had only been with her for a short while, but he helped her with all of her travel plans and also helped her with all of her winter coats as she went from one palace to another for her many visits. Because, you know, England is so cold. 'And has he been thoroughly searched along with all of his luggage?' the consulting detective asked Officer Jones. 'Oh, of course,' the police officer said. 'His room and all of his things. Everything here in the whole house has been searched.'"

"Sounds like the trail is cold," Sneak commented.

"Just wait," I encouraged. "So then, the consulting detective asked Sadvi Demopopulous why he wasn't with the others earlier – when they had interviewed each person. And Sadvi, in a really old voice said, 'I guess I didn't hear you. I was upstairs getting Princess Cressida's winter coats ready.' Then the consulting detective asked the Princess: 'Is that true you sent him upstairs to get your winter coats ready?' And she said, 'Yes, I did send him upstairs.' So, then the consulting detective asked, 'Princess Cressida, what were your plans for tonight? What were you originally planning to do before the jewel went missing?' Then, Princess Cressida told him, 'Well, Lady Lisa and I were planning on going to a piano concert at the London Hall.'"

"Maybe the Royal Albert Hall?" Uncle Charlie wondered.

"Maybe," I replied. "But then Princess Cressida said, 'We could never go out to a concert at a time like this. Everything is all messed up since the jewel has gone missing! I could never go to a concert now.' But then the consulting detective turned to her and said, 'I insist! You must go to the concert as planned!'"

"Interesting," Sneak replied.

"So, a little while later," I continued, "Princess Cressida and her cousin Lady Lisa were ready to leave for the concert at..." I paused, then asked, "Where did you call it, Uncle Charlie?"

"The Royal Albert Hall. I think that's the name of one of the big concert halls in London."

"Okay," I continued. "So, they all went there – to the Royal Albert Hall – in a couple of big horse-drawn carriages. Everyone went – Lady Lisa's servants and the people Princess Cressida brought from Bohemia – and, of course, the Doctor and the great consulting detective went too. And Athelney Jones who brought a bunch of soldiers and police officers who changed into regular clothes so they could be undercover at the concert."

"Nice," Sneak replied in approval.

"So, they went into the fancy concert hall with hundreds of plush seats and plush velvet carpets and giant chandeliers hanging from the ceiling. And eventually, Princess Cressida and Lady Lisa and all the people they came with made their way to one of those really big and expensive box seats in the balcony along the side of the concert hall. And then, the conductor came out and waved to the audience. And you'll be interested to know that the conductor in my story was someone who looked just like..."

"Joel!" Sneak guessed.

"Yep," I smiled, as we remembered our friend who loved music. "And so, after he waved to the audience, he turned and went to his music stand and he picked up his baton and started conducting the orchestra. And the musicians started playing some beautiful symphony music."

"I thought it was a piano concert, right?" Sneak asked.

"No, I thought it was an orchestra." Uncle Charlie added.

"What?" I asked.

"Earlier, you said they were going to a piano concert," Sneak explained. "Not a big symphony concert."

"I can't remember what I said earlier," I replied. "But, anyways, it was an orchestra concert, not a piano concert, and then, just before half time –."

"Intermission," Uncle Charlie corrected.

"Right. Intermission," I clarified. "So, just before intermission a couple of mean-looking thugs came up to the box where Princess Cressida and Lady Lisa were sitting."

"Did they look like anyone we know?" Sneak asked with a smile.

"No, no," I laughed. "Just your normal-looking thugs." I paused for a moment, as I considered having the two criminals look like some people I didn't like, but then continued. "So the thugs went up to the place where Lady Lisa and Princess Cressida were sitting and saw Princess Cressida's purse that she had left hanging on her chair. It was light blue and matched the puffy dress that she wore...crin..."

"Crinoline," Uncle Charlie corrected. "I *still* can't believe I know that!"

"Right," I continued. "So anyway, these two big thugs came rushing over and one of them tried to take Princess Cressida's purse, but she was able to hold on to part of it. And then, Lady Lisa started yelling, 'Stop thief!' really loud, as the one thug was wrestling the purse away from Princess Cressida and the other thug was fighting off some of the soldiers who were there in the balcony. So, there was a loud commotion, and everyone in the concert hall looked up at the fighting between the two bad guys and the soldiers – and even Joel looked up from the stage and the music stopped. And then, a bunch of people tried to help the princess and all the undercover detectives started swarming the area. And they all started wrestling with the two big thugs. But one of the thugs was really strong and was able to grab Princess Cressida's purse. And then, a few seconds later, he jumped down off the balcony and onto the first floor of the concert hall."

"That's awesome," Sneak replied.

"After that first guy jumped down, the second thug jumped down too, and they started running towards the stage. And all of the undercover police detectives started yelling, '*Stop thief!*' and '*Hey! Stop those guys!*' And all the people in the audience stood up and started pointing to them and a few people tried to stop them, but the thugs pushed them out of the way. And then, the two bad guys jumped up onto the stage where Joel was standing and knocked him over as well as a bunch of music stands and some of the musicians' instruments as they were running around the stage, trying to get out of the concert hall through a side door."

"This is great," Sneak commented.

"Yeah," Uncle Charlie agreed.

"So after the thugs had run away, everyone around Lady Lisa and Princess Cressida asked if they were okay and Princess Cressida said, 'In all of this commotion, not only did I lose my purse but I also lost my coat.'"

"You must like that word, 'commotion'," Sneak observed.

"I guess so," I replied quickly before returning to the story. "So… I forgot to tell you, the doctor arrived by then and asked, 'Your coat? How could that be missing too? The thieves only stole your purse, right?' And then Princess Cressida explained, 'Well, when the thug was wrestling my purse away from me, I saw Sadvi Demo…'" I paused as I looked down at the name in my notebook.

"Demopopulous," Uncle Charlie said firmly.

"Right, Sadvi Demopopulous," I continued. "The princess said, 'I saw Sadvi Demopopulous walk away with my coat.' 'But why would the old man walk away with your coat?' the doctor asked. 'Where would he go with it?' And then Athelney Jones said, 'Well, it looks like your coat isn't the only thing missing. It looks like the consulting detective is gone too!' At this, Officer Jones started to become angry. 'Princess, in one day you've lost your purse, your coat, your assistant who helps with your winter coats and the consulting detective who was helping with this case! Not to mention one of the most famous jewels in the world! I knew I should have arrested everybody!'"

"Oh, oh," Uncle Charlie said.

"But just then," I explained, "everyone in the auditorium heard the voice of the world famous consulting detective yell, '*Stop thief!*' and they could see that he was chasing the old man through the auditorium. And the old man was running with Princess Cressida's coat in his hands. But the old guy, it turns out, was running really fast – a lot faster than most old guys could – and was getting away from the consulting detective and the police officers who were following them."

"Nice," Sneak Ryerson replied.

"But, then, just as it looked like the old man was going to get away, a police inspector, Inspector Lestrade – who looked a lot like Hailey Cotton – stepped in his path and said in a loud voice, 'Arrest this man!'"

"Hmm, that's an interesting twist," Sneak said.

"But, it turned out that the old man not only could run fast, but was also really strong, and eluded the grasp of Inspector Lestrade and the police officers around her."

"So, the old guy wasn't really old after all?" Uncle Charlie summarized, as I ignored his question.

"And then, just when it looked like the old guy would get away from everyone at the concert hall, a noise was heard from the highest balcony – high above them all. And a figure could be seen doing three somersaults and then three backflips around a railing."

"Excellent," Sneak said approvingly.

"'That's my brother!' said Inspector Lestrade."

"He ain't heavy," Uncle Charlie said quietly to himself.

"And then the figure from high above – the one doing the somersaults – yelled in a loud voice, 'Get out of the way!' And in an instant the Inspector's brother, who was the greatest acrobat in all of London in the 1880's – and who also looked a lot like…"

"Moscow Cotton!" Sneak and Uncle Charlie said together.

"…did three more back flips and landed right on top of the old man as he was trying to get away."

"So the criminal wasn't really old, then?" Uncle Charlie asked again.

"Exactly," I explained. "So, when Moscow – Moscow Lestrade, that is – caught him, the entire audience applauded and cheered and all of the people in the story gathered around. There was Princess Cressida and her cousin Lady Lisa. Joel – the symphony conductor. And Athelney Jones – the policeman who looked a lot like you, Uncle Charlie. Even Mycroft was there."

"And the doctor and the consulting detective, right?" Sneak asked.

"Right," I answered. "So as Moscow was holding onto the old guy, the consulting detective said, 'Please take off that horrible excuse for a disguise! You haven't fooled me at all – pretending to look like an elderly man! I spent an entire winter in a nursing home dressed as a ninety-year-old and no one had the foggiest idea I was in disguise! But your disguise is disgusting!'"

At this remark, the car rang with peals of laughter from Sneak and his uncle – encouraging me to further embellish my story.

"'Your disguise is so horrible!' the consulting detective continued to shout. 'You should send it back to the shop where you got it from and ask for a refund!'"

My additional words brought even more laughter from the front of the car.

"So," I continued. "After everyone was around him, Moscow Lestrade took off the mask that Sadvi Demopopulous was wearing. And you know what they saw?"

"I'm not sure," Sneak said apprehensively.

"What?" Uncle Charlie asked anxiously. "What did they see?"

"You don't want to guess?" I asked.

"Not on this one," Sneak replied. "I don't have enough information."

"How about you, Uncle Charlie?" I asked. "Want to guess what they saw?"

"I have no idea," he admitted. "I can't think of anyone else. It seems like you've already gone through all of the *Sunday School Detectives* – except for Jennie's imaginary friend, Mr. Knick Knack."

"Okay, okay," I said, continuing my story. "Moscow pulled the disguise off and it turned out to be a guy... who looked just like... Julian Davis!" I cried, referring to the young prisoner we had visited earlier that morning.

"Julian Davis!" Sneak exclaimed. "What's he doing in the story?"

"Was he looking for space aliens, back in the 1880's?" Uncle Charlie said with a smile.

"I guess I got you guys pretty good on this one," I replied smugly, ignoring the question.

"You got us?" Sneak asked. "How did you *get us*?"

"Well," I continued. "If you rearrange the letters in *Sadvi* it spells Julian."

"Julian?" Sneak asked. "No it doesn't!"

"Er," I said sheepishly. "Sorry, did I say Julian? I meant to say: if you rearrange the letters in Sadvi." I paused dramatically before continuing, "It spells *Davis* – as in *Julian Davis*."

"Ahh," Sneak replied. "*Davis... Sadvi*. I can't believe I didn't notice that. I must be tired from our drive."

"Wait a second!" I said loudly, after realizing what had happened. "I can't believe it! I actually tricked the amazing Sneak Ryerson! This must be a first for me!"

"I can't believe it either," said Uncle Charlie.

"That was pretty clever," Sneak replied. "I like it."

"Is that the end of the story?" Uncle Charlie asked with a frown.

"Oh, no, no," I continued. "So, after they had Julian Davis – or Sadvi Demopopulous – in handcuffs, Inspector Lestrade returned the coat to Princess Cressida as well as her purse. 'We caught the two thugs just outside the auditorium,' the Inspector told her. 'They were trying to get away with your purse.'"

"That's some good police work," Uncle Charlie added.

"Just then," I continued, "the great consulting detective turned to Princess Cressida and asked her, 'Do you mind if I borrow your winter coat for a moment?'"

Sneak and Uncle Charlie laughed at this comment.

"Was he cold or something?" my friend asked.

"No, no, you'll see," I told my friend. "So Princess Cressida says, 'I guess so,' and she handed her light blue cra…"

"Crinoline," Uncle Charlie added.

"…crinoline coat to the great consulting detective, who then reached into a secret compartment under the collar. A moment later he said, 'Just as I suspected,' and he pulled out *The Blue Cressida* – the beautiful sapphire jewel – that had been missing."

"Nice," Sneak replied.

"And then Lady Lisa yelled, 'It's *The Blue Cressida*! You found it! You found it!'"

"That sounds like Lisa," Sneak added. "She can yell pretty loud sometimes."

"Then the astonished doctor turned to the great consulting detective and asked, 'That was amazing! How did you know the ring was in a secret compartment of the coat?' And then the great detective said, 'Well, Doctor, it was….'"

"Elementary!" all three of us said at the same time with a laugh.

"How did he solve it?" Sneak asked.

"Yeah, when did he know it was Sadvi who took the ring?" Uncle Charlie asked.

"The consulting detective then said to the doctor and all the others who were gathered around, 'When I saw the *supposedly* old man at Lady Lisa's house, I knew right away he was guilty. Sadvi's disguise was obviously a fake. And when I heard he was in charge of the princess' winter coats, I deduced that he had sewn a secret hiding place into one of her coats in order to hide the jewel. He probably took it from her during the commotion when she arrived – either when the horses were bucking when they saw the *Hound of the Baskervilles* or during the mix-up with the luggage at the front door or when they were trying to get that guy from the *Red Headed League* to leave. And he must have known that everyone would be searching for it as soon as the princess discovered the ring was missing, so he couldn't put it in his pocket or hide it in his room – because someone might find it there and know he took it. So, hiding it inside the coat was a perfect place. No one would ever find it there, because he was in charge of the coats! I knew he was guilty the first time I saw him, but I didn't know where he had hidden the jewel or how he was planning to escape with it. But, once I learned that the original plan was for Lady Lisa and Princess Cressida to attend the concert, I knew that must be the place where he would make his escape. When I saw everyone chasing the two thugs who had taken the Princess' purse – thugs, who I'm sure Davis had hired – I knew that was going to be the perfect time for him to make his escape with the coat, with the jewel inside. No one would be looking for the coat – they'd all be looking for the guys who took the Princess' purse. So, when I saw him run off with the coat, I went after him.'"

"That's pretty good," Sneak explained.

"Is that the end?" Uncle Charlie asked.

"No, no," I told him. "Not quite."

"Good," came the reply from our driver.

"But then the great consulting detective turned to Inspector Lestrade and asked her, 'Hailey, we've worked together a lot over the years and solved a lot of cases together. I'm really glad you and your brother – London's greatest acrobat – were here to catch Sadvi. But you'll have to tell us why you and your brother were here at the concert tonight? I thought we were only working with Officer Jones and his group of police officers. Why did you come to the concert too?'"

"Good question," Uncle Charlie added.

"It was then that Inspector Lestrade told the group an interesting tale," I began.

"Excellent," my friend replied.

"Was it a *Tale of Woe*?" Uncle Charlie asked with a laugh.

"No, no," I said as I continued the story. "'Well,' Inspector Lestrade began. 'We've been following those two thugs for a while now. And they led us here to the concert hall. We knew they weren't here to listen to music, so we stationed our police officers all around the hall – at all of the exits. And I asked my brother, Moscow – the world's most famous acrobat – to hide in a spot where he could jump down on them if they did anything bad."

"Cool," Sneak said.

"Then, the consulting detective asked Inspector Lestrade, 'But why were you here with so many police officers? They are just a couple of thugs, right? You and Moscow could have handled them on your own.'"

"Another good question," Sneak told me.

"Then, Inspector Lestrade gave an answer that shocked everyone," I explained.

"Oh, oh," Uncle Charlie replied ominously. "This doesn't sound good."

"'The reason,' the Inspector explained, 'is because those two thugs work for a criminal network led by someone called Moriarty."

"Dun, dun, dun!" Uncle Charlie intoned.

"I love it!" Sneak exclaimed.

"'We thought they could lead us to him,' the Inspector explained. Then the great consulting detective added, 'That makes perfect sense! Only a devious criminal mastermind like Moriarty would have tried something like this.' Then Moscow said, 'He almost started another war by stealing that jewel! It's a good thing we stopped him!' And then Mycroft turned to the princess and said, 'Since there still might be some criminals around here, I'd like to escort you personally to Buckingham Palace right now, so you can give the ring to the queen straight away.'"

"That's a good idea," Sneak said.

"The princess said, 'That is a great idea,' and Mycroft and most of the group left to take Princess Cressida to the queen while the other policemen took Sadvi to jail."

"Exit stage right," Uncle Charlie said softly.

"So then," I continued.

"...oh, it's not over yet?" Uncle Charlie said in a surprised voice.

"No, not quite," I told him. "So then," I continued, "there were a few people who did not go to the police station or palace, but were still in the auditorium. There was Joel, the orchestra conductor, who was helping his musicians get the stage cleaned up after the thugs had pushed over the instruments and the music stands. And the great consulting detective and the doctor and Inspector Lestrade were still there too."

"Just a couple of them stayed behind," my friend summarized.

"Right!" I continued. "So then, Inspector Hailey – I mean, Inspector Lestrade – turned to the doctor and the consulting detective and said, 'You two should really watch out for Moriarty; he's really dangerous. And now that you've stopped him from making a fortune by stealing *The Blue Cressida*, he'll stop at nothing to get you.'"

"I like it," Sneak added.

"Then the consulting detective turned to Inspector Lestrade and said, 'I'll be careful.' 'Me too,' said the doctor, and they all started walking out of the auditorium with all of the other people who were leaving the concert."

"I guess they cut the concert short because of all of the excitement," Uncle Charlie added.

"Right!" I affirmed. "So, they were in the big crowd of people leaving the concert hall, and the doctor was talking to Hailey Lestrade, when all of a sudden, he turned around and said, 'Where's my friend? Where's the great consulting detective? He was right here, walking right beside us just a moment ago!' And soon they were looking all through the crowd for their friend but couldn't find him."

"This doesn't sound good," Uncle Charlie added.

"So then," I continued. "Later that night, the great consulting detective woke up in a dark room and all he could remember was walking out of the auditorium with his friends – but couldn't remember getting hit on the head by one of Moriarty's henchmen. And he couldn't remember getting shoved into a dark carriage that was waiting outside the auditorium. And he didn't remember riding to a secret location – a big dark house on the other side of London – or being carried down to an ancient underground dungeon or being tied up."

"Woah," Sneak replied. "That's actually sort of scary."

"When he finally woke up," I continued, "he was greeted by an older man who was not wearing a disguise. 'Well, hello Mr. Holmes,' he said in a creepy voice. 'I see we finally get to meet face to face.' The old man paused for a moment, then said, 'I am very disappointed. You see, I was at the concert tonight and I saw you ruin my plans. I really wanted that jewel – *The Blue Cressida*. I could have made a lot of money from it... and maybe even started a war. But it's okay, I've got something even bigger planned in a few days, so I'm going to need you to be tied up for a while.' The criminal mastermind then let out a loud creepy laugh."

"What was it that Moriarty said?" Sneak Ryerson inquired. "That he's got something *bigger* planned in a couple of days?"

"Oh brother," Uncle Charlie replied. "This is starting to sound familiar."

Sneak continued his line of questioning, "Pep, what did the great criminal mastermind look like?"

"Like Mr. Crenshaw of course," I explained, referring to the older prisoner we'd met earlier, as I heard a groan come from Uncle Charlie.

"And what exactly were his big plans? Those things that are supposed to happen in a few days?" Sneak asked.

"I don't know," I admitted. "I'm still trying to figure out that part of the story."

"Just like us," Sneak said remorsefully. "Just... like... us."

CHAPTER 21

"That was a really good story, Pep," Sneak Ryerson complimented me in a serious voice after I completed my story.

"Yeah, definitely a good one," his Uncle Charlie added.

"Thanks," I replied meekly.

"You were able to get most of the *Sunday School Detectives* in it too," Sneak added.

"Yeah," I agreed. "I tried to. I was going to have Jennie and Michelle make an appearance – along with Mr. Knick Knack – as the Baker Street Irregulars, but I couldn't figure out a way to work them in."

"Hmm….maybe if you…" my friend began, thinking of a place to add them to the story and he added the words, "What if…" but he soon grew silent as he studied the wide fields that surrounded the interstate as we continued driving north.

We remained in silence as the car continued its path toward home and I slowly realized I had made a mistake. I hadn't noticed it initially, but I soon realized that the mood in the car had slowly changed when I mentioned Mr. Crenshaw. The others had been laughing and joking, but had stopped when I mentioned the older prisoner. And I came to regret the ending of my mystery. My friend had asked me to tell a story to take his mind off our visit with the convicted criminal. And initially, my funny detective story about a missing jewel had done just that. But the ending had reminded my friend again of Mr. Crenshaw and the words he had spoken to us earlier – warning us that *something big* would happen tomorrow in our hometown. Something *so big*, that all of the criminals in Hancock County should have an alibi.

Eventually, I leaned back in the seat and rested my head on my folded sports coat while listening to the car's loud engine and the wind that once again poured in through the car's open windows.

We drove in silence for the remainder of our drive back to Findlay, passing the city of Wapakoneta – with its domed Armstrong Air and Space Museum – then the outskirts of Lima and the small college town of Bluffton, Ohio. Eventually, we reached the Findlay city limits and I tried to lift the mood of the others by saying, "Wow! That sure was a relaxing drive!" But Uncle Charlie and his nephew in the front seats were quiet. "I didn't sleep, but I had a good time looking out the window, how about you Sneak?" I asked, again getting no response. Finally, still smiling, I leaned forward and asked, "Sneak, what have you been thinking about?"

"I've been thinking about our visit to the prison," my friend said in a serious voice – his mood now dark and gloomy.

"About what, exactly?" I wondered, hoping to help, surprised by the change in my friend's mood.

"About how Mr. Crenshaw said he's been one step ahead of me."

"Aw, you can't believe that? He was just trying to get to you, right?"

"Maybe," my friend muttered as we approached the exit for Route 12 and West Main Cross, a street that cut through the heart of our city. Uncle Charlie quickly took the exit and turned right onto the busy city street near the large and dramatic oval sign for the Imperial House Motel topped with a golden crown.

"Hey Uncle Charlie," my friend said seriously, turning to his uncle. "Can you turn left here?"

"Into the cemetery?" his uncle questioned with a surprised voice.

"Yeah, I just need to check something out – it's important."

"Uh... well... sure," Uncle Charlie reluctantly agreed. "I need to check in with my detectives as soon as I can, but I guess we can stop here for a few minutes... if it's important."

"It's important," his nephew said tersely.

The police captain quickly turned into the cemetery entrance, next to the parking lot for the Bill Knapp's restaurant. After the car passed the heavy green gates of the entrance, Sneak said, "You can stop here. I need to retrace my steps."

"Retrace your steps?" I wondered.

"You sure about this?" Uncle Charlie asked, as he halted the car next to several large old monuments near the cemetery's entrance.

"Yeah," came the reply from the young detective, who was lost in thought as his mind processed details not only from our morning's visit to the prison but also from events that had occurred several months earlier. Opening the car door, my friend swiftly exited before the car came to a stop. "Leave a correct eulogy," I heard him say as he walked rapidly down a narrow road between cemetery plots. "Leave a correct eulogy," he said again before turning at a large monument, and was soon out of sight.

"What's this all about?" Uncle Charlie asked from the driver's seat.

"I have no idea," I admitted.

"He makes me nervous when he gets like this – all moody and somber. A kid his age shouldn't be so depressed."

"Yeah," I agreed.

We paused for a moment as Uncle Charlie turned the car around to face the street, then turned off the car's engine.

"I think my dad has depression too," I admitted after a minute or two of silence.

"You're dad, huh?" Uncle Charlie replied. "I wouldn't have guessed that."

"Yeah, he's been really down in the dumps for a long time."

"I'm sorry to hear that," came the empathic response.

"Did you know he's trying to learn French?"

"Your dad? Really? I didn't know that."

"Yeah, he's got a lot of old books. He's trying to teach himself, but it's not working out too well."

"Hmm."

"He'd rather be a high school French teacher instead of selling appliances. But, like I said, it's not working out so well."

"And the one thing he's really trying to do is learn French?" Uncle Charlie asked.

"Yeah, it's crazy, right? Becoming a French Teacher instead of selling washers and dryers," I laughed.

"Well, believe it or not, my wife's whole family speaks French!" Uncle Charlie admitted.

"They... they do?" I said surprised. "I thought they were from Vietnam?"

"They are, but Vietnam used to be a French colony. So, a lot of Vietnamese still speak French. In fact, my wife's family liked the French a whole lot more than those Communists that took over the country after we left. It might sound crazy, but every year the family still celebrates Bastille Day!"

"I think my dad's mentioned Bastille Day."

"It's the French National Holiday – like our Fourth of July. They go all out with sandwiches and desserts. It's a lot of fun and it's actually coming up in a few days – on the 14th. You and your dad should come over. We're going to have a big party and I can introduce him to my father-in-law. I'm sure they'd hit it off. My father-in-law was a high ranking official in the South Vietnamese government, but now he mostly just tends to his garden. I'm sure he'd be glad to give your dad some language lessons. Who knows, it might even help your father become a high school teacher someday!"

"W… Wow, really?" I stammered, shocked by the news. "That… would be… great! I'm not even sure I know what to say."

"I guess *merci* would be the word, right?" Uncle Charlie laughed.

"Yeah, I guess so," I replied. "We'll definitely be at the party," I added quickly. "This will be so good for him."

"It sounds like it could be good for both of them."

I was overjoyed by the offer. *Maybe now Dad will be happy*, I thought. *He's been down for such a long time. This could be so great! He's got all those old books with words and phrases that people don't even use anymore. It's been so hard for him to teach himself. But having someone actually give him lessons on how people talk and what people actually say would be so great!* I was so overwhelmed and grateful to Uncle Charlie for his offer and euphoric with hopes for my dad that I could barely contain myself. I wanted to jump out of the car and race over to the appliance store and tell him the good news. I could just picture my dad's smiling face when I told him that I lined up a teacher for him. His face would be so full of joy and hope – so different than how it had looked recently.

I was smiling and laughing a little to myself at how amazingly things were turning out when I heard the scream. It was loud and guttural – like an animal in great pain.

"What was that?" I quickly asked Uncle Charlie, concerned at what we had just heard.

"I think that's Sneak. Hold on back there!"

In an instant, Charles Foster turned on the powerful engine, put the car in drive, stomped on the accelerator and jammed the car's steering wheel clockwise, spinning the vehicle to the right in the direction of his nephew. My body slammed against the small backseat window as the force moved us quickly along the narrow road. Headstones and monuments flashed before us as we continued down the narrow path. Coming to the end of the small road, Uncle Charlie jammed on the brakes and the tires screamed as we turned again. This time, I braced for the turn as we sped down another narrow drive until finally coming to a stop when we saw Sneak Ryerson standing alone in front of a headstone and an arrangement of gaudy purple and white plastic flowers.

The car stopped and I quickly exited, racing forward toward my friend. "Sneak, Sneak! Are you okay?" I yelled, running at full speed as Uncle Charlie followed close behind. The young detective slowly turned to us, looking weary and a little confused, all emotion drained from his face. "What's wrong?" I asked rapidly. "You look horrible."

"Did you guys have a friend who died?" Uncle Charlie asked, after seeing his nephew's sudden change in appearance.

The young detective's body seemed to have been sapped of its energy. His head and shoulders slumped forward as he turned back to stare at the headstone and the large bouquet of plastic flowers. "Sneak, you're not lookin' too good," Uncle Charlie observed. "You... you look like you've just seen a ghost."

I had to agree after seeing my friend's pale and distressed face.

"Sneak," I asked when I reached his side. "Are you okay?"

"Crenshaw said he's been one step ahead of me," the distressed boy said in a somber voice.

"Yeah, but you got him," I said calmly. "Mr. Crenshaw's in jail now."

"In prison," Uncle Charlie gently corrected.

"Remember that letter Julian Davis read to us this morning?" Sneak asked after a moment's pause.

"Well, yeah," I replied, uncertain why my friend had even asked.

"Do you remember what it said?"

"No," I admitted.

"Eulogy," my friend said slowly. "Please leave a correct *eulogy*."

"Yeah, your uncle said that's what people say at a funeral."

He paused again.

"It could have been over so much sooner," my friend finally said in a dejected and defeated voice. "I just didn't see the clues. I feel so stupid," he added, shaking his head.

"What do you mean you feel so stupid!" I protested. "You're the smartest person I know!"

"Not as clever as Mr. Crenshaw!" my friend said, spitting out the words. "He was one step ahead of me. Maybe he still is!"

"Maybe he still is!" I said, astonished. "The old guy's in jail! Er, I mean… prison! How in the world could he be ahead of you now?"

"That's what I'm trying to figure out!" my friend said angrily. "Our new mystery – about something *big* happening tomorrow – I'm sure there's so much more Crenshaw didn't tell us about it. And since I'm going on vacation tomorrow, I don't have any way to find out what he's up to."

"Well, we can leave it all to the police," I replied confidently. "Why are you so tough on yourself anyway?"

"I'm so tough on myself," my friend began angrily, "because this is the exact headstone where Mr. Crenshaw hid that note for Julian Davis. This is where I almost caught Julian on the night I was staking out the cemetery. This is where things could have ended."

"So?" I asked. "You *almost* caught him that night, right? That's more than anybody else did in the *Case of the Mysterious Circles*. And we did catch him at the seed barn, right?" I added, attempting to reassure my friend. "Jennie and Hailey got Mr. Crenshaw while you and I and your dad got Julian Davis."

"I should have been more observant," Sneak declared remorsefully, ignoring my encouraging pleas.

"More observant!" I protested. "There's no one else on the planet who's got a photographic memory like yours!"

And then, with a sigh – in his deep and profound sadness – he pointed to the gravestone in front of us. It was a granite monument with a bouquet of gaudy purple and white plastic flowers. "What… " I began to say, as my eyes focused first on the plastic flowers until I finally noticed the letters engraved upon the gravestone:

Loving Wife
Margaret Crenshaw
1923 - 1979

"This is the grave of Mr. Crenshaw's wife?" Uncle Charlie said slowly in disbelief. "Wow!"

It took me a moment to register what Uncle Charlie was saying and what I was seeing with my own eyes.

"This… This is the grave of Mrs. Crenshaw?" I echoed. "I… I can't believe it!"

"It could have been over so much sooner," repeated my friend. "I just didn't see the clues."

"Anyone…" I started, before my friend interrupted me.

"The notes Mr. Crenshaw left for Julian Davis were placed *behind* this headstone," the young detective explained in a somber tone. "Look back there now."

Slowly, Uncle Charlie and I walked a few feet farther to look behind the headstone of Mrs. Crenshaw. To our shock, we saw a small bouquet of black lilies. They were arranged in a circle with a black cloth banner strung from one side of the circle to the other. Printed in gold lettering on the banner were the words:

RIP
Sneak Ryerson, Detective
1968 – 1980
I'll See You Under the Ground

PART TWO

CHAPTER 22

Wednesday, 3:18 pm

Jeremiah Denlon walked rapidly through the office building's wide and uncrowded lobby, his cowboy boots making loud tap-tap-taps as he crossed the long red marble floor in front of the large silver sculpture of an oil well derrick and pump. After passing the receptionists' desk – with a quick nod to the three workers who sat at the wide marble counter – Jeremiah quickly exited the building through the lobby's fast-moving revolving glass doors. Moving with purpose – as he always did – the forty-nine year old walked rapidly over the hot sidewalks to Main Street, knowing he only had a few minutes to partake in a cold chocolate dessert before the demands of his busy schedule required him to return to the office for another meeting. Although he did not usually indulge in ice cream, the short walk and ice-cold malt sounded refreshing to him on that hot summer afternoon.

A short and powerful man, Jeremiah Denlon had heard taunts about the dark color of his skin in his early years, but as an adult, his physical strength, military bearing and steady, piercing eyes persuaded those who might be menacing to steer well clear of him. Jeremiah's long tenure at Peloponnesian Oil had been marked by a steady rise up the corporate ladder. After starting as a roughneck in one of Peloponnesian's oil fields, Jeremiah soon was promoted to foreman before being drafted into the U.S. Army during the Korean War. After his discharge, he returned to

Peloponnesian and quickly took responsibility for security at the massive Bates Field outside of Midland, Texas. Then, only a few years later, Jeremiah was given the responsibility of managing the security for all the company's Texas oil fields and refineries. Soon after that, he was promoted to his current role as head of corporate security. Jeremiah's many years as Peloponnesian's corporate security chief had been unremarkable – which was just the way he liked it – as he tried to stop most major problems before they ever occurred.

Like his Old Testament namesake, Jeremiah believed deeply in the Law – in following the rules and in swift justice to those who broke them. Which was why, on his way to enjoy an ice-cold malt on a hot summer's day, he felt such a deep sense of moral indignation upon seeing two Peloponnesian managers conferring with several "kid detectives" at the downtown sandwich shop. *You gotta be kiddin' me*, he said to himself.

After spying the group through the restaurant's large glass windows, Jeremiah quickly opened the glass doors and walked directly to the orange booth where the group was meeting. "Bobbie," the corporate security chief said in his deep Texas drawl to the well-dressed woman seated with the others at the orange booth.

"Jeremiah," the woman replied in a professional tone, following the unspoken company rule that all coworkers – even managers and directors – were to be addressed by their first names or nicknames.

"Girls," Jeremiah said next, nodding in the direction of three *Sunday School Detectives* – Hailey Cotton, Lisa Lavin and Cressida Hudson – who were seated across from the woman in the booth.

"M.C.," Jeremiah rapidly addressed a lanky middle-aged man dressed in a light grey suit who had stood quickly when Jeremiah arrived.

"Jeremiah," the middle-aged man said in a halting but friendly manner as he shook the security chief's hand. "How are you these days?"

"I've been better, M.C.," the corporate security chief said coolly. "Looks like y'all are having a pretty serious discussion."

"Well, nothing too serious," the tall middle-aged man said with a nervous laugh. "Let me introduce you to my daughter and her friends," he added, as he was none other than Hailey's father, Mr. Cotton.

"I recognize y'all from the newspaper," the security chief said slowly to the young investigators. "You're part of the *Sunday School Detectives*, if I'm not mistaken."

"That's right!" interrupted Mr. Cotton, unable to stop the corporate security chief's comments.

"...and seein' as how you're meetin' here with Mrs. Duncan from our Law Department, I reckon you're talkin' about a case we resolved earlier this week."

"Well," Hailey began.

"A case about an intern, if I'm not mistaken," the security chief continued in his deep Texas voice. "By the name of Andrew Bayhill." The girls quickly glanced at each other, signaling to Jeremiah Denlon that his assumptions were correct.

"Well, I guess there's no beating around the bush with you, Jeremiah," Mr. Cotton said with a laugh. "Is there, now?"

"No," Mr. Denlon said slowly, looming over the table with a renewed and serious expression. "I like to come to the point," he added, wiping his lower lip with his index finger as the girls sat staring nervously at their examiner. "I reckon you've taken young Andy Bayhill on as your client," the security chief continued in his deep southern drawl as he looked intently at the three detectives.

"Uh," Hailey gulped nervously, trying to answer in the affirmative but finding herself intimidated by the unfriendly questions.

"And, I'm also gonna reckon that young Andy's told you that he's as innocent as a lamb on Easter Sunday."

"Well," Lisa started, hoping to do better than her friend, but also not finding the words.

"Let me tell you young detectives somethin' you need to know," Jeremiah Denlon said in a firm, unwavering voice. "We caught that boy. We caught him red-handed. He had that ole' hand of his deep in the cookie jar. And, I don't know what he told you, but we caught him *stealin'*." Mr. Denlon paused while the girls continued looking up at their interrogator. "I'm sorry to be the bearer of bad news, but that boy is guilty," the security chief continued, now shaking his head. "It's too bad too, 'cause Bobbie said he was a nice young man and a good worker – all except about that part about stealin' from the cookie jar."

"Uh... " Hailey began again, trying to interrupt.

"If I were you," the security chief continued, looking directly at the three detectives. "And I was some hot-shot young *Sunday School Detective* or someone like that, tryin' to make a name for myself, I'd leave this case well enough alone. 'Cause that boy's gonna be more trouble to you than he's worth."

"Now Jeremiah," began Roberta Duncan who, until then, had been listening quietly to the security chief.

"Now, Bobbie," Jeremiah interrupted. "We both know these kids mean well. They've done a good job helping out their other clients here in town – I know that. I've read about them in the paper and I've heard about them from my sources. And I'm sure they want to do good by young Andy too. But you know as well as I do, that boy's as guilty as the sky is blue and the benches in here are no color that exists out in God's nature. There's no denying it. You even saw the evidence with your own eyes!"

"Well, I did see him take the papers *out* of his briefcase, but I didn't see –" Roberta Duncan began with precise clipped words.

"These kids don't need to be goin' on some wild goose chase," Jeremiah Denlon interrupted, now speaking more passionately. "Right? They'd be chasin' after what? Nothin'! Findin' what? Nothin'!" He paused dramatically. "What date is it today?" Mr. Denlon asked, momentarily looking up to the ceiling. "The beginnin' of July, right? Who knows, these kids could be spending the rest of their summer vacation lookin' for clues – only to find out that all the evidence leads right back to where they started. And who might that be? Their own client, Andrew Bayhill! It'd be a waste of time! Why don't you kids just enjoy your summer, if you know what's good for ya," he added ominously.

"Jeremiah… " Roberta Duncan tried again.

"Their client's as guilty as sin," Mr. Denlon said firmly to his coworker. "I know it. You know it. And, I think they should know it too."

"But, maybe he's not," Roberta Duncan began.

"But he is. He is," the corporate security chief said, shaking his head. "There's nothin' that will make me change my mind. Sometimes we get a rotten apple in the apple barrel. Sometimes we don't! But this time we did, and his name was Andrew Bayhill. It'd be a pity for these kids to waste their time tryin' to prove otherwise." He stopped and again paused dramatically. "And another thing," Mr. Denlon added, looking first at Mr. Cotton, then to Mrs. Duncan. "It'd be a pity to waste the valuable time of the good people of Peloponnesian Oil too, don't you think? Our time is *valuable* – we shouldn't be helpin' some kids go off on some wild goose chase that's tryin' to help a boy who we've already proven is guilty. Right?" Then, turning again to the three detectives he warned, "I'd leave well enough alone if I were you."

"Jeremiah!" Roberta Duncan protested.

"We've got bigger fish to worry about than Andy Bayhill," the security chief resolved. "There's that mess in Iran we've got to keep our eyes on," he said, referring to the Iranian Revolution and the hostage crisis. "And there's all those refugees comin' in from Cuba over the last few months. Who knows what that's gonna do to the price of oil! Plus, we're doin' everything we can to avoid another crisis with O.P.E.C. and another round of embargos. I just don't want these kids wastin' their time and gettin' in the way of the good work our people at Peloponnesian are tryin' to do across the street!"

Jeremiah Denlon paused for a moment as his audience remained quiet. Then, letting out a deep breath he concluded, "Well, I've said my piece. I'm gonna skedaddle. It seems I've lost my appetite for my malted. Just thinkin' about you fool hardy kids has taken my appetite away."

"Jeremiah!" Roberta Duncan protested again.

"Bobbie, girls, M.C.," the security chief said, nodding his head to the group. "I'll be on my way."

"Let... let me walk with you back to the office." Mr. Cotton said quickly, as he followed the security chief to the front door of the restaurant. "See ya Hailey," her father said rapidly, as he turned his head to flash a smile to his daughter.

The four who remained at the table paused momentarily as they watched the two middle-aged men exit the restaurant and cross the street.

"Wow," Lisa Lavin eventually said. "That was so intense. Is he always like that?"

"Oh, don't worry about Jeremiah," Roberta Duncan said in a calm voice. "I'm sure he's got a lot on his mind. He's got an awful lot of things to worry about."

"Like those things he mentioned?" asked Lisa.

"Yeah," agreed the older woman with a reassuring smile. "There's always a lot going on – mostly with our gas stations, but sometimes with our oil wells and refineries." Her voice dropped as her expression became serious. "And sometimes even here at the General Office, too. And, I'm sure, walking in here and seeing me talking with you three detectives probably didn't sit too well with him either," she added with a laugh.

"I don't think it did," agreed Hailey as the others laughed.

"That's okay. But, you heard him, right? He thinks he's got *his man*."

"Yeah, he seemed pretty certain," said Hailey.

"But, we've just got to convince him otherwise, right?" Roberta Duncan added. "I'm glad you kids are looking into it."

"Well, that's good to hear!" Hailey said, smiling. "For a minute there, I thought we were going to be off the case!"

CHAPTER 23

Wednesday, 2:55 pm

The three *Sunday School Detectives* – Hailey Cotton, Lisa Lavin and Cressida Hudson – arrived at Wilson's Hamburgers a few minutes before three o'clock on Wednesday afternoon. After meeting with Dr. Bayhill at his office in the morning, Alice Williams, the young scientist, drove the three downtown where they had lunch and shopped at a shoe store called The Children's Place – with its distinctive yellow shopping bags – before Alice returned to her work at the biology lab. "It's too bad Alice decided to go back to the lab," Lisa said to the others when they arrived at the famous hamburger shop. "I think she's really gonna miss out."

"Yeah, this afternoon should be interesting," Hailey agreed.

"Here comes your dad," Cressida said softly to Hailey when she saw Mr. Cotton enter through the glass doors at the entrance of the restaurant.

"Hey girls," smiled Mr. Cotton.

"Hi Mr. Cotton," Lisa and her cousin said in near unison.

"Hey Dad," Hailey smiled as she welcomed her father.

"Wow, it sure is hot out there," Mr. Cotton declared, wiping his forehead below short salt and pepper hair, parted to the left and recently cut by Smitty, a downtown barber. Soon, he was pulling on the lapel of his light grey suit, trying to get more air to a starched white shirt under a bright red tie. "I tell ya, it's not as hot as working out in the hayfields of Colorado, but today sure is a hot one. Out there I needed a water bag to stay cool," he added with a smile as Hailey rolled her eyes at hearing the familiar story. "It sure is a good thing it's air conditioned in most of these places," her father added with a laugh.

"Yeah," one of the girls agreed.

"Thanks again for doing this, Dad," Hailey smiled encouragingly.

"It'll be okay, as long as I don't get fired for this crazy stunt of yours," laughed Mr. Cotton.

"It's not as crazy as some of Moscow's stunts, right?" quizzed Lisa knowingly.

"No, no. It's not as crazy as some of the stuff he's pulled," replied Mr. Cotton as the other girls laughed. "That showboat," Hailey's father mused. "But, this plan of yours doesn't seem to be the wisest thing I've agreed to."

"Now Dad," Hailey said seriously. "There's absolutely nothing wrong with you running into an old friend of yours *and* your daughter *and* her friends at the same time, right?"

"I guess not," replied Mr. Cotton before pausing. "You kids," he added, shaking his head.

"So, you're all set on the plan, right Dad?" Hailey asked quickly.

"I guess so," her father chuckled.

"She'll be here at three o'clock, sharp, right?"

"She said she would."

"Is that her crossing the street?" Lisa Lavin asked suddenly, seeing a well-dressed woman approach from Main Street.

"Yep, that's her – she's right on time," Mr. Cotton affirmed.

"Okay," Hailey said calmly. "We'll walk around the building and meet you back here in a few minutes."

"I hope this crazy plan of yours works," Mr. Cotton lamented, as he smiled at his daughter. "If not, I'm a goner."

"I'm... I'm sure it will all work out," said Hailey, trying to sound confident. "What could go wrong?"

"I can think of a few things!" her father exclaimed, wide-eyed. "But, I guess I could always go back to the Colorado hayfields!"

"Thanks again, Dad!" Hailey said as she gave her father a hug and then rapidly followed her friends out the side exit of the restaurant.

CHAPTER 24

Wednesday, 2:58 pm

Roberta Duncan had legal procedures on her mind as she walked across the lobby of the Peloponnesian Oil Company headquarters. Her expensive shoes – purple dress pumps with rounded toes – matched the color of the wool blend Saks Fifth Avenue long skirt and blazer that she wore over a white blouse. The noise of her shoes echoed throughout the open space of the nearly empty lobby as they hit the red marble floor and she passed the large silver sculpture of an oil derrick and pump on her way to the revolving doors. Roberta, who was known as Bobbie to her friends, loved her work, and had been with the company for over thirty years. She enjoyed spending her days assisting paralegals in their work for the company attorneys. With her many years of experience, she found it easy to help solve problems and coach the younger workers through the difficult challenges they faced with legal briefs or research. She almost always found the work interesting – *something different every day*, she told her friends. But recently, she had found herself feeling melancholy as her mind drifted to thoughts of retirement, something she knew would be coming soon – even though her preference would be to work at the company forever.

Crossing Main Street, Mrs. Duncan was deep in thought, recalling a recent conversation with a young paralegal regarding a tricky case on trademark infringement. She barely noticed the three young women who were quickly exiting the side door of the iconic restaurant in front of her. Hoping to avoid the gaze of the Law Department manager, the three hastily retreated to the rear of the building near the drive-through. *When I return, I need to tell Diana about that case from Spartanburg,* Mrs. Duncan thought as she entered the sandwich shop, recalling a similar trademark case from several years earlier. *My notes from that old case could really help her now.* "Marcus Claudius!" Mrs. Duncan soon exclaimed with a smile as she approached Mr. Cotton who was standing near the entrance. Although most people used his initials, his old friends, including Roberta Duncan, continued to use Mr. Cotton's given name. "I was surprised to get your call," she added. "It's so good to see you. It's been far too long."

"It's good to see you too, Bobbie," said Mr. Cotton. "You haven't changed a bit since I started working for Peloponnesian in 1966!"

"Well, I know that's not true! But it's not every day I get invited to get a malt at Wilson's! What are you up to these days? You're not in any kind of legal trouble, are you?"

"Oh no, no," Mr. Cotton said, shaking his head as they walked closer to the loud clangs of the cash register. "I'm not in any kind of trouble." He paused for a moment, then asked, "Can't an old friend just invite another old friend to get a malt on a hot summer's day?"

"Well, I guess so," Mrs. Duncan said doubtfully as they joined the line to place their orders. "So, how are those kids of yours?" she asked.

"Oh, they're good, they're good," Mr. Cotton replied hesitantly as the two moved forward in the fast-moving line. They quickly ordered and Mr. Cotton paid the cashier from a silver money clip that he took from his pocket.

"And how about that daredevil son of yours?" Mrs. Duncan asked after they received their malts and moved to an empty orange booth in the restaurant. "How's he getting along?"

"He's good," Mr. Cotton explained as they took seats across from each other. "Moscow hasn't broken any bones this entire week!"

"Well that is good!" Mrs. Duncan affirmed, as they both laughed.

"Actually, it's been a while since he's broken anything," continued Mr. Cotton. "But, you know him – he's always racing something or jumping over one thing or another, trying to be a showboat. Just give him some time and something else will break!"

"Yeah," Mrs. Duncan said whimsically. "And how about your daughter? I'll bet she's turning into quite a young lady."

"She is, she is," replied Mr. Cotton, before quickly changing the subject. "And how about your kids?"

"Oh, you know," Roberta Duncan replied as her voice changed from light-hearted to a more serious tone. "I don't see them too often. One's in Cleveland and the other is in Chicago. They don't make it home too often. I try to see the grandkids when I can – but they're all so busy."

"Oh, that's too bad."

"Yeah... Well, what can you do about it? So, now Marcus, what did you want to talk about this afternoon?" Mrs. Duncan asked matter-of-factly, leaning forward as her spoon swirled her chocolate malt.

"Well, it's always good to catch up," Mr. Cotton said cautiously. "And give you an update about my kids and all..."

"Yes?"

"And... Oh hey," Mr. Cotton said in a surprised voice. "Speaking of my kids – wouldn't you know it, my daughter just walked in!"

Soon, the three girls bounded up to the orange restaurant booth.

"Hi Dad!" Hailey said with a wide smile, as she gave her father a hug.

"Well, isn't this a surprise!" said Mr. Cotton enthusiastically.

"Hi Mr. Cotton!" Lisa and Cressida said in unison.

"Do you remember Mrs. Duncan?" Mr. Cotton asked his daughter. "You might have met her at a Christmas party, or barbeque or someplace like that."

"Oh, I think so," said Hailey in a friendly tone as she smiled at her father's guest. "These are my friends, Lisa and Cressida."

"Nice to meet you," said Lisa.

"Yes, nice to meet you, Mrs. Duncan," Cressida added quietly.

"Nice to meet you young ladies too," Roberta Duncan said cautiously. "But please, call me Bobbie. No need for you kids to use formalities with me."

"Can we join you?" Hailey asked hopefully.

"Well... sure," said Mr. Cotton in a halting manner. "We were just talking about you and Moscow and Bobbie's kids."

"That's great!" declared Hailey as the three girls took seats at the booth.

"Well, this is *quite* a coincidence if you ask me, M.C.," the Law Department manager said with a laugh as she looked at Mr. Cotton and then to his daughter and then to her friends.

"What do you mean?" Hailey asked innocently.

"Well, the odds of this are just incredible!"

"The odds?" Hailey asked surprised.

"The odds of me meeting Findlay's own *Sunday School Detectives* here, today."

"Oh, well, uh," Hailey began.

"And the timing of it!" Mrs. Duncan continued.

"The... what?" gulped Hailey.

"The timing," Mrs. Duncan said laughing. "Meeting you – some of our city's most famous detectives – just a few days after I've had one of the most interesting cases of theft that I've ever encountered in my thirty years at work!"

"Really?" asked Hailey.

"You don't say?" asked Lisa.

"If I didn't know any better, I'd say this was an ambush!" Roberta Duncan laughed.

"A what?" Lisa asked loudly.

"A *set up*," said the older woman. "You know, to try to get some information out of me. Maybe for a case you're working on?"

"I think she's on to us!" Mr. Cotton said to the girls with a smile.

"You're probably right," Lisa admitted.

"I'm sorry," Hailey said quickly. "We didn't think you'd want to meet with us up in your office if we had called to make an appointment. And I knew that you and Dad were old friends, so I thought this would be the best way for us to talk."

"Oh, it's alright," Roberta Duncan said reassuringly. "I should have figured someone would be looking into the case for Andrew. I just didn't think it would be the *Sunday School Detectives*. Why don't you go and get yourselves a malt or a pop or something to drink and come back here and we'll talk about it."

"Great!" said Hailey.

"Cool beans," said Cressida softly as the three girls stood.

"Uh, can I have some money Dad?" Hailey asked.

"You sound just like my grandkids!" Roberta Duncan laughed.

"Wow, you're a lot of work today!" Mr. Cotton said to his daughter with a laugh, but soon he was getting money from his silver money clip – a clip with a large Peloponnesian Oil logo on its front. The back of the metal clip was equipped with a small nail file, pen knife, and golf ball marker also in the shape of the company logo.

"So, you tried to pull a *fast one*, huh, M.C.?" Roberta Duncan laughed when the young women left to order their malts and drinks.

"A fast one?" Mr. Cotton said innocently. "Of course not! The girls just wanted to talk to you about the case. And I was pretty sure you wouldn't want them up to your office."

"Well that's true! They would have had a hard time getting through all the new security on the eighth floor!" Roberta Duncan added, referring to the location of the Law Department.

"I heard Jeremiah put someone up there."

"Actually, he put *several* people up there with us," Mrs. Duncan replied in a serious tone. "But, I'm glad you contacted me. This corporate espionage case has been bothering me all week."

"Why's that?" asked Mr. Cotton.

"Because I'm not so sure Andrew Bayhill – the boy we caught with the files – is guilty."

CHAPTER 25

Wednesday, 3:08 pm

The three *Sunday School Detectives* – Hailey Cotton, Lisa Lavin and Cressida Hudson – returned with their chocolate malts to an orange booth at Wilson's Hamburgers to join Mr. Cotton and Roberta Duncan, the manager from the Law Department, who were deep in conversation.

"Mrs. Duncan's just told me something really interesting," Hailey's father informed the group.

"What's that, Dad?" Hailey asked.

"She said she's not sure your client is guilty."

"Really?" Lisa asked, leaning forward.

"Why not?" Cressida asked, as the girls put their black notepads on the table.

"Well, there are a couple of reasons," Mrs. Duncan replied. "But mostly based on the documents that Andrew had in his possession."

"He told us they were all marked with words like TOP SECRET, but he didn't know what they were about," said Hailey.

Andrew's manager laughed at the comments. "We don't have any documents stamped TOP SECRET! That sounds more like a government document, or a spy thing, or something like that. We use stamps that say CONFIDENTIAL and FOR INTERNAL USE ONLY." Mrs. Duncan paused for a moment before asking, "What else did Andrew tell you about the documents?"

"He said he just saw the big stamps on the front page," Lisa replied.

"Oh, and who they were written *to*," Hailey explained in a hushed tone. "The Company President."

"And who wrote them," added Cressida. "The Director of the Law Department."

"Right," Hailey agreed.

"Well, I can't tell you all of the specific details," Roberta Duncan said carefully. "But I can tell you that he was correct with that description. And they were definitely confidential and for our internal use."

"Okay," said Hailey, writing some words in her black notepad.

"And," Mrs. Duncan continued. "It's been communicated to other managers, so I can tell you, Marcus. A few of those memos had to do with *Project 81*."

"Oh yeah, I did hear about that," said Mr. Cotton knowingly.

"You're a *Project 81 manager*, right Dad?" asked Hailey.

"In the Accounting Department," Mr. Cotton clarified.

"Plus," Mrs. Duncan continued, speaking in a hushed tone to Mr. Cotton. "Another one of the memos had to do with potential takeover scenarios – through a hostile acquisition."

"About us taking over another company?" Mr. Cotton asked in a surprised tone.

"No, the opposite – if someone were to try to take us over. It even listed potential *white knights*," she added, referring to friendly companies who might buy Peloponnesian in the event of a hostile takeover.

"Wow, that is interesting," said Mr. Cotton.

"Why would your company want to keep all that secret?" asked Lisa.

"Well," Mrs. Duncan began. "Other companies would find that kind of information really valuable. If they were planning on taking over Peloponnesian, they would know exactly how we would respond."

"So, they'd know the company's…" Hailey began.

"Strategy," said Mr. Cotton.

"Right… strategy," Hailey summarized.

"Knowing how we'd respond to different situations could really be helpful to our competitors," Mr. Cotton explained.

"Exactly," Roberta Duncan agreed.

"It's like a spy giving plans to the other side," Cressida said quietly.

"That's right," confirmed Roberta Duncan. "That's exactly what's happened… or almost happened. We don't really know the full extent of the information getting out to our competitors."

"So, Mrs. Duncan," Lisa interrupted. "You told Hailey's dad that you didn't think Andrew Bayhill took the papers?"

"Well, the evidence against him looks pretty bad," confirmed the manager from the Law Department. "But – the interesting thing is – he never would have processed any of those files at his desk."

"What do you mean?" asked Hailey.

"Well, I don't know if he explained his job to you... " Roberta Duncan began.

"He did," Lisa interrupted quickly, hoping not to hear the detailed description of Andrew's work again. "He told us how he moved papers from old file folders and put them into new folders with new numbers."

"That's right! And did he tell you how old those files were?" Mrs. Duncan asked with a smile.

"I don't think so," Lisa answered.

"They were *ancient*," Roberta Duncan continued as the girls laughed. "I mean, they were *really* old. I would *never* let one of our new interns handle any confidential documents. So, if Andrew happened to process any files that had a *Confidential* or *Internal Use Only* stamp, they would have been out-of-date by at least twenty years!"

"Twenty years!" Lisa exclaimed.

"So, he didn't work with any new files?" Hailey asked.

"No," said Andrew's manager. "He was only assigned to work with the *old* ones, at least that's what I told the Records Department to bring him."

"That is really interesting," said Hailey as she wrote some words in her black notepad.

"You see," Mrs. Duncan continued. "All of the *new* files are stored in a locked room inside of our Records Department. And only our long-term employees have a key. Because, as you can imagine, the contents of those files are quite important to our company. We wouldn't want them in the hands of inexperienced summer interns."

"Makes sense," replied Mr. Cotton.

"So, you're positive that Andrew didn't work with any of the files he was caught with?" Hailey asked.

"Those files should never have crossed his desk," Roberta Duncan confirmed.

"How about... Jimmy... Jimmy Mannix?" Lisa asked, looking at her notepad.

"Yes?" Mrs. Duncan asked with a surprised look, astonished that the young detectives had already gathered the names of her other employees. "What about Jimmy?"

"Jimmy works on *Project 81* stuff, right?" Lisa wondered. "And it sounds like there was *Project 81* stuff in some of the stolen papers."

"Right. Well, he does work on *Project 81*," confirmed Roberta Duncan matter-of-factly. "But, he's an intern too. So, he wouldn't have access to those confidential files either."

"Oh... okay, thanks," said Lisa, as she turned back to the pages in her notepad to words that she had written earlier in the day from their interview with the young intern. "And how about the other people in Andrew's office – Jason and Paula?"

"Jason and Paula are both long-term employees with Peloponnesian," Roberta Duncan continued in her matter-of-fact tone. "They have access to that locked area."

"So, Jason and Paula have keys. How many other people have a key?" Hailey wondered. "You know, to that locked room in the Records Department?"

"Well, a lot of people actually," explained Mrs. Duncan. "Nearly all of the employees in the Law Department have a key and most of the employees in the Records Department too."

"Oh," Hailey replied with a frown as she looked at the other *Sunday School Detectives*, dreading the news that the number of suspects had just increased by a large number.

"We're going to change that policy soon," Mrs. Duncan explained. "So it is limited to only a few managers."

"That sounds like a good plan," Mr. Cotton said encouragingly.

"Going back to Andrew Bayhill," Lisa interjected. "You said he didn't work with the papers he got caught with."

"But that still doesn't mean he didn't take them," Hailey's father added, now keenly interested in the investigation.

"Hey Dad, you're supposed to be *helping* us with the case," Hailey said with a smile.

"Oh, sorry," Mr. Cotton laughed.

"Marcus is right," Roberta Duncan added. "Andrew still could have taken those documents."

"But how?" Lisa asked with a furrowed brow.

"Well, there could have been a lot of different ways. I've talked with several supervisors about this over the last few days and we've thought of a couple of scenarios. First, the door to the Records Room could have been unlocked – that happens sometimes – so, Andrew could have just walked in there and grabbed the memos. A second scenario is that someone in the Records Department could have accidentally sent them up to him. He was receiving cart after cart of files every day, so, there could have been a mix-up. Even though I told them to bring him the oldest files, they could have brought him the newest ones instead. And a third scenario we've considered is that he could have been working with someone in the Records Department – maybe a *partner in crime* who gave him the documents to take out of the office."

"Wow," said Lisa. "Explaining it like that makes it sound like he really did steal the papers. But you still think he's innocent?"

"I do," Roberta Duncan said in a serious voice, leaning in towards the others. "And let me tell you why. First, Andrew just started with us and didn't have too many friends at the office, so the idea of him working with an *accomplice*, like someone from the Records Department, really doesn't make sense to me. So, if that option is eliminated, that just leaves the possibility of him working alone to commit the crime. But, here's the thing that makes me really doubt he was involved: if he took the papers from the Records Department, he would have had to know the *precise* location of the files within that locked room in different file cabinets. It's not like we have a big sign that says '*Look here for our important files*'. Those memos are some of the most important things our company wants to keep secret."

"Well, that and our daily production totals," Mr. Cotton added.

"You're definitely right about that, M.C." Roberta Duncan added. "And actually, one of the memos had some information about that too."

"Really?" Mr. Cotton said in surprise.

"Yeah," Mrs. Duncan affirmed, shaking her head.

"Wow, that's amazing," Mr. Cotton added.

"And what's so important about the daily production totals, Mr. Cotton?" Lisa asked, looking at her notes.

"Well, they're really, really important for us," Hailey's father explained. "You see, our stock price is based on our oil production. So, if someone knew that information in advance – before we reported out our quarterly numbers – they could do all kinds of things that could hurt our company. If our production totals were lower than expected, the person could take a *short position* – which means they would make money when our stock price decreases. Or, vice-versa. And that's just assuming we're talking about one individual knowing that information in advance. It's pretty amazing to think about, but if a *big company* got that information, they could make even bigger kinds of trouble for us. They could take huge stakes in our company knowing that our stock price would increase in the future. It could really make us vulnerable for a takeover, or even put us out of business."

"Got it," said Lisa as she wrote more words in her notepad. "So, your company really wanted to keep these memos a secret."

"Oh yes, absolutely," confirmed Mrs. Duncan. "We really want to keep that information secret. And… speaking of *not* keeping something secret," she added in a measured tone, looking past the girls to the glass window at the front of the restaurant. "Here comes Jeremiah Denlon. He's not going to be too happy to see me talking with you young ladies about the case."

"Who's that?" asked Lisa, turning to look at the man in a black suit who was quickly opening the glass door to the restaurant.

"He's our chief of security," Mr. Cotton said with a sigh as they turned to watch the man quickly walk toward them. "Hailey, why don't you let me handle this," Mr. Cotton added. "You girls don't need to say anything. Jeremiah and I go back a long time. We first met when I had to audit the books out on a small Texas oil field where he was working. And, we actually have a tee time together at *Wayside* this Saturday."

"Okay Dad," Hailey said as the security chief approached.

CHAPTER 26

Wednesday, 3:25 pm

Hailey Cotton's hands were trembling as she held her cold malt at the hamburger shop. Just moments before, Jeremiah Denlon – the chief of security at Peloponnesian Oil – had departed the restaurant with her father. *I hope Dad doesn't get fired for this,* she thought as she watched her father walk out of the sandwich shop, concerned about the consequences of being caught interviewing Roberta Duncan – a manager in the company's Law Department and an important witness in their case.

The four who remained at the table paused momentarily as they watched the two middle-aged men exit the restaurant and cross the street.

"Wow," Lisa Lavin eventually said. "That was so intense. Is he always like that?"

"Oh, don't worry about Jeremiah," Roberta Duncan said in a calm voice. "I'm sure he's got a lot on his mind. He's got an awful lot of things to worry about."

"Like those things he mentioned?" asked Lisa.

"Yeah," agreed the older woman with a reassuring smile. "There's always a lot going on – mostly with our gas stations, but sometimes with our oil wells and refineries." Her voice dropped as her expression became serious. "And sometimes even here at the General Office, too. And, I'm sure, walking in here and seeing me talking with you three detectives probably didn't sit too well with him either," she added with a laugh.

"I don't think it did," agreed Hailey as the others laughed.

"That's okay. But, you heard him, right? He thinks he's *got his man*."

"Yeah, he seemed pretty certain," said Hailey.

"But, we've just got to convince him otherwise, right?" Roberta Duncan added. "I'm glad you kids are looking into it."

"Well, that's good to hear!" Hailey said, smiling. "For a minute there, I thought we were going to be off the case!"

"Oh no," Mrs. Duncan said with a smile. "Not if I have anything to do with it!"

"Andrew Bayhill will be glad to hear that," said Lisa.

"He'd be happier if you could clear his name," said Andrew's supervisor matter-of-factly. "You girls better get cracking."

"Right," Hailey replied as she quickly looked in her black notepad on the table. "Let's get going with more questions."

"Sounds good," Roberta Duncan said with a smile, as Lisa Lavin and Cressida Hudson readied their pens above their notepads while Hailey quickly turned to the inside cover of her notepad and read eight questions:

What is the mystery?

When did it happen?

Who did it happen to?

What evidence has been gathered?

Who are the witnesses?

What really happened?

Why did it happen?

Who did it?

"So, I think we're clear on what the mystery is, right? We're trying to figure out why Andrew had a bunch of documents in his briefcase."

"Right," Andrew's supervisor replied.

"Oh, Mrs. Duncan," said Lisa. "We were wondering earlier, has anything like that ever happened before? You know, before Andrew started working there?"

"No, not that I'm aware of. We were all so shocked when it happened. Andrew seemed like such a nice boy. He really was a good worker. We just couldn't believe he would be involved in something like that."

"Andrew said it happened on Monday," Hailey continued. "On his way out of work, right?"

"That's right," Roberta Duncan replied. "A security guard stopped him in the lobby, on his way out."

"And," Hailey continued hesitantly, "Andrew told us that you rode down on the same elevator with him as he was leaving." At this question, Lisa and Cressida glanced at each other, remembering their earlier theory that Mrs. Duncan had put the papers in Andrew's briefcase.

"Right, we rode down together."

"Did you see anything suspicious while you were on the elevator?" Lisa asked.

"No," Mrs. Duncan replied firmly.

"And how about when he got stopped? Did you see him when the security guard stopped him in the lobby?" Hailey asked.

"I... did," Andrew's manager admitted slowly. "I was sort of standing back... near the elevators... watching."

"That's quite a coincidence," said Hailey.

"Well, not exactly," Roberta Duncan admitted.

"Why's that?" asked Lisa, confused.

"Because I was the one who pointed out Andrew to the security guard!" Andrew's manager confessed with a sigh.

"What!" the three girls replied in unison.

"It sounds kind of funny now," said Mrs. Duncan. "You know, because *now* I'm telling you that I think Andrew is innocent. But it's true, I was the one who called security on him."

"Why was that?" asked Hailey abruptly.

"Were the papers sticking out of his briefcase, or something like that?" Lisa questioned.

"No, no," Mrs. Duncan replied, holding up her hands. "I didn't see the papers, or anything like that. It's actually because of the man we were just talking to – Jeremiah Denlon. He asked me to be on the lookout."

"Really," said Hailey, who was now busily taking notes.

"He called me that morning," Roberta Duncan explained.

"Monday morning?" Hailey asked.

"Correct," the manager from the Law Department continued. "He told me that one of his contacts at another company – I think someone at SOHIO in Cleveland, or maybe someone in Indiana – I can't remember where. But anyway, someone told Jeremiah that they had been contacted about buying our company secrets."

"Wow," the girls nearly said in unison.

"Did Mr. Denlon's friend say they were going to buy the papers?" Lisa asked quickly.

"No, no. They probably knew it was a pretty risky thing to do."

"And the wrong thing to do too," said Cressida.

"Correct," said Roberta Duncan. "Maybe Jeremiah's contact didn't want to get into trouble. I don't know. But the bottom line was, they didn't want to buy the stolen documents, so they called Jeremiah instead."

"Got it," said Lisa.

"So, anyway," Mrs. Duncan continued. "When Jeremiah asked his contact what types of documents were being offered, his contact told him about the things we've been talking about – memos about our most important project..."

"*Project 81*, right?" asked Lisa.

"Correct, plus documents about how we'd respond to a hostile takeover, our production totals and those sorts of things."

"Wow," said Hailey.

"Wow is right!" said Roberta Duncan. "I was flabbergasted when I heard the news. Anyway, with all of the specific things that Jeremiah had learned from his contact, he was able to narrow down a list of personnel to only three departments."

"How's that?" asked Lisa.

"Because only three departments have access to *all* of that information. Other departments would only know pieces. So, Production Accounting, for example, would only have access to the production totals, but not to the information about hostile takeovers. It's the same with the Tax Department or Revenue Accounting – people in those departments would only know about *some* of those things, but not all of them."

"Ah, got it," said Lisa. "So, what were those departments that would have access to everything?" she asked, writing quickly in her notepad.

"Legal," Roberta Duncan explained slowly as the girls wrote down the words. "The Records Department and the Executive suite."

"Thanks," said Lisa.

"So, after Jeremiah told me the news," Mrs. Duncan continued, "he asked me to report anyone who was acting suspiciously in the Law Department and he said he would contact the managers in the Records Department and ask them to do the same thing."

"So, report anyone, huh?" said Lisa.

"Right!" said Mrs. Duncan. "I think I even laughed and said something like, 'How in the world am I supposed to figure that out?'"

"That couldn't have been easy, right?" asked Hailey.

"Right! And it was really strange, too! You know, looking at all of the people who work for me and wondering, 'Is this person stealing our documents? Is that the one who called SOHIO to sell our company secrets?' It was weird! And I wasn't even sure if the documents had been stolen and already out the door – or, if the culprit was planning on taking them sometime in the future. Or, if it was all a big joke! I just didn't know!" The Law Department manager paused. "I have to admit, it was quite unsettling – not knowing if one of our colleagues was stealing corporate secrets."

"And there are a lot of people who work for you, right?" asked Lisa.

"Right. All of the paralegals, clerks, summer interns… "

"So, with so many people working for you," Hailey interrupted, "how did you notice Andrew? When did he become a suspect? Did he do something suspicious?"

"Well," Roberta Duncan began. "I want to make it clear – I never saw him take the papers or anything like that. In fact – like I said – he was a really good worker. Every day he'd process those old files – one after another. Most days, he'd get done with his work so quickly that he'd have to wait around for the Records Department to bring him more."

"So what was it?" Lisa asked impatiently. "What made you suspect Andrew?"

"Well, it wasn't me, exactly. It was actually his coworkers. First, there was Paula – her desk is right next to Andrew's. She asked me if I had noticed that Andrew was acting funny. And I told her, 'No, I hadn't'. And she said, 'He sure is acting nervous.'"

"Nervous?" Lisa said, writing in her notepad.

"Then, not too long after that, Jason – one of his other coworkers – came into my office and told me nearly the exact same thing!"

"So, both Paula Bigelow and Jason Compton told you that Andrew was acting nervous?" Hailey asked, adding the last names of Andrew's coworkers after consulting her notes from earlier in the day.

"Right! It was really strange."

"Had they ever told you that before?" Lisa asked.

"No," said Roberta Duncan. "And I hadn't really noticed Andrew acting that way. But they said he was doing all kinds of strange things – loudly tapping a pencil for a long time, nervously shuffling papers and a few other things."

"So, that's what made you suspect Andrew?" Lisa asked.

"Yes, that was all! I didn't think it was a big deal. But, Jeremiah asked me to report anything that seemed out of the ordinary. And what Paula and Jason told me was definitely out of the ordinary. So, near the end of the afternoon, I called Jeremiah. It was just before Andrew was ready to leave, so Jeremiah arranged for a security guard to meet me in the lobby. And, because the guard didn't know what Andrew looked like, he asked me to identify Andrew. I honestly thought it would take a minute or two for them to see that Andrew was innocent of anything and send him on his way – I had no idea those papers were in his briefcase. I watched in disbelief as the whole thing unfolded right in front of me: the security guard stopping him… then asking him to open up his brief-case… then finding the documents in there! It was shocking! I followed them down to the basement where there's a room with a two-way mirror that we use for our interviews, sometimes. And I watched them question Andrew. And girls, if you thought Jeremiah was angry when he spoke with you earlier, imagine him at about ten times that level. He was so upset with Andrew and those papers they found."

"Wow," one of the young detectives replied. "That must have been intense."

"It was," explained Andrew's supervisor. "But, after watching for only a few minutes, I knew that Andrew was innocent. He had absolutely no idea what was going on. He didn't know anything about the impor-tance of the memos or how they got in his briefcase."

"So now that you've had a few days to think about it… " Hailey began.

"Who do *I* think did it?" Roberta Duncan interrupted.

"Right," said Hailey, impressed that the woman had anticipated her question.

"That's the million-dollar question, right? And to be honest, I have no idea."

"Oh," said Hailey, disappointed. "I was hoping you could point us to another suspect."

"Sorry," Roberta Duncan said, shaking her head. "I can't think of anybody – and I've spent a lot of time thinking about it! I don't know who else it could be. Part of me wonders if the whole thing with Andrew might have been a set-up – you know, to distract us from the real person."

"What do you mean?" asked Lisa.

"Well, think about it," Mrs. Duncan continued. "We were so focused on investigating Andrew and going through *his* briefcase and interviewing *him* and looking at who *he* might have been working with in the Records Department, that the real corporate spy could have copied those memos and just waltzed on out the door on Monday afternoon without anyone noticing."

"Hmm, that's an interesting theory," said Hailey as she wrote some words in her notepad. "So, catching Andrew might have been a distraction from looking at the real criminal?"

"Maybe," Mrs. Duncan replied. "I wish I could give you some more suspects, but I don't think I can."

"Well," Lisa began as she studied her notes. "Your idea actually gives us *two* really important suspects."

"Two?" asked Mrs. Duncan. "Who would that be?"

"Paula and Jason," explained Lisa.

"How could they be…. suspects?" asked the manager from the Law Department.

"Because they're the ones who encouraged you to turn your attention *towards* Andrew and *away* from everyone else," explained Lisa.

"Well, I don't know about that," said Roberta Duncan, shaking her head. "I can't imagine they'd be involved in this."

"Could they be working together?" Cressida asked in her quiet voice.

"Jason and Paula?" Roberta laughed. "I don't think so." She paused to consider the idea. "I mean, they get along fine at work, but they aren't the best of friends or anything like that."

"Well, it looks like Paula and Jason are at the top of our list of suspects," said Hailey. "Is there anyone else who comes to mind?"

"No," said Roberta Duncan. "I really can't picture anyone in my department doing this."

"One of the things I was wondering about… " Lisa continued.

"Yes?" asked Mrs. Duncan.

"…is what about the *other* people processing the files? You said that you didn't suspect Andrew because he was working with the *old* files –

and the papers he was caught with were newer – right? So, who in your department was working with the *new* files?"

"Ah, well," Roberta Duncan paused for a moment. "That would be Paula and Jason."

"Paula and Jason?" Lisa said loudly. "So, you're telling us that they told you that Andrew was acting strange *and* they were also the ones who worked on the files Andrew got caught with?"

"Yes, that's right," Andrew's supervisor said quickly. "They would have worked with those files at some point over the past few months and put them into new folders with our new numbering system. I'm not sure which papers passed through which one's desk, but they definitely would have worked with those documents."

"It sounds like they're definitely our Number One suspects," said Lisa as she looked at her fellow detectives.

"And you said their desks are right next to his," Cressida said softly. "Right?"

"Right," Lisa agreed forcefully. Then, addressing Roberta Duncan, she added, "It would have been pretty easy for them to put those papers in Andrew's briefcase when he was away from the office and then go tell you that Andrew was acting really weird."

"I don't know," doubted Mrs. Duncan, shaking her head. "Like I said, I just can't see either one of them doing something like that. I mean, Paula's a mother of three young kids. She and her husband are strapped for cash a lot of the time, but I can't see her risking her job over this. And Jason, he lives with his grandparents! They aren't in very good health. I think he spends a lot of time taking care of them. I know they have a lot of medical bills, but I can't see him risking going to jail and leaving his grandparents' care to someone else. It just doesn't make sense."

"Well, we've seen people do some pretty crazy things," Lisa said, referring to some of the criminals the *Sunday School Detectives* had tracked down. "And those things haven't made a lot of sense either."

"I know people can do crazy things," Roberta Duncan agreed. "But I just don't see it with Paula and Jason."

"Well, we'll need to check them out," said Hailey confidently. "We could even get started by interviewing them today."

"Well, Paula will be on her way home by now," Roberta Duncan said, looking at her narrow silver wristwatch. "I can call her when she gets home and let her know you'd like to talk to her. Do you have some-one who can drive you out to her place? She lives out in Benton Ridge."

"We've got a friend who's coming to pick us up in a few minutes," Lisa said. "She could drive us."

"Okay," Roberta continued. "But let me warn you: Paula will talk your ear off. She's a very nice woman – salt of the earth if you know what I mean."

"And Jason?" Lisa wondered.

"I think he's got a F.E.E.T. meeting tonight. He's in that group that talks to UFOs – or tries to! Have you heard of them?"

"Yeah, we have," Lisa said, shaking her head, as she looked to Cressida and then Hailey. "We've heard a lot about them."

"Oh, right, of course you have," replied Mrs. Duncan, remember-ing the *Sunday School Detectives* case that was featured in several newspa-pers. "You can probably catch him at home after work, before he goes to that meeting."

"Could we just talk to him this afternoon at your office?" Lisa asked.

"Not with the way Jeremiah is carrying on," Roberta Duncan said. "There are security guards on the eighth floor now. So, I think it would be best if you talked to Jason at home."

"That's okay," said Hailey with a smile. "We can talk to him at his house. How about anyone else?"

"There's really no one I can think of," Roberta replied.

"How about the paralegals?" Lisa asked, looking at her notes from earlier in the day. "Andrew said there could be up to forty that work there?"

"That's about right," said Roberta Duncan.

"And they all passed by Andrew's desk to meet with you in your office?" Lisa asked.

"Well, yes, that is correct. They all report to me, so they come to me with questions or updates on the work they're doing."

"And a lot of them walked right by Andrew's desk?" Lisa asked.

"Right," Mrs. Duncan replied in agreement. "We're a pretty busy place."

"That makes it hard to identify a suspect in all the paralegals," Hailey said.

"I guess it would," said Roberta Duncan.

"Is there anyone in that group that you'd suspect? Maybe someone who had worked with those papers or might need to make some extra money by selling company secrets?" Lisa asked.

"I can't think of anyone in that group."

"Well, we might have set up some interviews with them," Hailey explained. "Especially if we don't get any clues from Paula and Jason."

"And," Lisa began, reviewing her notes, "I think there might be one more witness we'd want to question. Andrew said that Jimmy Mannix had a desk in the office too?"

"Right," Roberta agreed. "But I didn't see him in the office on Monday. In fact, I hardly ever see him. He's also got a desk on the floor below us."

"Andrew said his dad is a big shot at Peloponnesian."

"Well, yes – his father is a senior vice president," Mrs. Duncan said. "James Mannix, have you heard of him?"

"No, I don't think so."

"He and his wife are in the newspaper sometimes – for fundraisers and that sort of thing."

"Maybe we could talk with him too?" Hailey suggested.

"To James Mannix?" Roberta Duncan replied in a shocked voice. "I don't think you could get time with a senior V.P."

"No, sorry," said Hailey. "I was thinking we could get time with Jimmy Mannix, to see if he saw anything on Monday."

"Oh, sure," replied Roberta Duncan, now calmly. "That makes sense. I'll call him before he leaves work today and let him know you'll try to contact him for an interview at his house. I can get you those three addresses. Your best bet is to go to Paula's first, since she'll already be home. Then go see Jimmy because he usually leaves early. Then go see Jason, because he sometimes stays late. Who knows, you might find out that one of those three saw something on Monday. That could help with Andrew's case, right?"

"It could," Lisa agreed.

"Did you have any more questions, Lisa?" Hailey asked her friend.

"No, I think those were all of the questions I had."

"Cressida, do you have any more questions?" Hailey asked.

"I don't think so," Cressida replied softly.

"I think I'm out of questions too," said Hailey. "Thanks so much for meeting with us, Mrs. Duncan. We really appreciate it."

"Good luck with the investigation, girls," Mrs. Duncan smiled. "I'm not sure you'll be able to prove that Andrew is innocent, but I'm glad you're going to give it a try."

"Thanks!" the girls replied.

"Oh, and Hailey," Roberta Duncan said, turning to the young detective. "That dad of yours is one of the best. You're lucky to have him."

"I know," Hailey Cotton said, smiling broadly.

"He's so friendly and warm, always making everyone feel welcome and at ease."

"Yeah," Hailey agreed. Then her voice turned to a more serious tone. "But he worries about me a lot – with the detective work we're doing."

"I could see him doing that," the legal supervisor replied knowingly. "That's what all good dads do."

CHAPTER 27

"Over here! It's this way!" the woman yelled, after seeing the orange Volkswagen Beetle pause at her parents' newer, red-brick ranch-style house. "Keep going, keep going," she directed, trying to get the young driver's attention as she stood on her toes above the warped boards of an uneven wooden porch. Seeing the car pause again, she stepped off the front porch to wave the small car forward while carrying a small toddler. "It's over this way!" she added loudly. "You're almost here!"

Following the instructions, Alice Williams – a young scientist helping the *Sunday School Detectives* – drove her car slowly down a narrow gravel driveway until she entered a lush green yard containing several pieces of large, brightly painted metal artwork, all crafted from old farm equipment. "Wow, look at that!" one of her passengers said. "That looks like an airplane!"

"Yeah, and that looks like a Brontosaurus!" said another, impressed at the different shapes of the freshly painted sculptures.

Alice parked and after exiting, she and her three young passengers – Hailey Cotton, Lisa Lavin and Cressida Hudson – stared in surprise at the structure that barely stood in front of them: a dilapidated two-story brick farmhouse. It was easy for them to spot the temporary fixtures that silently proclaimed the need for major repairs. Nearest to them, three long silver metal braces held up the front porch's sagging roof. On the second floor of the farmhouse, they observed sheets of plywood covering many old, cracked and deteriorated windows. Shutters that had likely hung resolutely for many years were now missing or in pieces on the ground. Also on the ground, rocks were piled unevenly against several walls to support a crumbling foundation. "This place looks like it's falling apart," Alice said quietly to the girls.

"Yeah," one of them agreed.

"You found us!" the woman said loudly as she approached the car, still holding her toddler in one arm. "People are always having trouble finding this place!" she added in a sing-song voice, as an older girl followed, occasionally peering out from behind the woman's denim skirt. "This used to be my grandparents' house and my great-grandparents' house before that. And now my husband and I rent it from my parents. But ever since my folks built their new place out by the road, people have a hard time finding us."

"We didn't have too much trouble," Alice Williams admitted. "But I'm glad you were there to help."

"Oh, sure, that's no problem."

"Are you Paula?" Hailey Cotton asked, as the young investigators walked towards the woman.

"Yep, that's me! I'm Paula Bigelow!" she replied cheerfully. "I'm a little busy at the moment – getting ready for dinner. But, why don't you girls come on in. Don't mind the mess. With three kids under six, it can get a little out of control around here. But, come on in!" she added, and soon held open a broken screen door for the young women.

A steep staircase appeared in front of them as they moved inside the farmhouse while the pleasing smells of simmering pork chops and green beans filled the air. In a large living room, a young boy played on a worn carpeted floor and glanced up quickly at the visitors, his wide eyes soon returning to the dozens of multi-colored Legos, wood blocks and small metal Matchbox cars that surrounded the area where he knelt. "Watch your sister," Paula quickly instructed as she sat the toddler down in the living room next to the boy.

"Come this way," Paula directed her guests, as she led the young women to a nearby kitchen. Soon, Paula and the investigators were all seated around a rustic pine table.

"So, I'm Hailey," Hailey Cotton began. "And this is Lisa and Cressida and Alice."

"Nice to meet you," Paula Bigelow said as she greeted the young women. "Can I get you anything? Coffee or juice? Milk, maybe?"

"No, no, we're fine," one of the young women replied.

"Yeah, we're okay," said another, as they took the opportunity to observe the plainly dressed worker from Andrew's office – a woman in her early thirties, lacking jewelry or makeup, wearing her dark hair messily in a bun above her head.

"Okay, well," Paula Bigelow said haltingly, pausing briefly to look behind her to check on her oldest daughter who was now hiding behind her chair, listening to the conversation. "Bobbie – er, uh, Mrs. Duncan – telephoned and told me you'd be coming. I don't have a lot of time to talk before dinner, but I'll try to help answer your questions. She said you wanted to talk about Andrew." She grimaced when she said her former coworker's name. "But, Mrs. Duncan didn't really tell me anything else."

"That's right," Hailey confirmed in a serious tone. "We're part of the *Sunday School Detectives* and we have a few questions."

"Oh, *The Sunday School Detectives!*" Paula Bigelow replied in a knowing, cheery voice. "Well, isn't this a treat! I've read about your group in the paper! Are you the ones connected with *Youth for Christ?*"

"No, no," replied Hailey. "We just know each other from our church's Sunday School class and work on mysteries together."

"Oh, well, it's great what you're doing," Paula Bigelow said smiling. "We could use more Christian groups for kids in this crazy world of ours. My husband and I, we go to an *Immanent-Return* Church. Do you know what that is?"

"I don't think so," said Hailey.

"Well, it means we believe that Jesus is coming back at any moment. So, we've got to be ready, right?" Paula said, raising her voice and eyebrows, seeking agreement from the young women. "He could return so quickly – like *a thief in the night*, as He explained it."

"Hmm," one of the young detectives pondered.

"I'm actually going to put my notice in to Mrs. Duncan soon."

"Really? You're going to give your notice to quit your job?" Alice clarified, surprised by Paula's comments.

"Well sure," Paula Bigelow continued in her friendly tone. "If Jesus is coming back soon, I'd rather spend my last few months on earth with my kids than in some boring office."

"Oh?" Hailey said, thinking about Paula's explanation. "I guess that makes sense? I've never heard of that before."

"Well," Paula said cheerily as she moved a few strands of hair that had fallen into her eyes. "You might not have heard much about us *Immanent-Returners* so far, but you soon will!"

"Yeah, but nobody knows the exact time, right?" Cressida asked doubtfully.

"You're right! Jesus explained that we wouldn't know the *day* or the *hour* – but he didn't say anything about the *year*! And everyone in my church is pretty sure *1980* is going to be when it happens! There's a lot of prophecies that point to it – you know – nineteen hundred and eighty years after Jesus, and all that. Plus, if you add up the numbers, they equal eighteen, which is pretty significant too. Most of us think He'll return this *September* – which is the ninth month and that can be divided evenly into eighteen. And that's coming right up! It's all pretty exciting! If you want to check it out for yourselves, just look in the Bible. If you read the eighteenth verse or the eighteenth chapter of most books of the Bible, you'll see what I'm talking about."

"Hmm," Hailey said uncertainly, unsure of how to respond.

"Well, enough about me and my church," Paula said with a laugh as she looked at the unresponsive young women and then to the brown lacquered clock made from a tree stump showing the time on a nearby kitchen wall. "*You* just got started telling me that you are part of the *Sunday School Detectives* and then *I* just went on and on and on talking about my church. I'm just a Chatty Cathy this afternoon, aren't I! Sorry about that! So, what exactly did you girls want to talk about?"

"Andrew," Hailey said matter-of-factly, as she retrieved her notepad from her purse. "Andrew Bayhill."

"Ah, Andrew," Paula said sweetly. "He sure is a strange duck."

"That's what we were wondering about," Lisa interrupted. "What was so strange about him? Especially on Monday?"

"Well, you probably heard he's no longer with us at Peloponnesian," Paula said in a quieter tone as she picked up her youngest child who had crawled in from the living room. The child immediately began to squirm on her lap.

"Yes, well, that's what we'd like to talk to you about," said Hailey.

"Right," Lisa added. "So, what was so strange about him?"

"Ah, well, where should I begin?" Paula Bigelow asked with a laugh. "He was a *Nervous Norvus*, if you know what I mean – tapping his foot real loud, making lots of nervous noises, things like that. It was so weird."

"And, he was like that on Monday?" Lisa asked, writing some words in her notepad.

"Yes, for most of the day."

"Did you ever notice Andrew acting like that before?" Hailey asked.

"No, not exactly like that. That's why I – just a minute – Jubal!" she yelled to the boy in the living room. "Come take your sisters. See if they'll play with you while I talk to these nice young... girls."

Soon the young boy arrived in the kitchen and took his two sisters into the living room.

"So, on Monday," Alice, the young scientist, inquired. "Other than Andrew acting strange, was there anything else out of the ordinary?"

"No, I don't think so."

"And what about Andrew's briefcase – did you see anyone else around it? Maybe someone borrowed it or something like that?" Lisa asked.

"Well... " Paula Bigelow said sheepishly. "I actually knocked it over."

"You knocked it over?" Lisa said surprised, then quickly glanced at the others.

"Yeah," Paula continued. "Andrew kept it on the floor, right by his desk – in the walkway a little bit – and I ran into it with my foot walking to Roberta's office."

"Ah, got it," said Hailey. "Did you move it or notice anything different about it? Like, was it open or anything like that?"

"No, I think it was closed. I just moved it back to where Andrew kept it. He wasn't around, but I think I put it back in the place where he usually keeps it." Paula paused upon hearing her children arguing in the living room. "Jubal! Stop doing that! Be a big boy and play with your sisters!"

"But she's moving *my* cars around!" the young boy said from the room next door.

"It's okay to let her play with those for a few minutes," Paula yelled. "Just a few more minutes!"

"Aww, Mom!" the boy replied.

"Do you remember what time you kicked his briefcase?" Hailey interrupted.

"I'm not sure... Maybe around three o'clock or so."

The young investigators exchanged glances, recalling that Andrew told them he was away from the office at that time.

"Andrew was fired from his job on Monday because of some papers they found in his briefcase," Alice said sharply. "Do you know anything about that?"

"Well, I heard a few things – rumors, I guess you'd call them – about how he had taken some confidential papers or something like that, but I don't really know anything about it."

"So, you have no idea how the papers got in his briefcase?" Alice asked.

"No, sorry," said Paula Bigelow, shaking her head.

"Do you think Andrew would be the type of person to take them?" Alice quickly asked, impressing the other investigators with her questions.

"Well," Paula said thoughtfully, "if the papers were in his briefcase, he must have taken them, right?"

"Maybe," replied the young scientist. "That's what we're trying to figure out."

"Jubal!" Paula Bigelow yelled again from the kitchen after hearing more noises and crying from the living room. "Knock that off!"

"Well, I think we're probably done here," said Alice quickly. "I don't have any more questions."

"Okay, well, many blessings to you," Paula said sweetly as she quickly stood up. "Sorry I couldn't be of any further help."

"Actually," said Lisa. "I was wondering about a couple more things. Do you have time for a few more questions?"

"Well, okay," Paula said impatiently as she returned to her chair. Then, she quickly stood. "Actually, I think I have something burning on the stove – let me go check on that." She moved to the kitchen stove where the clatter of pots and pans could be heard briefly before Paula returned to her chair at the table.

"Now, normally, you don't work on Mondays, right?" Lisa asked.

"That's right," Paula Bigelow said with a smile. "I normally work Tuesdays through Thursdays. Why?"

"Well," Lisa continued. "You were in the office when Andrew got caught – and that was on Monday. So, why were you in the office then?"

"Well," Paula hesitated, long enough for the girls to glance again at each other. "I'm trying to save up for a trip with my husband and the kids. I'd like to take them to F-L-O-R-I-D-A," she said, spelling out the word. "And, since I was off – because of the July Fourth holiday – I wanted to make up some time. So, I got my mother – who normally watches the kids Tuesday through Thursday – to watch the kids on Monday for me, to help me get some extra spending money for our trip to D-I-S-N...,"

"I think we got it," said Alice. "You're going to see the M-O-U-S-E."

Upon hearing Alice's words, Jubal – the boy in the living room – began singing the theme song to the *Mickey Mouse Club*. "Who's the leader of the club?" he began to shout loudly.

"Oh, no," said Alice. "I forgot they spell out that word on the TV show."

"I was trying to keep it a secret!" Paula Bigelow said with pursed lips. "I'm not sure how much of a secret it's going to be now! I hope you haven't ruined our vacation!"

"I am so sorry," Alice said apologetically as she held out her hands, palms toward Paula Bigelow. "I didn't mean to let them know about that – I'm so sorry," she added, as Paula shot the young scientist another scornful look.

"Maybe I can get him to do something to take his mind off that," Paula said quickly, as Jubal continued his singing.

"And one more question for you," Lisa said, as they remained seated at the table.

"Yes?" Paula Bigelow asked in a frustrated tone, looking again at the clock on the wall.

"Mrs. Duncan said that you and Jason Compton were the only ones in the office who would have worked with the *Top Secret* – or, I mean, *Confidential* – company papers. Do you think Jason would have taken the papers and put them in Andrew's briefcase?"

"Jason!" Paula Bigelow exclaimed. "W… why would he take them?"

"Well," Lisa continued. "We heard that his grandparents aren't in good health. Maybe he was looking to sell the papers to pay for their medical bills, or something like that?"

"Jason? I don't think so. I can't picture that!"

"Well, we've got to treat everyone in the office as a suspect," Hailey explained.

"Everyone in the office!" Paula Bigelow shrieked. "I hope I'm not a suspect!"

"Well, we've got to look at all the possibilities," Hailey said calmly. "You know, to figure out why the papers were in Andrew's briefcase."

"Well, *I* didn't have anything to do with those files being in that briefcase!" Paula Bigelow said indignantly. "And I seriously doubt Jason did either."

"But Mrs. Duncan said the summer interns weren't allowed to work with them," Lisa explained. "And, that you and Jason were the only ones in the office who were allowed to work with the newer files marked *Confidential* or *Internal Use.*"

"What does that matter!" Paula Bigelow exclaimed loudly. "Jason and I process hundreds – even thousands – of documents each week, and a lot of them are marked *CONFIDENTIAL* or something like that! Mrs. Duncan can look through all the files we've worked on and see that they're *all* there. We didn't take anything!"

"Right," said Hailey. "But, you understand, we've got to look at everyone as a potential suspect."

"I don't like what you're hinting at," Paula Bigelow said as she abruptly moved away from the wooden table. "I didn't take any confidential files! Or put any papers in Andrew's briefcase!"

"We're not accusing you of anything," Lisa began.

"I think you better get going," Paula Bigelow said indignantly as she walked toward the living room. "I'd start looking into why *Andrew* had the papers inside *his* briefcase instead of accusing all of his coworkers of taking them! He's the one who had them!"

"I guess we better be going," said Hailey as she stood. "Thanks for talking with us."

Jubal continued singing in the living room as the young investigators entered the room.

"Your son has an interesting name," Alice said to their host as they were leaving. "Is it a family name?"

The woman stopped. Smiling proudly, she asked her son, "Jubal, can you tell the nice lady where your name is from?"

The boy stopped his singing and looked at the group of young investigators.

"Can you tell the nice ladies where in the Bible you can find Jubal?" His mother clarified.

"Genesis," the boy said. "Jubal was the son of Lamech."

"Wow," several of the girls replied.

"And what did he make?" Paula asked her son.

"Instruments!" the boy said as he moved to an old black upright piano against one wall.

"That's right, he made musical instruments!" said Paula, as her cheerful mood returned.

Soon, the boy was playing notes on the piano that sounded like *Twinkle Twinkle Little Star*. "Girls, do you want to sing along?" Paula asked her young daughters. "...up above the world so high, like a diamond in the sky," she sang as the girls watched their brother. Next, Jubal played notes on the piano that were similar to *Old McDonald Had a Farm* as his mother sang along. "Here a quack, there a quack, everywhere a quack quack!" she sang as her daughters looked on. "Can you play *Jesus Loves Me*?" Paula asked her son after he had finished with his second song, and immediately the boy began playing the famous children's song as several of the young investigators sang along.

CHAPTER 28

The orange Volkswagen Beetle filled with laughter as its driver, Alice Williams, pulled away from the old farmhouse and the newly built long brick ranch-style house. "That was not what I was expecting!" the young scientist said to the others in her car. "Are all your interviews like that one?"

"No, no," admitted Hailey Cotton, one of Alice's passengers. "Most of our interviews are pretty boring. We just ask people questions and try to write down as much stuff as we can in our notebooks. But, hearing Paula Bigelow's son play the piano was really sweet. And her daughters were pretty cute too."

"And, I thought her husband's metal art in the yard was interesting too," Lisa Lavin added.

"Yeah," agreed Hailey. "I'm glad she showed us some of those when we were leaving. Who knew you could make such cool sculptures from old farm machinery?"

"But she was really upset with our questions," said Cressida Hudson softly.

"Yeah," her cousin, Lisa agreed.

"Methinks the lady doth protest too much," Alice said as they reached State Route 12 and headed east towards Findlay.

"What does that mean?" asked Lisa.

"It's Shakespeare," laughed Alice. "It means that she sure complained a lot when we started asking her more questions – a lot more than I thought she would! And, we didn't even accuse her of taking the papers, did we?"

"No, not really," said Lisa.

"But she was sure upset," added the young scientist.

"Yeah, that was weird," said Hailey. "All I told her is that we needed to treat everyone as a potential suspect – which we do! It could have been any of those workers in the office who stole those papers – including her."

"Do you think it was an act?" asked Lisa. "You know, to throw us off the trail?"

"I'm not so sure," said Cressida softly. "She seemed pretty nice. I don't think she would steal the papers."

"But she needs money to fix up that house and to take her family to D-I-S-N... " Lisa began.

"I feel so bad about that," Alice interrupted as the girls laughed. "Hopefully she can still keep her secret and it won't ruin their vacation!"

"The kids will probably forget all about it," said Lisa.

"I hope so," Alice confessed.

"So, should we keep Paula Bigelow at the top of our list of suspects?" Hailey asked, directing the conversation back to the case.

"I don't think so," asserted Cressida. "I thought she was telling the truth."

"Yeah," agreed Lisa. "I think so too."

"Okay," replied Hailey. "Well, that means we'll keep on looking."

The group was quiet for a moment.

"Whoa," Alice declared suddenly, as her hands grabbed the car's black plastic steering wheel even tighter than they had a moment earlier. "I just thought of something!"

"What?" asked one of her surprised passengers.

"What if she wasn't telling the truth?" the young scientist said loudly.

"What do you mean?" asked Lisa.

"Think about what Paula Bigelow told us when we asked her why she was working on Monday!"

"She said that she worked on Monday because she missed work last week because of the Fourth of July holiday," Hailey recalled.

"Yeah, and what days does she normally work?" Alice asked with a smile, while looking at the rearview mirror to see the girls in the car's backseat.

"Tuesdays through Thursdays, right?" Lisa answered in a serious tone.

"And what day was July Fourth on last week?" Alice asked.

"I'm not sure," said Cressida.

"Me either," said Lisa, while Hailey shrugged her shoulders to indicate she did not know the answer.

"It was on a day she wasn't even supposed to be working!" Alice explained loudly.

"What?" Lisa asked, surprised.

"July Fourth was on Friday," Alice said with a smile.

CHAPTER 29

"I could get used to this detective work," Alice Williams said with a smile from the driver's seat of her orange Volkswagen Beetle. "So, who's next?" she asked her passengers – three *Sunday School Detectives* – as they travelled back to Findlay, Ohio on State Route 12, on their way to their next interview.

"Jimmy Mannix," Hailey Cotton said, looking at her notebook. "He lives out by the mall."

"I've got his address," Lisa Lavin added. "Mrs. Duncan said he should be home a little after five 'cause he never stays late at work." Soon, the three *Sunday School Detectives* were reviewing a city map and directing Alice through the heavy downtown traffic to Tiffin Avenue.

Eventually, they approached a neighborhood with long, open lawns. After passing the Country Club's driving range and signs for the golf club's 14th tee, they came to a large two-story modern brick house set back from the street.

"Oh no," groaned Lisa as they approached Jimmy Mannix's house.

"Isn't that?" Hailey Cotton asked.

"Yes," said Lisa in a clipped voice – shaking her head.

"Who?" Alice asked from the driver's seat. "Who is it?"

"It's Brad," Lisa continued. "He's my brother."

Brad Lavin, a high school junior, was dressed like most teenage boys that summer – wearing track shorts, a colorful tank-top, long white tube socks and basketball shoes. He stood on the edge of the Mannix family's long driveway, holding a clipboard and stopwatch. Standing next to Brad were two young women a few years older than the high schooler – one was wearing a floral-patterned sundress while the other wore a long dark skirt and white blouse, popular in many professional offices. The young women were both barefoot – their flat sandals and black high-heeled shoes rested nearby in the freshly cut and well-manicured grass.

"What are *you* doing here?" Brad asked when he saw his sister exit Alice Williams' car, followed by the others.

"I was going to ask you the same thing!" Lisa nearly shouted. "I thought you couldn't drive us around today because you had to *work*!"

"Well... I do... Later," Brad said awkwardly, referring to his part-time job at a local ice cream store.

"What are you doing?" Lisa asked, looking at her brother's clipboard and stopwatch.

"It's none of your business," Brad stated in a condescending tone, as the two women next to him laughed.

"We're timing Jimmy," the professionally dressed young woman explained with a smile. "Brad's going next. He thinks he can beat some kind of record or something."

"Record?" asked Lisa.

"It's the neighborhood land-speed record," Brad admitted. "Now, be quiet and let me concentrate – I want to make sure I turn off this stopwatch right when Jimmy passes the mailbox. You better get out of the street," he warned.

The four investigators quickly moved to the neatly manicured grass and a moment later heard the roar of a car engine on a nearby street. In a flash, a light blue Subaru zipped by the house and Brad Lavin quickly held up the stopwatch high above his head.

The driver slowed, turned at the next intersection, and then returned to the house. "Wow!" he yelled from the car window. "That was sweet! Let me look at my time!" Pulling into the Mannix driveway, the young driver quickly leapt out of the car and grabbed the stopwatch from Brad Lavin's hand. "Aw man, I thought I was faster! My car's so slow!" he said of his late 70's light blue Subaru RX – a two door sedan with a trunk and bumper covered with stickers from private schools and islands in the Great Lakes.

"It sure seemed fast," the young woman in the floral print dress said with a smile.

"Naw! This jock's gonna crush me!" the young driver complained, looking at Brad.

"Alright! Alright!" said Brad. "Let me give it a try!" he added, handing his clipboard to the young woman in the floral dress.

"You remember the route, right?"

"Yeah, I got it," Brad replied confidently as he walked to the street.

The young driver, wearing khakis and an untucked blue Oxford shirt, looked skeptically at the young investigators who stood nearby, knowing they weren't neighborhood kids or anyone he had summered with at the Lake.

After seeing the driver's wary look, one of the young women asked, "Hey Brad, who are these kids?"

"It's my bratty sister and my cousin and some of their friends," Lisa's brother said derisively as he walked to his car – a glistening brown two-door 1972 Buick Skylark parked nearby.

"Are you Jimmy Mannix?" Lisa asked impertinently to the young college-aged driver who was now holding the stopwatch.

"The one and only," Jimmy Mannix said with a smile, then patted his chest. The young women with him laughed.

"I'm Lisa – Brad's sister."

"Hey," Jimmy Mannix replied in a cool tone, nodding to Lisa, before turning to see Brad start his car.

"This is our cousin Cressida," Lisa added. "And our friends Hailey and Alice."

Ignoring Lisa's introductions, Jimmy Mannix paused to look down at the stopwatch, then shouted to Brad. "Alright Ace! Pull around."

Soon, Brad drove his car down the street, turned at a nearby intersection, and then returned slowly, idling his car a few feet away from the Mannix mailbox. The young woman in the floral-patterned dress – who was now holding the clipboard – yelled to Brad above the engine noise, "You can pull forward just a little bit."

"Not too much!" yelled Jimmy Mannix. "You can't start beyond the mailbox."

"Am I past it now?" Brad called back loudly above the noise of his car engine.

"No, no," said Jimmy in a serious voice. "You're cool."

Soon, they watched Brad reposition his body in the leather driver's seat of the Skylark, then grip the steering wheel with both hands.

"You ready?" Jimmy yelled, holding the stopwatch in front of him.

"Yeah," Brad shouted in response.

"Okay, do the countdown!" Jimmy directed, as the woman in the floral print dress quickly moved the clipboard above her head.

"Three, two, one!" the woman yelled, and then dropped the clipboard like a starting flag at a race. In an instant the Buick Skylark flew down the street and turned the corner.

"Where's he going?" Lisa asked.

"All over the place," Jimmy Mannix said, checking the stopwatch. "The most fun is going around Circle Drive. One time I almost got my car up on two wheels!"

"What?" Hailey questioned. "Can you go that fast?"

"Sure," said Jimmy. "It's a lot of fun. It's a pretty tight turn."

"Sounds pretty stupid," said Alice, the young scientist. "You could wreck into someone's house!"

"Or into another car," Lisa added.

"Or a kid on a bike," Cressida noted softly.

"Not me," Jimmy Mannix replied confidently as he shook his head. "I'm a great driver."

"Maybe you are," Lisa answered, unconvinced. "But I'm not so sure about Brad!"

The young women laughed.

"So you're Brad's sister?" Jimmy asked.

"Yep," replied Lisa.

"Brad's car is pretty fast," Jimmy added. "He's going to beat me by a mile."

"He got it from our grandpa," Lisa explained.

"It runs pretty good," admired Jimmy. "So, you came over to see if your brother could beat our neighborhood record, huh? He said he already beat the one in *your* neighborhood."

"Our neighborhood! I hadn't heard about that," said Lisa.

"Yeah, Brad told us he ticked off a few of your neighbors."

"Doesn't surprise me," Lisa laughed.

"Yeah," her cousin, Cressida, agreed.

"Actually, we didn't come over here to see Brad," explained Lisa. "We actually wanted to see you."

"Me? What for?" Jimmy Mannix questioned, glancing quickly at the stopwatch.

"Well, we were told that you have a desk near Andrew's..."

"Who?" Jimmy asked incredulously.

"Andrew – Andrew Bayhill. Over at Peloponnesian," Lisa continued. "But he's not with the company any longer."

"Oh, yeah," said Jimmy, changing to a serious tone. "I heard about that. Too bad, huh? He was sort of a weird kid – if I'm thinking of the same guy. I heard he took some papers or something."

"Yeah, something like that," said Lisa. "We wanted to ask you a few questions about that."

"Wait a second!" Jimmy Mannix smiled, then let out a loud laugh. "It's you! Mrs. Duncan called and told me some detectives would be asking me some questions! I didn't know it would be a bunch of kids!"

Lisa ignored the comment and continued with her questions, "Do you know anyone who might have put the papers in Andrew's briefcase?"

"So, you think *someone else* put the papers in his briefcase?" Jimmy asked, then quickly glanced at the stopwatch again.

"Right," replied Lisa.

"Why would someone do that?"

"It's just an… idea," said Hailey nearby.

"A theory that we're working on," Alice clarified.

"I have no idea," Jimmy said in a nonchalant tone. "Your brother should be getting close," he explained as they heard the roar of an engine and the squeal of tires in the distance. A moment later Brad's car flew by and Jimmy held up the stopwatch.

"Wow, that was close," said Jimmy Mannix as his two friends drew closer to look. "That was really close," he added admiringly while looking at the stopwatch. "He almost beat the neighborhood record."

Brad Lavin slowed the car, turned at the next intersection, and slowly returned as Jimmy and their two friends quickly walked to meet him on the street.

"How'd I do?" Brad asked from inside the car.

"You beat me," said Jimmy Mannix. "By a lot. And you almost beat the record."

"You were off by just a few seconds," one of the young women said.

"But, I'm gonna leave you in the dust when I get my Alpha Romeo," Jimmy Mannix laughed as the four soon began conversing about different types of cars and the different races throughout our city's different neighborhoods.

While Jimmy and his friends were talking by Brad's car, Alice and the *Sunday School Detectives* noticed a long four-door light-blue Cadillac slowly drive down the quiet street and eventually pull into the Mannix's long driveway. The driveway was wide enough for two or three cars, so the Cadillac easy maneuvered around Jimmy's light blue Subaru and eventually pulled into the property's detached three car garage. A stately white-haired gentleman exited and walked down the driveway to his mailbox, eventually greeting the four young investigators who stood nearby. "Girls," the man said, nodding. He stood for a moment, looking at his son laughing with Brad and the two young women on the street. "What seems to be going on here?" he asked in a professional tone.

"The boys are trying to beat some sort of record," Lisa said matter-of-factly.

"Ah, yes, *The Canterbury Trails* record," the older man smiled as he took a large stack of mail from his mailbox. "Can you believe that name?" he added with a laugh. "That's been going on for quite some time, I'm told. I'd guess if Jimmy gets that car he's been talking about, he'll be able to beat the record by a pretty good clip – but that's a big *if* on him getting the car!" The older man laughed again, then paused for a moment. "Sorry ladies, I didn't introduce myself – James Mannix."

The girls quickly introduced themselves to the older gentleman.

"Hmm, Cotton," Mr. Mannix said after meeting Hailey. "Is your Dad over at Peloponnesian?"

"Yes, he is," Hailey smiled. "He works in Accounting. On *Project 81*."

"Very good," said Mr. Mannix. "That's a good team they've got in Production Accounting. And M.C.'s one of the best."

"I like to think so," Hailey said, still smiling.

"So, did you come to watch my son race around the block?" Mr. Mannix questioned. "Or are you with that other boy?"

"No, no," explained Hailey. "We're part of the *Sunday School Detectives*. We just stopped by to ask your son a few questions."

"Well, he's a little headstrong, if you know what I mean. That sometimes comes with the privileges of wealth. But he's a good son. You don't think he did anything wrong, do you?"

"No, no," Hailey added with a laugh. "We're just following up with a case we're working on and had some questions to ask him."

"Well, good luck with that," Mr. Mannix said before taking a deep breath. "Sounds like you've got some work to do."

"Yeah," agreed Hailey.

"For me, I'm done with work for a couple of days. Gonna take my mind off the pressures of the old nine to five and go fishin' with some old friends."

"That sounds like fun," said Lisa.

"It should be," Mr. Mannix agreed with a smile.

Soon, the investigators noticed a well-dressed woman walk out of the house. "Jamie," she called to the older gentleman. "I've got your clothes laid out."

"In a minute Cheryl!" Mr. Mannix yelled to the woman standing near the garage. "I'm being summoned," the older man explained in a quiet voice. "The little missus needs to make sure I'm all ready for a party tonight and I'm all packed for my trip tomorrow. Well, it was a pleasure to meet you all."

"Nice to meet you too," the girls said, nearly in unison.

"Alright Brad's gonna go again – he's going to try to beat the record," Jimmy Mannix explained to the young detectives when he returned a few minutes later. "Did you have more questions or somethin' like that, or do you just want to stay and watch Brad race?"

"No, we've got more questions," Lisa said with a smile. "And I'm not interested in watching watch Brad do something stupid."

"Okay, okay," said Jimmy Mannix as the two young women joined him near the mailbox while Brad readied his car, going slowly down the street again.

"We talked with your boss, Mrs. Duncan, earlier today," said Lisa. "And she said you have a desk near Andrew's. In the same office as Paula and Jason."

"Yeah," Jimmy Mannix explained. "But I'm never there. I've got another desk on the floor below them."

"Okay," said Lisa. "So how about Monday?"

"What about Monday?" Jimmy Mannix asked in an annoyed voice, glancing first at the investigators, then to Brad's car.

"Can you tell us anything you remember about the day?" asked Lisa. "That's when Andrew was caught with the files."

"This past Monday?" Jimmy Mannix asked.

"Yes," one of the Sunday School Detectives confirmed.

"Well, I wasn't at work on Monday, if that's what you're wondering about. I was up at the lake with my dad and stepmom. We had a long Fourth of July weekend and didn't get back until late in the afternoon."

"So, you weren't in the office at *all* on Monday?" Lisa asked.

"Nope," Jimmy replied quickly, as he glanced at Lisa, then again at Brad's car.

"How about last week?" Lisa continued with her questions. "Did you see anything out of the ordinary?"

"No, I don't think so. Nothing really comes to mind," Jimmy explained with a shrug. "I was off work on Friday because of the Fourth of July."

"Can you think of how those important papers got into Andrew's briefcase?" asked Lisa.

"Maybe someone put them there, like you said earlier," he began. "Or maybe a UFO landed and an alien put the papers in his briefcase!" Jimmy added loudly, as his two friends laughed. "Oh, wait, sorry," he paused for a moment. "That's *Jason* who's into that weird UFO stuff – not *Andrew*. I get those two guys mixed up."

"Very funny," said Alice, unsmiling at the joke about her friend Jason Compton.

"Okay, okay. In all seriousness," Jimmy Mannix continued, "I have no idea how those papers got into the guy's briefcase. Maybe you should ask him to explain it."

"Yeah, well, we have," said Lisa. "And Andrew Bayhill doesn't have a clue how those papers got there either."

CHAPTER 30

The young detectives – Hailey Cotton, Lisa Lavin and Cressida Hudson – along with their driver, the young scientist Alice Williams – waited for Brad Lavin to finish his race around the neighborhood before driving away from Jimmy Mannix's house. "I don't want my car to get hit while he's speeding around the neighborhood!" Alice explained while they waited. Once Brad had returned from his race, Alice and her passengers left the neighborhood.

A few streets away, they saw two police cars driving rapidly in their direction. "Someone probably called the police on Brad!" Lisa laughed as the police vehicles sped by. "He doesn't always think things through."

"No, he doesn't," her cousin Cressida agreed.

"My brother can be a few fries short of a Circus Wagon Happy Meal!" Lisa added, as the car filled with laughter.

While Alice drove her car down a busy Tiffin Avenue, Lisa, who was sitting in the front passenger seat, turned to the others. "It's got to be either Paula or Jason, right?" she asked bluntly.

"I don't know," said Hailey. "Why do you say that?"

"Well, Jimmy Mannix didn't have any information to give us," Lisa summarized. "He said he wasn't even at work on Monday and barely even knew Andrew. But Paula and Jason? Think about it: They worked with the papers that were stolen, right? Plus, they were the ones who told Mrs. Duncan that Andrew was acting weird."

"Right," said Cressida. "And selling those important memos could have helped Paula for her trip to F-L-O-R-I-D-A...to see the M-O-U-S-E."

"I still feel really bad about that!" Alice protested. "I didn't know her son would start singing that song!"

"Well, she is definitely a top suspect," said Hailey. "But let's see if Jason Compton gives us any more clues."

"Yeah," Lisa agreed. "Mrs. Duncan told us his grandparents have a lot of medical bills. Maybe he wanted to steal the papers and sell them to help pay for those bills?"

"Right," Cressida affirmed.

"I don't think he's guilty," said Alice as she turned her car onto North Blanchard Street at the local Wendy's. "I know Jason from F.E.E.T. and he's really a nice guy. He couldn't be involved."

"We'll see," said Lisa skeptically.

"Why don't you let me ask the questions," Alice suggested. "I mean, since I've known him for a couple of years, Jason might be willing to tell me more about the case than he might tell you."

"Sure," said Hailey. "You did a great job asking Paula questions earlier today."

"Yeah," agreed Lisa.

"Thanks!" the young scientist smiled.

"So where does Jason live?" Hailey asked. "It looks like we're going towards Jacobs Elementary?"

"Well, he's not too far away from there," said Alice.

"You don't need our help with the map?" Lisa asked her older friend.

"No, no, I've driven Jason home after some meetings," Alice explained as she took the street's wide turn after crossing a pair of railroad tracks. "He's over on East Foulke Avenue, down the street from the Church of God."

"Oh, what's that church called?" Hailey asked.

"I think that would be the East Foulke Avenue Church of God," Alice explained, as the others laughed.

Soon, the four arrived at a tall white two-story wood framed house where Jason Compton lived with his grandparents. Hailey knocked on a metal screen door positioned outside a heavy wooden door as the others stood behind her on the stairs of a short stoop, anxious to conclude their final interview of the day.

"Hey," Jason mumbled nonchalantly as he opened the door.

"Hi," Hailey cheerily said with a smile. "I'm Hailey Cotton of the *Sunday School Detectives*. These are my friends Lisa and Cressida – and I think you know – "

"Alice!" Jason Compton said surprised. "I didn't know you'd be coming over."

"Well, I'm sort of helping out the *Sunday School Detectives* – if they'll take me."

"Oh," he said with a concerned look. "Well, come in – I guess. Mrs. Duncan said there would be people stopping over. She said I didn't have to talk to you if I didn't want to. But I guess that'd make me look pretty guilty if I didn't say anything, huh?"

"Well, maybe," said Hailey as she and the investigators entered the living room, quickly noticing that the lights were off and the heavy shades covering the windows were lowered. "But, uh, we're not the police or anything like that," Hailey added, cautiously watching her footing as she stepped into the darkened room. "We're just trying to get to the bottom of a mystery."

"Okay," said Jason Compton. "I've got to go to a F.E.E.T. meeting in a little while, but we could talk for a few minutes."

"Great," said Hailey enthusiastically.

"Shhh," said Jason.

"Oh, sorry," Hailey apologized.

"My grandparents are upstairs," Jason explained, as he pointed to the ceiling above them. "They're probably asleep already. Why don't we go down to the basement where you can talk louder and you can ask your questions?"

The girls agreed, and they soon followed Jason to a nearby doorway where they descended a flight of steep and narrow wooden stairs. Soon, they entered a brightly-lit basement, where they were immediately overcome by the many sights and sounds of numerous ticking clocks.

"Wow," said Lisa.

"Cool," Hailey agreed.

"This is... incredible," Cressida added in wonder.

"Jason!" exclaimed Alice to her friend. "I didn't know you had all of this! You've talked about your clocks a few times, but this is an amazing collection!"

"Well, they're my grandfather's... clocks," Jason said smiling, pleased with his joke.

The room, as the young detectives quickly discovered, was filled with dozens of clocks. Tall, narrow grandfather clocks lined two basement walls, some with open faces allowing the young visitors to see the many heavy metallic weights, chains and pendulums swing back and forth. Other grandfather clocks were closed, displaying beautiful wooden panels elaborately designed with carvings depicting historical scenes or rectangular shapes or depictions of flora, fauna and landscapes. Meanwhile, smaller tables throughout the basement held other types of clocks – old anniversary-style clocks encased in glass cylinders, wooden cuckoo clocks and many other timepieces of various shapes and sizes that whirred and spun and ticked loudly. Along another wall, clocks affixed to neon signs glowed brightly in red and blue and green, showing the names and logos of famous companies or products popular many decades before, each next to large dials displaying the time.

"This is really cool," Cressida said in a louder-than-usual voice, as she took in the sights of the many clocks.

"Thanks," said Jason Compton. "I can show you some of them." Soon, Jason gave the young women a tour of the basement, first showing them the grandfather clocks, then the neon clocks and then the anniversary clocks, "These are actually called Four Hundred Day clocks," Jason explained before describing in detail the pendulum and the springs that kept the time.

As Jason was about to describe another set of clocks, Alice finally interrupted. "Do you mind if we take a break? I know you've got a F.E.E.T. meeting to go to tonight, right?"

"Right," Jason confirmed.

"Do you mind if we ask you a few questions about Andrew Bayhill?" the young scientist began. "He's been accused of taking some important papers and we've been asked to help him. Can we ask you a few things?"

"Sure," Jason agreed. "That's fine."

"So, on Monday," Alice continued. "You were at work, right?"

"Right."

"Did you see anything suspicious – you know, anything out of the ordinary with Andrew or his briefcase, or anything like that?"

"No," said Jason Compton. "The only thing I saw that was weird on that day was Andrew. He was so nervous... tapping his pencil really hard on his desk... and even sweating a lot more than normal... it was sort of gross. I went and told my manager about it."

"So, nothing out of the ordinary with the files or with other people? There weren't any different people in the office or anything like that?"

"No, just the same people as I see every day. There was my boss, Mrs. Duncan, you know, and the other workers: Andrew, Jimmy, Paula; a bunch of paralegals. You know, there's always a lot of people coming in and out of the office to see Mrs. Duncan. It's like Grand Central Station around there. It's hard to concentrate sometimes."

"Wait a minute!" Lisa interrupted. "Did you say you saw Jimmy Mannix on Monday? Because he just told us he wasn't at work!"

"Oh, ah," stammered Jason. "I guess I was just listing off the people I usually see. I don't exactly remember seeing him there on Monday."

"Okay, okay," said Lisa with a grimace.

"And you didn't see anybody put anything in Andrew's briefcase?" Alice continued with her questioning.

"No," Jason said adamantly. "I mean, it was kind of funny – Paula kicked the briefcase over, but that was it."

"After she kicked it over, did the briefcase look any different or anything like that?" Alice asked. "Did it look any heavier, or have papers sticking out of it?"

"No. Do you think Paula did something to his briefcase?" Jason asked quickly with a concerned look.

"No, no," Hailey interjected. "We just need to check it out."

"Okay."

"Okay, then," said Alice. "Let's talk about Andrew Bayhill for a minute. Would you say that Andrew got along with people at the office?"

"Well," Jason Compton paused. "Not really… I mean he's a lot younger than Paula and me… He just graduated high school. I mean, he's okay, but he's not, like, best friends with people. He wasn't really interested in the stuff I'm interested in, like clocks or alien encounters, or anything like that."

"Okay," replied Alice.

"And now… " Jason confessed, moving closer to the others. "Well, now it's really crazy at work. They've put some extra security guards around our offices. I guess to make sure no one else takes anything."

"Would you suspect anyone else of taking anything?" asked Alice.

"Like who?" Jason wondered.

"Well, we're looking at everyone. You know, as a – a suspect who might have put those papers in Andrew's briefcase. So, is there anyone else who could, you know, use the money from selling the stolen documents, or anything like that?"

"Use the money!" Jason said incredulously as he began angrily spitting a reply. "We all could use the money! Paula lives in a run-down house outside of town... she's always telling us how things are breaking down and how expensive it is to fix them... and how she wants to take her family on vacation... and how her husband is spending all of their money making his sculptures! Then, there was Andrew. He needed money for school. And my grandparents upstairs are really sick and I'm wondering how we're going to pay for their medical bills, so yeah, everyone could use the money – I guess that means *everyone's* a suspect if that's where you're going with this! Except Jimmy, I guess... and Mrs. Duncan. They couldn't *use the money* – as you like to call it."

"Okay, sorry," said Alice. "I was just wondering."

"Well, I don't like someone coming in here and accusing me of stuff I didn't do."

"We're just trying to figure out how the papers got in Andrew Bayhill's briefcase," Alice reassured him.

"How should I know how they got there!" Jason loudly protested. "I didn't have anything to do with it!"

While Alice and Jason continued their enthusiastic dialogue about the case, Cressida turned to her cousin and said in her soft voice, "Hey Lisa, I don't think this interview is going anywhere, do you?"

"No," Lisa quietly replied with a frown. "We haven't learned one thing."

"I think I'll excuse myself and check around upstairs," Cressida proposed.

"That sounds good," her cousin told her.

"Jason, is your bathroom upstairs?" Cressida asked, interrupting Jason's discussion with Alice.

"Yeah, go to the top of the stairs and turn right," he told her sharply, before returning to his heated exchange with Alice. "So, like I was telling you, there are like thirty paralegals that come and go in and out of that office all day long! I'm sure some of them could use the money too! Are you going to question every one of them like you're questioning me!"

"We've got to look at everyone," Alice explained.

While Jason Compton was protesting the investigation, Cressida quietly walked up the flight of stairs and opened the door into the darkened first floor of the house. Passing the open door to the bathroom, she slowly turned the doorknob of the next door she found – a closet. After looking up and down at the many towels and linens, she closed the door and quietly walked down the hallway.

Suddenly, she heard a noise and stopped.

"Ahhhh," she heard faintly. "Ahhh," she heard again. She felt a chill and shuddered at the strangeness of the noise.

She waited, holding her breath as she tried to listen again to the faint voice.

"Pills! I need my pills!" she heard a weak, elderly voice call out. "My pills!" she heard again, now detecting that the voice was coming from above her on the second floor of the house.

"I'll tell Jason!" Cressida called out to the person on the floor above her – unsure if they could hear her or not.

Cressida turned the doorknob to the next room, momentarily forgetting how to return to the basement in the darkened hallway. Opening the door, she could see in the dim light two posters on the wall. One pictured our solar system, with planets circling the sun, while the other was of the Starship Enterprise, from the television show *Star Trek*.

Cressida Hudson knew that she had found Jason Compton's bedroom.

Like the other rooms on the first floor, the bedroom was dark, and for a few moments, Cressida fumbled to work a small lamp on a nearby desk. Eventually, she turned on the lamp and illuminated the space.

She wanted to leave quickly, now that there was some light to illumine her path through the hallway to the basement, but something caught her eye on a nearby desk piled high with books and plastic models of rockets and spacecraft. She stopped to look at the items. *Mostly books*, she said to herself. *Mostly about astronomy*, she added. And then, to her surprise, she saw that under the pile of books sat a stack of papers. Shocked at her discovery, she had to do a double take to confirm that her eyes were really seeing what her brain was registering. She moved the books to reveal, to her surprise, a stack of stapled documents. After looking at a few of the documents, she soon discovered that the top pages all displayed the familiar Peloponnesian logo – a black hexagon surrounding a red letter "P". Some of the first pages, she observed, were even stamped in red and blue ink with the word CONFIDENTIAL. *That's the same word Andrew Bayhill and Roberta Duncan used when they were talking about the stolen documents*, Cressida thought.

Amazed at her discovery, Cressida spent several minutes quickly reading through the documents, trying to understand their contents, but struggled to understand the many technical words used throughout the memos. So focused was her reading of the many details in the dim light of the bedroom that she failed to hear a set of footsteps climbing the stairs from the basement. Soon, the footsteps were walking down the hallway. Having neglected to close the door behind her, the light from the desk lamp shone brightly throughout the darkened hallway – revealing her presence in the bedroom.

The footsteps stopped when they reached the bedroom.

While hunched over, reading one of the documents in the dim light, Cressida realized that someone was next to her. Startled, she turned and dropped the company memo she was holding.

"You shouldn't be here!" Jason Compton said forcefully, holding a long wooden stick several feet above his head.

Cressida Hudson screamed.

PART THREE

CHAPTER 31

I was resting on the living room floor, having just finished a second episode of *Hogan's Heroes*, when the telephone rang. It was a few minutes after eight o'clock on the night of Wednesday, July 9th and I was in a bit of a daze. A prison visit earlier that morning and an ominous message left for my friend at the cemetery had left me worn out and mentally drained from the day's events.

"Pep, it's for you," my mother called from the kitchen.

"Stiles Residence," I said automatically after hurrying to the phone, forgetting that my mother had already answered.

"Hey, it's Sneak," my friend said somberly. "You still awake?"

"Barely," I confessed. "I'm so exhausted from everything that's happened today."

"Hailey just called and wants to meet us tonight. She's gonna be with the other *Sunday School Detectives* over at Riverside Park and they want to talk about the case of the stolen papers they've been working on. Do you want to go with me to see what they want?"

"S… sure!" I stammered quickly, instantly feeling energized and interested in hearing about their adventures. "I can change my clothes and bike over to your house in a few minutes."

"Okay," my friend replied, unenergetically. "See you then."

I quickly told my mom of our new plans and changed out of my pajamas, while she directed me to "not be out too late." Racing to the garage, I grabbed my bike and began pedaling to my friend's house as fast as I could. *They want to talk about the case of the stolen papers they've been working on,* I repeated to myself. *This should be so cool! They only met with our client this morning! I wonder if they've already solved the mystery?*

On my way, I began thinking about the newspaper article I would write about the case. I was proud of my first article called *The Adventure at Riverside Park* and quickly began thinking of titles for this new story. *The Case of the Stolen Documents* was the first to come to mind – echoing the words of my friend. *No, no, how about The Case of the Pilfered Papers,* I thought, and soon imagined the bold uppercase letters on the front page of *The Republican Courier.* Then, suddenly, another title came to mind – a title that sounded really good – *The Missing Memos.*

Inventing a title for a detective story takes some imagination. Early in my writing career, I thought it best to begin with the word "The", followed by an explanation of what the mystery entailed – either listing the crime or the geographic location. For example, "The Case of..." or "The Mystery at..." or "The Adventure at..." all sounded like great mysteries to me. I wanted my stories to be just like a Sherlock Holmes or a Hardy Boys story and I couldn't imagine writing a mystery without having a title like theirs. It is funny to note that my favorite title for this latest mystery, *The Missing Memos,* broke most of my rules.

I rode my bike to my friend's house at breakneck speed, even though only a few minutes earlier, I had been exhausted and ready for bed. Now, I amazingly found myself energized and excited to hear what Hailey and the other *Sunday School Detectives* had learned. I was curious, too, to discover why they wanted to talk to us so late on a Wednesday night!

When I arrived at Sneak's house on Decker Avenue, I found it bustling with activity as the Ryerson family prepared to leave for their long fourteen-day vacation the following morning. In the driveway, Mr. Ryerson was struggling to connect a plastic car top carrier to the roof of the *Maroon Monster,* pulling and tugging small black bungee cords tightly around the silver roof rack of the station wagon. Meanwhile, Mr. Ryerson's father, who we all called Grandfather Ryerson, stood nearby offering advice to his son as he leaned on a cane made of dark wood. I quickly greeted the two men, parked my bike along the side of the house, and knocked on the back door before heading inside. The scene was chaotic. Mrs. Ryerson and Cousin Sara were in the kitchen cutting vegetables to place in a red and white Igloo cooler and readying other snacks for the first day's long drive. Sneak's sister, Jennie, meanwhile, had just returned from Day Camp and was laying out stuffed toy giraffes on the living room floor and negotiating with her mother on how many she would be allowed to take with her on the trip. "No, absolutely not! That's too many," her mother kept saying. Meanwhile, Grandma Ryerson sat in a chair at the dining room table, reading interesting quotes and anecdotes from *The Reader's Digest* to those nearby.

"My bike's still out at The Farm," Sneak explained as he raced down the stairs from his bedroom. "So, I'll have to borrow Jennie's."

"I'll trade you my bike for some space in your suitcase," Jennie Ryerson said with a smile.

"You're on," Sneak replied as he hastily made his way out of the kitchen. "We'll be back in a little while, Mom. We're just riding up to Riverside Park," he explained to his mother as we quickly took the three steps down from the kitchen and were soon out the back door.

Continuing his burst of energy, my friend rushed to the nearby garage and came out with a small girl's bicycle painted pink with long plastic ribbons extending from the handlebars. He jumped onto the bike's long banana seat and began pedaling away from the house as I quickly followed.

Riding down the street, I reflected on the great contrast between the bicycle my friend was current riding and his cool three-speed racing bike that I had followed, only the day before as we traversed over many miles of empty country roads. I didn't tease my friend about riding his sister's bike because I knew that his day had been long and difficult, and assumed he was still in a bad mood.

When we reached the edge of a small corn field on Osborne Avenue, I asked my friend, "Did Hailey tell you what's going on?"

"No," my friend replied moodily.

We soon crossed the narrow Blanchard River bridge and approached the large swimming pool at Riverside Park. Turning right on a sidewalk, then sharply left near the community pool's chain link fence, we passed several kids walking home with towels around their shoulders, their lips and cheeks revealing signs of recently devoured red and blue snow cones. Ahead of us, an exodus of lifeguards, parents and children made their way out of the pool's gated area to nearby sidewalks and parking lots. Most of the people were unhurried, smiling as they strolled and chatted under a slowly setting sun. The night was calm and quiet as the pool's loudspeakers were suddenly silenced. The blare of popular songs from *Fleetwood Mac*, *REO Speedwagon* and the *Eagles* would have to wait until the pool reopened the following day.

My friend and I continued biking near the large concrete band shell before arriving at a playground where many of the *Sunday School Detectives* had already gathered. Hailey Cotton was there with her brother Moscow. Lisa Lavin and her cousin Cressida Hudson were in attendance, as was Joel Hemlinger, who was unable to join the others earlier in the day because of his music practice.

"Hey guys!" Hailey greeted us in her confident and friendly tone. "No Jennie tonight?"

"Nice bike!" Moscow laughed, when he saw Sneak riding up on the pink bike with pink ribbons.

My friend, the great detective, was silent, so I explained. "Jennie's not coming tonight. She just got back from Day Camp and she's busy packing for their trip tomorrow… and arguing with her Mom about how many stuffed animals she can bring."

"Ah, I can see her doing that," Joel laughed.

"Me too," smiled Hailey.

"How about Mr. Knick Knack?" Moscow wondered. "Did Jennie send him along?"

"Nope," I replied with a laugh. "She was so busy she didn't even remember to send him."

"Tell him I said 'Hi' if you see him," Moscow smiled.

"I'll do that!" I laughed.

"Alright. Okay, let's get started," Hailey interrupted, matter-of-factly. "We've got a lot to talk about tonight."

Soon, we all found places around the playground. Four of us – Hailey, Cressida, Sneak and I – sat at a metal picnic table, while Hailey's brother moved to the top of a nearby metal slide that looked like a wooden parapet from an old fort. Meanwhile, Joel and Lisa sat nearby on swinging metal gliders that could be made to go faster by pushing forward and pulling backward with handles located near their shoulders.

"Thanks for coming over," Hailey began. "We've had quite a long day."

"No kidding," Lisa said as her cousin nodded in agreement.

"We've had the craziest day too!" I exclaimed. "You wouldn't believe all the stuff that happened at the prison!"

"I can't wait to hear all about it," Hailey affirmed.

"Yeah, me either," said Moscow from above us.

"But, why don't we go first?" Hailey recommended. "We need to decide some stuff tonight. Then, we'd love to hear what happened at the prison. Okay?"

"Sure," I agreed, as my friend the great detective remained silent, studying the ground around his Chuck Taylor shoes, dark hair falling into his eyes.

"Okay," Hailey said with a smile. "So, let's start from the beginning."

Soon the three investigators – Hailey, Lisa and Cressida – began telling us of their morning meeting with Alice Williams at her biology lab at the college and her offer to help the *Sunday School Detectives.*

"Another scientist in the group!" Joel exclaimed. "That would be cool."

"Boring," said Moscow from his perch high above us.

"What do you think about that?" I asked Sneak, who was sitting next to me at the metal picnic table.

"Uh, what? Sorry, I wasn't paying attention," he said, lost in other thoughts.

"We might get another scientist in the *Sunday School Detectives,*" I explained.

"Oh… Great," he added, before looking to the ground again.

The three *Sunday School Detectives* then described their interview with Andrew Bayhill at his grandfather's office at the seminary, and included a long description of Andrew's work and his shock at being accused of the crime.

"So, did you take Andrew on as a client?" I asked eagerly.

"Yes, we did," said Hailey.

"And he says he's totally innocent. And had nothing to do with stealing the files," I summarized.

"He does," Hailey confirmed.

"He's probably guilty," Moscow smirked from above us.

"Why do you say that?" questioned Lisa.

"Just to make things interesting!" Moscow laughed as he jumped from one wooden beam to another above the metal slide.

"Well, there's enough people who think he's guilty already," said Hailey.

"Like Mr. Denlon, right!" said Lisa.

"Exactly!" Hailey agreed.

"Who?" asked Joel.

Soon, Hailey and the others described the late afternoon meeting at the hamburger shop with Andrew Bayhill's manager, Roberta Duncan, and the interruption by the chief of security, Jeremiah Denlon.

"He doesn't sound like a nice guy," I concluded.

"Well, he wasn't very friendly to us today!" Hailey said with a laugh. "But our dad is good friends with him, and he said he was just upset with some stuff going on at work."

"Yeah," Moscow agreed. "Dad told me they're playing golf at Wayside on Saturday. And I might get to drive the golf cart!"

"You hit a tree last time!" Hailey laughed.

"Yeah, but I was still learning how to back up!" Moscow explained, while many of us laughed.

Next, Hailey described their interview with Paula Bigelow at her old farmhouse outside of Benton Ridge. Then, Hailey described the brief interview with Jimmy Mannix at his family's house near the Country Club.

"So, really nothing from those two," Moscow Cotton concluded.

"Well, we're not so sure," said Hailey.

"We didn't think Paula was telling us the whole truth," Lisa added.

"Oh, yeah, Alice did pick up on that," said Hailey.

"Why's that?" I asked.

"Because Paula usually doesn't work on Mondays, but she did this week," Lisa began.

"And the files were stolen on Monday," Joel finished.

"Yep," said Lisa. "You got it."

"But, there are still like fifty other people you need to interview, right?" Moscow asked. "All of the paragliders."

"Paralegals," Lisa corrected.

"Moscow, I'm not done yet," Hailey said curtly to her brother. "If you could just be patient, you'll be able to hear the rest of the story."

"Okay, okay," he said from above.

"So, the last place we went was Joel's house..."

"What?" Joel asked.

"Sorry," Hailey apologized to our friend as we laughed. "It's been a long day! The last place we went was *Jason's* house – his name is Jason Compton. And like Paula and Jimmy, he worked in the office with Andrew Bayhill. Anyway, *Jason* lives with his grandparents over on East Foulke Avenue near the Church of God."

"What church is that?" I interrupted.

"The East Foulke Avenue Church of God," the girls said in unison as they laughed.

"Ah, right," I replied.

"So, anyway, we got to his house," Hailey continued.

"It was so creepy," said Lisa.

"Yeah," her cousin agreed.

"What was creepy about it?" Moscow asked, now quite interested in the story.

"I didn't think it was *that* creepy," said Hailey. "It's just that Jason kept all the lights off and the blinds shut so his grandparents could sleep."

"Sounds pretty creepy to me," I admitted.

"No kidding," Joel agreed.

"And then he invited us down to his basement where he has hundreds of clocks," Hailey continued.

"Now that *is* creepy!" said Moscow.

"Really, it wasn't too bad," his sister admitted. "It was actually kind of interesting."

"Did he keep the lights off there too?" I laughed.

"No, no," said Hailey. "He had lots of lights on, to see all of the clocks. There were a bunch of grandfather clocks and clocks in glass cases…"

"Cuckoo clocks too," Cressida said softly.

"Boring!" Moscow added. "Not creepy – just boring!"

"It was boring – after a while," said Lisa from her swing. "I was definitely feeling tired when he was telling us about all of the different clocks that he was working on."

"So, did *he* see who put the papers in Andrew's briefcase?" Joel asked.

"Well, not exactly," said Hailey.

"Not exactly?"

"I'll get to that part in a minute," Hailey explained. "But he definitely said he didn't see anyone put anything in Andrew's briefcase."

"Okay?" asked Joel. "So, what's the big deal?"

"Well," Hailey explained. "While we were interviewing Jason, Cressida went upstairs to use the restroom."

"And I found his bedroom," Cressida admitted quickly.

"Wow!" exclaimed an impressed Moscow Cotton. "What did you find?"

"Wait just a second Moscow," said Hailey.

"So," Lisa interrupted. "Right in the middle of our interview with Jason – while we were asking him all kinds of questions about the office and the missing files – he said he needed to go upstairs to get something. So, he bolts up the stairs and leaves Hailey and me in the basement."

"While Cressida was looking around upstairs?" I asked in a concerned tone.

"Yep," said Lisa.

"I wasn't thinking," said Hailey. "We should have followed him upstairs right away – instead we looked at some clocks for a minute or so."

"Anyway," said Lisa. "All of a sudden we heard this really loud scream."

"A scream?" I asked.

"From Cressida," Hailey revealed. "It was super loud."

"From Cressida?" Moscow, Joel and I nearly said in unison, surprised that such a quiet person could make such a loud noise.

"He was so mad at me," Cressida explained in her quiet voice.

"At you snooping in his room?" I asked.

"No, actually, not for that – for screaming so loud."

"What?" I asked. "I don't get it."

"He said he was sure I woke up his grandparents on the second floor!" Cressida explained, as the rest of our group laughed. "You have to understand," she continued. "The place was really dark and all of a sudden I saw Jason standing in the doorway with a big stick over his head. I thought for sure he was going to slam it down on me! So I ducked and covered my head and let out a big scream."

"Did he hit you?" I asked, concerned.

"Oh, no," said Cressida. "He didn't. He just stood there and asked why I was screaming so loud."

"You were screaming really loud," Lisa admitted.

"Yeah," Hailey agreed.

"What was he doing with the stick?" asked Moscow. "Was he waiting for all three of you to get there, and have a big fight?"

"No," Hailey replied in a serious tone and then mouthed the words: "Moscow, stop!" to her brother, as she shook her head.

"He said he needed it to get some of the grandfather clocks going," said Cressida.

"Yeah," Hailey explained in a more scientific tone. "He said he noticed several pendulums not moving on the clocks in the basement, so he went upstairs to get the long wooden stick he uses to push them along – to get them going."

"Couldn't he just push them with his hand?" I asked.

"Well, the ones he noticed were back behind some other clocks, and he said he needed the long wooden stick to reach them," explained Lisa.

"Makes sense," I said.

"Did you believe him?" Joel asked.

"Yeah, I did," said Lisa. "About that anyway."

"But just before Cressida thought she was going to get hit by the stick, she found some pretty interesting evidence," Hailey continued.

"Evidence? Really?" Moscow questioned. "What kind of evidence?"

"More papers," Cressida explained. "From the company. Like the ones Andrew told us about this morning."

"Like the ones *someone* put in Andrew Bayhill's bag," her cousin added.

"Dun dun dunn!" Joel hummed loudly. "And with that – the case is solved!"

"Nice work!" I congratulated Cressida. "All done in one day!"

"Technically, less than a day," said Moscow in a cheery voice. "That's awesome!" he added, jumping off the wooden platform and onto the metal slide, then landing quickly on the dusty ground.

"Well, don't be too quick to celebrate," said Hailey. "We ran into a slight problem."

"No search warrant?" Sneak said gloomily from his seat at the picnic table. "Or, did he destroy the evidence?" he asked, surprising the rest of us, because he was now paying attention to the conversation.

"No, no, nothing like that," Hailey said. "You see, when Cressida screamed, Lisa and I ran up the stairs and we saw the papers on the desk – so we are witnesses to what was there."

"There was a big stack of them," Lisa explained. "And they looked a lot like the ones they found in Andrew's briefcase," Lisa confirmed. "With the company name on them."

"And a few even had big stamps that said 'CONFIDENTIAL' and things like that," said Cressida.

"But," said Hailey, "after Jason got back to his room…"

"Where did he go?" I asked.

"Oh, he went upstairs to help his grandparents go back to bed," Hailey explained. "And give them their pills."

"Oh," I replied.

"So… once he came back," Hailey continued, "and we confronted him with the evidence, he said that the papers really didn't prove anything."

"What do you mean?" Moscow asked. "That doesn't make any sense."

"That's what we said at first," said Lisa.

"But," Hailey continued. "After Jason turned on more lights…"

"And put the big stick down," said Lisa.

"He had us look at the papers," Hailey continued. "He showed us that they were like thirty…"

"…or forty," said Lisa.

"…years old."

"Thirty years old?" I asked.

"Right," said Hailey. "They were really old."

"That's ancient," said Moscow, as he pondered his next trick.

"Why did Jason have those old papers at his house?" asked Joel.

"Well," Lisa said, as she exhaled deeply. "Jason said they were for his grandfather. He said that he found them while he was doing the file transfer work at Peloponnesian – you know, like we explained earlier about Andrew's job – taking papers from an old folder and putting them into a new one. Anyway, Jason said that his grandfather used to work at Peloponnesian and the papers had his name on them and were about the work he did a long time ago. So, he took them home to show them to his grandfather."

"He took his grandfather's forty-year-old files home?" Joel asked. "Why would he do that?"

"He said his grandfather has memory issues," Hailey explained. "It's called dementia. He has a really hard time remembering things. Jason thought that seeing the papers might help him remember those things that happened thirty or forty years ago."

"Jason said he was going to bring the files back," said Cressida. "After he had finished showing them to his grandfather."

"Were there any *new* files in that stack?" Joel asked. "Like the ones Mrs. Duncan told you about?"

"No," said Hailey. "It looked like Jason was telling the truth. They were all really, really old."

"What did you do then? Did you just leave the files there for him to get rid of?" Joel continued.

"Was that when he came at you with that long stick?" Moscow asked as he pretended to swing a stick in the air. "Did you have to duck and jump to get away from him and do some ninja moves?" he questioned as he pretended to defend himself against an attack – first bobbing his head down, then jumping up on a small plastic horse that was set on a metal coil located in the middle of the playground. "Jason Compton!"

Moscow yelled. "You can't hurt us with that wooden stick! Stay away from us or we'll wake up your Grandma!" Soon, the young daredevil jumped off one piece of equipment and then onto another before running around the dusty playground. "You'll never catch us with those alarm clocks!" Moscow exclaimed, as we laughed.

"He didn't come after us with a stick," said Hailey as she smiled at her brother. "Or his alarm clocks!"

"We really weren't sure what to do after Jason told us the papers he had in his room were different than the ones they found in Andrew's briefcase," Lisa admitted.

"We were afraid that if we left the papers there, he would get rid of them – or sneak them back into the office tomorrow morning and then there would be no way to prove that he took them," Hailey added.

"Right," said Joel.

"So, we actually took them," Lisa began.

"Oh, really?" Joel said, surprised.

"We told Jason that this could prove that Andrew Bayhill is innocent, and we needed to show them to his manager, Mrs. Duncan," Hailey explained. "We were thinking we'd go to her office tomorrow and show her the papers."

"Yeah," said Cressida. "We thought it might help Andrew get his job back."

"And that's what we wanted to talk to you guys about tonight," said Hailey. "Do you think we should take them to Mrs. Duncan first thing tomorrow morning, or should we do more investigating? There are a few other leads we could look into, but I think Cressida might be right – if Mrs. Duncan sees those papers, it might help Andrew get his job back."

"Well, maybe," Joel said doubtfully. "It doesn't really prove that Andrew is innocent, right?"

"What?" I questioned.

"You're right, Joel," Hailey affirmed. "We didn't find papers *exactly* like the ones Andrew was caught with. But, it does show there's at least one person in the office who's taking papers – and it's not Andrew Bayhill."

"Yeah, you're right," Joel agreed. "But from what you told us about your meeting at Wilson's, Mrs. Duncan already thinks Andrew is innocent, right? So, showing her the papers wouldn't really change *her* mind, right?"

"Right," Hailey said tentatively. "But, I don't think I know what you're getting at."

"Well, I don't think it's Mrs. Duncan you need to see at Peloponnesian tomorrow morning," Joel stated confidently. "It's that security chief."

"Mr. Denlon?" Lisa asked.

"Yep," said Joel. "From what you told us, *he's* the one who thinks Andrew is guilty and *he's* the one who thinks he's already solved the case. So, if you showed him the papers you found at Jason's house, it would show the chief of security that he's got it all wrong. And once he sees that he's wrong, he might give Andrew his job back, don't you think? So, it's *Mr.* – uh, *Denlon* that you need to convince, not Andrew's manager, Mrs. Duncan."

"That makes a lot of sense," Hailey agreed.

"I think you're right, Joel," said Lisa.

"Okay, well... Let's take the papers to Mr. Denlon in the morning," Hailey concluded, then paused before asking, "Who wants to go with? We could try to meet at Peloponnesian around eight o'clock, when people start coming to the office – that way Jason wouldn't have a chance to make up a story about the missing papers. If we can show them to Mr. Denlon first, then meet with Mrs. Duncan after that, who knows, maybe Andrew will get his job back by tomorrow afternoon?"

"That would be cool," said Lisa.

"Yeah," several of us agreed.

"That would be really cool," I added. "Do you have those papers you took from Jason's house?" I asked, eager to see the company's confidential documents.

"They're in my mom's car," Hailey explained. "She dropped us off and is coming back in a little while. I thought they might be hard to read out here."

"Oh, got it," I agreed, surprised by the growing darkness of the long summer's day.

CHAPTER 32

"Well, that was our day," Hailey Cotton sighed, after describing the opening investigation into the discovery of stolen company documents. "I wanted to make sure everyone had all the information… if you wanted to help." She paused, then questioned her long-time friend. "Sneak, after hearing about the case, are there any other angles you think we should look at?"

"No," Sneak Ryerson replied glumly.

"How about you, Pep?"

"Naw, I can't think of anything either," I admitted.

"Okay, well, let us know if there's anything we might have missed. We're all still pretty new at this detective business! Sneak, you've got the most experience of us all!"

Hailey expected the young detective to reply, but he was quiet, silently studying the dusty playground.

"Okay, so, how about you two?" Hailey eventually asked, looking first to me and then to the great young detective. "How was your visit to the jail?"

"Prison," Sneak Ryerson clarified gloomily.

"What?" Hailey asked.

"It wasn't a jail that we went to. It was a prison. And it was… uh… hard. Why don't you explain it, Pep?"

Even though the hour was getting late, and I had been through so much during the day, I felt a sudden rush of energy at my friend's request. Reminding the others of a Labrador Retriever, I quickly leapt from my seat and began a rapid explanation of the day's events – first describing our drive south to the Lebanon Correctional Facility and then the meeting with the warden who wanted to talk about Sneak's old cases, and then our interview with the young prisoner named Julian Davis.

"Julian Davis!" several of the *Sunday School Detectives* exclaimed upon hearing his name.

"He's there too?" Lisa asked incredulously.

"Yeah," I said maturely. "Of course, he's in a different unit than Mr. Crenshaw, but he's there too."

"Wow," said a surprised Hailey Cotton. "Alice will be really sad to hear that. She was hoping he'd be placed in a mental facility, or somewhere he could get some help."

"Well, he's definitely still crazy," I explained. "He still thinks the UFOs are coming to rescue him."

"Oh brother," said Moscow, as he again climbed up the metal slide – this time grabbing the bottom of the slide and climbing up underneath the structure until he reached the top high above us.

"He even had a note," I continued, knowledgably, "from *The Great Peggu*."

"Oh no," said Hailey. "Mr. Crenshaw's still trying to warp his mind?"

"Yep," I replied. "I think so."

"Bummer," came the responses from several in our group.

"What did it say?" asked Hailey, referring to the note.

"It was just a bunch of gibberish about UFO's and stuff like that," I explained. "But it did have a lady's name: Mary…"

"York," Sneak added.

"Right! Mary York was the name," I clarified. "Sneak's Uncle Charlie is checking to see if there's anyone around here with that name. And the warden is checking on any visitors or prison workers with that name too. So far, they haven't found anyone." I paused. "The note also said something about a funeral – and I can tell you more about that later."

"A funeral?" Hailey asked, puzzled.

"Yeah, I'll get to that in just a minute," I continued. "So, after we met with Julian Davis, we met with Mr. Crenshaw. And… he's got a screw loose too if you ask me."

"What's he like?" questioned Lisa.

"Well, he's old," I explained, as the others laughed. "And pretty creepy."

"What did he want to talk about?" Hailey asked about the man she had seen only briefly – after pulling a space alien mask from his face.

"He was really interested in knowing more about our work on *The Case of the Mysterious Circles.*"

"What exactly did he want to know?" Hailey asked warily.

"He wanted to know how he got caught!" I exclaimed. "You know, like when did Sneak figure out it was him – stuff like that."

"Oh," said Lisa. "So, *that's* why he wanted you to come visit him!"

"Well, I think that was a big part of it. But he also said he had some information for us."

"Oh, right," said Hailey. "I remember you guys telling us that at the pool party. What was it?"

"Well," I began, before pausing dramatically. "He said that *something big* is going to happen tomorrow here in Findlay – something *really* big."

"Something big?" Hailey asked, as her face contorted.

"Yeah," I confirmed.

"Dun dun dunn!" Joel said loudly, his eyes glimmering with joy.

"So, what's gonna happen tomorrow?" Moscow Cotton asked, now hanging upside down from the top of the slide.

"Mr. Crenshaw didn't know," I replied.

"Or at least he didn't say," Sneak added morosely.

"So, you think he probably *does* know what's going to happen, but he's just not saying?" Hailey asked her friend.

"Yeah," the young detective replied in his somber tone. "He's up to something, I just don't know what it is… yet."

"Hmm," said Hailey. "But it would be hard to do something *big* from prison, right?"

"That's what I said," came my confident reply. "I'd be surprised if he has anything to do with it."

"So, he just told you guys that something is going to happen tomorrow, but he didn't tell you what it was," Lisa summarized bluntly.

"Right," I confirmed.

"Did he at least tell you *where* he got his information?" Lisa asked in a more frustrated voice.

"He did," I continued. "Mr. Crenshaw said he heard it while he was here in the Hancock County Jail. He said he tried to use it to get less prison time, but nobody took him up on his offer. So, he waited until this morning to tell us. He said the word around the jail was that all of the criminals should have alibis tomorrow."

"Hmm," Hailey said again. "Alibis..."

"Sounds kind of fishy, if you ask me," Moscow added.

"Yeah, definitely fishy," Joel agreed.

"So, what do you think's gonna happen?" Lisa asked quickly. "Did Sneak's Uncle Charlie know? 'Cause he drove you down there, right?"

"He drove us," I confirmed. "But Uncle Charlie didn't know either – it was the first time he'd heard about anything big happening tomorrow. Once we left the interview with Mr. Crenshaw, Uncle Charlie called the police department to check on it, but none of the officers had heard about anything happening tomorrow either. They were going to check with their – what did he call them, C.L.s?"

"C.I.s," Sneak explained. "The confidential informants."

"Ah," said Lisa.

"I was thinking maybe it's gonna be a bank robbery or something like that – that would be something really *big*," I suggested.

"Definitely," Moscow agreed in an excited voice from the slide. "Maybe they'll blow up a safe at a bank and take all the money! BAM! BAM!" he shouted excitedly.

"I just hope they don't take any of my money from the *Squirrel Club*," I confessed, as the others laughed at my mention of the local Diamond Savings and Loan's program for young investors – a program featuring a bank employee dressed in a squirrel costume who made appearances at local parades and events. "I've been saving up for a long time," I added.

"Even though he didn't tell you much, I'm sure you got a bunch of clues from the interview with Mr. Crenshaw, right Sneak?" Hailey asked her old friend.

"Ah, not really," the young detective replied, his mood still dark and unchanged. "Like Pep said, Mr. Crenshaw just gave us that basic information, but when I started to press him to try to get more information, he got mad and stormed out."

"I would have paid money to see that!" said Moscow.

"It was kind of funny," I admitted.

"There was really only one clue that I could do anything with," Sneak Ryerson admitted. "And it wasn't much."

"What was it?" Moscow asked.

"Well, it was from that note that Julian Davis read to us – from *The Great Peggu*," Sneak explained.

"But really it was from Mr. Crenshaw, right?" quizzed Lisa.

"Correct," I confirmed.

"In the note," Sneak continued. "It said to *please leave a correct eulogy*."

"A what?" asked Moscow.

"A eulogy. It's something they say at a funeral," I explained knowingly.

"Right," the great detective agreed. "When someone dies, it's the speech that friends say about the dead person."

"Oh," said Moscow.

"So, it got me thinking," Sneak continued. "Where would we leave a eulogy?"

"Maybe at a church?" said Moscow. "Duh?"

"Or a funeral home, right?" said Lisa.

"Or a cemetery," Joel added.

"A cemetery is what I thought of first," Sneak agreed. "So, with that clue – plus the fact that Mr. Crenshaw said he had seen me at the cemetery and was always one step ahead of..."

"Wait, what?" Hailey interrupted. "Mr. Crenshaw said that he had seen you?"

"Yeah," admitted the famous detective. "He said that he saw me at the cemetery a few months ago – when I almost caught Julian Davis with his note. He even claimed that he saw me fall off of Julian's bumper and encouraged a lady to call the police on me."

"That's creepy," said Joel.

"Definitely," Lisa agreed.

"So, because of those clues, we returned to the cemetery this afternoon and I went to the headstone where Julian Davis grabbed that note. And guess what?" Sneak asked, now in a more animated tone.

"What?" Moscow asked excitedly. "Did you go bumper hopping again?"

"We found two more clues," the great detective explained, ignoring Hailey's brother.

"Two clues?" Hailey confirmed.

"Yeah, the first one was actually written on the headstone, where he left the note," Sneak continued. "Does anyone want to guess who is buried underneath that marker?"

"I have no idea," said Moscow. "It wasn't your headstone was it?"

"Now that would be creepy!" said Lisa.

"No, no. It was Margaret Crenshaw," Sneak explained.

"Mrs. Crenshaw?" Hailey asked, surprised.

"What?" someone gasped.

"Yep," confirmed Sneak Ryerson, before quickly returning to his dejected tone. "If I would have just stopped and looked at the name on that headstone, I could have solved that case so much sooner."

"You think?" Lisa asked.

"Well sure. At the time, I wasn't sure how Russell Crenshaw was involved in the mystery. He could have been just another victim of the fires. But if I would have known that his wife's grave was the drop-off location for the notes to Julian Davis... That would have put Mr. Crenshaw at the top of my list of suspects. I would have quickly seen that he was the mastermind behind all of the fires and those letters to the editor."

"Well, maybe," Lisa doubted.

"Knowing that information would have changed a lot of things about the investigation," the young detective responded in an annoyed tone. "And I failed to see it."

"So, what was the second clue?" Hailey asked.

"The other clue was actually *behind* the headstone," I interrupted, barely able to contain myself, eager to share the dramatic evidence with our friends.

"Yeah, it was behind the headstone," Sneak Ryerson agreed.

"Was it another note, like the kind Mr. Crenshaw left for Julian Davis?" Hailey asked.

"Not exactly," said Sneak. "It was for me."

"For you?" Hailey clarified.

"For me," Sneak said again.

"Was it written in code, like the notes for Julian Davis from *The Great Peggu*?" Hailey asked.

"No, it was pretty clear," Sneak replied.

"It was flowers," I explained quickly. "Black flowers with a banner. And the words on it said – what did it say exactly?"

Sneak told them.

"Ugh," several said in shock.

"It actually said 'RIP Sneak Ryerson'...like Rest in Peace?" asked Lisa.

"Yep, with the year I was born through this year."

"So, it was saying you're going to die this year?" Lisa asked.

"That's terrible," said Hailey. "Can your uncle prove that Mr. Crenshaw sent that from prison?"

"He's going to look into it," said the young detective. "As you can guess, he wasn't too happy about it. But so far, there's no evidence of where they came from."

"Wow," said Moscow from the wooden platform above us. "That is crazy."

"Yeah, and scary," I added. "That part about 'I'll see you under the ground' wasn't very nice either, was it?"

"Like you'll be buried, right?" said Moscow.

"We'll have time to figure all that out later," the famous young detective said quickly. "What I really want to do is figure out what's going to happen *tomorrow* – and maybe try to stop it. We're supposed to go on our family vacation tomorrow and be gone for two weeks, but I'm gonna try to explain all of this to my parents and see if they'll cancel our plans, or at least delay our vacation by a day or two. If they don't do that, I'll see if they will let me stay at home to work on the case. But, it's pretty unlikely they'll change things, since they've been planning the trip with my grandparents for a while, so that just leaves *tonight* for me to try to work it out. To be honest, I have no idea what the *big thing* will be tomorrow, but I still have a few hours to work on it. And… that means if I can't figure out the mystery tonight, you'll have to figure it out tomorrow."

"Now, how exactly are *we* going to figure it out?" questioned Moscow.

"There probably won't be anything *big* happening tomorrow anyway," I said, trying to reassure my friend. "Mr. Crenshaw probably just made up all that stuff to get us to come visit him today."

"Maybe," Sneak replied doubtfully.

"What do you think it is?" Hailey asked her longtime friend. "Do you think it will be a bank robbery, like Pep said earlier, or something else?"

"I'm not sure. I don't have a lot to go on," the young detective admitted as he pushed back the hair on his forehead, revealing eyes that were tired and bloodshot from the enormous strain he had put himself under to unravel the secret. Sneak Ryerson paused. "We've already seen Mr. Crenshaw commit arson and a bunch of other crimes. He's capable of a lot of bad things."

"Yeah, like getting someone to run you over with their car," Moscow said somberly.

Moscow's comments quieted our discussion, as the sounds of cicadas, grasshoppers and distant fireworks filled the air. Suddenly, two quick honks of a car horn were heard from the parking lot near the band shell.

"That's probably my mom," Hailey Cotton told us. "We should get going."

Several of the *Sunday School Detectives* agreed.

"So, should I meet you in the lobby of the big building tomorrow?" I asked apprehensively.

"Sure, that would be great!" Hailey smiled. "Let's try to get there around eight o'clock or so, okay?"

Several *Sunday School Detectives* agreed with sleepy voices.

"Okay, I'll see you there," I replied.

CHAPTER 33

Darkness had fallen on Riverside Park and the *Sunday School Detectives* slowly navigated broken and uneven sidewalks on our way to the parking lot. Illumined by the orange glow of streetlights, we saw that both Mrs. Cotton and Mrs. Lavin had arrived and were waiting to take two carloads of investigators home.

Sneak Ryerson and I carefully walked our bicycles toward Mrs. Cotton's station wagon and were warmly greeted by the mother of our friends, Hailey and Moscow. We gathered around the copper-colored car and talked to Mrs. Cotton for a few minutes. Near the end of our conversation, Mrs. Cotton said to the young detective, "I bet you're really looking forward to your big family vacation tomorrow. Your Mom told me you'll be visiting a lot of places. It sounds really interesting. I think she said your first stop will be Niagara Falls, right?"

"Yeah," Sneak Ryerson admitted. "We'll probably leave in the morning."

"Well, I hope you have a great trip," Mrs. Cotton said encouragingly.

"I do too," Hailey Cotton added. "And… we'll try to do what we can while you're gone."

"Yeah, we'll try to figure out that case without you," said Hailey's brother. "And if *we* can't do it – I guess that means *you'll* have to figure it out when you get back in September!"

The famous detective laughed – the first I had seen him smile all evening. "Moscow, you're ridiculous!" he exclaimed. "I'm not gonna be gone that long!"

After the cars pulled away, my friend and I stayed in the parking lot for a moment, watching the water roll over the long waterfall of the Blanchard River dam.

"Your parents *might* let you stay," I said hopefully, trying to offer some encouragement to my friend as the water gurgled and splashed nearby.

"They won't," Sneak calculated.

"Yeah, but if they do, you can stay at my place. My mom won't mind."

"Thanks," said my friend. "Maybe I can call you from a pay phone tomorrow night to see what happened – we'll be in Canada, so I'll have to get some Canadian money, but I think I should be able to reach you."

"Okay," I replied, feeling a great sadness about my friend's situation. "Really try to talk them into it," I pleaded. "Tell them how important it is."

"They won't let me," my friend concluded.

We were quiet for a moment, staring at the water as it dropped from the higher elevation into the lower part of the river while a collection of sticks and logs swirled aimlessly near the river's edge.

Soon, we stepped onto our bikes and began the slow ride home along darkened streets and sidewalks. After crossing the Blanchard River bridge and reaching Osborne Avenue, I said goodbye to my friend and promised to see the great detective off in the morning.

Within a few minutes of arriving home, I was fast asleep.

CHAPTER 34

Maybe there's a way to convince my parents to change our vacation plans, Sneak Ryerson thought as he rode home on his sister's bicycle. *We're supposed to leave at seven or eight tomorrow morning – maybe I can convince them that waiting a day would be better. Or maybe I can encourage them to wait two days and leave on Saturday? The odds are against me,* he thought. *But it might prevent a major crime.*

As he rode, he thought about how different the Ryerson house would be when he came home. Arriving home on most any other night, he might find his father napping in his recliner, surrounded by newspapers and magazines, his dark glasses askew on his face below a tight crew cut. His sister, Jennie, might be watching television, or already in bed listening to repeating music on her small red and black ladybug-shaped turntable, to help her memorize her piano lessons. His mother, meanwhile, might be busy sewing at the dark wooden dining room table or baking cookies in the kitchen.

Tonight, however, the Ryerson house would be very different, with his parents and grandparents, his sister and cousin all readying for their long trip. *Maybe they haven't made much progress,* Sneak thought. *If they aren't ready, it will be easier to convince them to stay.*

Pulling into the driveway, however, the young detective discovered that the plastic car top carrier was now affixed to the roof of the *Maroon Monster*, held securely in place by multiple black bungee cords and ropes. On the driveway, near the car's back bumper, a collection of hard-shell Samsonite suitcases sat waiting to be loaded.

Wow, Dad's made a lot of progress, observed the young detective. *Since he's been working so hard on the vacation plans, maybe I should talk to Mom first.*

Sneak quickly returned his sister's pink bicycle to the garage and entered the back door of the house, where he was immediately greeted by his mother carrying a laundry basket filled with clothes.

"Ah, Steven, you're back!" his mother exclaimed wearily as she climbed the stairs from the basement. "Something smells absolutely awful down there! I thought I told you to get rid of all those experiments!"

"I guess there still must be one or two animal or plant samples," the young detective acknowledged, trying to remember where in the basement he had placed the remaining items that were decomposing.

"Well, throw them out tonight!" his mother directed. "If the laundry room smells that bad now, just think about how bad the whole house is going to smell in two weeks!"

"Okay, okay," Sneak replied quickly.

"And you need to help your father with those suitcases too," she added. "They're pretty heavy, and he wants to get them loaded tonight so we can get an early start tomorrow."

"Sure," the young detective replied, as he quickly decided to shift tactics and talk to his father about changing their vacation plans instead.

He waited for his mother to pass, then took the three steps up to the kitchen where Cousin Sara was helping Mr. Ryerson and Grandpa Ryerson wash and dry dishes at the kitchen sink.

"Hey Sneak," Cousin Sara greeted the young detective with a smile.

"Well hullo!" Grandpa Ryerson said, when he suddenly saw his grandson.

"Hiya Sneak," said Mr. Ryerson, with a towel over his shoulder and a large metal pot in his hands. "I'm glad you're back. I could use your help with loading some suitcases tonight. I'm going to try to get those up into the car top carrier tonight, so we don't have to worry about it in the morning."

"Oh, okay," Sneak replied morosely as the three continued washing and drying cups and mugs and pots and pans as they laughed and told stories while the smell of Palmolive dish soap filled the air. Moving into the dining room, the young detective saw that the wooden dining room table was covered with small maps, travel books and a tall U.S. atlas, while the recliner and sofa in the nearby living room contained piles of folded and unfolded clean laundry, ready to be packed into waiting suit-cases. On the living room floor, Jennie Ryerson had placed a number of her stuffed toy giraffes in a long line, hoping to get permission to take most of them on the trip.

"Hey, Dad," the young detective asked a few moments later, inter-rupting his father's work in the kitchen.

"Yes?" his father questioned, turning to his son.

"Can I talk to you for a few minutes?"

"Now?"

"Yeah, it's kind of important," his son explained, looking around the crowded kitchen. "Maybe we can go out to the burning barrel?" he added.

"Uh… Well, sure," Mr. Ryerson replied. "We do need to take out the trash before we leave tomorrow morning."

Soon, father and son were walking to the back yard, carrying waste-paper baskets filled with the family's trash. Upon reaching the *burning barrel*, an old, rusted oil drum located behind the family's garage, the pair emptied the wastepaper baskets into the large barrel. Mr. Ryerson lit a match and dropped it inside and the pair stood and watched the flames dance through the debris. "So, Dad," Sneak Ryerson said to his father. "I was wondering about tomorrow. Is there any way we could leave later in the morning?"

"I don't think so," Mr. Ryerson replied, shaking his head. "You know our first stop on the trip is Niagara Falls and everyone is looking forward to it. We really need to leave around eight or so to be able to see everything up there. After we look around there tomorrow night and Friday morning, we've got to hit the road again, because it's a long drive to New Hampshire. It will take us at least seven hours to get over there."

"Yeah, but do we have to leave at eight tomorrow morning? Could we leave later, like ten o'clock or eleven? Or maybe sometime in the afternoon?"

"I don't think so," Mr. Ryerson explained. "It's six hours to get to the Falls from here. And with all of the stops your grandparents might want to make, it could take even longer."

"I could ask them not to stop," the young detective proposed.

"I'm not sure if that will help," Mr. Ryerson said with a laugh. "You know how they like to see things – and there's a lot to see on the way – even before we get to the Ambassador Bridge in Detroit! There's Fort Meigs outside of Toledo, The Henry Ford Museum and Greenfield Village too."

"Yeah, but..."

"Then, from Detroit, it's another four hours to the Falls – and they'll probably want to stop somewhere in Ontario, like London or Stratford or Niagara-on-the-Lake. They've even mentioned getting a picture next to a sign for Ryerson Polytechnical Institute in Toronto."

"But I could..."

"We'll need to get an early start if we want to get to the Falls by the evening," his father said solidly. "'Cause we'll want to look around there too."

"Is it possible for us to wait a day or two before we leave?"

"No," his father said firmly, shaking his head and remaining focused on the details of the family's trip. "I don't see how we could. We need to be in Keene, New Hampshire by Friday night for the start of the family reunion – and, like I said, that's a good seven hours from Niagara Falls – even more with our stops! I don't see how we could leave any later."

"Urg," Sneak said with a pout.

"I thought you were looking forward to the trip! There are some really interesting places that we're going to see. What's with the sudden change of plans?"

"It was something one of the prisoners said this morning," Sneak explained.

"Ah, I figured we'd have some time to talk about that over the next two weeks in the car!"

"Yeah, probably," Sneak Ryerson said in a resigned voice, thinking again about the long trip with the family.

"So, what did he say?" Mr. Ryerson asked.

"He said that something *big* is going to happen tomorrow."

"Something *big*, huh?"

"Yeah."

"What is it? Did he tell you?" his father asked.

"No," said the young detective. "And I couldn't get any clues out of him about it."

"That's too bad," said Mr. Ryerson. "But your Uncle Charlie was there, right?"

"Yeah."

"And he couldn't get any more details out of him either?"

"No," Sneak said again, in a resigned voice.

"Well, I guess you'll just have to trust your uncle to find out what it is. If we leave when I hope we do tomorrow, we'll be a couple hundred miles away by noon. So, there's not much you could do. Plus, you're still grounded from doing detective work for a little while longer, right?"

"Yeah," Sneak said, his voice weak, disheartened that he could not continue the investigation.

The pair continued to watch the flames whip through the trash in the darkness of the night. A moment later, they were startled by a noise nearby and soon saw Sneak's Grandfather Ryerson walking through the yard toward them – one hand holding a wooden cane while his other hand held onto a plastic wastebasket.

Sneak's Grandfather Ryerson was an elderly man – turning eighty on Christmas Day later in the year – who favored plaid western shirts and cowboy hats over his bald head. Grandfather Ryerson had worked tending oil and gas pumps for over forty years in eastern Wyoming. And, like his son, he loved reading, but their magazines differed, with Grandfather Ryerson enjoying *The Saturday Evening Post*, *Popular Mechanics* and *National Geographic*. Although he had not finished high school – only achieving an eighth grade education – Sneak thought of his grandfather as one of the smartest people he had ever met: someone who knew a lot, it seemed, about everything.

"You forgot a can," Grandfather Ryerson explained as he handed the plastic trash can to his son.

"Thanks," Sneak's father replied. "I guess I did."

As they added more trash to the fire, Sneak decided to tell the men about the events of the day, hoping that his father or grandfather might spot a clue he had missed. Soon, the young detective was describing the visit to the prison and the interviews with the two prisoners.

"So, can you think of any clues from that?" Sneak asked, after he had concluded his descriptions of the meetings with Julian Davis and Mr. Crenshaw, as they stood before the rusted burning barrel.

"Well, I should be able to figure it out!" Sneak's father exclaimed with a laugh. "I was the smartest kid in the fourth grade!"

"Yeah, and the only one!" Grandfather Ryerson laughed, as the two men shared a joke about their life in rural Wyoming, where Sneak's father had been the only member of his grade in a small three room elementary school.

They paused for a moment.

"I can't really think of anything," Sneak's father replied.

"How about you, Grandpa?" Sneak asked.

"Well," his grandfather began. "I was just thinking how strange that clue was."

"Which one?" asked the young detective.

"About the eulogy," said his grandfather.

"Why's that?" asked Sneak.

"Well, I guess when you get to be my age, you get to see a lot of funerals," he said with a chuckle. "And I've been a pallbearer for a lot of them with our Masonic order and for the Eastern Star chapter too," he informed his grandson. "But, I've always thought of a eulogy as something that is *given*," Grandfather Ryerson explained. "Or something that is *said*. It's not something that someone *leaves*."

"That's interesting," said his grandson.

"Do you think that might help?" Grandfather Ryerson asked.

"I'm not sure."

The three paused for a moment.

"Did I ever tell you the story of *Special Order 191*?" Grandfather Ryerson asked. "It's sometimes called *The Lost Dispatch* or *The Lost Order*. Now that was a communication that was left at the wrong place and the wrong time. It is quite interesting. It changed the course of the Civil War – or at least the Battle of Antietam."

A short time later, Sneak followed his father and grandfather back into the house and began making plans to leave for their family vacation the following morning.

CHAPTER 35

On the morning of Thursday, July 10th, I rode my bicycle to Decker Avenue to say goodbye to my friend. I arrived a little after eight o'clock and found the Ryerson family in the final stages of their departure. Jennie Ryerson was arguing with her father about the number of stuffed toy giraffes she could bring, while Sneak Ryerson was receiving a lecture from his mother about not packing enough clothes. Meanwhile, Grandma and Grandfather Ryerson finished their cups of coffee on the back porch with Cousin Sara. Eventually, after several more trips back into the house, the family found seats in the long station wagon they called the *Maroon Monster*.

"Did you figure out what's supposed to happen today?" I asked my friend, moments before he departed. "Is the *big thing* a bank robbery or something else?"

"I wasn't able to figure it out," he replied, his face showing the weariness of a late night attempt to solve the problem with his computer-like mind. "I'll try to call you tonight from Canada," he added hopefully, from inside the long station wagon.

"Okay, I'll let you know what happens," I reassured the young detective. "It probably won't be anything."

I followed the car on my bicycle as Mr. Ryerson erratically backed out of the driveway and then quickly pulled away from the house on Decker Avenue. After stopping at the stop sign at the end of the street, the car turned north on Osborne Avenue, heading towards Riverside Park. After crossing the Blanchard River bridge, the Ryerson's *Maroon*

Monster was out of sight and I paused for a moment trying to remember the many places the family would be visiting: Niagara Falls.... Keene, New Hampshire.... Caribou, Maine.... Boston... Philadelphia.... Washington, D.C. I couldn't remember all of the cities, or the exact days they would be there – but I wished I could be going with them.

Turning left at the stop sign, I waved to the workers at *C&R Auto Body*, who had their garage door opened to the bright morning sun. At the stoplight, I turned west on Sandusky Street, riding quickly down the sidewalk as my green Whittier Elementary gym bag, attached to the handlebars of the bike, flapped in the wind.

Eventually, I arrived at the tall office building of the Peloponnesian Oil Company and leaned my bicycle against the side of the building. Approaching the large glass windows of the lobby, I nervously joined a group of workers who entered the building through the fast-moving revolving doors.

After entering the large lobby, I soon found several of my friends.

Hailey Cotton, Lisa Lavin and Cressida Hudson were all seated in plush green chairs next to an expensive glass table and having an intense discussion.

"We shouldn't have gotten here so early," Lisa protested in a hushed voice.

"It's fine," Hailey reassured her, as many office workers filed past them through the large lobby to a bank of elevators. "I'm sure it won't be too much longer," she added optimistically.

"Have you seen Andrew's boss come in?" I questioned.

"There are so many people coming through here," said Lisa. "I don't think we'll see Mrs. Duncan."

"How about the other people from the office?" I asked.

"I've been looking for Paula and Jason too," Lisa added. "But I haven't seen them."

"Jason Compton's not going to like us being here," said Hailey as she looked down at the large manila envelope bulging with papers in her hands.

"Are those the papers you got from his house?" I asked as Hailey confirmed with a nod of her head. "Can I take a look?" I asked.

"Not now," Hailey said in a serious voice. "Let's wait."

"I thought Moscow was going to be here too," I wondered, changing the subject.

"He's riding his unicycle outside," Hailey said as I looked out the window and saw Moscow Cotton fly by on the sidewalk across the street, with Joel Hemlinger racing behind. "I think Joel's out there too," Hailey added.

"I'll go hang out with them," I told my friends.

I went outside to look for my two friends but could not find them. They had apparently turned a corner and were on another street, but I was unsure which direction they went, so I returned to the lobby.

I found an empty green chair next to my friends and placed my green Whittier Elementary gym bag at my feet. Looking forward, I was immediately mesmerized by the large silver sculpture of an oil well derrick and pump. My eyes, transfixed by the large, shimmering metal artwork, initially followed the intricate shadows and shapes of the large installation, but a few moments later I could not keep them open, and I fell asleep.

I awoke around nine o'clock when a rush of workers arrived. After their loud and boisterous entrance, only a few other workers entered the lobby, followed by delivery drivers with packages. And then, for a while, the lobby was quiet.

I fell asleep again and was awakened when a well-dressed woman approached our group. "Are you the ones who want to see Mr. Denlon?" she asked, talking quickly.

"Yes," Hailey confirmed.

"Mr. Denlon has a very tight schedule today," the woman stated rapidly, sounding distressed. "Very tight. And he doesn't really have time for any unscheduled visitors."

"But we have," Hailey began, looking down at the manilla envelope containing numerous documents.

"Is there anything I can help you with?" the woman interrupted.

"No," Hailey insisted. "We need to speak to Mr. Denlon personally."

"Okay, let me see what I can do," the woman replied and then quickly left.

Ten minutes later she returned.

"Follow me," the woman quickly directed.

"A couple of our friends are outside," Hailey explained. "Can you give us a minute to go get them?"

"I suppose so," the woman said, swiftly looking at her watch.

"Can you go get them?" Hailey asked me, and I soon walked with great speed across the lobby to the revolving doors. Exiting the building,

I was glad to see that Moscow and Joel were now across the street, in an empty alley behind the Elk's Club.

"Hey guys," I yelled when I ran up to Moscow, who was still riding his unicycle, and Joel, who was singing a popular song. "They're ready to see us!"

Moscow swiftly hid his unicycle behind a large planter of flowers, and we crossed the street. We entered the long lobby, passing the large silver sculpture of the oil well derrick and pump, and quickly caught up with the others who had gathered at the bank of elevators.

"We're all here," Hailey smiled, and we soon followed Mr. Denlon's assistant into an open elevator where she pushed the button for the basement.

After exiting the elevator, we walked quickly behind the assistant to a room that was located below the lobby.

"Mr. Denlon will meet you here," the woman said hastily. "He may be awhile," she added before promptly leaving.

"I thought we'd go up to the top floor to some fancy office!" Moscow complained, when we were alone and seated around a long table. "Dad told us Mr. Denlon's office is right next to the Executive Dining Room. He even said you can see it from the street, if you know where to look. Dad said the dining room's got a big curved glass window that overlooks the city."

"That's cool," I said, nodding.

"But instead, they've taken us to the *basement*," Moscow protested.

"Yeah, what gives?" I agreed. "I thought Mr. Denlon was a big shot?"

"He is," said Hailey as she looked around the simple white room that contained only plain plastic chairs, a long table, and a plain cream-colored touch-tone office telephone. A large mirror covered one of the walls. "Hey, wait a minute!" Hailey exclaimed. "This must be the room where they brought Andrew Bayhill on Monday!"

"What?" I wondered.

"Oh yeah!" said Lisa. "This must be the room with the two-way mirror!"

"A two-way mirror!" I said in a shocked voice. "I've only seen those on TV."

Moscow and I rapidly approached the mirror and tried to spy who or what was on the other side. "I think I see someone!" I said excitedly. "No, wait a minute," I added. "That's just me."

Joel Hemlinger sang popular songs and laughed with the girls while Moscow Cotton and I continued to make faces and look at the edges of the mirror to try to see into the next room, but we tired of the effort after about ten minutes.

After another few minutes of waiting in the basement room, the door suddenly flew open and Jeremiah Denlon entered, followed closely by his assistant who was now carrying a stack of papers.

This was the first time I had seen the chief of security, and he looked angry. "Peeved," he said quickly as he walked into the room, while his assistant shut the door. "Mighty peeved, is how I'm feelin' right now," the chief of security clarified in his deep Texan drawl. "When I last saw y'all yesterday, I asked you to leave the good people of Peloponnesian alone," Mr. Denlon explained, his piercing stare going through us. "And I thought... well... maybe they'll wait *a year* or so before bothering us again. Those *Sunday School Detectives*, they're good folks, they're smart, they mean well, maybe it will be 365 days or so before I hear from them again. And then I got to thinkin' that maybe one year is probably too long – maybe it will be six months before we hear from them. Then, I thought, naw, maybe it won't be half a year. Maybe it will be just *one month* before we hear from those *Sunday School Detectives* again. And then I thought, maybe that's too long, maybe not thirty days, maybe it will be *one week* – those *Sunday School Detectives* will wait at least a week before contactin' me again!" He paused. "And then, what do you know? Here I am today, busy in meetin' after meetin', and all of a sudden, my assistant comes in an' tells me I've got some uninvited visitors who didn't wait one year, they didn't wait one month or even one week! You all waited exactly *one day* to start pestering me again! I already told you I didn't want you kids snooping around here! We've got a lot of important things to take care of. But now you're all back! I'm sure, y'all just want to talk more about ole' Andy Bayhill! You all probably talked to him, and he gave you some more information, or something like that. But I've already told you what he did! I've already told you he's guilty! He's as guilty as sin! So, if I were you, I'd go back to lookin' for those lost pets like you were doin' last month! You're never gonna find out anything important helpin' ole' Andrew Bayhill! That case is shut tight!"

During Mr. Denlon's long speech, Hailey tried to explain why we had come to the office but could not interrupt the focused security chief. "But, we found something really important... " she was finally able to say, holding her manilla envelope filled with company papers.

"I don't care if you found *Jimmy Hoffa*!" Mr. Denlon replied sharply. "I don't want you kids foolin' around with our company. We've got important things to do here! This isn't a place for kids! There's so many other things we need to take care of! You kids need to skedaddle!" Turning to go, he addressed his assistant. "Escort these children upstairs, and make sure they leave the building. I'm runnin' late for my next appointment with two board members."

"Of course, Mr. Denlon," replied his assistant. "I'll take them to the lobby and then be right up." Several in our group stood to leave but suddenly sat down because of the shock of what happened next.

To our surprise, a middle-aged woman suddenly burst into the room. She wore expensive summer clothes and fine jewelry, but was visibly distraught, her cheeks streaked with makeup from tears of worry and distress. "Jeremiah! They told me I could find you here!" she said loudly, looking straight at the security chief as she clutched tightly to a crumpled piece of paper.

Like us, Mr. Denlon was surprised to see the visitor and was momentarily speechless.

Hailey Cotton, however, immediately said, "Mrs. Mannix?", quickly recognizing the woman. "We saw you yesterday, when we went to interview Jimmy."

"Ch... Cheryl?" Mr. Denlon finally replied, in a surprised voice. "Wh... what are you doing here?"

"You've got to help me!" she cried. "You've got to help *us*—Jeremiah!"

"What's happened?" the security chief asked, his voice concerned.

"It's Jamie!"

"What's happened to him?" questioned the security chief.

"He's... he's been... *kidnapped*!" the woman sobbed.

"What?" the security chief asked in visible shock. "Are you sure?"

"Someone took him!" The woman explained, as tears rolled down her face. "Someone took him and his friends, while they were on their fishing trip."

Several of us gasped at the news.

"Jeremiah, I need your help!" the woman pleaded while clutching the piece of paper.

"Absolutely," Mr. Denlon said, his initial shock diminished, as his voice changed to a calm and reassuring tone. "We'll do whatever it takes to get James and the others back."

"This note says there are some people we need to find. It says they can help us! They aren't listed in the phone book," the woman explained in a quick burst of words between sobs. "I've... I've looked all over for them this morning. But I can't track them down. I desperately need your help on this!"

"We'll put all our resources on it," the security chief said supportively.

"That's such a relief, Jeremiah," the woman sighed, wiping her cheek with a beautifully manicured finger. "I've been so upset about this."

"You have my full cooperation," Mr. Denlon replied. "So, tell me, who is it exactly that we should be looking for?"

"They're called the *Sunday School Detectives*," the woman explained.

PART FOUR

CHAPTER 36

James Mannix was smiling as he drove his long, light-blue Cadillac down his long driveway next to his professionally manicured lawn. Most mornings, his drive followed the same routine – pulling out of the garage beside his son's blue Subaru with its window stickers of private schools and yacht clubs, then deep thoughts about corporate strategy on his drive downtown before eventually pulling into the executive parking garage, secured by a tall silver garage door that opened to a parking area within one of the company's buildings, designated for only the most senior company leaders.

But, on the morning of Thursday, July 10th, James Mannix's drive was very different. He left his driveway well before sunrise, but instead of bolting over to a busy Tiffin Avenue and then towards downtown, he followed the streets that wound around the Country Club, passing several holes of the well-maintained golf course, and then driving past the clay tennis courts and the long white clubhouse. Soon, his car was zooming along the twisting, curve-filled Country Club Drive as the senior executive smiled, delighting in the plans he had made for the next three days. His wealth had provided him with many comforts, including several beautiful places to relax – a large house in Florida and a cabin in the mountains out west – but James Mannix was a man who enjoyed routines. And so, just as he had done in previous years, he had scheduled four days with friends to go fishing on Lake Erie.

The older executive – only a year or two away from retirement – had packed his fishing gear in the trunk of his long four-door car along with a small suitcase, that noisily shifted back and forth as he took the sharp turns that followed the bends of the Blanchard River. Slowing his car at a stop sign, the executive turned left at a softball field and then took a sharp right, quickly pulling into the driveway of a tall two-story blue house, near the parking lot for the pool at Riverside Park.

"Mr. Mayor," James Mannix said in his matter-of-fact voice when he exited the car and saw the city's mayor, Kevin Runyon, standing inside his garage filled with old campaign signs and cardboard boxes overflowing with old door-to-door campaign flyers.

"Mr. Mannix!" the mayor replied heartily as he looked at his watch. "James, you're a few minutes early, but I'm not surprised!"

"I guess you can tell I can't wait to get out on the water!"

"But I'm not quite ready!" the mayor protested. "I noticed someone had disturbed the wishing well last night. They pushed over part of the stone wall, so I tried to rope it off. It's pretty deep down there – been dry ever since I've owned the place, but I wouldn't want anybody to fall in."

"Probably some kids, huh?"

"Yeah, no doubt. Just let me finish up here," the mayor said as he loaded fishing supplies into a plastic container on the floor of his garage. "I've got just a few more things to load. The guys should be here soon."

James Mannix and Mayor Runyan talked for several minutes about their plans as the mayor continued packing items into a plastic storage container. Soon, a newer model Ford Mustang pulled into an open parking space along the street.

"He's got a different car every time I see him," James Mannix joked.

"I think you're right, James," the mayor laughed.

After parking, the driver yelled from his car. "Hey Kevin," he beckoned to the mayor. "Is it okay for me to park here on the street since we'll be gone for a few days? Or should I park over in the parking lot by the pool?"

"Where you're at should be fine," the mayor replied. "No one will care if your car is there for a few days."

"I guess I know who to talk to if I get a ticket, right?" the driver laughed, as the mayor quickly said, "I'm not promising that!"

Soon, the driver turned off the loud car engine as he and his passenger exited. After gathering their fishing gear, tackle and several duffel bags from the car's trunk and backseat, they approached the blue Cadillac in the driveway.

"Morning James," the car's passenger said, addressing James Mannix as he brought his equipment to the car.

"Morning Larry," came the executive's reply. "There should be plenty of room in the trunk for your gear."

"Looks like a good morning to be out on the water," the driver of the Mustang said as he joined the others and placed his gear into the trunk of Mr. Mannix's Cadillac.

"Definitely a good day to be out on the water, Dan," James Mannix declared. "I checked the forecast, and I think we'll have a really good couple of days."

"Are we all ready to go?" Dan, the driver of the Mustang, asked impatiently.

"I still need a few minutes! I'm running late!" Mayor Runyon said as he dashed back into his house.

A short time later the four were in the blue Cadillac heading northeast on Route 12 with James Mannix driving and Mayor Kevin Runyon in the passenger seat. In the wide backseat were the two occupants of the Mustang, two middle-aged men named Dan and Larry who worked as barbers at a shop at the mall. The pair had closed their barbershop, as they had done for a number of years each July, to go fishing on Lake Erie.

Larry, the older of the two barbers, was quiet and sometimes appeared nervous, frequently adjusting his silver wire-rimmed glasses. When asked about his family, he would disclose the smallest amount of information about his wife, who was a teacher, and his daughters, who were students at Findlay High School. On rare occasions, the older barber would display great wit, and offer a joke in response to something said by his colleague.

Dan, the younger of the two barbers, was effusive and kept the others occupied for most of their hour-and-a-half drive with stories about cars – updating his fellow passengers on a newly purchased car he would be using for drag racing and an older car he was preparing to drive at the upcoming Demolition Derby at the Hancock County Fair.

"I think you could talk about cars all day!" James Mannix laughed as they approached a marina near Sandusky, Ohio.

"He does," Larry said ruefully, as he adjusted his glasses and gazed at the many boats in dry-dock and on the water. "Haven't you been over to the barber shop?"

"I think that's it," said Mayor Runyon, pointing to a boat moored along one of the long wooden piers. "The captain called me last night with the ship's name. It looks like there's a parking spot right in front!"

Soon, James Mannix pulled into a parking spot next to the large vessel as the four gazed at the gleaming golden letters on the ship's stern – *The Ichabob*.

The four quickly exited the car with their hands filled with fishing gear and supplies. "Permission to come aboard!" James Mannix said loudly to the broad-chested captain on the ship's deck who had watched them approach.

"Permission granted," the captain replied.

Soon, the quartet carefully walked up a narrow plank to the boat.

"You found us," the captain said in a raspy yet hearty voice.

"Your directions were very good," said Mayor Runyon.

"Good," said the captain, as he scratched his scraggly blonde beard, then adjusted a worn and tattered Greek fisherman's cap. "Watch your step as you come aboard. I can send my mates down to help bring up the rest of your things."

"Mates?" asked the mayor.

"Well, just two fellas that need a lift to Kelly's Island."

Soon, two scruffy looking mates descended and emptied the car of fishing gear as James Mannix supervised, and soon all were back onboard.

"Hey, do I have time to run down to the restaurant and get some breakfast?" Dan asked quickly. "I'm starving."

"I'll have one of the mates make you something once we've shoved off," the Captain replied. "It won't be a problem for him. He's a good cook."

"Right," the mate said with a smile. "I'm a good cook."

"Why don't you have him do that, Dan?" Larry, his fellow barber, suggested. "That way we can get out on the water sooner. The weather is beautiful. It's gonna be a great day."

"Well, okay," said Dan. "I don't want to hold us up."

The boat was quickly unmoored from the dock and was soon floating past several red buoys. James Mannix moved towards a seat on the bow as the other passengers made their way to the cabins below deck.

Unexpectedly, the captain jammed the throttle forward with his strong and weathered hand, momentarily disorienting the passengers as the boat thrust ahead while still in the marina's no-wake zone.

"This is gonna be a good weekend," Dan said to Larry, his coworker, after regaining his balance, and began unpacking a few items from his duffel bag in a cabin below deck.

"Hey Dan, why are there so many family pictures in here?" Larry asked, looking around the cabin. "The other boats we've rented didn't have all this personal stuff on the walls."

"Hmm, that's weird," his coworker replied. "I don't know."

Soon, Mayor Runyon knocked on the frame of the open cabin door.

"You guys notice anything strange about this cruise?" the mayor asked.

"Yeah," Dan answered. "Larry noticed all of the pictures on the walls."

"Yeah, and I thought it was strange there aren't that many supplies onboard for four days on the water," the mayor explained.

"Let me check the dressers," Dan said before opening a clothes drawer. "There's someone's clothes in here!"

"What do you think is going on?" Larry asked as he readjusted his glasses.

A married couple was eating breakfast on the outdoor patio of a nearby restaurant when they spotted *The Ichabob* pull away from the marina. They both waved and shouted a friendly hello. Then the man turned to his wife with a confused look and asked, "Who are those people on Bob Crane's boat?"

James Mannix sat in one of the large comfortable chairs on the bow of the boat as the vessel rocked up and down, swiftly leaving the marina. *The sun's out – a perfect morning*, he thought, as his mind marveled at the glorious day. A few moments later his thoughts turned to Cheryl, his young wife – and his third – who had made such an impression on the society ladies of Findlay with her many parties and charity galas. *She's a keeper*, he said to himself.

James Mannix then thought about Jimmy, his son from a previous marriage, who seemed to be settling in well in his summer job and not acting as rebellious as he had the previous summers. *They like him at work*, James thought. *He's even involved in some music concerts*, he added happily.

The executive then turned his thoughts to his real estate holdings – the large house in Findlay, the cabin in the mountains and place at the beach. *Who would have thought I'd have so much?* he wondered, remembering his humble beginnings. *Mannix, you old dog, you've come a long way,* he mused as his face lit up with a grin.

"Mr. Mannix, could you come here for a moment?" the captain beckoned. "We need you on the bridge."

"Sure," the executive replied in a relaxed tone and soon lazily lumbered to the port side of the boat. After a few unsteady steps, Mr. Mannix grabbed a railing and pulled himself up the few stairs that led to the bridge platform, careful not to spill a drink he had in his hand.

Reaching the bridge, Mr. Mannix stopped abruptly, seeing that the captain was joined by the two mates who were now carrying firearms.

"We won't be going walleye fishing today," the muscular captain explained.

CHAPTER 37

In the basement interview room at the headquarters of Peloponnesian Oil, Jeremiah Denlon stared at the distraught woman, Cheryl Mannix, and tried to make sense of her comments. "Cheryl," he said. "Did I hear you right? You're saying that your husband has been kidnapped and you need to find the *Sunday School Detectives*?"

"That's right, Jeremiah," she confirmed. "I'm desperate to locate them. I just found this note on my front door," she said, quickly placing the crumpled piece of paper down on the table. "I need to find the *Sunday School Detectives* to know where to leave the money!"

Mr. Denlon flattened the crumpled note as we scurried around the table to read it.

We have kidnapped four people including:
James Mannix of Peloponnesian Oil
Mayor Kevin Runyon of Findlay
Leave $131,578.95 in unmarked large bills at the
cave at Riverside Park by one o'clock today
The Sunday School Detectives will know
where to leave the money
The prisoners will be released unharmed after our escape

"What do you know about this?" came the swift question from Mr. Denlon as he moved from staring at the note on the table to staring at each of us.

"Nothing," said Hailey quickly.

"Yeah, we swear," Lisa added. "We don't know anything about this."

"Why are you questioning these kids, Jeremiah?" Mrs. Mannix asked.

For a moment the room was quiet.

"You're not going to believe it, Cheryl," Mr. Denlon began, shaking his head.

"We... we're actually the *Sunday School Detectives*," Hailey admitted cautiously.

"You!" Mrs. Mannix nearly shouted.

"Yes," Hailey confirmed.

"What have you done with my husband!" Mrs. Mannix said loudly. "This isn't funny. I need him back – safely."

Hearing these comments, Cressida, who was turning pale, quickly left the room.

"Where is she going? What's going on here?" Mrs. Mannix questioned.

"I don't know," said Hailey. "Honestly."

"None of us knows what's going on," Lisa added, concerned for her cousin who had suddenly left the room.

"I didn't know you were just a bunch of kids!" Mrs. Mannix shouted.

"Cheryl," Mr. Denlon said in a calm voice. "We'll get to the bottom of this and get your husband back safely. You have my word on it."

"This might be the *big thing* we heard about yesterday," I said quickly to Hailey and the others.

"What *big thing*?" Jeremiah Denlon asked me firmly.

"We were in prison yesterday... in Lebanon," I said haltingly. "Not the country, but the city near Dayton. And one of the prisoners told us that something big was going to happen today... and... I was worried they'd take my money from the Squirrel Club, because I keep a lot of money there... I mean it's mostly spare change from my allowance... but it's been adding up over the years."

"What are you talking about?" the security chief interrupted.

"We were told a *big thing* was supposed to happen today and it looks like this is it," I summarized. "It wasn't a bank robbery after all."

"Who told you this information?" Mr. Denlon asked forcefully. "About the *big thing*?"

"Mr. Crenshaw," I replied quickly. "Mr. Russell Crenshaw. But he didn't tell just me... he told our friend Sneak Ryerson... who's a famous detective... an' who's on his way with his family to Canada right now… probably already at Niagara Falls… then they're going to New Hampshire."

"What?" Mr. Denlon asked, confused.

"Oh, and Mr. Crenshaw told Sneak's uncle – Charles Foster," I added.

In an instant Jeremiah Denlon grabbed the telephone on the table and dialed a number.

"Captain Charles Foster, please," he said calmly, then waited a moment as the operator connected him to the police captain. "Charlie? Jeremiah Denlon here. Could you come over to the General Office right away? We've got a situation I need your help with. It's going to probably take all of your officers, but we can't let it get out over the airwaves yet. It probably would be best if you came over in an unmarked car, too. I'll meet you in the lobby." He listened to the police captain's response, and then said a quick, "Thanks."

After hanging up the phone, the security chief let out a deep breath.

"Charles Foster will be here in a few minutes," Mr. Denlon told us. Turning to Mrs. Mannix he said, "Cheryl, let's get you to someplace comfortable – you've had quite a shock." Then turning back to us, he added, "I'll be back in a few minutes with Captain Foster and we'll sort this whole thing out. I hope you've been telling the truth."

Instantly, the security chief grabbed the note from the table and left the room with his assistant, as Mrs. Mannix feebly walked between them.

"You can cancel my appointment with those two board members," we heard Mr. Denlon say as they walked down the hall.

CHAPTER 38

We waited quietly for about fifteen minutes in the basement inter-view room at Peloponnesian Oil, talking in hushed tones and whispers – unsure of who was behind the two-way mirror on the other side of the wall. Soon, Jeremiah Denlon returned to the basement room with Charles Foster.

"Hey kids," Uncle Charlie said in a somber voice, while Mr. Denlon stood just inside the room, near a wall by the closed door, quietly observing the conversation. "We've got a pretty serious situation here. As I think you heard, our mayor – Mayor Runyon – and Mr. Mannix from this office, left on a fishing trip earlier this morning. Then, a short time ago, Mrs. Mannix received a note about them being kidnapped. The boat they went out on has been recovered and was empty. So, it seems like the story checks out... at least so far. The ransom is to be paid by one o'clock this afternoon, which doesn't give us much time. The ransom note says that you kids know where to leave the money. The drop off location is to be at Riverside Park... at a cave?"

Instead of holding the note, as Mrs. Mannix and Mr. Denlon had done, Uncle Charlie held the edge with a tissue and sat it down on a white piece of paper on the table. We moved closer to read the note again.

"So, to begin," Uncle Charlie continued. "Can you kids tell me anything that you know about this case? Did you know anything about a kidnapping being planned? Or anything like that?"

"No," Hailey admitted to our friend's uncle. "We were surprised to hear about it."

"I was surprised too," the police captain confessed.

"This must be the *big thing* that was supposed to happen today, don't ya think Uncle Charlie?" I said, knowingly.

"It looks like it, Pep," the police captain agreed. "But I wouldn't have guessed this in a million years. If anything was going to happen... I thought it was going to be a robbery."

"Me too," I agreed.

Our conversation paused for a moment.

"Okay, then," Uncle Charlie continued. "The note says you kids know where this cave is located?"

"We found it during our last case," Hailey explained.

"I wrote about it in the newspaper," I added.

"I don't think I've ever seen a cave at Riverside Park and I've been over there a lot. Where exactly is it?"

"It's under two cherry trees that overlook the river," Hailey explained. "It's real close to the memorial for that famous songwriter."

"Ah, okay, the Tell Taylor Memorial! I know where that is," confirmed Uncle Charlie.

The police captain paused, as he thought about the park.

"Like I said, I've been there a lot, but I haven't seen a cave," he confessed.

"It's below the trees," Lisa explained.

"But the ground is just flat there. I've seen the shelter house and some trees but not a cave entrance. I don't get it."

"The entrance is actually on the hillside below the trees," Hailey clarified. "And above the walking path that goes by the river."

"Above the path?" Uncle Charlie asked quickly.

"Right," Hailey affirmed. "It's at least ten feet above the walking path on the side of the hill, so it's really hard to notice."

"And it's covered with moss and ivy too," Lisa added.

"We had to lift Moscow up on someone's shoulders to reach it," Hailey clarified.

"Yeah, it's pretty high up," Moscow Cotton explained. "And above the cave entrance are those two cherry trees and the memorial – at the very top of the hill."

"Okay, got it," Uncle Charlie said, nodding his head. "I guess I forgot there's such a big elevation change from where the monument is by the street and where the river is there. There's a long set of steps going down to the river that's not too far from there, right?"

"Yeah," someone said.

"Well, now that I know what I'm looking for I'm pretty sure I could find it. It's basically right there at the bend in the river." The police captain paused for a moment, as he considered how the kidnappers might retrieve the requested money. "So to get to any money that was placed there, someone could either rappel down, maybe by tying a rope to one of those cherry trees and sliding down to the cave. Or, they could jump up to it, if they were down at the walking path by the river. Is that what you're telling me?"

"Yep," confirmed Moscow. "There's only two ways to get there."

"How did they ever pick this place?" Mr. Denlon interrupted, still standing near the door. "And how did they know that *you* kids would know where it is?"

"I wrote about it in the newspaper, in the article called *The Adventure at Riverside Park*," I explained. "When Moscow got up there, on the edge of the cave, he could see farther out into the river, and solved the case."

"Yeah," Moscow Cotton confirmed. "We thought it was a rock ledge on the side of the hill, but when I looked, I could see it was actually a cave."

"Okay, got it," replied the security chief. "So, anyone who read that article in the newspaper would have known about it – and they would have learned that you kids knew about it too."

"Yeah, I guess so," confirmed Hailey Cotton.

"Hey," Uncle Charlie said quickly. "Can someone draw me a map, just to make sure I know exactly where I'm going. I think I can find it from your description, but I want to make doubly sure I can find it."

"Sure, I can," Moscow Cotton volunteered and a few moments later, Mr. Denlon located a pen and paper from a nearby room.

"So, here is the big bend in the river," Moscow began, as his left hand drew a wide semi-circle in the shape of an uppercase letter C, in the middle of the page. "Way up here is the softball diamond," he said, adding a few words and a diamond at the top left of the page. "And from there, the street goes straight down…. what's the name of it?"

"McManness," Uncle Charlie noted.

"Right," said Moscow, as he drew a straight line for the north-south street on the left side of the paper. "And there is the monument."

"The Tell Taylor Memorial," clarified Hailey, identifying the monument that contained a stone plaque and three large rocks engraved with the lyrics from the famous 1908 song, *Down by the Old Mill Stream*.

"Right," agreed Moscow, and he quickly drew three rocks, south of the softball diamond. "And to the right of the monument are those two cherry trees," Moscow explained, as he drew two trees to the east on the monument, next to the bend in the river.

"Makes sense," said Uncle Charlie.

"And below those trees," Moscow continued, "on the side of the hill is the entrance to the cave."

"Copy that," Uncle Charlie said, to let us know he understood.

"Then to the south of that is the parking lot for the pool," Moscow added, drawing an oval parking lot. "And next to that, on the right, is a picnic shelter and all of the concession stands."

"Okay, I think I've got it!" said Uncle Charlie. "Thanks again for your help. This map has been helpful."

"Sure," several of us affirmed.

"If you think of anything else, give me a call."

"Okay," several Sunday School Detectives agreed.

The room was momentarily silent.

"Do you need anything else?" Hailey inquired.

"I don't think so," said Uncle Charlie. "We'll take it from here. We don't have much time to get that money together, but there are people who are working on that now. The bank should be able to get it all soon – especially since one of the people kidnapped is on their Board. We'll get Mrs. Mannix and the other family members over to the police station so we can get their statements. You never know if someone might have seen something unusual or spotted one of the perpetrators earlier in the week loitering around one of their houses. And, based on your map, if the drop zone is there at the cave, I think we'll set up our overwatch position across the river, on the roof of the Kodak building. That spot should give us a good view of everything happening across from there."

"Oh, yeah, that would be a good spot," I agreed.

"Thanks for your help, kids. You done good," Uncle Charlie affirmed in a serious voice. "Like I said, we'll take it from here."

"Great!" Hailey and several of the *Sunday School Detectives* replied.

"I'll have my assistant take you back to the lobby," Mr. Denlon clarified.

"Let's try to keep all this quiet today," the police captain said in a firm voice as we concluded. "There's no need to get people panicked if we can resolve it quickly, right?"

Several of us agreed.

"Oh, and kids, needless to say... Let us do our jobs and stay away from that entrance to the cave."

CHAPTER 39

We waited for a few minutes in the company lobby, now busy with an early lunchtime crowd, as Hailey Cotton called her mother to pick us up. Once Hailey returned from a bank of phones near the elevators, we walked quickly past the large silver sculpture of an oil well derrick and pump and exited through a fast-moving revolving glass door and into the warmth of the sun on a busy downtown sidewalk.

"That was so crazy!" I said excitedly after we exited the company lobby. "I'm so relieved to get out of there!" I said in a loud ecstatic voice, overjoyed to be out of the building and into the fresh air. "That was so intense!"

"I'll say so," said Moscow.

"Do you think they're going to take Mr. Mannix and the mayor to the cave when they go to get the money?" I wondered.

"Pep, you shouldn't be talking so loud," Hailey scolded. "It's still an ongoing police investigation. Plus, we don't want anyone to know about it until everyone is home safe, right?"

"Yeah, right," I agreed.

As we waited for Mrs. Cotton, we discussed how hungry many of us were and soon Moscow suggested that we get lunch.

"I want to get as far away from here as I can," Lisa suggested with a sigh. "My mind needs to think about something else."

"Mine too," I agreed.

"I know a place that is far away from here that has a good lunch!" Moscow smiled, and soon it was decided that we would have lunch at Friendly's, a restaurant near the mall.

Mrs. Cotton arrived in her copper-colored station wagon and agreed to take us to Friendly's on Tiffin Avenue and we quickly entered the car. Hailey Cotton took the front passenger seat, still holding onto the manilla envelope containing company memos that Jason Compton had taken from his office. Her brother, Moscow, found a seat in the back of the station wagon after having retrieved his unicycle parked nearby. Joel Hemlinger, Lisa Lavin and I found places in the second row, behind Mrs. Cotton and her daughter.

"Sounds like you've had a long day already!" Mrs. Cotton said with a smile, after we shared the many details with her on the way to the restaurant.

After arriving at the restaurant, we had to wait near the entrance for a few minutes as our table was being prepared. While we waited, Mrs. Cotton went to talk to a friend at a nearby booth.

A few minutes later, our hostess informed us that a table was ready.

Mrs. Cotton was still talking to her friend as we walked past her and the ice cream counter to a wide oval table at the back of the restaurant. "Hailey, could you ask Patsy to bring me a coffee?" Mrs. Cotton requested.

Soon Patsy, our server, took our order for drinks – starting first with Hailey and Moscow, who were her customers every Sunday after church, along with the Ryersons. Moscow ordered a root beer while several others at our table ordered milkshakes.

Mrs. Cotton soon returned to the table and explained, "I'm glad I was able to speak with Marilyn! The women's circles are planning our church's annual summer Bazaar – and we're in charge of the Soup and Salad Lunch in a few weeks! We actually have a meeting to talk about it this afternoon, so it was great to discuss a few things just now! We raise quite a lot of money for the Red Bird Mission, but there's a lot that goes into it."

A few minutes later Patsy took our food order. I ordered chicken tenders while Moscow Cotton ordered the clam boat special, leading Joel to sing the hit song from 1974, "Don't Rock the Boat".

"Maybe we can go swimming this afternoon?" Moscow suggested after we placed our orders, as Joel and I heartily agreed. "I've got a few more dives I can show you guys!"

"Awesome!" Joel exclaimed. "I didn't show you guys all the ones I can do either."

"Can you take us to the pool afterwards, Mom?" Moscow asked his mother.

"Sure, but remember, I've got that meeting later this afternoon to help plan the Soup and Salad Lunch, so you'll need to get a ride home from someone else."

"Oh, I'm sure we can do that," her son said confidently.

We were silent for a moment, as a loud ring of a bell indicated an order was "up" from the nearby kitchen.

"Swimming and diving will be good," Moscow sighed. "I just want to think about something different than that office."

"Yeah, me too," I agreed.

"Me three," said Joel.

"I can't believe that the *big thing* was," I began, before remembering that we were asked to keep the information quiet. "You know, the *big thing*," I added in a quieter tone.

"Yeah, it's *so* weird," Lisa agreed. "I think I'll go with you guys to the pool," she added. "I don't think I'll swim, but it would be good to do something different this afternoon and not investigate anything."

"Yeah," several of us agreed.

"I don't think we helped Sneak's Uncle Charlie very much," Hailey explained to Mrs. Cotton. "Except for giving him the location of the cave." She paused for a minute, then said in a quiet voice, "It's weird that we actually met Mr. Mannix yesterday. And now today, he's been kidnapped."

"Yeah," a few of us agreed.

"Wait? What?" Mrs. Cotton said, as she quickly put down her cup of coffee. "You saw Mr. Mannix yesterday?"

"Yeah," Hailey confirmed. "We were at his house. I thought I told you that last night."

"I don't remember you saying that."

"It's just a big coincidence, I guess, huh?"

"Hmm," Mrs. Cotton replied. "I don't know."

"Well, it doesn't matter now," said Moscow. "We're going swimming and gonna let the police take care of it!" He paused for a moment. "But, they might come after me because a couple of my dives are illegal in three states!"

We laughed at his comment, as his mother was deep in thought, focused on the information from her daughter.

"Are you sure you've told them everything?" Mrs. Cotton asked. "It seems like you'd have a lot more to tell them, since you were at the Mannix's house yesterday. Are you sure you don't want to review that again?"

"I don't always say this," Mrs. Cotton's daughter said with a smile. "But I think that Moscow may be right, Mom. Maybe we should just take a break and let our minds think about something completely different."

"But Hailey, there are four lives at stake," Mrs. Cotton said passionately. "This seems pretty important."

"I don't know," said Lisa. "We're all feeling pretty tired."

"I don't know if you all know that I grew up on a farm north of Bowling Green," Mrs. Cotton explained. "My dad was a farmer – a dairyman – and also the local butcher, until he sold his farm to my oldest brother. And he still likes telling farming stories to anyone who will listen. He's always been full of great phrases and expressions – some of them are funny, about life on the farm; some of them are serious. But, they've helped me quite a lot over the years."

"That seems lucky," I said.

"Well, yes, that's one way of putting it," Mrs. Cotton smiled. "I think some of the phrases were even passed down from his family from Austria."

"Australia!" I asked, "With the kangaroos?"

"No, no, Austria, the country in Europe," Mrs. Cotton explained. "My dad came from a long line of farmers. And he really had to work hard to keep the family farm going. He'd have to wake at five in the morning to milk the cows and always encouraged all of us kids to be diligent and work hard too. Over the years, he's said things like, 'Better get out there kids, the hay isn't in the barn yet' or 'The early bird catches the worm' or sometimes when we'd really have to focus and persevere through some difficulty, he'd say, 'Sometimes you've just got to bite the bullet'."

"Those are funny sayings," Hailey agreed.

"Those sayings of his actually reminded me of the study we've been doing in our adult Sunday School class on the Old Testament."

"How's that, Mom?" asked Moscow.

"Well, we just finished our study of the Book of Joshua. And I was really taken by the beginning – the first chapter, actually – where we learned about Joshua's leading the Israelites into the Promised Land. What I thought was really interesting was that God told Joshua three times to 'be strong and courageous', and the third time God told Joshua to 'be strong and very courageous, do not be afraid, or discouraged, for the Lord your God will be with you wherever you go'. I memorized that passage, because it really spoke to me."

"Wow, that's really good," declared Hailey.

"Yeah," several of us agreed.

"So," Mrs. Cotton continued, "I would encourage you to think about Joshua – and my father's advice – and keep going with your investigation. God has given you all some amazing gifts. I have a feeling that there might be more to this case that you can help with."

"That sounds really good, Mrs. Cotton," Lisa affirmed.

"Okay," said Hailey. "I guess we should take another look at what we told Sneak's Uncle Charlie."

"Yeah, and then maybe we can go swimming?" Moscow asked.

"Sure," said Hailey. "I don't want to stop you guys from showing off your dives!"

The discussion paused for a moment.

"Moscow, maybe you can redraw that map you gave to Uncle Charlie?" his sister proposed. "Maybe we'll see something we missed?"

"Sure," said her brother.

A few moments later, Moscow Cotton flipped over a paper placemat and found a crayon from a kid's meal and was redrawing the map of Riverside Park. "Here's the bend in the river," Moscow began, as he drew a large semi-circle "C".

"Here's the softball diamonds," he said, drawing the diamond at the top left of the page. "Here's the street that runs past the diamonds and the park," he explained as he drew a straight line from the diamonds down the page. "Here's the memorial…"

"The Tell Taylor memorial," Hailey explained.

"And over here are the two cherry trees," Moscow continued.

"Do you guys think we told Sneak's uncle everything we knew?" asked Hailey.

"I think so," I replied.

"We told him that Moscow had to get on someone's shoulders to reach the entrance," said Lisa.

"We didn't really tell him what the inside of the cave was like," said Hailey.

"Well, I couldn't really tell," Moscow admitted. "I was looking out to the river for that missing canoe to solve that case."

"Right," said Hailey. "But is there anything you *remember*. Do you have any specific memories of when you were up there?"

"The cave was really dark," Moscow admitted. "I couldn't really see in because of all the moss and ivy. Plus, there was a pretty good breeze blowing on my shoulders, so I didn't want to stay up there very long."

"Wait... You said a breeze was blowing on your shoulder?" said Hailey.

"Yeah, that was all I remember," her brother admitted.

"A breeze that was coming from inside the cave?" Hailey clarified.

"Well, yeah!" said Moscow. "Duh! It was a cold breeze – I mean we don't get those coming in off the river at the start of the summer."

"I didn't know you felt a breeze," Hailey began. "A breeze might mean...."

"That there's another opening to the cave!" Lisa exclaimed.

"That's what I was going to say too!" said Joel.

"I think we might be on to something!" admitted Hailey.

"We probably should call Chief Foster," Lisa recommended.

"424-7150", I chanted as Hailey Cotton rushed to the payphone at the back of the restaurant while Patsy brought our lunch to the table.

CHAPTER 40

Hailey Cotton returned from the payphone at the back of the Friendly's restaurant to tell us that she wasn't able to speak with Sneak's Uncle Charlie directly, but had left a message telling the police captain that there was likely another entrance to the cave.

"I'm glad we were able to help him out!" her brother, Moscow Cotton, said with a grin. "Now we can go swimming!"

Our food had arrived while Hailey was making her phone call, and before eating, Mrs. Cotton said a brief prayer for the speedy recovery of the men who had been kidnapped earlier that morning.

After our meal, which was filled with jokes and laughter, Mrs. Cotton offered to drive us home to get our swim trunks. Stopping at my house to change clothes, I was curious as to why my bicycle wasn't in the garage where I usually kept it. Later in the day, I remembered that I had left my bicycle downtown, and hoped it was still leaning against the outside wall of the Peloponnesian Office Building.

As Mrs. Cotton drove us to Joel's house, we discussed several options for exhibiting our diving and swimming talents, including the Canterbury Club and the YMCA, but ultimately decided on the pool at Riverside Park, with its tall high dive and smaller springboards – which were much higher than the other pools in the community.

Turning at the light at Tiffin Avenue, we passed Fire Station Number 3 and a softball diamond on the left and Mayor Runyon's house on the right. "Hey, it looks like the mayor has put some rope up around his wishing well," Joel said, pointing to the local landmark that we were all familiar with. At some point in our lives, most of us had stopped by the wishing well and thrown in a coin and made a wish. Even though the well was on his private property, across from the historic Riverside Park, the mayor welcomed visitors, and sometimes left campaign flyers on the well's brick wall that extended several feet above the ground.

"He's such a friendly guy," I said of the mayor, who many of us knew from his lectures on public service at our elementary schools and his guided tours of the old courthouse.

"It looks like part of the wall is knocked over," Hailey commented, as we quickly drove past the mayor's house on the right and then the Tell Taylor Memorial on the left.

A few moments later, Mrs. Cotton pulled into the parking lot for the swimming pool.

"You'll call someone to get a ride home, right?" Mrs. Cotton asked as we exited the car.

"My mom can come and get us," assured Joel.

"Or, my mom could get us too," Lisa said with a smile.

"Okay, have fun kids!" Mrs. Cotton replied.

After Mrs. Cotton drove away, we quickly made our way to the short brick building where lifeguards and the pool staff were busy at the front desk. Moscow, Joel and I paid for our admission, received our hand stamps and were directed into the boys locker room, filled with showers and a large wooden rack of wire baskets, that were each secured in place by combination locks. We exited the locker room and entered the pool area, and were quickly greeted by the many sights and sounds of dozens of kids swimming and playing at the long community pool.

After giving my towel and green Whittier Elementary bag to Hailey, who had followed Lisa through the girls' entrance – and had also decided not to swim – I followed the guys to the long line for the tall high dive. "You are not going to believe the trick I'm going to do," said Moscow as we waited. "You guys will be so impressed."

I tried to choreograph my dives with the popular songs that blasted from the pool's loudspeaker, while Moscow and Joel and I tried different dives from the different diving boards – showing off our abilities to do corkscrews and cannon balls, belly flops and jackknives.

Meanwhile, Hailey and Lisa took our towels and my gym bag to an open space near the pool's chain link fence and sat down in the grass to enjoy the summer sun.

As they watched us and the other swimmers, Hailey pulled out the folded paper placemat from Friendly's, containing the map that her brother had drawn earlier. "Where do you think the other entrance to the cave is?" Lisa asked, as her friend put the map in the grass between them.

"Maybe we should think about north, south, east and west directions?" Hailey proposed.

"Sure."

"Well," said Hailey, "if you start at the cave entrance, and go north…" she began, and soon made a line with her index finger from the cave entrance to the top of the paper. "You end up in the outfield of the softball diamond or the tennis courts by the fire station! I don't think another cave entrance would be there. I've never seen anything like that over there."

"You're probably right about that," said Lisa.

"And if there was another entrance to the south of the cave…" She pointed to the cave entrance on the map and moved her index finger down the page. "I guess that it would be under some picnic shelters or concession booths, maybe the playground or even the pool. There isn't any kind of cave entrance over here, right?"

"Not that I've ever seen," Lisa confirmed.

"And we know it can't be to the east, because that's where the river is – so, I guess that means that the other entrance to the cave has got to be to the west."

"That makes sense to me," Lisa agreed.

Slowly, Hailey traced a line from the cave entrance towards the left side of the paper.

"So, if we start at the cave entrance and move west… we come to the two cherry trees and then the Tell Taylor Memorial."

"And we know that there's not an entrance there," confirmed Lisa. "Because everyone would see it!"

"But if we keep going…" Hailey paused. "Moscow didn't add it to his drawing and it's not exactly a straight line across… but…"

"But what?" Lisa asked, puzzled.

"If you keep going in almost a straight line from the cave entrance to the cherry trees and then to the memorial, you'd come to Mayor Runyon's house! I guess that would be near the corner of… what is that… Cherry Street and McManness? We just drove by it! And right there in his side yard is the wishing well! That's got to be the other entrance to the cave!"

"Hailey, that's brilliant!" cried Lisa. "I think you've figured it out!"

"Well, it's only a hunch still, right?"

"Let's go tell the guys."

CHAPTER 41

We had only completed a few dives when Lisa Lavin and Hailey Cotton approached us, carrying our towels and my green Whittier Elementary bag. "What's going on?" Moscow asked, as he and Joel Hemlinger and I waited in the line to jump off the high dive.

"Guys, we've got some important stuff to tell you. Let's go!" Hailey directed.

"What! Come on Hailey!" Moscow protested. "We just got here!"

"Do one more dive and meet us out front," his sister instructed.

Soon, we each did a final dive and joined Lisa and Hailey at the pay phones outside the entrance to the pool, where they quickly told us what they had discovered.

"So, Mayor Runyon's wishing well is directly across from the cave entrance!" Joel summarized.

"It is!" said Hailey. "It's got to be the other entrance that leads to the cave."

Going to the nearby payphone, Hailey tried to reach Sneak's Uncle Charlie, but again was told that he was not in the office. She then attempted to explain the additional details she had discovered, but had some difficulty communicating with the operator, as the music from the pool's loudspeaker was quite loud. While she was talking, our friend Joel was also talking to her, saying, "Remember, Uncle Charlie's probably on a stakeout already and Mr. Denlon said he didn't want anything out over the airwaves, so you need to tell them not to do a big broadcast about the second cave entrance."

After hanging up the payphone, Hailey sighed and said, "I don't think she understood what I was saying."

"Well," grinned Moscow, "I guess that means we should go over to the wishing well and check it out ourselves."

"But Sneak's uncle told us not to get involved," said Hailey.

"Technically, Uncle Charlie told us not to go to the *entrance* of the cave near the river," Joel added. "The wishing well is pretty far away from that."

"Yeah, what would be the problem with us going there to take a look?" Moscow Cotton reasoned. "We can just go home if we don't find anything, right?"

"Okay, okay," Hailey relented. "Let's go check it out."

Leaving the busy pool area, we followed the sidewalk north and walked the short distance up McManness Street to Mayor Runyon's house. The blue two-story house looked empty. No cars were in the driveway and the only vehicle nearby was a newer model Ford Mustang parked on the street.

We walked through the well-maintained grass of the mayor's yard to the wishing well, and saw that part of it was roped off, where the exposed above-ground brick had been toppled over.

Gathering at the top of the well, we looked down, hoping to see the second entrance to the cave, but all we saw was darkness.

"Helloooo," Joel said into the dark well.

I was concerned that the echo lasted a long time. "How deep do you think that is?" I wondered.

"Prolly not too far," Moscow estimated, and he was soon climbing over the short above-ground wall and down into the well.

"I'm not sure we should be doing this," Lisa said, with a concerned voice.

"There's lots of places for me to put my hands and feet," Moscow explained. "This should be a cinch. Or, you can lower that bucket from the roof and use that."

"I guess there's only one way to find out if this is a second entrance to the cave," Hailey reasoned.

"I don't think Moscow should be the only one going down there," Lisa protested, and soon she pulled herself over the wall and started to climb down into the well.

"Maybe, we should *all* go and check it out," Hailey suggested to Joel and me. "If there are different tunnels, or someone needs help, there's no way to know it from way up here."

Soon, I was concerned that I could no longer see Moscow or Lisa.

"Moscow, what's down there?" I asked, looking down into the well.

"I'm almost there," said Moscow. "I'm almost at the bottom. Holding onto the rocks got harder, because my hands are pruney from being in the water."

"Moscow, I don't think pruney is a word," his sister laughed.

"Well, it is today!" said Moscow. "Ouch!" he soon cried.

"What's wrong?" Hailey called.

"Oh, Lisa's foot just hit me on the head! I guess she's a little faster at this than I am!"

Soon, both Moscow and Lisa called up to us, and told us that they had arrived at the bottom of the well.

"Is there any water down there?" Hailey asked.

"Nope," said her brother.

"There's plenty of room for everyone, if you want to join us," Lisa commented.

"Look for a tunnel," directed Hailey. "Or some kind of opening that would take us to the cave."

"There are two!" her brother called up. "Which one do you think we should take?"

"Take the one that goes east!" Hailey instructed. "That's the direction of the cave."

Moscow and Lisa's discussion soon came up to us at the top of the well.

"Okay," Moscow eventually yelled. "We've decided which one to take. The tunnel is kind of small right here, but it will probably get bigger. I'll start and then Lisa will show the next person which tunnel we've decided to take. And then, she can go. Then, the next person can tell the next one, until it gets to Pep."

"Be careful!" Hailey called to her brother.

"I'll see you at the other cave entrance!" Moscow yelled up hopefully, as his sister shook her head.

"Okay, I'll go next," Joel said, as he climbed over the wall and began his trek down the side of the well. "It's pretty dark in here," he confessed as we soon lost sight of him, but heard him humming a popular song.

Hailey and I remained at the top.

"Are you climbing down?" Hailey asked me.

"I could stay up here," I said nervously. "You know, to direct the police on where to go."

"I don't think they're coming," Hailey admitted. "The phone connection was pretty bad, and the music from the pool was really loud and Joel was saying something at the same time I was talking! I don't think the police operator understood what I was saying."

"So, we're on our own?" I asked.

"I think so," said Hailey.

"Well, maybe I should wait here."

"We might need your help down there," said Hailey.

I paused, thinking about the different possibilities and said a short prayer.

"Okay," I finally agreed with a sigh. "I'll do it."

"Great!" smiled Hailey as she climbed over the wall, then made her way down the side of the well. "This isn't too bad," she said encouragingly. "Give me another minute, then you can start."

"Okay," I said nervously. *Pep, why did you agree to this*, I said to myself. *This is not safe!*

I waited a few moments, then pulled myself up and over the wall, as my arms and legs began to shake nervously. Like my friend, Moscow Cotton, my hands were wrinkled from our recent swim, and I grabbed tightly to the different rocks that surrounded the well as my feet found footholds.

In an instant my right hand slipped, and the green Whittier Elementary gym bag that had been wrapped around my wrist dropped into the well below me.

"Ouch!" I heard someone say after hearing a loud thud. "What was that!"

"Sorry," I said. "It was my gym bag with a tape recorder inside," I explained.

"Pep!" my name echoed throughout the deep well.

I wasn't sure if I could hold onto the rocks on the inside of the well, so I pulled myself back up and sat for a moment outside of the well. Looking up, I saw that there was a bucket tied to a long rope, so I carefully lowered the bucket into the deep well.

"I'm sending the bucket down first," I told Hailey. "Watch out for it."

"What?" she asked, as the bucket arrived at the bottom of the well at the same time she did.

I pulled myself up and over the wall again and steadied myself as one hand grabbed tightly to the rope while my other hand and feet found places in the wall to hold onto. Time seemed to pass slowly as I inched my way farther and farther underground, making minute progress as I took one small step after another.

Finally, after what seemed to be many minutes, I arrived at the bottom.

Hailey had waited for me as I descended and was carefully studying the ground that was littered with pop cans and coins. "Hey, look at that," she said, pointing to a faint boot print, with small pebbles within it. "I don't think that came from any of us," she said. Instinctively, she grabbed a handful of the dirt and put it into a pocket of her sundress, which she quickly buttoned shut. "Sneak Ryerson always says that you never know when important soil samples will turn up at crime scenes."

"Right!" I said, already out of breath.

"The other *Sunday School Detectives* went this way," Hailey said, pointing to a nearby opening at the floor of the well. "They're way ahead of us, but I'm sure we can catch up. Are you ready?"

"S... sure," I agreed, even though a part of me did not want to continue.

A few moments later I followed Hailey as she crawled into the underground tunnel.

CHAPTER 42

Holding a pair of *Bausch + Lomb Zephyr 9x35* binoculars to his eyes, Captain Charles Foster slowly scanned the wide bend of the muddy Blanchard River. As his hands slowly moved from left to right, the police captain examined the many details of the river and the nearby public park. Both were busy, with teens and adults enjoying canoes, pedal boats, playgrounds, and walking paths on the sunny summer Thursday afternoon.

"Anything happening?" asked Jeremiah Denlon, the security chief who stood nearby.

"Nothing yet," Sneak Ryerson's Uncle Charlie said calmly from his observation post on the roof of the Kodak building. "But we've got a lot of undercover folks down there. If the kidnappers make a move, we'll see them."

"They should have picked up the money by now, don't you think?" Mr. Denlon asked in a concerned tone.

"I'm not sure what they have in mind," said Uncle Charlie.

Soon, voices were heard from behind the two men as a young sheriff's deputy arrived. A few moments later, Uncle Charlie handed his binoculars to another officer and promptly introduced the young deputy to the group of police officers on the rooftop.

"Deputy Curtis," Uncle Charlie said to the young deputy wearing the grey uniform of the county sheriff's office that included a black leather holster and wide belt. "I'd like to introduce you to Jeremiah Denlon. He's the security chief over at Peloponnesian."

"Nice to meet you, sir," said the young deputy.

"The sheriff has appointed Anthony – er, Deputy Curtis to be his liaison," Uncle Charlie explained to the security chief. "If the kidnappers go outside of the city limits, we'll need to work with them."

"Makes sense," said Mr. Denlon.

"We've got people standing by," said the deputy.

"I've invited Mr. Denlon to come along as an observer," Uncle Charlie explained to Deputy Curtis. "One of the victims who's been kidnapped is an executive with his company."

"Yes, I heard that," said the young deputy. "I also heard that the FBI is sending some agents down from their Chicago office."

"Ahhh," the police captain sighed. "They don't like being second fiddle to any of us locals, do they?"

"Maybe the case will be all wrapped up before they get here," the young deputy offered optimistically.

CHAPTER 43

I was having a number of doubts about my decision to follow my friends as I crawled behind Hailey Cotton in a dark tunnel far below the well-maintained lawn of our city's mayor. I had only crawled a few feet away from the bottom of the wishing well, but was already feeling claustrophobic and was having difficulty breathing. The tunnel was narrow – too narrow for my liking – and I moved at a slow pace, unable to see anything ahead of me.

As I crawled through the dark passage, my knees and elbows scraped against dusty rocks, aching more and more as I progressed farther. *We could be crawling through mud or water*, I thought, trying to remain optimistic and think about positive things. "I can't see anything," I finally said to Hailey, feeling dizzy as my head spun from the lack of light. *At least the bottom of the wishing well had some sunlight*, I thought. *This tunnel is pitch black*. "I hope we don't fall over an underground cliff or anything," I told my friend. "Are you still up there?" I asked. "That's you, right Hailey?"

"Of course, it's me," Hailey said quickly. "I'm just trying to crawl as fast as I can. The roof isn't very high, but I haven't hit my head yet, have you?"

"No," I replied, not telling her that I was keeping my head quite low to avoid any rocks above me and drag my towel and gym bag behind me.

I paused for a moment, suddenly feeling even more claustrophobic. I looked nervously behind me, then in front. Darkness was all around. *I'm going to get stuck here!* I thought as I panicked, feeling the walls closing in tighter and tighter. *There's no way out of here! How am I ever going to turn around in this narrow tunnel? I've got to turn around! But how can I do that? Plus, what kind of animals are down here?* I added to my worry. *I'm sure there's got to be a snake den or a nest of spiders!*

"Come on Pep," Hailey encouraged, when she sensed that I had stopped moving forward. "I'm sure it's not too much farther."

"Okay, okay," I replied. "I was just taking a break."

Eventually, I continued crawling forward, hoping to catch up to my friend. A few moments later, Hailey began estimating the land-marks above us. "This is probably where the street begins above us," she explained, after we had crawled ten or fifteen feet. A few minutes later she encouraged me by saying, "Pep, we're probably right below the monument now, don't you think."

"I don't know," I added, as my knees and elbows became more and more tender from crawling over the rocks and dirt, and the Whittier Elementary gym bag that I dragged behind me felt heavier and heavier. *I took out most of the stuff when we visited the prison*, I reminded myself. *I wish I had kept my flashlight!*

We continued crawling for several more minutes.

"I can't go on much longer," I told my friend as my lungs gasped for deeper and deeper breaths.

"It can't be much farther," Hailey said. "Just a couple minutes longer. You can do it Pep!"

To my relief, after a few more minutes of crawling forward, Hailey yelled, "Pep, I see a light. I see a light! There's a light at the end of the tunnel!"

With these words, I started crawling faster, and was surprised to hear the faint sounds of Joel's singing. "I saw the light!" our friend sang. When we were a little closer to Joel in the tunnel, he called out, "Hey Hailey and Pep, what's taking you guys so long?"

"We're coming," I heard Hailey say. "I think we're almost to you."

"You're not going to believe this place!" Joel said, as we soon joined him.

To our surprise, the narrow tunnel ended, giving way to a large dimly lit cavern. As our eyes adjusted to the light, we observed that a glow of sunshine was coming from a wide opening at the far end of the cave – a wide opening that was covered by moss.

"That must be the entrance where we were before," Hailey said, as we stood and welcomed the sunlight. "Because of the moss and the way the light was shining, Moscow probably couldn't see how big this place is!"

"Where are the others?" Hailey asked Joel, as she dusted off the dirt from her sundress and I checked on my bruised elbows.

"They went over to explore that area over there," our friend explained, pointing to our left. "It's huge. But I decided to wait here for you two."

"Thanks!" Hailey appreciatively.

"Yeah," I agreed. "You don't know how glad I am to see you!"

As we looked around, even though there were many shadows cast along the floor and walls of the cave, we could tell that the cavern was indeed vast.

"They went this way," Joel explained, and we followed the young musician to a large underground boulder field that stretched into the distance where Moscow and Lisa were having fun climbing up and down the big rocks.

"Oh, hey Hailey," Moscow shouted when he saw his sister. "Isn't this so cool! I wish I would have come in here, before. This is like my own playground!" he said, jumping from one boulder to another, enjoying the many features of the cavern.

"Why don't you come over here, so we can talk about the case first," Hailey requested. "I'm sure you'll have time to come back here."

Soon Moscow and Lisa joined us.

"So, do you think that's the same entrance that you came up to, Moscow?" Hailey asked, pointing to the wide entrance covered with moss. "The one that's under the two cherry trees?"

"Yeah, definitely," Moscow Cotton explained. "I can't believe I didn't take a few more steps and check this place out!"

"Well, we were busy that day with an important case," his sister replied.

"Yeah, but this is such a cool place to explore."

Hailey walked closer to the entrance as we followed.

"Hmm," she said loudly, as she looked around the moss-covered entrance. "So, Mrs. Mannix... or the police, or someone was supposed to drop the money off here, right?"

"Right," I agreed. "That's what the note said they were supposed to do."

"So, I guess I'm wondering," Hailey paused, then continued. "Where is it?"

"The money?" Joel asked.

"Yeah, all those dollars..."

"Plus, ninety-five cents," I added.

"Right," affirmed Hailey. "I don't see it anywhere. Does that mean that the kidnappers got it already, or does it mean that Mrs. Mannix didn't put the money here? I don't get it."

"Do you think that Uncle Charlie couldn't find the cave?" Lisa asked, in a concerned voice.

"I'd be surprised if that happened," said Hailey. "Moscow did a pretty good job of drawing the map and explaining where this is."

"Maybe, instead of putting the money at the entrance, they put it inside the cave?" Moscow suggested.

"Let's look for it!" said Joel. "There's a lot of crevices and places that we haven't explored yet."

"There's only a few possibilities," I heard Hailey say softly. "Either the kidnappers have the money, or they don't."

Soon, we split up and began looking around the cavern.

"Pep, why don't you look over there," Hailey asked. And soon, I was looking near the tunnel we had recently exited. The area was dark and covered in shadows, and my eyes were having a hard time adjusting back to the darkness.

We were all silently searching for the money when suddenly, the loud chuff, chuff, chuff of a helicopter's blades echoed throughout the cavern walls.

CHAPTER 44

The low-flying helicopter took up the entire field of Uncle Charlie's *Bausch + Lomb Zephyr 9x35* binoculars as it slowly held its position outside of the cave entrance above the river and across from the two cherry trees. The wind from the helicopter rotors disturbed several of the trees in the park, dislodging limbs from branches, while creating small white caps on the surface of the river. Canoes on the river looked like they might tip over and a teenager in a pedal boat lost his baseball cap as it flew away.

"What are they doing?" Uncle Charlie complained, as he saw the low-flying helicopter hover above the water, the yellow FBI signs on the doors gleaming in the afternoon sun. "Well," Uncle Charlie continued. "If the kidnappers didn't know earlier that the police and law enforcement were involved, they sure do now!"

CHAPTER 45

Inside the cave, we had been quietly searching for the ransom money, when suddenly the helicopter appeared outside, creating windy conditions at the cave entrance. Instantly, vines and moss and ivy were shifting, and different shadows appeared on the floors and walls.

With the vines and moss in different positions, areas that had been in darkness were now illuminated. *Could that be?* I wondered, as my eyes adjusted to see what looked like a man standing against the cave wall in an area that had previously been shrouded in darkness. Two duffel bags, I noticed, were at his feet.

Making eye contact with me, he quickly grabbed one of the bags and lunged toward me.

I could hear the coins rattling inside the bag but could not react in time as the man swung the duffel bag from the shadows and hit me. "Urgh," I cried loudly when I fell.

"Pep, what's going on over there?" Hailey wondered, as she heard the scuffle, and several *Sunday School Detectives* rushed to my side. They were also soon hit by the swinging duffel bag as the man moved in and out of the shadows to make his attack.

"My ankle," I heard Hailey say, grabbing her leg after falling.

Moscow attempted to escape the attack but was hit from behind by a swinging duffel bag. He staggered many steps forward, tripping over several rocks, unable to catch himself.

CHAPTER 46

"Could this day get any worse?" Charles Foster asked as he turned to Mr. Denlon and the other officers standing with him on the roof of the Kodak building.

From their observation post high above the Blanchard River, they had watched in disbelief as an FBI helicopter hovered next to the cave entrance, then swoop down over the public park and community pool, looking for a place to land.

"I'll say it again," said Charles Foster, shaking his head. "Could this day get any worse?"

"I think so," said Deputy Curtis, as he gave the binoculars to the police captain. "Take a look, sir."

Raising the binoculars to his eyes, Uncle Charlie was alarmed to see Moscow Cotton of the *Sunday School Detectives* hanging by one hand to the edge of the entrance to the cave, his feet dangling in mid-air, high above the walking path that followed the river.

CHAPTER 47

Needless to say, the plainclothes police officers were not amused when they arrived to help Moscow Cotton off the edge of the cave entrance, ensuring that he did not drop and hurt himself on the walking path or fall into the nearby Blanchard River.

Soon, Uncle Charlie and other officers arrived and assisted in getting us out of the cave.

"I thought I told you kids to stay out of this!" Sneak's uncle said loudly as we gathered around him near the Tell Taylor memorial above the river. "Didn't I specifically say, 'Let us investigate this' and 'Stay away from the entrance to the cave'? I'm pretty sure I said both of those things!"

Soon, we described what had happened, explaining that the kidnapper had used the tunnel from the wishing well in Mayor Runyon's yard to enter the cave undetected and then exit the cave using the same tunnel to make his escape.

"We weren't planning on messing things up, Uncle Charlie," said Moscow.

"Well, I can't be too upset," the police captain admitted. "If you kids hadn't stumbled upon that tunnel, we'd still be waiting outside, thinking that the kidnapper hadn't even taken the money. He's long gone now, but at least we know he hasn't gotten far. We've got people out on the roads leading out of town, and I wouldn't be surprised if the sheriff decides to put up roadblocks too."

The police captain paused for a moment, then asked, "Is there anything you can tell me about the kidnapper? Was there anything distinctive that you noticed?"

"He came out of nowhere," said Hailey.

"Yeah," several of us agreed.

"And hit us pretty hard," I acknowledged.

"He must have been hiding there for a while," said Joel. "Waiting for his chance to get back into the tunnel. When the helicopter showed up, he must have thought that was his best chance to leave, because we were so distracted by the noise. He probably could have gotten away with it without us noticing, but Pep saw him."

"I bet we really surprised him when we showed up!" said Moscow.

"I'm sure we did," said his sister.

"Well, thanks kids. We've got an ambulance coming if anyone needs to get checked out. It'll be over at the parking lot by the pool. There's a bunch of things I need to get working on, so I need to get going," Uncle Charlie explained. "Let me know if you think of anything."

After Sneak's uncle confirmed we all could arrange for rides to get home, he rapidly walked to an awaiting police car and sped away, as the search for the kidnappers continued.

We paused for a moment at the memorial, each of us bruised from the surprise attack we had received in the cavern.

"That was bad," Hailey said, carefully trying to put weight on her foot. "My ankle is going to be swollen for a while."

"Yeah, my hand is messed up too," Joel explained. "I'm going to need to go home and get some ice on this, so I can play in my concert on Sunday."

We walked to the payphones outside of the entrance to the pool and listened to Joel as he called his mom and asked her to come pick him up.

"I hope you feel better, *Joelsie!*" Lisa smiled, using the nickname for Joel that our friend Michelle had used.

"I do too," said Joel, too tired and sore to complain.

We were quiet for a few moments at the payphones as the music blared from a nearby loudspeaker.

"So, do you guys want my mom to take you home too?" Joel asked us.

"Actually, I was thinking we'd go see Alice," Hailey smiled. "Does anyone want to go with me?"

CHAPTER 48

We waited for about fifteen minutes for Alice Williams, our young scientist friend, to arrive after she received the phone call from Hailey Cotton. Her orange Volkswagen Beetle impressed many of the kids who were standing near the payphones outside of the entrance to the pool at Riverside Park. But the car was not big, and we found it to be a tight fit with Alice in the driver's seat, Hailey in the passenger seat, and Moscow Cotton, Lisa Lavin and I squeezed into the backseat.

Moscow Cotton and I had not met Alice previously and were happy to meet the young scientist. We were also still in our swim trunks, and I asked Hailey if it would be alright if we stopped at our homes to change clothes. Hailey, however, said that time was "of the essence" in catching the kidnappers and asked us to wait.

A short time later, we arrived at the Science Building on the university campus and made our way to the third floor. "So, what exactly is this all about?" Alice asked when we arrived outside her lab.

"I've got a sample of dirt," Hailey Cotton explained. "And I'm wondering if you can analyze it in your lab. Our friend Sneak Ryerson always says that you never know when important soil samples might show up at a crime scene."

"Or ashes from pipes," I added. "He studies that too – and decomposing stuff."

"Okay," Alice said hesitantly. "I'm not sure what we'll find with your dirt, but we can give it a try. Give me just a minute…"

Soon, the young scientist returned with two circular petri dishes. "So, where is your sample?" Alice asked.

"It's here in my pocket," Hailey admitted as she pointed to a pocket on her sundress.

"Well, I'm not sure *what* we'll be able to do with that, but we'll do our best," Alice smiled, as she had Hailey place the dirt from her pocket into the clear plastic petri dishes. "This might take a while," she added, before taking the samples into the lab.

We waited in the hallway, and a few minutes later Alice returned. "I've given the samples to some scientists in our lab who will be better at analyzing that than me! If there's something to find in those samples, they'll find it!"

"Thanks!" said Hailey.

"Yeah, thanks!" Lisa added.

"So, while I've got y'all here... or, at least some of y'all from the *Sunday School Detectives*, I wanted to tell you about what's happened since yesterday," Alice began.

"What's that?" asked Lisa.

"Well, I've actually been doing an awful lot of thinkin' and prayin' since we were together," the young scientist explained. "And a lot of the things that y'all and Dr. Bayhill were sayin' yesterday morning really hit home. Honestly, I can't fully explain it, but... before I left with you to go over to the seminary, I wouldn't have called myself a Christian. And now, well, I guess I do."

"Wow!" said Hailey, "That's great!"

"Woo hoo!" shouted Lisa. "I'm so happy for you!"

"Very cool," Moscow Cotton agreed, while I smiled in agreement as well.

"Yeah," Alice continued. "I've even scheduled a meeting with Pastor Thomas from your church to talk more about it. I'm looking forward to learning more." She paused thoughtfully for a moment. "The best way I can describe it, is that I've found something that really makes sense – something that I'd longed for, for a really long time."

"I'm so happy for you," said Hailey.

We talked with the young scientist about her newly found faith for a few more minutes when eventually, one of the scientists in the lab called Alice in.

A short time later, Alice returned to the hallway. "Okay, so I've got some good news and some bad news on that sample," Alice explained.

"Okay," Hailey said hesitantly.

"The bad news is, we couldn't really definitively identify what types of soil we were looking at. It seemed to be a mix of several different types."

"That's a bummer," said Moscow.

"Yeah," I agreed.

"What's the good news?" Hailey asked.

"The good news is that there were several particles in the soil sample."

"Particles?"

"Yep, and they appeared to be small seeds – or fragments of seeds. Probably the kind used by farmers to plant corn. They definitely seemed more for agricultural use, versus something that someone would put into a pot on a windowsill."

"Agricultural seeds?" Hailey confirmed.

"Yeah, that's the best guess of the scientists in our lab."

We were quiet for a moment.

"Pep," Hailey said, turning to me. "You said that it was Mr. Crenshaw who told you about the *big thing* happening today, right?"

"Right," I confirmed, unsure about the direction of the conversation. "I thought they were going to rob the *Squirrel Club*," I told Alice.

"And the evidence from the well is that someone was in the well, who had recently been in contact with agricultural seeds, right?"

"Right," I affirmed.

"And who owned a seed business, before they were sent to jail?" she asked.

"Mr. Crenshaw!" several of us exclaimed.

CHAPTER 49

It was late on Thursday afternoon when Alice Williams drove us to Mr. Crenshaw's farm.

"I remember hearing that his seed operation was on the north side of town," Hailey Cotton told us, as Alice's orange Volkswagen Beetle sped north.

"I heard it's been run by his brother ever since Mr. Crenshaw was arrested," Lisa told us and we soon arrived at Mr. Crenshaw's property, exiting the small car like clowns at a circus: Alice, our driver, from the driver's side, Hailey Cotton from the passenger side, followed by Lisa Lavin, then Moscow Cotton, and then me.

We first raced to Mr. Crenshaw's old farmhouse, where we found the back door unlocked. We knocked and rang the doorbell but no one answered, so we slowly opened the door and found ourselves in the kitchen.

"We've got to find those victims of the kidnapping," said Hailey quickly. "Before something bad happens to them. Let's see if they are here."

Soon, we began looking throughout the first floor of the house and then the second floor, and then the attic. Not wanting to send anyone to the basement alone, we all went down the creaky slanted stairs and looked through each room in the underground space.

"They're not here," Hailey said dejectedly. "I thought for sure this is where we'd find them."

"It doesn't look like anyone has been here in months," Lisa observed, pointing to the dust that had built up on many of the surfaces in the house.

"So, not here, huh?" Hailey admitted.

"There's still the barns to go through," said Lisa.

Soon, we raced across the yard to the two barns, deciding to split up in our search for the victims of the kidnapping. We searched through haylofts and corn cribs, animal pens and old corrals.

"They aren't here," I concluded once we had searched the area thoroughly and returned to the car.

"Where could they be?" Hailey wondered. "This has got to be the place, right? It all makes sense."

"So, what are our clues again?" asked Alice.

Hailey summarized the evidence: "Pep and Sneak were told by Mr. Russell Crenshaw yesterday that something *big* was going to happen today. Now, today, after the kidnapping, we've found some seeds in a footprint, probably made by the kidnapper. And since Mr. Crenshaw had a seed barn, I figured that's where they've been hiding the victims."

We were quiet for a moment.

"We didn't see a seed barn in any of the places we've looked at," Lisa observed.

"Wait, what?" asked Hailey.

"We've checked in animal pens and corrals and places like that – and inside the old farmhouse. But we didn't see any storage places for seeds. There's nothing that looks like that seed place on Warrington Avenue."

"Urgh," Hailey said, exhaling quickly. "We've been checking Mr. Crenshaw's house and barn – but those towers for storing the seeds are up the road."

We rapidly returned to our places in the Volkswagen Beetle and rushed up the county road to a building with a sign that read *Crenshaw Seeds* next to three large towers, similar to the towers we had seen in our earlier case.

Similar to the farmhouse and barn, the one-story office building and storage towers all looked abandoned. After checking several doors in the office building, we finally found one that was unlocked.

We went inside.

"I'm glad we don't have to worry about a raging fire or smoke inside this building, like we did at the other seed place," I said, as I began checking doors throughout the office building.

"No kidding," Moscow Cotton agreed.

"I'm not sure if anyone is here… " I began, when suddenly we heard noises down the hallway.

We quickly rushed to the area where we heard noises.

"That sounds like people talking!" said Hailey.

The door leading to the voices was locked.

"I'll go find a crowbar," Moscow said excitedly. "Or we could try to kick it open."

"Actually," his sister said, "it looks like the lock is on the outside."

Upon saying these words, she turned the lock and opened the door. Four men – Mr. Mannix, our city's mayor and two of Findlay's barbers were seated around a small wooden table. Their faces were tired, but all were smiling.

"Ah, you must be the *Sunday School Detectives!*" Mr. Mannix exclaimed. "They told us you'd be here to rescue us."

CHAPTER 50

A short time later, Mr. Crenshaw's old seed company was swarming with police and fire vehicles. Even the FBI helicopter found a place to land in an open field nearby.

After the police had taken everyone's statements, we gathered around the four men, whose fishing trip had been severely interrupted.

"I'm glad you kids found us when you did," Mr. Mannix smiled, as the mayor and the two barbers agreed.

"I'm not sure if I could have withstood hearing more car stories from Dan!" the mayor joked.

"They weren't too bad," Larry smiled.

"If I had to hear another story about a car that needed a replacement for a high head gasket, I would have surely lost my mind!" the mayor confessed.

"Now you know what it's like for me everyday at the barber shop!" laughed Larry.

"Oh, come on now," said Dan. "I was just trying to make conversation!"

Uncle Charlie joined the group, and soon asked the victims, "So, the kidnappers told you that the *Sunday School Detectives* would rescue you, huh?"

"That's right," said Mr. Mannix.

"They specifically said the group's name?"

"That's right," Mr. Mannix affirmed.

"Did they say the name of any other group?"

"No," said the executive.

"Do you have any idea how they knew it would be the *Sunday School Detectives* who would be here to rescue you?" asked Uncle Charlie.

"I have no idea," Mr. Mannix admitted.

"Me either," said the mayor.

"We know the kids from cutting the boys' hair," Dan explained. "But I don't know how they could have predicted who would get to us first."

"Do you know?" the police captain asked, turning his question to Hailey Cotton.

"I have no idea either," she laughed as she shrugged her shoulders.

"Well, we'll review everyone's statements. Who knows, with all the details you've provided, hopefully we can catch those turkeys."

A short while later, my mom arrived. "You look like the wreck of the Hesperus," she said with a concerned voice, after seeing my dirty and bruised knees and elbows, scratched from crawling through the tunnel from the wishing well to the cave. Then, after examining my fat lip, from being hit with a duffel bag full of money, she added, "I need to get you home, young man,"

"I think I'll be okay," I told her.

"I'm taking a break from investigating cases for at least one day!" I told my friends, just before following my mom to her car.

"Maybe we can go swimming tomorrow?" Moscow suggested.

"Oh, no! I don't think so! I'll pass on that, thank you very much!" I said loudly. "The last time you asked me to go swimming, I had to climb down a well and then crawl through a super narrow tunnel – and then get clobbered by a bad guy! You can go swimming by yourself, Moscow," I added, as my friends laughed.

CHAPTER 51

I did not see my *Sunday School Detective* friends again until Sunday, July 13th, a few days after finding the victims of the kidnapping at Mr. Crenshaw's property. On that Sunday, we attended church in the morning and talked briefly after Sunday School, agreeing to support our friend Joel Hemlinger at his concert later that afternoon.

Most of us arrived a few minutes before the piano recital was to start and took our seats at the back of the chapel – the same chapel where we met on Thursday nights during the school year for Children's Choir practice.

The hard wooden pews were not very comfortable, and I stared at the multicolored tiles on the floor as I waited for the concert to start. Looking up, I was surprised at how different the walls appeared in the warm afternoon sun compared to the darkness of winter nights. I was greatly impressed by the cheeriness of the windows, as they popped with red, blue and green colors.

The Ryersons were still on vacation, but the other *Sunday School Detectives* were there. Joel Hemlinger took a seat with the other performers in the front row. Meanwhile, Michelle, even though she was not playing in the concert, also sat in the front row, ready to cheer on Joel. "I can't wait to hear you, *Joelsie*," she told him with a smile, as the musician frowned. In the back row, Lisa Lavin and her cousin Cressida Hudson sat with me, along with Hailey and Moscow Cotton.

I really missed my friend Sneak Ryerson, the great detective, who was somewhere in the Eastern United States or Canada. There were some questions I had about the recent kidnapping that I was sure he would be able to answer.

Eventually, the small chapel filled with people. Mrs. Kulchar, the student's piano teacher, stood in front of the collection of performers, parents, and friends and greeted many as they walked in.

The room quieted as she warmly greeted those in attendance. "I am so, so glad that you are here. We have a wonderful group of very talented students. Some of these students, you will see, are just beginners, while others have been playing for a very, very long time. It is so wonderful to see them all using their God-given gifts. Please give them all a warm welcome and applause as we begin."

We clapped, and soon the first student, a four-year-old approached the black Kimball piano and hoisted himself up onto the leather piano bench.

"That kid can't even touch the pedals," said Moscow Cotton.

The boy played a variation of "Twinkle Twinkle Little Star" and soon returned to his seat in the front row.

Next, another young student was introduced and played a variation of "Twinkle Twinkle Little Star".

"We do some repetition," Mrs. Kulchar explained after a third student followed the others and played the same song. "You'll hear a lot of similar songs. And I appreciate everyone's patience with the repetition. In fact, we have one young lady who listens to her album of repeated songs every single night to help her with her piano lessons. I am so proud of her. It's too bad her family is on vacation this week, because otherwise you would hear from her now. The young lady I'm referring to is Jennie Ryerson."

Soon, another younger student was introduced and played the same song as the first three.

"Well, that was a tune you've heard already," Mrs. Kulchar said after the fourth student performed. "But, as I mentioned, we do a lot of repetition. We do memorization too, and it helps to have songs that are similar."

Moscow Cotton squirmed in his seat, bored from the many similar songs. "Can we go?" he pleaded with his sister. "If I hear one more 'Twinkle Twinkle Little Star', I'm going to lose my mind."

I had grabbed a program on the way in, and had made it into a paper airplane, but Hailey soon asked me to pass it to her so she could see what other songs the younger kids would play. "The program says there are other songs coming up: 'Fur Elise' by Beethoven and 'Eine Kleine Nachtmusik' by Mozart," she told her brother.

"Boooring," Moscow replied as I chuckled, and Hailey handed the program back to me.

"Shush, Moscow. Just wait for Joel," Hailey insisted. "You know he's going to be really good."

Suddenly, Hailey jolted back in her chair. "Why are they here?" she asked, after seeing someone across the room. Instantly, she grabbed the printed program from me. "Ah," she exclaimed, studying the information. "It's all starting to make sense now. I know who stole the papers and put them in Andrew Bayhill's briefcase."

Hailey thinks she's figured it out. How about you, dear reader? Do you have a suspect in mind? You've been given the same information as Hailey received. Who do you think put the papers in Andrew's briefcase? Why did they do that? What do you think the solution is to *The Case of the Missing Memos*?

If you have an idea, write it in the space below:

_____

_____

_____

_____

_____

_____

_____

_____

CHAPTER 52

"Did you notice that Dr. Bayhill is here?" Hailey quickly asked Lisa Lavin, pointing to the older seminary professor in a pew across the room.

"No, I didn't see him come in," Lisa replied. "I wonder why he's here?"

Soon, Mrs. Kulchar stood and said, "And now it's time for our older students. The first student is Andrew Bayhill. He's a recent graduate from Findlay High School, and he'll be playing 'Clair de Lune' for you this afternoon."

Andrew Bayhill nervously walked to the Kimball piano and sat quickly on the black leather seat in front of the keys.

Turning to Moscow and me, Hailey told us quietly, "Do you see that Andrew Bayhill's playing?"

"Huh?" I replied.

Andrew nervously played his piece, and we clapped as he quickly returned to his seat.

Mrs. Kulchar rose and addressed the crowd. "Next, is another older student. He is brand new to learning the piano and our company of pianists. It's important at concerts like this to give everyone a chance to show what they know so they get used to performing. Next time, I'm sure you'll be quite impressed!" She paused. "Our next student is Jimmy Mannix, who will be playing 'Long, Long Ago' for you today."

"It's Jimmy Mannix!" Lisa said to Hailey.

"Yeah, I saw his name in the program," Hailey replied.

Soon, the young man approached the piano and sat on the black leather seat in front of the keys.

Jimmy then began to play a song that was not easily identifiable. Many of the younger students looked at each other and turned up their noses. Audience members turned to the program to see his name and the name of the uneven, mistake-filled music. Jimmy, I thought, might be good at some things, like racing his car, but his piano playing was atrocious. I wondered if I would be getting a headache from listening to the music and rubbed my ears several times, hoping to block some of the sounds. Eventually, Jimmy completed the piece and sat down.

"Well – uh, like I said, he's a new student," Mrs. Kulchar said haltingly, before changing the subject. "For our final piece, we have Joel Hemlinger, who will be playing Shostakovich's Piano Sonata Number 1. It will take Joel just a minute to get set up. The piece is rather long – about eleven minutes – so, why don't we have everyone stand up and stretch for a minute. You younger kids can get your wiggles out now."

Soon, the attendees stood and the room was abuzz with voices talking.

Hailey went quickly to Andrew Bayhill who was watching as Mrs. Kulchar helped Joel arrange long sheet music across the piano.

"Hi Andrew," said Hailey.

"Oh, hey," said the young intern. "Do you have a friend who's playing today?"

"Yes, I do. It's... Joel... who's coming up next."

"Oh, he's really good," Andrew admitted. "I'm just learning, but I would love to play as good as him, sometime. Are you enjoying the concert?"

"Yes, very much," Hailey replied. "But I have a couple quick questions for you."

"Sure. Are you interested in becoming a student?"

"Well, no. I'm actually interested in your schedule."

"Oh, okay," Andrew replied, surprised.

"When do you have your piano lesson?"

"Let's see... That would be on Mondays... At 5:15."

"And who comes after you?"

"Oh, that's Jimmy. Just like for our performance today. I'm first and he is second. His lesson is at 5:45."

"And do you take your briefcase with you to your piano lesson?" Hailey asked.

"Well, of course I do, it has all my music in it."

"And do you have that briefcase with you the entire time you are at your lesson?"

"Of course it's with me the entire time, I do…" Andrew Bayhill began. "Well, actually, no – I leave it in the hallway, before I go into Mrs. Kulchar's piano room. It's kind of bulky with a book or two in it and all I need for my lesson is my piano music. So, I've been leaving my briefcase next to the chair in the hallway, where we all wait for the lesson before ours to finish and for our lesson to begin."

"And Jimmy Mannix is the next student waiting to go in?" Hailey asked. "Sitting right there next to your briefcase?"

"Well, yeah," Andrew Bayhill confirmed, before slowly realizing what Hailey was getting at with her questions. "So you think that…"

Soon, both Andrew and Hailey were staring at Jimmy Mannix who was at the end of a very long wooden pew on the other side of the chapel.

"Okay, let's get started," said Mrs. Kulchar, interrupting the many voices talking to friends or family members in the chapel. "The music that you are about to hear is in many ways magical – if I can say that here within the walls of the church. Or transcendent – that might be a better word to use here in the chapel. This young man has worked very, very hard on this piece. And I really think you will enjoy it. And now, without further ado, our very own Joel Hemlinger! Please give him your full attention."

The crowd clapped loudly for the musical prodigy as he stood and bowed, and then, returning to the piano bench, began playing Shostakovich's Piano Sonata Number 1.

CHAPTER 53

In our church's chapel, Joel Hemlinger energetically played Dimitri Shostakovich's Piano Sonata Number 1, a piece written in 1926. He struck the keys loudly and forcefully during the first movement, before the piece turned quieter. The atonal modernist sonata was full of dissonance and sounded unlike anything most of the younger performers (or their parents) had ever heard. Several of the younger children chuckled, or quickly became distracted. In the slower section, a few audience members even clapped, thinking the performance was over, as Joel repeatedly struck one key slowly.

Just before Joel's performance started, Hailey Cotton and Andrew Bayhill found seats, but continued staring at the young office worker named Jimmy Mannix. A moment later, once Joel's loud playing began, Jimmy Mannix jumped from his seat at the end of a long pew and ran to the exit. Swiftly taking the four stairs, Jimmy Mannix was out the door.

"We've got to be quick!" said Hailey, as she rose to follow Jimmy Mannix. Encouraging Michelle to leave her seat from the front row, Hailey soon arrived at the back row where the other *Sunday School Detectives* were sitting. "Come on," she said quickly. "As our friend Sneak Ryerson would say, 'The game is afoot'."

"I think that would be Sherl – ," I said, wanting to correct my friend, but was soon pushed out of the pew by the others who wanted to move quickly to the exit.

Following Hailey Cotton, we gathered outside the chapel. "Jimmy Mannix is the one who stole those documents and put them into Andrew Bayhill's briefcase," she told us rapidly. "We've got to find him before he gets away."

"There are so many ways he could have gone," I said. "The hallways look empty."

"Okay," said Hailey. "Lisa and Cressida, why don't you check outside. He might be out in the parking lot and driving away," she added.

"Will do," said Lisa as she and her cousin scurried down the stairs.

"Moscow, why don't you and I check upstairs – he might have gone up there to hide for a while, trying to trick us into thinking he had already left."

"Sure thing," said Moscow as he began up the stairs.

"Michelle and Pep, why don't you stay close by here to see if he returns, but check the sanctuary first – just to make sure he isn't hiding there."

"Okay," I agreed, as Michelle and I walked quickly down the hallway to the sanctuary.

The overhead lights were off above the long sanctuary, but we found the area brightly lit by the many stained glass windows that framed the sanctuary's stone walls. Slowly, Michelle and I checked every pew to ensure that Jimmy Mannix wasn't hiding beside or under them. "I guess he isn't here," I said with a shrug when we reached the tall wooden pulpit.

Suddenly, I saw a shadow jet across the balcony high above us, from one door to the other.

"Jimmy Mannix is up there!" I said to Michelle.

A few moments later, Hailey and Moscow appeared at the door where Jimmy had emerged.

"He went that way," I said, pointing to the open door on the other side of the balcony. "Towards the sixth grade Sunday School room."

"I'm going to go up there," I said to Michelle. "I might be able to help."

Soon we exited the sanctuary and were outside on the large main staircase that faced Main Street.

"I really wanted to hear *Joelsie*," Michelle pouted.

"Well, I'm sure he's still playing. You still have time," I said. "Why don't you go listen."

Soon, the young girl returned to the chapel and I was taking two steps at a time up the staircase.

I arrived at the hallway outside of the sixth grade Sunday School room, and peering in, I saw that the room was empty.

I must have missed them, I thought. *I wonder where they went?*

Looking up, I saw that a wooden panel had been removed from the ceiling and pigeon feathers were on the classroom floor. Suddenly, Hailey Cotton's head appeared in the opening above me.

"Pep, they've gone up to the bell tower," she explained. "I can help pull you up, but you need to get up here quickly. Just jump from the desk."

I quickly went to a nearby desk and flung myself upward, missing the opening in the ceiling and falling to the floor.

"Hurry, Pep," Hailey directed. "We need to catch up with them."

"Okay," I said quickly and stood on the desk again. My second attempt was more successful, and I clutched the opening in the ceiling as my friend grabbed my arm. Soon, I was able to get my other arm in and an elbow below me, before pulling the rest of my body through the opening with Hailey's assistance.

"They went that way," my friend explained, pointing up to the top of the tall bell tower.

"Oh boy," I said, seeing the great distance above me.

"Let's go try to help Moscow," Hailey smiled.

Climbing upwards on a narrow metal ladder, my hands and legs began to shake as I tried to keep moving and not look down – but that proved difficult.

The wind whipped through the tall bell tower as we climbed higher and higher. Soon, we saw Lisa and Cressida far below us on the lawn. Hailey and I yelled down to them, and soon they were joined by the church janitor who watched us climbing up the tall structure. "I'm calling the cops," the janitor said warily to our friends.

"I think Moscow is yelling something," Hailey said, as we heard a noise being carried away by the strong wind. Climbing a little farther, we could see that Moscow was just below Jimmy Mannix.

To our shock, Moscow Cotton was hanging on to the edge of the tall tower with just the fingertips of one hand. "Oh the humanity!" he yelled as he dangled from the tall bell tower. "Sanctuary! Sanctuary!" he added, quoting from the book about the Hunchback of Notre Dame. "I'm so scared of heights! Ahhhh! I almost fell with that last gust of wind! You've got to help me!"

"What's Moscow doing?" I asked his sister. "He's not afraid of heights – is he? Plus, there's a ledge right below him."

Jimmy Mannix was close to escape as he neared the top of the tower. There, a different ladder on the other side of the tower led away from the *Sunday School Detectives* giving chase and to his car in the parking lot below.

But instead of reaching for the other ladder, Jimmy Mannix stopped and looked down to see Moscow Cotton dangling from the edge of the tower. "I told you, you shouldn't have followed me!" he sneered.

"Ahh!" Moscow continued. "I'm so afraid of heights!"

"You're so stupid!" Jimmy Mannix called down. "You can't even climb up a ladder right."

"I'm so scared," Moscow yelled.

"Fine," we heard Jimmy Mannix say reluctantly, as he turned and climbed down a few feet to be closer to Moscow's hand. "Don't let go," he yelled. "I'm going to help you."

Observing my friend, I yelled, "Moscow, stop dangling your feet – the big ledge is right there! You won't fall!" My instructions, however, were lost to a gust of wind.

"I can't do this much longer," Moscow protested. "I can't hold on much longer!"

"Let me just grab your…" Jimmy began, as he moved to grab Moscow's wrist to bring him to safety, when instead, Moscow Cotton grabbed *Jimmy's* wrist and flipped over the surprised young man, putting both of Jimmy's wrists behind his back.

"Gotcha!" Moscow said proudly. "You're not going anywhere!"

CHAPTER 54

The following day was Monday, July 14ᵗʰ, and in the evening my father and I arrived at the Bastille Day celebration at Uncle Charlie's house on Winterberry Drive, located near the mall.

At the front door we were quickly greeted by Sneak and Jennie Ryerson's Aunt Marie, who invited us to a backyard filled with folding tables and chairs and decorated with plastic French tricolored flags of blue, white and red.

She gave us circular tricolor cockades to place on our shirts and introduced us to the party guests. We met many of Findlay's French speakers, including the French teachers from the middle schools and high school as well as Aunt Marie's parents.

"So, I hear you'd like a tutor?" Aunt Marie's father asked my dad.

"I would," my father smiled, and soon the two men began a friendly conversation, partially in French and partially in English, and made plans to start my father's language lessons. I was overjoyed.

To my delight, Uncle Charlie invited the other *Sunday School Detectives* to the party to celebrate the end of *The Case of the Missing Memos*. "Pep!" my friends yelled when I approached the group. Many of my friends were seated in folding chairs around a circular table near the back of the yard. Moscow Cotton, I noticed, was nearby, hanging upside down by his legs from the top of a swing set while swinging Uncle Charlie's son Trey in his arms. Trey's sister, Lilly, was enjoying the party too, running between tables and giggling.

We were missing our friends Sneak and Jennie Ryerson, who were still on vacation, but were happy to have our other friends at the circular table: Hailey Cotton, Joel Hemlinger, Lisa Lavin, Cressida Hudson and Jennie's friend Michelle.

We enjoyed the French appetizers and laughed when Moscow complained that he was expecting "French Toast" and "French Fries" at the party.

Soon, Uncle Charlie joined our group, pulling up a folding chair to the table.

"You've got a lot to be proud of this week!" said the police captain about our recent success.

"The Lord really helped us again," Hailey affirmed.

"He did!" Lisa agreed. "Moscow, you were in a tough spot up on the church bell tower."

"Yeah, I could have been a goner," Moscow admitted with a smile, still hanging upside down from the nearby swing set.

"And then finding the guys who were kidnapped," said Lisa.

"You kids done good," Uncle Charlie said encouragingly. "You drive me crazy sometimes, but you've done some good work."

"So, are you going to charge Jimmy Mannix with the theft of the company documents?" Hailey asked.

"No, unfortunately we're not," Uncle Charlie admitted. "We don't have enough evidence. I mean, the case that you've laid out is a very good one. It looks like Jimmy was working with someone in the Records Department to take the documents. And, to ensure he had an alibi for when the papers were stolen and being taken out of the office, he made sure he was still off work when it happened. It was probably his partner in the Records Department who put those papers in Andrew Bayhill's briefcase. Apparently there were people from the Records Department going into Andrew's office several times a day. And that idea of placing the documents in Andrew's bag was brilliant – it allowed Jimmy to have an alibi, and then get them during Andrew's piano lesson. It was a pretty clever plan."

The conversation paused for a moment.

"The good news," Uncle Charlie continued, "is that Andew Bayhill is getting his job back, he had an interesting 'vacation' last week, huh?"

"Right," I smiled.

"So, did Jimmy Mannix have anything to do with his dad getting kidnapped? Hailey asked. "That would be a pretty bad thing for a son to do to his dad."

"Yeah," several of us agreed.

"Well, that is interesting," Uncle Charlie explained. "I talked with Jeremiah Denlon, the security chief over at Peloponnesian, and he told me something really interesting."

"What's that?" asked Moscow Cotton, after letting go of Trey, who went to play with Lilly, his sister.

"Well, the amount of money that Jimmy was trying to sell those stolen papers for, was almost exactly the same amount as the ransom demand."

"Really?" one of the Sunday School Detectives questioned.

"So, I think what happened, was that a local criminal around here, or a criminal up at the lake, got wind of Jimmy Mannix's plan. They knew he'd have a windfall of cash and decided to kidnap his dad to get it. They probably had all of their plans in motion before the documents were found in Andrew's briefcase and not sold after all."

"Wow, that is so crazy!" said Lisa. "So, a theft turned into a kidnapping!"

"It looks that way," said Uncle Charlie.

"And.. It also turned into a twisted ankle for me," said Hailey, pointing to a nearby set of crutches.

"And a busted lip for me," I added.

"And a concert that none of my friends got to hear," Joel said glumly.

"I got to hear it, *Joelsie*," said Michelle, as we began laughing. "And I thought it was divine!"

We laughed and joked and enjoyed many desserts – bonbons and tarts, eclairs, macarons and madeleines. The music that played softly in the background, I later learned, was from a record by Edith Piaf. Aunt Marie played the song "La Vie En Rose" multiple times as people laughed and talked in her backyard.

For the evening's finale, we went to the driveway and held sparklers as Uncle Charlie set off fireworks. When the fireworks exploded over-head, the partygoers sang the song called "La Marseillaise", the French national anthem. To help the non-French speakers, Aunt Marie distributed the words on sheets of paper with her Avon card attached. "Aux armes, citoyens," we sang. "Formez vos bataillons, Marchons, marchons! Qu'un sang impur. Abreuve nos sillons!" I read the translation too: "To arms, citizens, Form your battalions, March, march! Let an impure blood water our furrows!"

I didn't know what it all meant, but it was very rousing.

Standing with my friends, fireworks exploding overhead, I saw my dad still talking with Uncle Charlie's father-in-law about language lessons, and I was happy.

SOLI DEI GLORIA

Sunday School Detectives Vol. 3
The Clever Mr. Crenshaw
Introduction

"He's been one step ahead of me the whole time," my friend Sneak Ryerson said with a distraught look.

"Who?" I asked.

"That Mastermind and Evil Genius," my friend said, as he hunched over several pieces of paper at his metal office desk cluttered with papers and open reference books.

"What do you mean?" I asked, as I lined up some of my friend's army men in his second floor bedroom of the Ryerson's house in Findlay, Ohio.

"No... That's not it," my friend said in a frustrated tone. Soon, he used a pencil to cross out a word on the paper and quickly replaced it with another. He paused to study the paper again. "He's been one step ahead," my friend repeated, without looking over at me. "Ever since the beginning!" He shook his head in disbelief. "It's incredible. I haven't been putting the pieces of this puzzle together like I should have."

"Pieces to what puzzle?" I wondered with a perplexed look, as I glanced around the room for a jigsaw puzzle.

"He laid out one clue after another for me to solve – and I missed them all."

"Like what?" I wondered, after setting up another two-inch tall green army soldier across from another one, then turned to study my friend who had just returned from a long family vacation, trying to discern why he was so agitated.

"Well, like at the cemetery – the grave – where he dropped the messages for Julian Davis. It was at the grave of his wife," my friend explained.

"Oh, right," I replied. "We saw that when we came back from visiting the prison. But that's an easy one to miss if you ask me. You were pretty busy trying to catch Julian Davis with that note. And it was dark, too – there's no way you could have noticed whose grave it was, right?"

"Right," my friend agreed, still looking at the words on the paper. "But there were other things, too," he continued, moving some dark hair that had fallen into his eyes.

"Like what?" I wondered.

"Well, there was that phrase: *leave a correct eulogy*."

"Right, but you figured that out, right? That's what pointed us to the cemetery," I confirmed.

"Yeah, but Grandfather Ryerson noticed how weird it was. He told me that '*leave a correct eulogy*' doesn't really make sense. Grandpa said that a eulogy is something someone *gives* or *says* at a funeral. It's not something that someone *leaves*."

"Hmm, okay," I replied.

"After Grandfather Ryerson pointed that out, I started thinking that Mr. Crenshaw was probably leaving more clues that I wasn't picking up on."

"Why's that?" I asked.

"Well, because sometimes when you have a weird series of words or phrases in a document or a letter, it might be there because it's a code, not a simple instruction or a greeting or something like that."

"Hmm," I said, considering his words, as I moved another plastic army man across from another.

"Like that amount of money for the ransom," my friend continued. "It took me a while to notice that."

"What does that have to do with anything?" I asked.

"The amount – of the ransom," he said, still concentrating on the papers on his desk.

"Well, I remember it was sort of a weird number," I confessed.

"Exactly," my friend said, as I recalled the recent *Sunday School Detectives* mystery, where four men – a company executive, our city's mayor and two barbers – were kidnapped. "It was a really big number, but it ended in, like, 490 something."

"578.95," my friend said.

"Yeah, that was definitely strange."

"I did some math on it," my friend said, still concentrating on the papers on his desk. "And, do you know what an exchange rate is, Pep?"

"I don't think so," I told him.

"Well, it's the amount of money one currency is worth compared to another one. So, like today, one English pound sterling is worth about two dollars and forty cents."

"What does that mean?"

"It means that if you gave me two dollars and forty cents, I could give you back an English pound and it would be an even exchange. They are the same amount. It would work the other way around, too. If you gave me an English pound and I gave you two dollars and forty cents, the exchange would be even. The currencies would be the same. I saw it in some of the stores when we were on vacation in Canada. But there, the currencies are almost exactly the same amount, so some stores on the border didn't even bother to try to calculate it. But, one Canadian dollar and fourteen cents equals one U.S. dollar."

"Hmm," I pondered. "So, if we were in Canada and I gave you a U.S. dollar and you gave me one Canadian dollar and fourteen cents, it would be an even exchange?"

"You got it," my friend confirmed.

"I think I'd take the Canadian money," I concluded. "Those red bills with the Queen and the Prime Ministers on them are pretty cool."

"They are," my friend agreed.

We were quiet for a moment, as he wrote a few words, then quickly erased them.

"But, Sneak," I finally asked my friend. "What does that have to do with the kidnapping case?"

He paused for a moment, studying the papers on his desk, then said off handedly: "I checked the exchange rates listed for different countries in the newspaper, and there's one that comes out evenly with the ransom amount."

"Evenly?"

"Yep," he confirmed, still studying the papers on his desk.

"So," I finally asked. "What was it?"

"Oh, uh…22.8."

"What?" I asked.

"The exchange rate was 22.8," my friend explained. "If you multiply the ransom amount by 22.8 it equals three million."

"Three million what?" I asked.

"Pesos," Sneak Ryerson explained. "Mexican Pesos. That's probably where the kidnappers went with the money."

"You've got to be kidding me, right?" I exclaimed.

"No, not at all," my friend said in a serious voice, as he turned his attention to me. "The exchange rate on March 31st of this year – the date when they probably started planning everything – was 22.8 Mexican Pesos to one U.S. Dollar."

My friend then turned to study the papers on his desk again.

"Man, that's weird," I said. "So, the kidnappers were from Mexico?"

"Hardly!" my friend said loudly.

"Oh," I replied, not feeling very smart about my conclusion. "Why not?"

"Because they're not!" my friend said loudly. "Russell Crenshaw just wanted us to know where they were taking the money! Where I'm sure three million pesos can go a long way!"

"Russell Crenshaw?" I asked, now taking my turn to speak loudly. "What does Russell Crenshaw have to do with the kidnapping? I mean, I know the kidnappers used his empty property, right? But, he's been in prison for a long time! There's no way he could be involved in the kidnapping! We just saw him last week!"

"Three weeks ago," my friend clarified.

"Right, three weeks ago," I agreed.

My friend paused again, studying the papers on his desk, then began writing more words and out crossing others. I waited a few moments in silence before my friend continued. "I didn't see it at first, but Mr. Crenshaw likes teasing us by holding out difficult clues for us to find – like, at the end of our interview with him in prison, do you remember what he said when he left us?"

"He said that 'something *big*' was going to happen on that Thursday."

"Right," my friend said.

"And it did," I added.

"It did," my friend agreed. "But after he gave us that clue, he said something really interesting when he said goodbye to us."

"When he said goodbye to us?" I asked.

"He said, *Adios*."

"Adios?"

"Yes, it means goodbye in Spanish and it was a *clue*. Russell Crenshaw put it right out there for us and I completely missed it."

"Saying *Adios* was a clue?" I said incredulously. "He wasn't just saying goodbye?"

"It was a clue," said my friend.

"But what was that clue supposed to tell us? I don't get it."

"It was supposed to tell us that there'd be at least one Spanish word in the case!"

"What?" I protested again, as I continued my observation of my friend with a perplexed look. "That doesn't make any sense! Just because Russell Crenshaw said *one* word in Spanish to us when he said goodbye, you're telling me that we were somehow supposed to know that there would be a Spanish clue in the case?"

"That's precisely what I'm telling you," said my friend, as he looked up from his papers to face me – his look serious and his eyes revealing that he was set on achieving his objective.

"Well…" I began, unsure of how to respond.

"Don't you remember it, Pep?" my friend asked.

"I guess not," I replied, as I reminded myself to check the audio cassette recording of the interview with Russell Crenshaw when I returned home.

"I've got it written down," my friend said, as he looked through his stack of papers, but I knew his great photographic memory had already captured all of the details from the conversation. "Here we go," he said. "Mr. Crenshaw's last words to us were actually sung to us. Do you remember when he sang the words, 'Au revoir, Adios, Auf Weidersein. Good night!'"

"Right, I remember that. That's how *The Lawrence Welk Show* ends. My grandma always makes me watch that show when we go visit her. Should we go watch the show next Saturday night on PBS and sing along to the polka music and dress in matching outfits, just because Russell Crenshaw sang those words?"

I was becoming more and more exasperated by my friend's outlandish ideas.

"Pep," my friend said sternly. "His words weren't exactly the *same* words as they sing on the show."

"I don't understand," I confessed.

"In *The Lawrence Welk Show*, the song actually ends with them singing, "Adios, Au Revoir, Auf Weidersein. Good night!" He paused. "So, the pattern for the words on the TV Show are: Spanish, French, then German."

"Okay?" I said, confused.

"But Mr. Crenshaw changed the order when he said goodbye to us. Instead of starting with a Spanish word, he started with a *French* word. Then, he used a *Spanish* word second."

"Okay, so his words were: French, Spanish, then German. What's the big deal?"

"Well, that's the clue," replied the great detective. "By starting with the wrong word – the French word – he was showing us he knew that a French word was part of our initial mystery with him. Remember, you told the *Sunday School Detectives* about that French phrase your dad sometimes says, and it helped figure out the mystery!"

"Yeah, but…" I began.

"And to reinforce the point, Mr. Crenshaw even gave us a clue in French when he said he was getting treatment from the nurse. Do you remember he said he needed to 'go to the infirmary and see Nurse Ratched, er, whatever her name is?'"

"Right, isn't that the name of a nurse in that movie about crazy people?" I replied quickly. "My friend told me about it. It's called One Flew Over the Something Nest."

"You are right about the movie," my friend affirmed. "But, he didn't say her name exactly like they do in the movie." The great young detective quickly pointed to a heavy book near his desk. "I looked in this French dictionary and *racheter* means ransom."

"So you're saying *how* he said goodbye was a huge clue that we missed?" I asked.

"Absolutely," my friend continued. "The first interaction with him was solved with a French word, and then our second dealings with him had to do with a Spanish word – the Mexican *Peso*."

"But you told me earlier that the kidnapper wasn't from Mexico?" I asked, confused.

"That's right. I don't think the kidnapper was from there."

"I don't get it," I confessed. "What's the point of the clue then?"

"It's Russell Crenshaw's way of being clever. He loves the puzzles. He was letting us know that he knew all about the kidnapping. Not only did he know that *something big* was going to happen the next day, but he also knew about the ransom amount!"

"So, he was sort of tipping his hat to the kidnapper, then, right?" I asked. "Letting us know he knew who the kidnapper was?"

"I think it was more than that!" said the young detective. "I think he was actually showing us that he was the one behind it all! He's the evil genius – the Criminal Mastermind – and I didn't even see it!"

"Come on," I protested. "Just because he said *Adios* to us and then it turned out that the number in the ransom note equals a Spanish Peso doesn't mean that Mr. Crenshaw was behind it all – does it? I mean, it could have just been a coincidence, right?"

"I don't think so."

"I mean," I continued, "the kidnapper could have been from Mexico, right? There were a couple of clues for that – right? You could explain it that way."

"No, you could not," my friend said sternly. "Think about what he said before he sang the creepy song. Do you remember that?"

"No," I admitted.

"He said, 'I'm one step ahead of you! I'll always be one step ahead! You better watch out for those UFOs! They'll get you sometime!'"

"Oh yeah," I admitted. "I remember that. It was pretty creepy."

"He said to watch out for the UFOs…" my friend began. "I'm so glad Hailey figured it out. Who knows how bad things could have been for those kidnapping victims."

"Figured out what?" I asked.

"Where the victims were located," my friend explained. "If my brain would have worked just a little harder, I could have helped."

"What do you mean?" I asked.

"Do you remember where we heard the phrase, 'UFOs…UFOs' before meeting with Mr. Crenshaw?"

"No," I replied, shaking my head.

"It was when we met with Julian Davis."

"Hmm, I don't exactly remember what he said."

"Well, he told us he had been contacted by aliens, and he read that letter he said he got from them."

"Oh yeah," I replied. "That Julian Davis really had a few screws loose."

"But that letter," my friend continued, "started with that phrase, 'UFOs… UFOs.'"

"So, what does that have to do with anything?" I wondered.

"It's another clue," said the great detective. "Mr. Crenshaw was telling us to study that letter, when he told us to watch out for the UFOs."

"Hmm," I replied doubtfully. "So, we were supposed to look at the letter he gave Julian Davis?"

"Right," my friend said. "I think Mr. Crenshaw assumed we would actually take the letter from Julian Davis and decipher it when we got back to Findlay – but we didn't."

"Really?" I questioned.

"I've recreated it here," he said, pointing to a paper on his deck. "And I just deciphered it."

"What did the letter say?" I wondered. "It was mostly gibberish, right? A poem or something?"

"It is a poem of sorts," said my friend. "Let me read it to you."

My friend picked up one of the papers he had scribbled on to get the words exactly right.

JUNE 1st, 1980
UFOs, UFOs, LOITERING ON OTHER KOSMOS
ASK THEM: MARY YORK?
PLEASE LEAVE A CORRECT EULOGY

"Right, I remember," I said. "Your Uncle Charlie was going to try to track down Mary York and see if she was part of Russell Crenshaw's group that started the fires. And that's when you decided to look at the cemetery because it said something about a eulogy, right?"

"Right," my friend said. "But there isn't a Mary York – at least there isn't one connected with this case."

"Okay?" I wondered. "If there's no Mary York, what are the other clues in the note?"

"Well," my friend began. "The first thing is the date – June 1st, 1980."

"Okay?" I wondered again.

"It's the key to the cypher. It's telling us to look for *firsts*."

"Firsts?" I asked.

"Right," said the great detective. "So, after studying the date on the first of June, I thought about *the other firsts* in the letter and underlined the first letter of each word."

He soon showed a second paper with all of the first letters underlined in the words that appeared after the date.

JUNE 1, 1980
<u>U</u>FOs, <u>U</u>FOs, <u>L</u>OITERING <u>O</u>N <u>O</u>THER <u>K</u>OSMOS
<u>A</u>SK <u>T</u>HEM: <u>M</u>ARY <u>Y</u>ORK?
<u>P</u>LEASE <u>L</u>EAVE <u>A</u> <u>C</u>ORRECT <u>E</u>ULOGY

"Okay?" I quizzed him again.

"So, then I wrote each of those letters down," Sneak Ryerson explained, and soon showed me another piece of paper with the following letters.

UULOOKATMYPLACE

"It still looks like gibberish to me," I admitted.

"Does it?" my friend replied. "What if you put a space between some of the letters to make them words?"

"Could it be?" I began. "No, it's possible!"

"It is," my friend said as he showed me another piece of paper with the full clue.

UU LOOK AT MY PLACE

"Mr. Crenshaw was telling us to look at his place?" I said with a gasp.

"Yep," my friend said, nodding his head.

"That's where we found those guys who were kidnapped!" I said, amazed. "I can't believe we found them without these clues from Mr. Crenshaw."

"I can't either," my friend admitted. "It really was an answer to prayer."

"But," I asked, "how were we ever supposed to know that? Why did he think we'd check for clues like that in the note to Julian, or in the other things he told us?"

"Well, that came at the beginning of our discussion with him," my friend explained. "Do you remember when he said he had a lot of money…"

"Oh, yeah," I said. "He said his family won some money in a trial or something."

"Exactly!" my friend said loudly. "Do you remember specifically what he told us?"

"Not the exact words," I admitted.

"He told us that his family was awarded a lot of money from a *jury* in a personal injury trial in England."

"Okay?" I said, repeating myself many, many times.

"So, I've done some research on that too," my friend explained, pointing to another large book on his desk. "And the thing that I've learned is, they don't have those kinds of jury trials in England."

"What?" I asked, surprised. "Do you think he was mistaken?"

"No," my friend smiled. "He was not mistaken. It's a *judge*, not a jury, who makes those awards in England. It was a lie," my friend explained, looking directly at me. "And he said that to show us that from the very beginning of the interview he was lying, so we should be on the lookout for clues and half-truths."

"But he was telling the truth when he told us 'Something big' was happening!"

"Right," my friend agreed. "That was probably one of the only things he said that was true when we met with him. But the other things – like he heard it from other prisoners in the Hancock County Jail – was all made up."

"Sneak," I said, shaking my head. "This all just seems too crazy – that somehow Mr. Crenshaw, who was in prison, figured out a way to kidnap those guys and give us a bunch of clues, even before it happened. That's what you're saying, right?"

"That's precisely what I'm saying," my friend said with a sigh. "The planning was incredible: putting the information into that weird note to Julian Davis… then putting that weird amount of money in the ransom note that was equal to a large amount of foreign currency… and of course, figuring out how to kidnap four people. Like I said, the planning was incredible."

"That is incredible," I agreed.

We paused for a moment.

"You should call your Uncle Charlie," I recommended, referring to my friend's uncle who was a captain in the Findlay Police Department.

"Yeah, I guess I should," my friend replied, and soon he was pushing buttons on a salmon-colored touch-tone phone.

"Hey Sneak!" his uncle replied heartily when he heard his nephew's voice. "How was your vacation?"

"Good, it was good, Uncle Charlie."

"Remind me again where you went?"

"Lots of places," my friend explained. "Niagara Falls, New Hampshire, Maine, then down through Boston, and Pennsylvania, then Washington, D.C. and Maryland. It was a really long trip."

"That sounds like a lot of driving," his uncle observed.

"Yeah, it was," my friend agreed wearily.

"So, what's going on?" his uncle asked. "Did you solve any cases by reading about them in the newspaper while you were on vacation?"

"No, no," his nephew grinned. "But I've been wanting to tell you some things I've discovered about Russell Crenshaw. You're not going to like it."

"Oh, hey, actually, I was going to call you today, now that you're back, and talk to you about him too."

"Oh, really?" my friend asked.

"Yeah," said his uncle. "The news is pretty amazing, isn't it."

"What news is that?" asked my friend.

"Oh, sorry, I thought you knew," said his uncle, in a serious tone. "It happened a few days ago."

"What happened a few days ago?"

"Russell Crenshaw died."

**Sneak Ryerson and the Sunday School Detectives plan to return!
Look for The Sunday School Detectives Mystery Vol. 3
"The Clever Mr. Crenshaw"**